I0760985

FALCON FLIGHT

CHRONICLE II

Azalea Dabill

Dynamos Press
Chiloquin Oregon

II

Dynamos Press
P. O. Box 942
Chiloquin, Oregon/97624
www.azaleadabill.com

Publisher's Note: This is a work of fiction. Names, characters, places, and incidents are a product of the author's imagination. Locales and public names are sometimes used for atmospheric purposes. Any resemblance to actual people, living or dead, or to businesses, companies, events, institutions, or locales is completely coincidental.

Cover Designer: Derek Murphy

Keywords: Crossover: Find the Eternal the Adventure, Teen and young adult fantasy books, Young adult fantasy series, Christian adventure books for teens, Epic fantasy romance, Coming of age fantasy, Fantasy literature for children and young adults.

Falcon Flight Chronicle II/ Azalea Dabill. -- 1st ed.
ISBN 978-1-943034-18-5

III

Contents

Ruse 1
Hostage 11
Traitor 27
Oaths 39
Struggles 49
Trickery 65
Flight 83
Persuasion 103
Bargains 121
Travels 139
Accused 151
Suspicions 165
Defenses 185
Confessions 199
Rangdo 213
Attacked 231
Countermeasure 247
Surprises 263
Challenges 279
Family 295
Hamal 309

Change.....325
Raid.....339
Wounds.....351
Strife.....367
Secrets.....381
War.....397
Siege.....413
Love.....429
Revelations.....441
Tested.....459
Blades.....475
More Books.....497
Story Chat.....499
Glossary.....500
Acknowledgements.....508

IV

Falcon Flight

To the Master of all who taught me through the steep learning curve of this book and brought it to completion. To my editor Margie Vawter, this book would not be in such excellent shape without you; and to Derek Murphy, for the wonderful covers and career training.

To my readers:

You are the best. I'm so glad you've chosen this journey with me.

Crossover - Find the Eternal, the Adventure!

V

The Falcon Chronicles

Falcon Heart Chronicle I

Falcon Flight Chronicle II

Falcon Dagger Chronicle III *

Lance and Qull - A Novella

Falcon's Ode - Poetry Companion

Suggested Reading Order

Two prequels in *Falcon Dagger* *Coming 2024

Falcon Heart a novel

Falcon Flight a novel

Lance and Quill a novella

Falcon Dagger three novellas.

1

A prince's ruin. ~Proverbs 14:28

Kyrin Cieri strode toward the curtains of the Blue Flower room. More than two years of slavery. No word of home, her Britannia of rushing streams and whispering oaks, or of her father, Lord Dain Cieri of Cierheld.

And no way of escape.

Tae said the circle of circumstance was incomplete. Alaina told her the next stitch in the Master of the stars's pattern was not clear. Ali Ben Aidon guarded his slaves too well.

Would she ever walk in Cierheld with her father again? It was five years since her twelfth name-day, when she took the oath of first daughter in Cierheld hall. Esther would say she never had a first daughter's qualities, one who bore the old blood in her veins, and maybe she had not. Yet no one from home could call her "sprite get" now. She was stronger than they dreamed, though she carried the blood of the hills in her slight bones, dark hair and eyes.

She could not return to her people and her land. Her stronghold key rusted away in Ali's possession. She would not see her father again, and Cierheld would die with him.

Stronghold first daughter. She had never entirely felt like one. Kyrin bit her lip. Two things of Britannia remained to her.

Alaina Ilen, dearer than blood, her sister of salt and sacrifice, forged under threat of death. Walking at her side, Alaina's red-gold braid swung with a soft swish against her leather and cane body armor, laced over her white *thawb.* The intricately embroidered tunic displayed swords and flowers in delicate silver, blue and green. The staff Alaina held across her body was a harsh line dividing blade and bloom.

Kyrin's lips quirked. But for its leather handgrips, the staff was smooth as silk from Alaina's use. Her sister gave her a smart blow during their last training bout, before she wrested the weapon away. What new trick would Alaina bring against her this night, besides her proven mastery of the scribe's pen and her embroidery needle?

Ali's first bodyguard, watchful as a leopard, paced before heavy curtains of dark silk. With a glower, Umar thumped the hilt of his sword against the stone arch of the Blue Flower room. The solid thunk of his hilt announced their presence to the feasters within, and to their master, Ali Ben Aidon, merchant and murderer. Mouth wry, Kyrin dipped her head to Umar.

He held out his hand, demanding Alaina's staff. She laid the weapon in his palm, his skin nearer gold than white.

Kyrin wrinkled her nose. Her master's unacknowledged son could never quite wash off the smell of meat, rice, and saluki: the scents of the kennels, and the savage beasts of his Hand. Umar ran with them often, teaching his hunters of men patience and endurance in the desert sands. He glanced at her, expressionless.

Had he forgiven her for her eye of evil intent he once swore tipped the glowing brazier on Ali's ship, that gave him the burn scar across his sword hand?

No matter. Umar never spoke of it since. She had grown strong. She'd stolen every moment she could from serving Ali's table the past two winters to learn the demanding ways of *Subak.*

Tae Chisun, her husband in name, a second father in fact, had taught her well his ancestral fighting art of the hands and feet. Also, under the tutelage of her master's second bodyguard, Jachin, she knew one end of a sword from the other.

Umar glared at Alaina, free of her blue veil and serving robe for this brief moment, as he examined her staff for hidden blades. Umar never sought to interfere with Kyrin's training with Jachin, knowing their master wished her and Alaina's skill to impress the *caliph* in Baghdad—and those the caliph favored. Such as the caliph's *wazir.* Kyrin clenched her hand at her side.

She and Alaina would demonstrate the fighting art of the East to Ali's guests at table—and Sirius Abdasir. Once guardsman to the caliph, now first wazir, Ali's most honored guest professed a liking for close-in combat. So it would be dagger work this night, among other things. Kyrin touched her blade.

The cool haft of the weapon in her sash did not have the balance of her bronze falcon, the second thing that remained to her of Britannia. She'd left her mother's falcon dagger in their quarters. Tae was right.

Ali Ben Aidon must never discover the Damascus steel under the bronzed surface. It was her last gift from her mother. Never was the weapon for common wear. The falcon drew interest to its piercing amber gaze and beautiful strength.

Umar's smile widened, unpleasant. He kept Alaina's staff. "Wait until the master calls you."

Alaina glanced at Kyrin, who frowned. When would he let them in? He loved to play the sand cat with the mouse, she knew. But they were not his prey.

Jackals, hyenas, these merchants and slavers. They preyed on the foolish, the weak, the needy—and the unknowing. This night her master's guests must see a dance of interweaving bodies mixed with the gleam of blade and the thud of weapons on flesh, executed in a moment. She and Alaina would teach them awe during the fall of a grain of sand. Kyrin's lip curled.

Alaina leaned toward her and whispered, "Our master's guests wish to see cunning artistry and flamboyant performance, do they not?"

Kyrin nodded, not giving back her sister's smile. They must see neither failure nor mastery of the warrior's art. The trick was not to betray Tae *or* her master. She did not intend to go to court, nor engage Tae or Alaina near that pit of eels.

In Britannia it was long after Compline, though no monks' bells rang in this land. She drew herself up as Umar lifted the curtain for a passing servant and caught a glimpse through a window within. Ali's fruitful wadi, before the hills with their stark mountains behind, the leagues of burning desert to the distant sea, all lay invisible. The patches of night in the high, thin windows of the Blue Flower room faced west, without stars.

Beneath the dark portals a pale hunter frozen in marble bent his head, listening. His bow hung in his hand above a gurgling fountain, his hunt forgotten. Like hers. Water flowed around his sandaled feet, chuckling with secrets.

Kyrin's skin pricked. She also held deadly knowledge. None in the Blue Flower room could know how deep her training in Subak had gone. Tae insisted the death touch was not for common talk about the hearth.

Beside the hunter a small naked tree stretched red branches toward the stars. It was dying. And with it, her hope.

"Do not disillusion our wazir." Umar grinned, a thin stretching of his mouth.

Kyrin's face twitched into a semblance of a smile. She and Alaina did not possess greater strength than a man. They *could* strike nerves the size of a needle's head, deal crippling pain, and take the senses of the strongest, then kill at need. Her master would call them soon.

No doubt, the waiting guests wondered if Ali Ben Aidon's boast of his foreign women, who wielded blades in the manner of the East, was true. Could they, would they, kill a man? Would they please the wazir this night? Enough to gain invitation to the caliph's court?

Umar need not fear. The moment had come for their training to bear fruit. Dancing from foot to foot, Kyrin's blood picked up. Her breath quickened in the familiar rhythm.

Umar swept open the curtain and called with a mocking flourish, "The warriors of the house of Ali Ben Aidon!"

Kyrin and Alaina stepped past him. Incense-laden warmth rolled around them. A breath of air hinting at winter frost touched Kyrin's cheek from the night.

Her master's guests, in flowing thawbs and spotless *kaffieyehs,* milled beyond a free-standing wood dais twenty paces away. They moved around the tall pillars that marched up the sides of the room. The grey columns flanked a long, low feasting table lined with cushions, where other guests sat crosslegged.

The chill grace of stone cast shadows against the walls. Tae did not linger near the marble hunter, his dark hair streaked with a pale, straight lock above his ear. His familiar, short figure and almond shaped eyes that set him apart did not meet her gaze.

At the end of the room, two last pillars loomed behind Ali's empty chair at the head of the table. Lamps flamed bright, fixed high on the pillars' sides.

Nine of the wazir's men in brilliant red thawbs, edged in black, waited in the shadows, nearly as still as the marble hunter. Sirius Abdasir rested near the dais, reclining on cushions near Ali's less formal seat right of the great chair. Her master would not insult his guest with a higher seat. Kyrin's mouth flattened.

The wazir's men watched her from under kaffiyeh and turban. Let them stare. She lifted her chin slightly. Was it the jet earring, the eye of evil in her ear? She looked away.

Lamp-light from the table skittered over the men and merchants of the caliph's court and local *souk.* They seated themselves on rugs and cushions about the low dais and the table as they pleased, their animated gestures and liquid tongue quick with anticipation.

Kyrin bit her lip. Tae was not among the shadows or the guests. Surely Ali had bid his *hakeem,* his esteemed healer and exiled warrior, the prize of his prowess, to be present to witness the triumph of the house of Ben Aidon.

A cry of challenge blasted in Kyrin's ear. Startled, she spun with a fierce yell. Guests glanced up sharply.

"It is time, sister!" Alaina's voice was welcome in the tongue of Britannia. Her sister leaped back. Her hands guarded her face, her left foot led, her green eyes were alight. She grinned at Kyrin. Her shout had caught her out well and truly.

Kyrin lifted her chin, and her smile bared her teeth as her spirit rose in answer. *Never give up.* Alaina cried low, "Seajok!" And kicked for Kyrin's head.

So it begins. Kyrin slipped forward and deflected the blow, then hit Alaina's shoulder with an open palm. Alaina's counter kick thumped her chest armor. Kyrin absorbed it with a grunt. They circled across the stone floor toward the dais. Each yell focused a strike. Kyrin sought an opening while Alaina pressed her back.

They moved down the aisle between the guests, toward the dais. Kyrin's heel touched polished wood.

She sprang up and back and her twisting momentum drove her back foot forward in a snapping roundkick. Her foot thunked into Alaina's side. Her sister reeled.

Kyrin grinned—too soon. Alaina turned to catch the staff Umar threw from the doorway. Kyrin attacked from high ground at the edge of the dais. Her dagger hand darted down. Alaina brought her weapon around and Kyrin's blade "tinged" on the iron band about the wood. She grimaced at the vibrating sting and flowed around Alaina's swift counter, blade darting for her side.

Alaina turned her instant evasion into a thrust for Kyrin's stomach then whirled her staff toward her legs. Kyrin sucked in her middle and jumped over the blurring wood. She slashed at Alaina's near hand with her dagger. Her sister evaded again, jerked her staff back, and flipped the opposite end at Kyrin's head. Kyrin leaned back—the tip whirred past her nose—and Alaina was open.

Kyrin leapt for her throat, flashing hand ready. Her palm lost most of its power against Alaina's arm, but her knee drove in beneath and found Alaina's stomach. Light cane flexed under leather.

Her sister bent, mouth open for air, and staggered. She dropped her staff, which rolled across the dais in staccato thunder. Zoltan darted from among Ali's watching slaves to pull the weapon clear.

The edges of Kyrin's mouth lifted. No chance of Alaina regaining it. Sweat sparkled on her face. Blade spine leading, Kyrin drove toward her sister's neck. With a high yell, Alaina surged in under her arm and shouldered upward. Her fingers dug behind Kyrin's knee, seeking her balance. Kyrin let her have her leg, dropped to her back, tucked a foot in Alaina's stomach, and heaved. Her sister flew over her head.

Alaina rolled and spun to her feet, but Kyrin had used her pull to follow her up. She smiled, with a low laugh of joy in the fight. Alaina drew her dagger, a small frown of focus on her heart-shaped face. As breathless as the marble hunter, Ali's guests leaned forward on their rugs.

Steel glittered and shrieked as they swung apart and together. Blades flashed low and quick. Resilient body armor strained against opposite armor, inner strips of cane bending with the force. Their feet pounded a small circle as they leaned against each other, searching for advantage or disadvantage of balance.

Kyrin broke free. Sweat trickled down her face. She brushed it aside. The smell of sweat masked sandalwood. Alaina breathed hard, and the guests murmured. No moment to rest. Ali would punish them with a day of fieldwork if they did not please. Not that Kyrin minded fieldwork. She simply hated Umar's fault-finding eye.

In again, feint and fumble with a purpose—to catch and lock Alaina's wrist. Kyrin took her dagger, slammed her to the wood. She gave her sister a courteous bow and returned the weapon. The dance began again. Attack and counterattack. With purposeful mistakes, where first she and then Alaina came away with a blade after a giving a blow that would maim or kill if it were delivered with the edge, at speed.

Kyrin's grip on her dagger hurt her fingers. Her stomach twisted. A true fight lasted but a moment—then one life would be left. But men such as these took no thought for that, only for the dance, the uncertainty, the lingering moment before the mock kill. Back to back, at last Kyrin and Alaina stopped. Slowly, with full respect, they pivoted to face the four cardinal points of the world, then bowed to their guests.

With a deep breath, they spun into their second display. Leaping in a kick as high as Alaina's head, Kyrin then swept across the dais in a series of jumps, counterpart to a mesmerizing glitter of light as Alaina wove dagger attacks around her that teased those near the dais into staring tension. *Never be unaware.* The words Tae said so often, pricked at her thought.

Right of the dais, Ali Ben Aidon sat on a low throne of cushions, out of the window's chill, his pale, wide lips pursed. He lifted the end of a water-pipe and drew a rumbling burble through his *nargeela.*

Kyrin rolled her enemy of air to the floor, and spun back toward Alaina, each in their own routine. Strike and strike and spin.

To her master's left, the wazir reclined on an elbow, a languid arm across his knee, clean nails meticulously pared on that broad hand that commanded so many. Sirius Abdasir's face bore the seal of his Greek mother and Arab father, rounded features blent with a high brow in a long face. His brown eyes were as light as his golden skin, his generous mouth gifting all with warm approval. That warmth could turn arrogant and cold in a moment.

Kyrin struck across the dais toward him. Only a brave man dared the wazir's displeasure, and took his head in his hands when he did—and the sword drank his blood—or it did not. She dared so, once. Now there was too much thought in Sirius Abdasir as he stroked his chin, watching her. What did the wazir seek? He frowned. His finger and thumb drew down his beardless chin again, a gesture she remembered from a day of ash and blood. Kyrin pressed her lips together. That day was not this, and it never would be.

In a swift lunge, almost without looking, she closed with Alaina and tapped the base of her sister's throat with darting fingers. A deft turn, and Alaina's blade lay against Kyrin's skin. She shivered at the cold touch on the scar in the hollow of her throat. Alaina gave her a mocking smile for the sake of their watchers. That smile belied her sister's white fingers on the hilt. The danger was known.

Kyrin's dagger clashed against Alaina's in high salute. She lowered her blade, sheathed it, and resisted the urge to gulp air. She bowed briefly to the enthralled guests. Instantly, heads turned and tongues wagged with astonishment. Kyrin held another bow for her master and the wazir, his thawb blood-red. Alaina was a silent, comforting shadow beside her.

"Oh, well done, O my host! Most excellent!" Sirius Abdasir inclined his head to Ali. His glance passed over Kyrin, a sudden tightness about his mouth. His nose flared with indrawn breath, intent as a saluki on the scent. If he had hackles they would be lifting.

Kyrin held herself rigidly straight.

Doubtless such a warrior as Sirius Abdasir was disappointed that there was no taking of a life. As when he gave his slave, Seliam, to her blade. But that did not end as either of them thought. Frankincense hung thick in the air.

A fig for what he thought. Ali was pleased. After her fight with Seliam, Sirius had asked about her falcon dagger. He had loosened it in its sheath, noted the bronze blade—then tossed it back to her. Kyrin's breath fled gently through her nose. This night she was wet with sweat—not red blood. She might always fail Sirius Abdasir in that, the taking of a life.

Sirius's mouth flattened with the faintest smile. Kyrin shivered. It was said he wove webs at court. There had been whispers about the sudden end of the old wazir. Did Sirius Abdasir weave a web this night?

2

Hostage

Assembly of treacherous men . . .
bend their tongue like a bow. ~Jeremiah 9:2-3

"O my guest"—Ali spread his arms expansively— "Are my *askars* not ready to delight the eyes of the Most Excellent?"

The wazir grunted.

Kyrin bit her lip hard. Ali's askar, *his* warrior—no—she was Tae's *rangdo,* a student of life and of the way of the warrior. For Tae, for Alaina, for the Master of the stars, and for herself. Never would she strive for one who embraced death and despair. And the caliph—

Sirius caught her angry gaze. The strength of him held her fast. His narrowed eyes searched her face.

A band of iron tightened about Kyrin's chest; her breath came shallow. She dropped her gaze. Did Sirius see one who could profit him? Or a slave who dared deceive him—or his master, giving a performance that defied them? His skills of the warrior differed from Tae's, but they were yet a warrior's, and he held a danger all his own.

A cold prickle crept over Kyrin's skin, and her breath caught. The tiger that haunted her dreams was loosed. It had been so long since he pursued her in the night.

Her old nemesis prowled the room, unseen; his huge paws noiseless; with a hide of blackness and flame, and green-gold eyes that devoured. She yanked her gaze from Sirius. Would the beast crouch behind her this night, his claws ready to sink into her back when she slept?

In her mind the tiger turned his head, locked hungry eyes with hers, and growled. A collar of silver winked about his throat, set with pieces of jet that gleamed like eyes. The amber eyes of slain falcons.

A wave of heat and dizziness passed over Kyrin. *But the falcon, my queen of the air, she broke the chain and rode your shoulders!* That also had been a dream.

"You have polished them, O my host, into jewels of the East; fair artisans, hard as diamond, pure as gold." Sirius Abdasir's teeth shone. He rested his chin on a meditative finger, regarding Ali. Kyrin caught at the wazir's voice as at a rope, staring hard at his sash. His words dissipated the roaring in her ears. "Their techniques bury true warfare within, I think."

Her breath caught. The words of the book darted through her mind. *Take every thought captive; think on whatsoever is true. The Master of the stars is here.*

"Where did you come upon such diamonds in the rock?" The wazir quirked an eyebrow at Kyrin, his face lean as a winter-hungry wolf, head tilted inquiringly. She straightened.

"Ahhh," Ali settled back on his cushions. "That is a very long tale."

"The night is old. Let your jewels rest. I am sure all ears here are interested in a tale of gold gained. Who trained them? He must be a warrior without match, and must carry the touch of death in his hands." Amid a chorus of the guests' agreement, Sirius crossed one knee over the other and rocked an elegant slippered foot, waiting.

In silent command, Ali waved Kyrin down as Alaina drew a startled breath at his words. Kyrin knelt obediently with her on the wood dais, hands clenched on her knees.

The tapestry above Ali's chair at the end of the table lay in shadow. The tiger had not hunted her dreams since mistress Shema passed. The lamps were too weak now, to see if the stalking beast had been moved, replaced with another tapestry. There was something of the tiger about Sirius. Her mouth stiffened in a pleasant mask. Why did the wazir speak of Tae?

When Seliam gained his captaincy under Sirius Abdasir, and she kept her Subak match of honor with him, there had been no word of warriors needed to serve the caliph at court. Tae forsaw the wazir's interest in her and Alaina's performance and provided concealment for their skill alone.

Surely Ali would not willingly sell his most valuable slave, the house healer or *hakeem,* and a skilled warrior. But where *was* Tae? It was strange Ali had not turned every room upside down to procure him to witness his triumph. Did her master seek to humble Tae yet again for his past defiance in the matter of her maidenhood?

Sirius surely suspected there was more to learn of Tae's skill. There was always more to learn. Kyrin's mouth dried. For the first time in a long season she wished for her veil; it would shield her from the wazir's brown gaze. He studied her as if he knew something she did not.

From what Zoltan said, the wazir kept his finger on the pulse of the slave trade in Baghdad. Did he want Tae to train fighters for him and the caliph? What did he desire from her?

Behind her one of the guests coughed. Kyrin clutched her knees, her only sign of startlement, stifling the impulse to strike down the threat.

Ali launched into his tale, regaling his expectant guests with Kyrin and Alaina's capture from Britannia's coast. He paused to cough, and winced. In his tale, he mastered the village in the night by wit and planning, and at last his men overcame all resistance in the name of Allah, sacking the stronghold on the cliffs. There he took a last, young captive.

How he had relished subduing the harm that followed her glance, naming the darkness and binding her evil eye with a jet earring carved in the shape of her corruption.

Kyrin clenched her jaw, keeping her hand from the heavy ring in her right ear; she would not hide from every gaze that pinned her. The hard wood under her knees was as old as the grief of three winters.

When Ali murdered her godfather and her mother, he burned their bodies in the razed stronghold, which he gave to the hungry, lonely gulls of the sea. Kyrin blinked back the sting in her eyes.

Did her father yet live? Was there gray in his hair, like the peppering about Tae's ears? Did his laugh bring joy to those around him, his deep voice approve of Cierheld's men for a task well done? He would have arrived from York soon after the burning of her godfather's hold. And if her father held to her godfather's plan, her inheritance now had walls of Roman stone. Cierheld would not fall easily to any, with Lord Dain Cieri's great bow and heavy sword to defend the walls.

She drew a deep breath. She was a daughter of Cierheld. Stronghold first daughter—and she *would* return.

Ali stretched his arm toward the dais. "And then, O my generous guests, my hakeem did what his hands do so well: healed my wounded and taught the art of war to the soft and to the fearful, to women."

Beside Kyrin, Alaina smiled and dipped her head, gentle and proud. Kyrin scowled.

Ali beckoned them forward. With an impatient hand he pointed to Kyrin. "Even this worthless one is now a treasure of my collection," he said, as they stepped from the dais and knelt before him, bowing their foreheads to the stone.

Sirius's voice was dry and mellow above Kyrin's head. "It was your wisdom, O my host, to take the hakeem on your last voyage. Though you did not find what you sought, not all was lost."

Wind blew from the windows, past the marble hunter, laden with incense from a brazier. Kyrin held her breath against a gathering sneeze.

"Yes, yes, it is so." Ali nudged a cushion aside with his embroidered slipper, and motioned Kyrin up distractedly. Her master's breath came short. Sweat dotted his forehead. His pupils were wide and black. The pain was taking him early. "Sit—no—make yourselves ready, then return to us." Ali's pale cheeks quivered, and he coughed again.

Kyrin swallowed her protest and quickly followed Alaina out. The blue curtain closed behind them.

Outside, his gaze dark, Umar watched. Kyrin nodded and walked numbly past him, through the long entry room, and right, into the passage. Her mind spun into place as her feet turned toward the quarters they shared with Tae.

After a feast Ali never asked them to return before he broke his fast in the morning.

Sinking onto her pallet, Alaina tugged at a damp leg pad. "What under the stars was that about? Ugghh, it's off. I hate damp leather." She poked the leg pad with disgust and propped it in a corner of the open chest against the wall of their small room, frowning. "I hope Tae gets back soon. I wonder when we'll perform for the caliph. The wazir seemed pleased."

"Yes. But our master's humor is—odd." It was long past mid of night. She curled a strand of hair about her finger and tugged. She did not relish going back, to Sirius Abdasir or Ali.

"It is the herbs, or the pain." Alaina shrugged. "But the wazir, why did he ask Ali about us? He knows our story and Tae's; everyone in the house does. He cannot want us for the caliph's guard; the caliph would never allow it."

No, but Tae would seldom bow to threat, or to a sword held by a tyrant. Kyrin kept her voice low, removed her damp arm pads, and set them in the chest. "If I knew what the wazir wished, I could be sure not to give it to him."

"Oh, Kyrin! Is Sirius so evil?"

"Yes. He counted Seliam of less worth than, than"—she struggled out of her chest protector and tossed it beside her pads—"his shoes. I do not think being wazir has changed him. Power is his poison."

Alaina slipped past the old argument. "There is something about Seliam this night, he did not see me. Did you see him by the pillars?"

Kyrin frowned. "No. I didn't. But Tae should have been there. Maybe he and Jachin found a sick sheep out in the wadi and had to tend it." She thoughtfully twisted a curl of hair until it was painfully tight.

Being a warrior himself, Sirius discerned too much of their skill. She must conceal what she could, without Tae's ready tongue to fend him off. Court had been dangerous when Alaina and Tae tended the late wazir, and he died. Now the wazir to the new caliph questioned them.

She said suddenly, brightly, "If Sirius wishes speech with us we can speak of Ali's roses. I love gardens and children. Our bodies have been trained as a man's—yet we remain women, we deal with gentler matters. The world of men and of war is a fearful thing. To open our mouths about such things in the presence of the gracious wazir to the most pure Emissary of Allah—it is most unthinkable. Don't you think?"

Alaina covered her laughing snort with her hand.

"Hah!" Kyrin pointed at her. "I knew you could do it. We will foil them. Until Tae comes." With a grin, she shoved Alaina's shoulder, and Alaina shoved back with a relieved laugh.

They pulled off their damp thawbs, scrubbed down with damp scented cloths, and donned their blue serving robes and veils again. Kyrin combed out her hair and twisted it up, struggling with her hairpins until Alaina whisked them from her fingers and anchored them deftly.

Kyrin touched her smooth, elegant coif and tapped the falcon heads of the pins Tae had carved for her. "With your nimble fingers you ought to serve the wife of the caliph."

Alaina grinned. "I would not serve the queen. *You* are my sister, graceful one."

Kyrin laughed at her and shrugged, turning to consider her blades, lying on her mat in a neat row, from a finger-length to a hand-span long. She sighed and slid the falcon dagger from under her pallet. It gleamed cold in her hands, warming to her touch as always. She wanted the falcon at her back tonight. Tae would catch that warning, if he saw none other before he entered the Blue Flower room.

Sliding the bare blade securely through her sash, she caught up her smallest dagger, shoved it from sight lengthwise in her sash beside the falcon, and tossed Alaina's short blade to her. "Don't forget this."

Alaina fished the finger-length dagger from the air and concealed it in her brown sash at her waist, her mischievous mouth flattening. They donned their half-veils, which ran across the bridge of the nose and fell sheer below the chin, leaving their eyes visible. What could one read in eyes alone, without the mouth to confirm or deny? Especially when the veil seam made her nose itch and she grimaced like fury? Kyrin grinned, hesitated, then picked up her neck pouch. The rabbit skin was soft, embroidered with a cross of red and blue.

Ali disliked the necklace within it that her father gave her. Her master would not let her wear the sign of the fish at his table. She reached in the pouch.

The oak beads were dark with age, and the carved fish of iridescent shell shone the brighter, if a little thinner for her constant stroking. She released the necklace and pulled out a pearl armlet.

Shema had given it to her after Seliam snapped her pearl and shell necklace Ali had awarded her for defeating him. The pearls in Shema's armlet shone, bits of cloud interspersed with blue shell. Kyrin slipped it up her left arm, below her sleeveless blue serving thawb. The shades of color graced each other. The sickness had taken Shema so quickly. She missed her mistress's smile. Kyrin gave the cool armlet a minute turn.

Shema was gone, Tae was not here, and Sirius was hunting. There was no escape, and there was also no help for it. Kyrin turned toward the door and tripped on the blue hem of her thawb. *Ha! Graceful, Alaina? Let us hope my words this night prove better.*

§

Sirius Abdasir's face was bland when they entered the Blue Flower room. Ali took his water pipe from his mouth, the carved end wet with spittle. His hand shook.

At his word, Kyrin approached, folded her legs beneath her, and sank beside him with a half-smile. She could be graceful in that, at least. But Alaina was the one with the golden tongue.

"Why have you veiled, worthless one? Remove it!" Ali's voice was sharp.

Tensing, Kyrin dropped her veil in her lap without a word.

The wazir chuckled and looked from her to Alaina. Kyrin's hands stilled on her veil, crumpled the blue into a ball in one fist.

"Come, my guest," Ali said, beckoning the wazir. "Closer, O my friend. I have a trifle for your ears."

Sirius leaned toward Ali's whisper, and cinnamon wafted from his red sleeves. Kyrin drew a deep breath of the warm sweetness in spite of herself then glared and dropped her gaze. Like her father, the wazir must keep the spice in his clothes chest. At least it did not choke her, as Ali's heavy scents sometimes did.

Rather than carry the leanness of a wolf, Sirius Abdasir ought to be as fat as those who wove webs upon webs. Did he carry poison in several places on his person, in a packet up his sleeve, or in one of his rings? She knew his kind, a grasper after power, a player of chess on the palace board. Long ally of her master, the guardsman, now he was wazir to the caliph, with the caliph's regard. Doubtless Ali sought that favor.

"Does she please you?" Ali said in Sirius's ear, with a low laugh. Kyrin froze.

The wazir did not answer. He drew back, waving for Nimah, who approached with a platter of stuffed dates. He lifted three sweets from her dish and presented one to Kyrin with a grin. Kyrin looked at Ali, her heart beating fast.

"Take it, shy one," Ali growled.

Not worthless one? Kyrin reached for the date, forcing the tremor from her fingers. Did the fruit hold poison, maybe not of the belly, but of some vital move on the court board? A chess move she had missed? A wazir did not bestow food on a slave, much less a woman—unless she was his possession. Or did his gesture but acknowledge her skill in the way of the warrior? But Sirius had long heard of it.

He waved Nimah away. Nimah scuttled back, a rabbit startled by a wolf. Kyrin twisted her damp veil. Even Nimah sensed something amiss.

At the tables the guests filled the last corners of their bellies with tidbits, drinking tea. Their stares wandered from Kyrin's black earring to her face, to the wazir and their host, then circled again. They noticed nothing. Kyrin smoothed her scowl to soberness.

Tae was away, unlike the day she had fought for her very breath, for him and for Alaina. When the falcon called to her to refuse the ashes of hate, she disobeyed her master and obeyed the ruler of all, and doomed her second father and her sister to lingering death. But for some reason Sirius approved her decision to spare Seliam's life, and saved her from Ali's punishment. The regard of an Arab, one in power—what did he want?

What were his words? *He must be a warrior without match and must carry the touch of death in his hands.* Kyrin twitched against a crushing weight in her chest. Power. Tae's power, his knowledge. The death touch. That was what the wazir sought.

Kyrin forced herself to breathe. She ate her date. The sweet goodness of it surprised her; it ought to be bitter, bitter as dying hope.

How could she persuade the wazir that Tae was a man with some training, but without the skill he desired? That he was a simple warrior and healer, best left in Ali's hand? She, Tae, and Alaina might grow old in the caliph's service.

Sirius offered a date to Ali with a gracious smile and tossed one to Alaina. Then he looked at her.

Kyrin eyed him sharply. Her words would not fit this danger. There was prey afoot, and the tiger prowled. Tae must come soon. She searched the shadows in the room, passing over the wazir's motionless men in red and black. Nimah had passed her uneasiness to Zoltan, Kyrin was sure. Zoltan would have sent the word out for Tae. But Tae did not watch from the pillars, from concealment among the guests, or from the door. Something shifted beside the pillar at Ali's back.

Straw-colored hair under a black turban, an elbow robed in red, and the hem of a black cloak slid into the light. Seliam. He turned his head and moved back into shadow. She stared at him hard but his agate gaze remained unchanging. He held nothing for her.

The guests' voices thrummed in her ears. It was as Alaina said. Seliam did not see them, not this night. He'd posted eight men around his master, one at each corner of the dais, two inside the door arch, and one on either side of Ali and the wazir. Sirius kept his men close.

Ali's guests began to wash in bowls of rosewater the slaves held for them then drift out of the Blue Flower room after compliments to their host, with low bows to the wazir.

Sirius turned from a last obsequious guest before he finished scraping the rug with his sleeves, to bend an approving smile on Alaina. "It came to my ears you listen to the poets. What words do you find most harmonious in your pursuit of the holy tongue? Which lend themselves well to our poets and to your pen?"

Kyrin's teeth caught on her lip. A hunter's tactic—diversion.

"I commanded she learn our tongue," Ali shouldered in, "and she knows it well, to fit her for the tasks of the Most Excellent. Enough. What of the court? How is Hippole?"

"Ah, as all women tend to be," said Sirius, his eyelids sliding almost shut, "Hippole is well, but she does not look as well as these. But her voice—she rivals the sand lark." He glanced at Kyrin.

Ali grinned. "Would you enjoy comparing this one's voice to Hippole's, O my guest?"

Kyrin almost choked and swallowed so she did not splutter. Arabs. *Her* mother tongue did not twist in the mouth, did not give itself to the deceit of flowing Arabic, to those who destroyed or killed whatever they touched. But that was not quite true; the Aneza in the desert were honorable. And Faisal . . . but her master was far less than he.

Ali's smile strained his mouth and his large eyes were cold as the deepest ocean, heartless as an eel's. The pipe in his hand bent in his fleshy grip. Kyrin swallowed.

"Ah," the wazir said, leaning back with a wave of his hand, "she is skilled at arms, and should keep to her gift. But, my generous host, I would be greatly favored to speak with your hakeem." His dark eyes were intent.

Kyrin held her breath.

"Ahh," Ali muttered, "but we should do this without the healer. My hakeem is their husband, you know."

"Husband in name, as all know." Sirius's voice was dry as bone left to the sands.

"Yes," Ali said low. "Yes. The season is short." He swayed a little, and pushed himself up straight where he sat. Sirius's eyebrows rose.

Ali grasped Kyrin's arm. "Would you savor the nectar of this dark flower?"

Kyrin scrambled up, breathing fast.

Ali gave her a push toward Sirius. "It will do her good, to serve the one favored of the caliph with a song." He laughed and coughed harshly. "This flower has never had a bee." He recovered his breath and hummed, a contented sound.

Kyrin felt cold. She could not carry a single line of a song, and a bee and a flower ... *Ali gives me to the wazir for his bed? Has he been into the poppy for his pain? He must think the wazir strong enough to best me—or does he play a dangerous game of bait and switch, seeking to make Tae amenable to the wazir?* If the wazir touched her—if he took her to court—Tae would kill Ali for his treachery. Then Jachin would force Tae to his knees in the courtyard, his hands bound behind him. Umar's blade would flash into Tae's neck, loosing his life in a red flood on the flags.

Kyrin took a step toward Sirius. If she did not resist she might learn much. Nimah had gone. Umar stood without, and he did not favor her this moment, if he ever had. The wind might also change. *And if I must, I will be alone with the wazir, to finish what I start.*

"Ah, no." Sirius held up his hand. "Let your jewel rest, O my host, she is doubtless weary, and will bless me this night."

"Then, O my brother, I take her," Ali said, "though she warble as a hyena in my ear." His rattling laugh ended in a choking snort. Kyrin blinked, and felt sick. Ali cleared his throat with rasping effort, and Alaina gave a small, smothered cry. He ignored them. "My hakeem must learn obedience to his master. This one will be sweet, and school him well to my taste."

Quiet fell over the room, though the guests had not heard the low exchange. Kyrin stood frozen between Ali and the wazir.

"Aahh, yes." Sirius's smile tilted to one side; his eyes warmed to cinnamon. Kyrin drew a shivery breath. He bowed his head, solemn. "I accept your favor, O my host. Her voice will give me pleasure." The wazir gripped Kyrin and pulled her down behind his shoulder. His callused hand was a manacle of iron. He did not fear her.

Kyrin sat as he bid and did not try to pull away from him. He released her. At home, the bell had rung for Lauds. Uncle Ulf would be on his knees.

Courage, Alaina mouthed, tension in every line of her.

Yes. Kyrin forced her body to loosen. *Falcon. Watch, wait. Rise on the wind.*

Sirius cocked his head. "O my host, you are weary. You have entertained us well—overlong perhaps—"

"Not so, not so! Blessed of the Most Excellent, you are my guest, you exalt my house." Ali paused, and dropped his pipe. He fumbled for the hose, tumbled the nargeela on its side, and flung the pipe after it in disgust.

There was the faintest twitch at the corner of Sirius's mouth.

Kyrin sought Alaina's eye and looked pointedly toward the door. Her sister's lips firmed in refusal. Kyrin glared. A quiver ran over Alaina's shoulders. At last she looked down, accepting.

"So, how have your pearl beds been growing on the coast, mine host?" Sirius sipped his tea.

Ali's mouth twisted. "Ahh, poor. Poorer than they should be . . ."

Kyrin rolled her veil with cold fingers and tucked it into her sash. There—the hard edge of her small dagger. Alaina should already be outside the door. Why did she not go?

Her sister fiddled with Ali's discarded pipe hose with uneasy fingers, sniffed at the end, and sniffed again. She put it to her mouth for a curious puff, swallowed—and coughed, tears welling.

Ali turned, his face blank. Then he suddenly laughed, and laughed, until he wheezed. Alaina held his nargeela tightly, her face flushed, and refused his coaxing to have another puff. At last, with a grimace, she bent to it—and coughed explosively. Ali slapped her shoulder and roared. Kyrin was sure he left the print of his fingers on her skin. What was in her master's cursed tea—or was it in the pipe? *Alaina, go!*

Alaina rubbed her face, her eyes glazed, and spilled Ali's cup of tea in his lap with an awkward arm. He knocked her sprawling with the back of his hand. "Out, out! Nimah!" Ali called and bent, wheezing.

Alaina lay limp. With a frown, Kyrin rose to her knees. It was not possible such a light blow took her senses. The other slaves were gone, and Sirius's men took no notice. She looked for Umar, but Sirius grabbed her arm hard, without turning. Kyrin sank back, motionless until he let go. Alaina breathed.

Nimah hurried in. A male slave Kyrin had never seen stalked at her heels, head down. A kaffiyeh hid most of his face, and his robe was white. At their master's order, Nimah slid a terrified glance at Kyrin, seized Alaina under the arms, and pulled her out past the curtain, the heels of her slippers whispering over the floor. A chill hit Kyrin as her sister disappeared beyond the door arch.

The male slave poured Ali more tea. Had Tae's herbs for their master been adulterated? But Ali had smoked much more of the pipe than Alaina and he had not slept. It could not be that.

A cup slid into Kyrin's hand and she jumped. Sirius smiled at her, steadied the clean, dry cup in her hand, and had the slave fill it with lukewarm tea. It was not the moment to face the wazir down. Kyrin turned her glare on the slave. He did not raise his eyes, but Kyrin rather thought the sudden quirk of Sirius's mouth was amusement.

Her master took a long drink of tea and sighed.

Sirius said briskly, "Your table has refreshed Allah's servant. With your gift, by the rising of the sun I will be renewed."

The slave blotted Ali's robe dry, and Kyrin watched Sirius drain his cup. She sipped from hers. It tasted only of tea as far as she could tell.

The last guest stood, groaned good-naturedly, and patted his ample stomach. He left, and Umar scowled into the room, peering around the door arch. The new slave gathered the last of the dishes, placing each utensil so as not to make a sound. Fixed to its pillar, a lamp sputtered. Its flame stretched tall, and taller, soon to flicker out with the others.

Inscrutable in the dimness, Sirius's men stood, statues at the four corners of the dais. Spears in their hands, black bishts over their shoulders, their faces were brown and still with a warrior's patience. A spider's patience. Then she knew.

They waited for Tae.

3

The lot is cast . . .

Every decision is from the Lord. ~Proverbs 16:33

Alaina ran, ran, laboring through wind-rustled grass up the long side of the wadi. Her shins stung from the dry stems. Her lungs ached with running and the sharp residue of smoke.

Ali's herbs were vile. She had distracted him, but only for her sister. Her mouth tasted of bile. Their master would not dare use Kyrin that way unless he was out of his wits. Tae would kill him—and then he would die.

She stumbled. A sliver of moon above the wadi lit her uneven way over the shadowy, rock-scattered ground.

Was the wazir forcing Kyrin into his guest room this moment, to his bed? She did not believe Sirius found beauty in Kyrin's voice. Did he come to Ali's feast on the caliph's business and accept Kyrin only to please his host? It might be.

And if she could find Tae . . . he could persuade an oyster to give up its pearl. Gasping, Alaina forced her leaden legs on. Over the rise, the herdsmen's hut lay concealed, a low blot in a bare grassy bowl of hillside. *Oh Tae—be there.*

§

It was a long way back to the house. Tae swiftly took the cart track that zigzagged down the side of the wadi. Alaina skidded across the ruts, running over dirt, grass, and stone behind his near noiseless feet.

Halfway down the valley below them, Ali's house lay quiet. Above the south gate the torch was a dying ember. At last Tae stepped into the dim light. "High is the house of Ali Ben Aidon!"

The guard jerked his head up, and his hand slipped to his sword. Then his shoulders sagged with relief. Tae slapped his back. "The night is good for a run, my friend. And the master calls." His chest heaved.

The guard nodded, caught sight of Alaina, and stiffened. Tae's dark gaze skewered him. "Our master commands it. Let Umar prepare his Hand quietly. There may be jackals seeking to flee our master's generous table with that which does not belong to them. They must find Umar's salukis bold and fleet." The guard blinked and his jaw hardened. He opened the gate and closed it behind them without a word, then locked it and strode across the flags to disappear into the dark breezeway toward the stables, his hand on his sword.

About the court nothing stirred, nothing but the rustling, bare fig tree on its island in the middle of the court pool and the ripple of a diving frog against the stone edge.

Alaina shivered. Before her, the dark tunnel of the breezeway joined the kitchen on one side and the long wing of Ali's house on the other. Beyond that, a gate led to the women's court, with Ali's stables to the right. Past the great gate, a walker could go along a passage between, outside the wall, and across the wadi to the far fields, or to the isolated garden where they practiced the way of the warrior. If Kyrin were free, and hunted, she would go to the garden.

Alaina's throat closed and she gripped the blade in her sash. *They must still be in the Blue Flower room. There is no voice or torch in these shadows.*

The window to their quarters opened on the pillared porch paces beyond Tae. Their windowsill was quiet and shadowed, the first of many beneath the colonnade. Tae hurried past the porch, into the breezeway, then darted left into the house storeroom, ignoring the kitchen opposite, and the men's quarters adjoining it.

Alaina pattered after him, glancing over her shoulder. A late lamp glimmered across the flags from the kitchen. Women's voices murmured faintly. The locked main gate completed the circle of protection about Ali's house and his courts. But their enemy lay within.

They slipped past stoneware jars of olive oil, vinegar, pickled vegetables, and stored bottles of myrrh and scented oils. Baskets of grain, bunches of dates, garlic, onions, and herbs hung carefully apart from one another. Tae swung open the inner door to the house, pulling up on it, silencing its squeaky hinge.

They crept down the stone passage. The wazir's guest room loomed on the right, soon after the storeroom. It was dark under the door and quiet within. Alaina sighed soundlessly, but hardly comforted.

Anyone could conceal themselves in the pools of darkness between the guttering lamps. Her dagger held tight in one damp palm, it was hard to keep herself from clutching the back of Tae's thawb with the other. They flitted by the curtained, wood-paneled doorways to Ali's rooms on the left, then the rest of the house, including Mistress Shema's unused quarters. The women's quarters loomed before them. Bright, new-filled lamps hung beside the lintel.

The last tiny room on the left, their quarters lay near the end of the passage. Alaina glanced inside. Kyrin was not there. She had not really thought she would be. Her feet whispered past it after Tae, into the entry room and the great front door that gave on the court they had just left.

The bare stone walls were well lit. The guard outside had his back to the closed wood portal, as usual. He was not alarmed.

Alaina's chest ached. Kyrin had not fled, or fought. A few sandals remained along the wall, awaiting their owners. Would Kyrin return for hers?

They crept right, toward the Eagles' arch and the scene of harvest carved over the arch of the Blue Flower room. Alaina stopped short before she ran into Tae's back. The heavy curtains of sky-blue silk rippled. They were shut and Umar was gone. She held her breath in the silence.

Tae took in the barred room, the passage they came from off to the side, the walls, floor, and back to the closed curtain, blowing in the draft from the windows within. Whitened hair followed the old blade scar down toward his left ear. Abruptly he lifted his head. Power and tension coiled inside him, every muscle acting with every other. He had a hunter's senses. One night after training, when she ran back to ask him a question, she saw him.

He fought the straw man on the garden wall almost silently, with thumps of impact directed by precise breaths of energy. His target disappeared in a whirlwind of flying straw. When the chaff settled, Tae knelt in the midst, head bowed. His shoulders shook once, then stilled, rigid. He fought something that could not be conquered with feet and fists. Even then he had not struck in hot anger. Alaina left more quietly than she came.

Now his mahogany face held that same hard stillness, his gaze focussed. His mouth pressed together. He glanced at her, pointed two fingers at the floor with a walking motion, and flicked his hand forward.

Alaina nodded. To Sirius she was a familiar, assessed threat. Tae was not. She scuffed a foot and pushed through the curtains, parting them slowly, the silk blinding her. Ali cursed within and there came the thump of a blow. Her heart thundered. The curtain fell away from her with a whisper.

A spear point quivered before her nose. Alaina stumbled to a halt with a squeak. Then a sword pressed against her side, and something else pricked her back.

The spear wavered. Alaina clenched her fists, wishing for her staff. The wazir's guard should control his weapon. Beaded with sweat, his strong face was unyielding. Chain mail peeped from his red and black sleeve. After he looked her over his mouth slackened. He spat to the side in disgust. The breath of the guard behind her came quick.

A strangled gurgle came from the far side of the dais, near the marble hunter. Alaina turned her head—foolish movement—but where was Kyrin?

The wazir braced himself behind her, holding her by the arms. Kyrin swayed, grimacing as if she were about to be sick. But she had not made the choking noise.

Ali lay sprawled at the foot of the dais. His overturned nargeela was leaking across the floor. And Seliam knelt behind him, his dagger at Ali's throat. His face was grim.

The guard lowered his spear from Alaina's nose to her middle. She stretched her lips in a small smile, as if Sirius Abdasir played a jest on his caliph's behalf. An expensive jest, for there was a dark stain on the floor near Ali's feet.

Where were Umar and the rest of the guests? Sirius's guards had clustered about the door behind her. There were no bodies.

Alaina closed her eyes briefly. They had been waiting. And she had brought Tae.

Beyond the curtains the cook's voice echoed distantly, "You know the master's hand!" Every back in the room stiffened. Her voice shrilled, "Go, slothful one!" Tae grumbled a reply, unseen.

The thick-bodied guard before Alaina raised his spear and flicked a hand-signal. Steady footsteps neared. Tae stepped through the curtains.

In a blink, Alaina's guard had poised his spear at the base of Tae's throat, while another man held a sword to his side. The guard behind Alaina pressed harder on his weapon. Alaina tried not to move.

Tae gaped at them all. He almost dropped the wide bowl in his hands, steaming water sloshing over his fingers, then he steadied it and inclined his head to the wazir. He held up the bowl with a worried smile that said the guards were mistaken if they deemed him a threat, a mere servant.

The spearman slid around Tae, his weapon never leaving Tae's throat, and stopped at his back. Tae did not move, though the tip surely pricked his spine.

Sirius said mildly, "My esteemed brothers have gone to their rest. There is no need of rosewater or of washing." He watched Tae, his eyes narrow.

"Yes—my master." Tae bowed and turned away, obedient.

Ali's angry grunt rasped loud in the room, and he glared at Tae, wordless under Seliam's blade.

The wazir rapped, "Stop!"

Tae froze. He did not flinch at the sword one of his guards readied to thrust into his side. "O my master?" Hope and fear warred in his face.

Alaina bit down on a wild laugh. He was a masterful storyteller, his body articulating the subservient tale he wished.

"What are you called?"

Alaina pressed her lips together. Burn the wazir. Sirius knew Tae's name. He looked the same as he always had.

"My master names me Tae Chisun." It appeared Tae would play his game.

Sirius beckoned, imperious, and Tae approached. The wazir's guards followed, the spearman's mouth working unhappily.

Tae stopped just out of Sirius's reach, his gaze on the floor.

The wazir grinned. "You have not lost your touch, tending those of this house." He held Kyrin without effort.

"My master?" Tae looked up, his brow creased.

"Those in the house of Ali Ben Aidon have felt your healing hand, and your—other attributes. You taught your wives the way of the warriors of the East. You taught them, and their skill can kill." His dark eyes challenged Tae.

"Yes." Tae moved in assent. In less than a breath he stood straight as a rod, shorter by a head than every man in the room, but calm and strong as a mountain.

Alaina found her own back straightening.

Sirius cocked his head quizzically, his voice soft. "I require your obedience and your knowledge. There is one touch, is there not, to take a life?"

Kyrin's face went white. "Do not—" She jerked against Sirius Abdasir's grip then dropped with a pained cry as he shoved her down again.

Alaina tensed. "No!" There was warning pain in her side from her remaining guard's sword.

Sirius lifted his hand. His men instantly stilled. A drop of blood rolled down the back of Tae's neck, over his collar. He had not moved.

Kyrin knelt, her forehead almost touching the floor from the force of Sirius's painful grip that twisted her toward the floor. She blinked, her lashes flickering.

Alaina swallowed, breathing fast.

"My master," Tae said quietly, "my women will hinder your travel. They cannot harm you, and I will not oppose you. Will you let us fetch what you require for your road? We will test that there is no harm in dish or drink for your journey."

"Why should there be harm in my good host's house? Where do you think I go, O slave of my enemy? You may come alone—or with them. Are they not your wives?"

The guard at Alaina's back lifted his blade to her neck.

Tae closed his eyes as if pained, and opened them again, staring at the wazir.

Brows arched, Sirius waited.

A stillness grew within Tae, grew and spilled outward. A quiet waiting.

The wazir's lips twitched into a knowing smile.

Alaina swallowed hard. Unlike Tae, the wazir's eyes neither hated nor laughed. They were dead. As if this were a small thing in a chain of things, few of which mattered.

The wazir wanted the touch of death. He had heard rumors, or there was a loose tongue and spying eyes in Ali's household. Tae had hidden his knowledge of the death touch from all, though Jachin had guessed, once. Alaina felt numb. She and Kyrin did not yet possess that knowledge. And the wazir knew it.

Sirius nodded at Tae's tight-lipped silence. He gave rapid orders in an Arabic dialect Alaina could not make out. Tae did not resist the cords the wazir's men drew tight about his elbows and wrists. They dug into his flesh.

Kyrin's breath came ragged. Sirius released her and dropped a hand to her waist to urge her to her feet. The haft of the falcon dagger peeped from Kyrin's blue sash under his fingers, the bird glaring at the world. Sirius paused, and his hand curled around the weapon.

Alaina's breath caught. The falcon drew trouble. Its courage either called evil, or met it. She shook her head. As if that thought mattered.

Kyrin staggered up. The wazir pulled the blade free. "I will put this in a place of safekeeping."

Kyrin's gaze glowed like jet. Her mouth opened and closed. Then she let out a breath and her shoulders slumped.

Oddly, her glare did not anger the wazir. Ignoring her, he slid the falcon through his own sash. Alaina thought the bird hunched between its feathered shoulders, amber gaze scornful, indignant at its position in the sash of the second highest ruler of the land.

As indignant as Kyrin.

Alaina put the back of her hand to her mouth to stifle a croak of sudden laughter.

Still in Seliam's grasp, Ali pounded his slippered feet against the floor in inarticulate triumph, straining forward. Seliam slid his arm further around his neck lest Ali inadvertantly open his throat against his blade. Caring nothing for anything else, their master bent a wide, thin smile on Tae, who ignored him. Ali coughed violently, and finally pressed back against Seliam to catch his breath.

Alaina went rigid. Seliam. It was plain enough. He had betrayed them, and her master was become enemy to the wazir.

Sirius's captain turned. His hair was straw-pale, and when his cold eyes landed on Alaina his mouth flattened. As if he would cut Ali's throat with pleasure. Alaina did not step back, but faced the menace in him.

Her master trained worthy slaves and had filled many important positions for the wazir and the caliph. For which of them was he condemned? Ali somehow thwarted the caliph's will. If the wazir wished it, their blood would not add much to the mess of overturned tables and scattered cushions between the pillars. His men stalked about the room, taking nothing, looking through everything.

One of the guards pushed over the marble statue. The hunter fell, shattering about the fountain, the crash reverberating through the stone under her feet. The guards picked through the marble pieces.

What did they search for? Most of the lamps on the pillars had gone out; only those over the dais lit the disarray, flames flickering weakly as if with shame.

Alaina breathed deep. It was not over. She loosened her muscles. Tae was with them, and she must be ready.

Finished with Tae's bonds at last, Sirius's guards urged him away from the seat at the end of the table and toward the door. They guarded him close, not trusting to the cords. As he passed, Tae gave no warning movement of fingers, feet, or brow. Alaina lifted her hand, like a small lost bird fluttering after him. He stared ahead, heedless of the guards, of the wazir's voice, of all around him. He did not look back.

She took a step, and hard hands walled her away. She found herself turning to plead, falling to her knees. "My master—Sirius! My Lord Wazir! We are not your enemy. Please! Let us go with him."

"My soul is pained to part you, but it must be so. In sha'allah." Satisfaction lurked about Sirius's mouth. He said something in that strange dialect once again. His men tightened their grip on Alaina and pulled her back toward the curtain, after Tae, despite her struggles.

Not resisting the wazir's grip on her arms, Kyrin eased her head from side to side—*don't fight.*

Anger rose in Alaina. They were not pulling her sister after Tae.

The curtains closed around him. With a sob, Alaina let the guards drag her where they would. She poured out her heart to Kyrin, silently willing her the strength and courage of a sister's love.

For Kyrin could kill the wazir, she could. If they did not bind her for his pleasure. Tae too, could have killed him—and he did not. For she and Kyrin would have died also.

Did Sirius count his pawns of so little value in the caliph's court? Alaina struggled to find her feet. This time she would walk out of her own will.

The curtains blurred through her tears. Her sister would kill if she had to.

Father above, give us grace. Fly high, falcon, my sister. Stoop swift, take the heart.

4

So are my ways higher than your ways. ~Isaiah 55:9

Kyrin gulped air, trying to steady her knees as Alaina stumbled out of the Blue Flower room after Tae and the guards. *Lord! Don't let them kill them!*

Sirius kept one hand on her arm while his men strode this way and that, shoes whispering over stone and wood, their robes trailing over cushions. Nothing left unturned, in moments they had gathered before the wazir again. Ignoring everyone, Seliam stared at the back of Ali's head, his mouth a grim line. The room held too much movement, pain, and anger trapped in stillness.

The wazir gave Kyrin into the care of a stocky guard and slid an ornate sword from a sheath another man in red and black held for him. The wazir turned the weapon, ran a finger along the edge. He grunted and replaced the blade, took the sheathed weapon in his hand. What did he mean to do with it? Kyrin's throat felt thick.

"Take Ali Ben Aidon to the court," Sirius Abdasir said to Seliam curtly. The captain urged Ali up.

Her master's shoulders were bowed. The north window above the shattered hunter seemed to hold his gaze. It was likely he went to his death, out in the court. A death deserved many times over. But no one should die alone. Would he listen to his worthless one?

Bitterness choked Kyrin like wormwood. *Worthless one.* But she was not the name he had given her. The Master of the stars gave her another. Kyrin opened her dry mouth and croaked, "My master—remember the mercy of Jesu!"

Sirius cuffed her absently, as if out of habit. Kyrin's ear burned. Ali did not move, as if he were already a shell of a man. Kyrin bowed her head. There was nothing more to be done.

Never glancing at her, Seliam forced her master out through the curtain, his breath wheezing. Kyrin's heart was heavy as stone. She had once spared Seliam's life. Was he ever her friend?

The wazir beckoned to a slender guard with a thin, pocked face as he strode toward the door after them.

The stocky man followed him, while the thin warrior fell in and moved with Kyrin, his dagger a steady pressure at her back. No escape from his vigilance.

After Seliam dealt with her master, the wazir would likely send his captain to hunt down Umar and Jachin. She did not know where he had put Alaina and Tae. The wazir might count on that, that unknowing, to bind them all to inaction.

Pausing under the arch of the Blue Flower room, Sirius turned his head to look at her. "It is done. Disloyalty has brought its price." He smiled thinly. "Bring her." He spun on his heel. "Let nothing be heard in the men's quarters."

The weasel guard nudged Kyrin between the shoulders with his blade, amusement tugging one side of his mouth. Wordless, mouth tense, Kyrin followed the wazir's straight back as Sirius ignored possible ambush in the passage and strode toward his guest room. He would not be so cheerful if he knew Jachin was about, as Jachin must be, and Umar. Kyrin's heart sank.

It was so quiet. Did Sirius know that Jachin was dead, and did Nara and the rest also lie still somewhere in the rooms they passed? He had ordered no noise to be heard from the men's quarters. He might have lied to Tae, and killed them all.

The wazir stepped aside. The guard's weapon forced Kyrin through the guestroom door ahead of his master. Her foot caught on the hem of her thawb, and she stumbled inside. The door creaked shut behind her and latched with a click. Sirius stood in front of it.

Kyrin pivoted away from him to conceal her right side, noting a stool and a small table beneath a window that looked over Ali's fields. A brazier flanked them. She stopped with her back to the window. A crisp kaffiyeh hung from a peg near the door. Under it a long pallet held baggage, bound with cord. He was leaving, soon.

Kyrin dragged in a harsh breath. Buried in her sash her small blade lay hard against her side. There was no time for quiet removal.

Sirius had been a warrior all his life. Likely he cut his teeth on a dagger. She would use the dagger and the stool, then if those failed, the baggage and the brazier—but first she must find out where he held Tae and Alaina.

Sirius leaned against the door and crossed his arms, a most un-wazir-like pose. The wood groaned. His eyes lingered on her with a slight frown, more disconcerting than if he looked at her in the usual way of men. Kyrin winced. He seemed to want to pierce her soul.

Something flickered in his eyes and his mouth turned down.

She willed her heart and breath to slow. *Lord, give me a solid strike before he closes. Last I grappled with Alaina, she won.*

Sirius sighed and stepped forward, his shoulders broad. "You have tangled my net, but this hour is mine."

Kyrin lunged aside, hit her shin against the stool. Then she had it, and her blade in her other hand, hidden by the wood seat, and she spun in a crouch.

"No!" Sirius wrenched his bare sword before him. "You will be here but a moment, and never there." He flicked the tip of his long blade at his pallet without dropping his vigilance.

He had refused Ali's offer of her once. But if he meant to question her about the touch of death . . . The stool trembled in her hand.

Sirius turned his back and moved to the table. Kyrin swiveled, a hound to the circling jackal, ready. The door was at her back now, a better prospect than the window. Or not, with the weasel guard outside.

"Good." Sirius reached a hand for the stool. Reached as if she could and would give it to the hand of her rightful master. She bit her lip, weighing his patience and her chances.

Sirius smiled, a straight gash in his face, and his voice was dry. "Men serve me, not wood. I leave you in your wisdom to divine which is the stronger."

Kyrin slid the stool across the floor. He sat with a bone-wracking sigh and laid his sword across the end of the table. Kyrin gaped at him. He glanced from her dagger to her face.

"I put your hakeem with my guards: for his life and for my own. Life is precious, do you not think?"

The back of Kyrin's neck tightened to the point of pain. He was laughing at her, with Tae and Alaina in his hand. Sirius leaned forward and the spark of amusement in him went out.

"I will speak a word in your ears. Open them."

Kyrin tightened her grip on her blade.

"You are from Britannia, the isle of cold fog. Do you wish to leave your bones here?" His dark eyes under his turban held her as fast as nails. "I think your hakeem does not desire his last breath in my fiery land, blessed as it is of Allah. He comes from the East, bound though he is not to return."

How did Sirius know of Huen's letters? No one else would have told him of Tae's exile—except Umar. In the last missive, Tae's wife, Huen, had sent her joy that Tae lived. She said that her father, Kuksun to the army, did not yet speak Tae's name.

Kyrin licked her lips. Longing, her's for home and Tae's for Huen had nothing to do with what the wazir wanted. Though she knew little of the death touch. better the wazir asked her than forced answers from Tae.

Sirius's face tightened. "Your husband will stay and teach the caliph's men to ward my master with his skill. I send you to your land."

Kyrin stared at him, her limbs stiff as a fly's that is dropped in honey.

Sirius raised his hand. "Your sister will go with you on your task. A traveler of the sands, whom the caliph seeks, is believed to be captive in Britannia. The light of my eyes—"Sirius's voice caught. He lowered his voice to a growl, "You will find this one. Named Hamal Abdasir, of my blood, he is a brother's son. The caliph has forbidden me this journey, blessed be he."

Words both proud and bitter. Yet there was something behind the twist of his mouth, the pain in his brown eyes. A plea. For what? Mercy for his lost nephew? Rose and smoky clouds colored the waking sky outside the window. Sirius did not seem after the death touch, not yet.

"My horses and men will take you to the Red Sea, then to Gaza and my ships. You will ride the waves to the land of fog. So it will go well with your hakeem." The wazir's brows drew down. "Ali Ben Aidon has betrayed the most Blessed of Allah. My hand will remove him from the earth; he is no longer your master. You have served well, with your sister. Find Hamal. It is your task, the last for the most Illustrious, blessed of Allah."

Kyrin's throat was too dry to swallow. She hesitated, ready to turn homeward on the dawn air wafting through the window. Escape. She could even hear Uncle Ulf's Benedictine bell. Prime. She shivered. *Is this the beginning of the way you make for me, Master of the stars? To leave Tae behind and go to find my father?* She would be free with Alaina and Cicero, with a bow in her hand.

At least Ali would harm no one again. If the wazir's tongue was true—*give me wisdom.*

A honeybee careened through the window with the morning coolness. It bumped against the wall. Buzzing, it escaped to a bunch of trumpet flowers nodding on the sill, a last bloom of honeysuckle kept awake by the house's warmth. Nothing and no one could keep him if he wished to leave. Like the bee, Tae could make it out on his own. Unless they chained him every moment. And even with chains, she would not wager on his captors. He would escape when the season was right.

The wazir waited, silent. The bee bumbled away. Kyrin walked to the table. Her eyes stung. She stretched out her arm.

When she pulled back, her blade lay on the wood. "I swear to you, with my God's help, to see Hamal return to you. I know what it is to see one close to you"—she swallowed hard—"lost. How will I know Hamal? Who had word of him, and where, in my land?" She leaned forward, gripping the table edge. "But I need Tae. He protects and heals and finds what is lost, none better."

Sirius cleared his throat, took her weapon from the table, and slid it in his sash beside the falcon. "Hamal is your height, with near twice your years." He stretched out a silk-shod foot and hooked the brazier nearer, cocked an eyebrow at her. Kyrin looked away from the falcon blade, a bronze flame against his blood-red thawb, the falcon's eyes dark and yearning. She flushed, and the wazir grinned. "Hamal is brown haired, and his eyes burn when he is stirred or his bag of coins is plucked. His anger would make you serve him, but also his good pleasure; he is quick as a flame and gentle as a gazelle. And what may catch the gazelle unaware?" The wazir leaned back, a bitter, pained curve touching his lips. "A snare, poison—or hard words." He stared out the window. Then his gaze pinned her again. "Hamal sought the lore of alchemists, in the service of his caliph. To create hot gold for the glory of Allah."

Kyrin stared at him. No wonder the tiger hunted among them in the Blue Flower room. How could a man bring such a thing as gold into being? Gold came out of the ground. It could not be created, only shaped.

Father once showed her how her mother's gold torque came from the mine. She had watched the jeweler heat it, mold it, and set it with a green stone for her mother's last birthday feast. Kyrin swallowed the ache in her throat. She would go to Cierheld and find her father. If only she could take the falcon dagger. Her mother would not return, but she would go to her someday, and rejoice with her in the kingdom of the Master of the stars.

The wazir stood slowly, watching her. "News of Hamal came to me from a house called Cedsel, which sells slaves. I do not know where it lies in your land. Your hakeem will serve the caliph until a year is gone. If honor is his, Tae Chisun will depart for his house and his land with gifts. I will keep him bound until messengers from my ships tell me you and your sister have boarded."

Kyrin said, "Is my word straw, that I will not keep my oath?"

"I know slaves. Your tongue may be true now. But later, your heart may change. Tae Chisun stays to seal the word of your mouth, and you go to secure the goodwill of the most blessed."

He handed her a small leather bag full of the hard roundness of coin.

Sirius was a stone wall and a barred window, and she a bee, beating against him. Did stone never crumble? Might she at least find where Tae and Alaina and Jachin were held? "O my master—"

He scowled, his patience at an end. "Be silent, and wait without."

Kyrin knelt, touched her forehead to stone. Would she ever be done bowing to men?

Sirius rose, stepped outside, and spoke low to the guard. He departed without another word. The guard beckoned. Kyrin dragged her feet as he escorted to the storeroom. Then she was inside, and the bolt thunked behind her. It was black. The door to the breezeway and the kitchen was locked also, and there was not the smallest crack around the frame because of rats.

Sirius did not trust her. Kyrin laughed, a snort that turned into a sob. That edge cut both ways.

She took a few cautious steps, sliding her feet over the floor. A bag of grain touched her ankles, and she sank onto it.

She was going home to the smell of oaks, the rustle of leaves; to gentle rain, chuckling streams, dew and heather; the call of robins and the hawk. She was returning to Cierheld and her falcons. She would find Father and Aunt Medaen and Uncle Ulf—but what could she have said to the wazir to free Tae? Never could she leave him in Sirius's hands. She did not trust power hungry Arabs, much less the caliph and those under him.

She knew who she could trust. It was unthinkable to do nothing. But the doors were shut. What did the Master of the stars want her to do? Did he mean for her to wait? Wait, at a time like this? At least the grain bag was softer than the floor. She sighed.

Abrupt feet moved beyond the door. Kyrin tensed. The steps faded into silence. For age-long moments her breath whispered in and out, and her blood thumped. The sharp odor of onions and the light scent of dates reached her nose. The rough sack beneath her did nothing to prevent the creeping chill. Her uncle would say the bell for Prime had passed.

But how to get Tae away from the wazir? She did not even know where her second father lay bound. Then he would help her find Alaina. But if Tae were chained, how would she find the key?

A hot tear slid down her cheek, and another. Tightness in her chest choked her in the darkness. Even if Tae could get free on his own, she would not forsake him to danger. She would not leave him, though it might be a hard fight for the key.

Tae did not take kindly to any man telling him what he should teach of his art, let alone the wazir. If he did not think a man's heart worthy of the knowledge, he would refuse him. Torture or no.

Lord of all . . . ahhh, why did it take her so long to ask? The Master of the stars knew her heart. She linked her hands behind her head and curled over her knees. *I cannot think.*

Plunked in the stream of life she was a whirled pebble. But surrounded by his power. The stars circled in the deep heavens, sap rose in tree and leaf, delicate flowers unfolded, suns were guided and ended, and the joyful water of life danced, given to all things by the One who made them. *Help.*

The heat in Kyrin eased, and she breathed less desperately. In this moment she need do nothing but trust. It was what he left her to do, in the circle of circumstance. Weariness sank into her bones like lead. Her nose itched, and she sneezed. The grain—she hoped her face did not swell as it often did at harvest.

Her stomach growled. Opening different sacks and containers, she found the dates and ate a handful, wiping her sticky fingers on the sack. Her hands stilled. They would need food in the desert. She would be sure it was only food. Rummaging around, she tasted contents as she gathered healing and cooking herbs for Tae, a sack of grains mixed to her and Alaina's taste, a sack full of dates, and a box of Ali's fine tea. Kyrin emptied a sack, wrapped her treasures in it, tucked it in another, and curled up.

The hollow scrape of the breezeway door woke her. She could barely see. Her face had swollen, sleeping on the grain sacks. She rolled over. Shadows against the light, two men pulled her to her feet. "Where do you take me?" Her skin buzzed as if a hive of bees lay under the surface.

They did not answer, but knocked her bag from her hand and tugged her out the opposite door. Warm sunlight bathed Kyrin between blurred shapes of dark and light. They hustled her from the main court into the echoing stable court. Camels complained; a donkey brayed. She drew a breath through her stuffy nose, and the odor of manure, feed, and straw mixed harshly. The stables needed cleaning, and the dogs—a low, inquiring whine rose close before her. Cicero!

"I will open the gate." It was one of Umar's stable boys. The guards released her a moment. She tripped over a dark bundle on the flags, and the corner of the kennel raked her thigh. Her hands scraped red stone.

The guards' fingers dug into her shoulders, and they yanked her up. One of them growled and slapped her. Eyes tearing, Kyrin cringed and kept her feet by feel. The tall wall of the kennels swam before her—and the shadow of the great back gate creaked open.

Sirius lied. Not a slave honored with an important task, but one marked for death.

5

Struggles

Because the days are evil. ~Ephesians 5:16

Unresisting, Kyrin sagged between the guards, bending her knees. And launched upward. Using their hold on her arms, she lifted and kicked out with both feet. Missing one guard, she struck the knee of the man on her left. She used that tenuous perch to leap toward the other guard, who'd slapped her.

The first man screamed as his leg broke with a crack, and she fell toward the gate atop the other man, with a knee in his gut. Reflexively, he grabbed her arm when she tried to run. Caught, she scrabbled for position at the guard's back, wrapping her legs around his middle, going for his neck from behind as they hit the flags. He smelled of garlic and oil.

"Help!" As the stable boy yelled, the gate crashed shut.

The guard grunted. He turned, strong as a bull, reaching for a good grip, but he was not accustomed to fighting on the ground. Kyrin turtled her chin against her chest to deny him her throat and turned her head to bite. Her teeth found flesh. He groaned and swore, trying to pull aside.

Using that momentum, she flattened him, and worked herself toward his head. She bore down with all her weight on his chest, pinning his arms and denying him the leverage to throw her off. By degrees, she edged around the curve of one arm. He fought furiously, his prone length trapped between her digging knees and elbows, as he strove to land a solid blow. She gave him no opening.

At last her elbow touched his neck. Like a crab, she spun across his torso to anchor her heels in his sides, and shoved her forearm across his throat as if to grind him into the stone. She could not see, only feel, her face turned to avoid his gouging fingers. She was almost there. Her breath came hard, counterpoint to his.

He gurgled harshly, straining to free himself. She worked her other arm beneath his neck, reached to clasp her forearm. Her fingers touched. *Grip, rotate*—and she had the headlock. In panic, he bucked against the sudden loss of both blood and air to his head. Kyrin held on with all her strength.

It would be but moments until the guard was senseless, but if the stable boy poised to strike her, she was undone. There were running feet, a questioning voice from Nara's kitchen.

Umar's salukis raised a sudden clamor in the farther kennel. The guard clawed at her, weakening. But she was close as a lover, her cheek to his. Though his nails scored her ribs, he could not dislodge her.

A body thumped into the kennel fence behind her. Kyrin jerked but held on grimly. Claws rasped as a whining saluki slid down on the other side. Cicero's paws pattered rapidly away, came flying closer: another thump and slide. An urgent whine of desperation. He hit the wood withes again, growling.

The guard went limp. Kyrin held him for six breaths, then pushed away and scrambled up. She did not have the three moments needed to make sure he never bothered her again. No time.

Nearby, the first guard gave a gasping shout. "You!" A dim shadow to the side, he staggered up on one leg.

The gate—

As she spun away, Kyrin's robe twisted about her ankles, taking her feet. A camel grunted when her shoulder slammed into its foreleg. She rolled under the beast, and scrubbed at her eyes. She must pry them open—must see.

The guard panted after her, cursing, his leg dragging. Vague shapes of men in red flowed toward her. Someone closer cried, "Shut the inner gates! No one must get out!"

The gate to her left was already closed. But the vines growing over the wall to her right would hold her. They would let her into the women's court. Kyrin rolled over.

Cloth of red filled her vision, close enough to touch. She gathered her legs under her. It couldn't be the camel's travel bags, not so rich a maroon. The red shifted. And Sirius cleared his throat. She was out of moments.

Kyrin made a small noise and stiffened against her instinctive strike. She could not see if the wazir held a sword above her head. Cinnamon tingled in her nose.

She put her hands on the flags carefully. "I'm sorry. They hit me. I can't see."

No blow fell. Her shaky voice was a crow's. Her throat itched as badly as her skin. She needed some of Nara's tea before her lungs swelled and her lips took on a bluish cast.

The second guard woke and made it to his feet, swaying. "You are dead, caster of evil!"

He drew nearer, and she couldn't see him.

Sudden heat boiled through Kyrin. "I want to *know* if a sword comes for me. Not be taken out the back gate to die like a dog!"

Sirius shouted, a word she could not understand. Kyrin tensed. To her surprise, the guards retreated.

The wazir put a hand on her arm. Kyrin caught her breath, but he simply guided her to her feet, his other hand on her waist. Not holding a blade, then.

"My thanks—O my master." She was glad of his hold. Her knees threatened to go. She was shaking with fear and anger both. Her side burned. She tried to look at him.

"Ah." Sirius's touch was cool and impersonal on her hot face. "What happened to your eyes?"

"The grain in the storeroom makes my face swell, but herb-water and tea help. And myrrh and pineapples. It will not keep me from riding."

"No, but you may slow Seliam if you cannot see. Still more if you cannot see your way to loyalty." He touched her bronze earring lightly, and the black earring shifted in her other ear. Cold skittered across her skin.

There was a loud bark, and a taut, hairy body hit Kyrin's legs and turned, growling. Her bones vibrated with the force of Cicero's rage. "Cicero, no!" As she pulled him back from the wazir, her hands found her saluki's head and one of his teeth. Cicero sat, muttering in his throat. Kyrin curled her slashed palm, ignoring the sharp pain.

Sirius's snort was almost a clipped laugh. "Seliam!" he called over his shoulder. He faced her. "For the loyalty of your hound, Ali's ring of ownership will bind you no more. You mistook my men's actions, is it not so? But you have said you will keep my trust."

"Yes, Excellent One." She was not to die. Kyrin let out a shaky breath. She curled her fingers around Cicero's silky ears, her heart almost breaking with warmth for him. When she was gone from this place, Cicero would eat like a king.

Seliam came. He did not meet her eyes, now open enough to clearly see the file in his hand. *Traitor.* She did not wish to ask *him* to fetch her bag from the storeroom. He let Tae go to undeserved bonds. How dared Seliam tell her nothing of the wazir's designs after she gave him his life and they practiced with the blade together?

Her back straight, she turned her head stiffly aside. Seliam filed at her master's bronze earring. He kept the ring in a careful vise grip, and it did not twist and hurt with the force.

In a moment, Ali's ring of ownership was broken. Seliam tugged it from her ear. Her head felt light.

The wazir nudged the jet earring of the evil eye with his finger. "Your word," he said, his voice full of challenge, "must break this one."

Kyrin lifted her chin and held Sirius's blurred frown in her vision. Surely he had heard Ali's suspicious mutters of his worthless one, and her casting of an evil eye. But the wazir wore no blue bead or token to ward its power. He did not fear it. Her eyes, which darkened almost to black with shock, pain, or fear, had not seemed to make him uneasy. Had he not noticed?

The wazir gave her a sharp nod and murmured orders to Seliam.

She shrugged. Mayhap it was better so. It seemed that little troubled the wazir. Seliam flinched almost imperceptibly as his gaze caught hers. He was a different matter. Did he fear the evil eye, or did he remember she had held his life as she did the guard's, with the same hold about his neck?

Kyrin ran her finger around the black earring, bitterness in her mouth. *Never free. I carry the taint of men's fear whether I bear the ring or no. The touch of death assures it.* The jet was as slick and heavy as a sun-warm snake to her touch. *No.* She would break it, the earring and the fear in Seliam's eyes. And she was always free, free to do right. Kyrin turned her back on Seliam. She was free to try as she could to keep her oaths and find her father.

Her father. She had not been able to improve her practice with the bow, as she'd sworn the night her mother fell. Father might scorn her ability to wield herself as a weapon, to serve a table, and not much else. She had barely begun the sword. Mastery took more years than she had lived. And embroidery needles and cooking spoons turned on her efforts with a vengeance, though her rice managed to fluff and not burn.

Kyrin stroked Cicero's smooth head. Would rice equal well cooked porridge in Aunt Medaen's eyes? And her robes: the abominable half-veil and the comfortable thawbs. Old Medaen would surely wish to burn *them.* Kyrin twisted the jet earring hard, the sting keeping back her tears.

Esther would lift her nose, her demure mouth would tilt, and her assured green gaze rake Kyrin from mussed hair to Arabian slippers. Poised Esther never missed an awkward moment in the lives of those around her. They were potential arrows in her quiver, every mistake a drop of blood guiding the wolf to prey.

Kyrin sighed, and glared at Seliam's back in regret. Why had he betrayed them? The Master of the stars would frown on her using the arrow of Seliam's fear against him. But to watch him sweat would be a boon.

§

Seliam stood guard over her in the kitchen, after bringing her bag from the storeroom across the breezeway. Her face felt thick, and she knew it was blotchy. Her cheeks heated that Seliam should see her so. *Fool, to sleep on the grain.*

Somewhere in the house, Alaina and Tae lay bound. Nara bathed Kyrin's face and bound her slashed hand and wounded side with myrrh and aloes. Kyrin's eyes opened further after the cook's dose of myrrh-water. She dried her face on a towel Nara handed her. The Egyptian grasped her elbow with her wide hand, her straight-cut black hair swaying forward, covering her cropped ear. "I would have your promised recipe before you leave, girl."

Kyrin blinked. Nara was as unshakable as ever. But to think of cooking at a moment like this?

Nara nodded slowly, her dark eyes catching glints of light. "Our hakeem has a taste for hart that runs free. Not for him, these hand-fed gazelle. As it is with your father, so it is with your master. Free air runs in their blood." She sniffed. "I must have a recipe to fit the need."

Kyrin's heart gave a great thump. Freedom, and Tae. But what did Nara mean by the wazir's need? He was not bound. But that was of no import now. "Which recipe do you desire?" She could think of nothing that would help.

Seliam grinned at Nara and drew a bit of paper from his sash. "This may fit *your* need." He glanced at Kyrin. "If you seek the ingredients for one of Alaina's dishes, we will feast well."

Kyrin glared, and his smile fell away. He understood written Arabic, being in the caliph's service. Forcing her fingers open, she accepted the coarse paper from him and a charcoal stick that Nara held out to her. He *should* shift his feet. Alaina would rather poison him.

One of her sister's dishes indeed! This was her own. Kyrin bent her head. At the top she wrote "Stew of Hart" in Latin. "Tae will know how to cut it" she scratched down after "one haunch of hart." Next she listed two hares, potatoes, carrots, and various restful herbs. Kyrin added, "Immerse the most Illustrious golden potato you may find, and marshall the red carrots to follow it in our master's longstanding herb mix, that they may marinate in long rest. Ready the hart. At evening, return the two browned hares to the pot. Cook without stirring. Add a pinch of rosemary and sage to the herbs—to improve taste. Add cloves and a bit of honey. Let all in the house eat of our 'Stew of Hart.' See that you sleep well, do not let yourself be burned! With all done, hang what remains of the hart in a white cloth in the sheep's hut, to age in the free air. The second morning's stew is best.

"Remember us, and cook well this 'Stew of Hart.' Kyrin Cieri of Cierheld."

The letters felt strange. The charcoal rasped across Seliam's paper. If this seed of a plan bore fruit, soon she would scribe messages on skin parchment in her father's stronghold, and send word to a hall called Cedsel, seeking news of Hamal.

Nara took the missive, mouthed the concealing words. Brows drawn, she looked at Kyrin.

"Tae will read it to you. It is Latin." She hoped he and Nara understood her buried instructions.

Seliam stepped forward to stare curiously over Nara's shoulder, and the cook whirled. "If you smudge my recipe, you will never taste a finger's drop!"

Seliam drew back, with an abashed shrug.

Cicero trotted in and lay down at Kyrin's feet, panting.

Dried blood speckled his paws about his nails. Kyrin rubbed his head. He had leaped the fence to defend her against Sirius—or the stable boy let him out.

Seliam frowned and strode over to grasp Cicero's neck and pull him away, though without violence. Kyrin stiffened. He dare not lay a hand on Cicero.

In the kitchen doorway, Zoltan reached out, crooning. "Come, my wind-runner, let us salve your paws, as your mistress would wish. You will run swift again."

Seliam released Cicero. His ears perked up at Zoltan. Then Cicero turned his head, and his almond eyes pierced Kyrin. He walked to her and his teeth closed on her hand, gentle. His tail waved to and fro, once. Then he released her and went to Zoltan, regal and solemn. Kyrin swallowed the lump in her throat and did not call him back.

"Go! All of you! Out! His hair, however noble, must not mix with the wazir's stew." Nara shepherded them out of the kitchen, an indignant wind. In the breezeway, Seliam turned to watch Zoltan lead Cicero away, his fingers tapping his sash thoughtfully.

Kyrin gave the cook a fierce hug. "You walk in my thoughts, Nara. The Master of the stars keep you."

"You will travel far, with him." Nara cupped Kyrin's face in her large hands, her smile wavering. "I also hold you in my heart. Fly high, Shaheen."

Shaheen—falcon. With more than a desert wind under her wings. "I will, Nara. You have all the feathers of my goodwill. And you will ever be in my prayers." Kyrin brushed at her wet cheek. She hadn't thought she could cry when she left Ali's house.

§

Alaina was in their quarters, guarded by a man named Hadden, who stood alert in the wazir's red outside the door. Tae was not there. Her sister rolled Tae's empty mat up, her face bleak, and laid it aside. She reached for his blanket, refusing to look up at Kyrin. Tae's sword and stick were gone, with every other weapon.

Kyrin knelt beside her. "Alaina, all is not lost. The wazir sends us on an errand—to Britannia."

Alaina froze, Tae's folded blanket in her hands.

Kyrin laid her finger on her lips and glanced at the door. "I will tell you the rest as we ride."

Alaina gave a choked giggle. She grimaced and said, louder, "Camels again. Whisper sweetly in Lilith's ear so she does not bite me. She may have forgotten me, though I take her dates every seven-day."

Kyrin took the falcon dagger's empty sheath from beneath her mat and tucked it inside her thawb. With few words, she and Alaina changed from Ali's blue to their desert garb, the old thawbs' hems now rising above their ankles. Their tumultuous journey across the sands with Ali's caravan against raiders, sand, wind, and war seemed endless seasons ago.

Kyrin's forehead furrowed. Nara had thrown out their tattered bishts, and Ali had long before taken away the woven green cloak her mother made her, with her stronghold key.

She took her neck pouch and in her other hand weighed the pearl and shell armlet Shema gave her, twin to the necklace Ali bestowed on her after her trial by sword. It more than reminded.

Alaina shook out her mat vigorously. "You may need that."

Kyrin nodded. The armlet joined Seliam's treachery with memory of sweet, fiery Shema and Ali. All she had of them was memory. She dropped the armlet in her pouch, tied it around her neck, and strode to the door.

She ignored Seliam, standing in the passage opposite, and gave a message to Hadden. She asked the wazir to return her key of Cierheld as proof of her inheritance, and her green cloak. Hadden left and returned swiftly. "The lady of the house keeps your cloak and key."

She ought to have known. As the eldest of Ali's concubines, wily old Qadira *would* have them. Kyrin kept her face expressionless. They finished packing their blankets, Subak gear, Alaina's needles and thread, and the carved hair sticks Tae had made them. Alaina added a few scrolls that they thought might be useful to their bundles.

Then it was time to face the ladies of the house. In the women's quarters, Seliam and Hadden peeled away and took up posts inside the door. The women were wary as red deer. Only Nimah smiled at Kyrin, small and uncertain, her radiant beauty fallen from her, muddied by fear and uncertainty. Clothes, bedding, and food were scattered about the room, painstaking needlework cast away like scraps destined for the midden. The women stood against the walls, veiled, their eyes on their feet, darting sidelong glances at Seliam and Hadden, hands clenched in their robes. Would it be their fate to be sold as concubines to the caliph's men, and what of Nimah . . . or had they been torn from life already, soiled beyond what Ali's treachery had wrought?

Kyrin swung toward Seliam. If they'd dared—

Seliam flushed. "None have been touched," he growled.

Kyrin hugged Nimah. "I go to my land, for the caliph. Tell Zoltan my heart will not forget his kindness to Cicero. Will he take him out to run in the desert—for me?"

Nimah's eyes widened and she glanced at Alaina, who spoke quietly to Qadira in the middle of the room. Alaina accepted an olive-green cloth bundle from the concubine's wrinkled hands. Kyrin nodded at Nimah's unspoken question. "Yes, Alaina goes also. I—we will miss you, Nimah." She felt cold and alone in the face of what she meant to do. It would be God's grace if she saw Nimah again, or anyone living, beyond the next hand of nights.

"You are both of my blood, my sister." Nimah hugged her, sweet jasmine wafting around them. Kyrin swallowed hard.

Nimah went to Qadira and gripped her bird-thin arm. Quadira's wrinkled face seemed shrunken and her eyes were red. Her carefully built life was ash. Unveiled, the ancient woman smiled.

Kyrin dropped her gaze. She had greatly disturbed Qadira's rule. These bare walls had heard so much laughter and had so often been a haven, though a cage. She was bound for home, and these women were left to slavery. They would go to the court or to any who would take them as lesser concubines. And she could do nothing. *Keep them, O my Lord, in your mercy.*

Qadira lifted her head, an ancient queen. "We will go outside, and watch one of our house leave for her own land." She waited, expectant.

Seliam lifted his chin in acquiescence and nudged Hadden to precede him.

The women of the house followed Kyrin and Alaina to the stables and lined up against the wall of the women's court in silent witness. Kyrin drew herself up straight and smiled at them. A tear trickled down her cheek. Though most of them had never understood her, some of them had been friends. And sharp-tongued Qadira revealed a good heart.

Kyrin gave her a bow of respect, and Qadira's tart old mouth worked. It might have been a smile. Kyrin touched her hand, and Qadira drew her into a short embrace. Alaina followed her, and then they hugged every one of their sisters.

At the end of the line, Kyrin faced Lilith, who groaned and blinked dark-lashed eyes, reaching her long head to lip at Kyrin's thawb. Beside her own camel, Alaina unwound Qadira's cloth bundle. Two cloaks, or desert bishts, lay rolled within. Both new-woven, of pine green.

Kyrin took the bisht Alaina offered her, held it up, and let it unroll to her ankles. Her iron key hit the flags with the sound of metal on stone. She picked it up. It glowed with oil, without a trace of rust. Her fingers closed around it, her throat tightened, and she put it in her pouch.

Thick and beautiful, the bisht was an exact copy of her mother's faded cloak, which had wrapped the bundle. Qadira watched her, old and bent, yet somehow erect, her eyes sharp. She would care for her sisters. Kyrin bowed to her, then donned the bisht with a flourish. She could give Qadira that triumph.

Autumn scented the air with ripe oranges. Kyrin shivered. The cloaks would help them through the winter. It was the third autumn since she'd stepped into this courtyard, a new slave, on her way to wash in the women's pool.

Now she was going home. Her father's brown eyes, his thick, clean-limbed strength, his oak-brown face were at last clear before her inner eye. He would hug her, call Cernalt to bring her hawk, Samson, and ply her with food and drink. The stronghold would feast—Kyrin swallowed.

She must tell him how her mother fell. Yet justice had been done; Ali was no more. Though her hand had not avenged Lady Willa of Cierheld. But that was as it should be. The knot grew in Kyrin's throat.

With a shuffle of feet, Tae limped from the breezeway into the stable court, his steps shortened by a length of cord between his ankles. His arms were bound behind him. The wazir followed, his men grouped around him. Tae swayed.

Kyrin was beside him in a moment. She shook him gently, holding him up when he sagged. At her shoulder, Alaina gasped in dismay. Tae turned his head. His brown eyes were near swallowed by their dark irises; he had been dosed with strong herbs, mayhap the poppy.

Kyrin's mouth flattened. She turned to Sirius and her voice was husky. "This was *not* necessary, O my master. As my oath is gold, his is of diamond."

"I do not gamble in my master's service." Sirius stood unbending, arms crossed. His men unfolded in a line of red and black and glittering spears along the breezeway and around the edge of the court. In the kennel, Cicero whined. His paws scrabbled.

Kyrin worked her dry mouth. "We—will find Hamal." This time she could not make her tongue call him "master." The wazir inclined his head, as if he expected no less.

Tae said thickly, "He—don' trust them, daughter . . ."

Kyrin pressed his shoulder. "Be easy. Alaina and I are not harmed. The wazir wishes us to find a certain traveler of his blood—as a last service for the caliph." Tae closed his eyes as if they were too heavy to hold open. Kyrin continued, "We go to Britannia, where we will search out Hamal Abdasir." Her voice hardened. "The wazir, worthy as he is, holds you to keep me to my word." Her voice dropped, and she leaned her head against Tae's. "I love you . . . Father." It was the name he wore in her heart.

His harsh-lined face softened in the bright sunlight, and he kissed her on the forehead. Kyrin wrapped him in her arms, kissed him on each cheek, and stepped back. Stiff and straight in indignation at his treatment.

"Tae . . ." Alaina clung to him, tears gleaming on her cheeks, her face twisting in pain.

Kyrin envied her. *She* could shed no tears, not before the wazir. Sirius Abdasir must see only strength—and her sister's grief-torn leave taking.

Scattered among the gathered household, the wazir's men kept their eyes on her, Tae, and Alaina. Doubtless they'd been warned. Kyrin's mouth twisted. *There is only so much flesh and bone can do. But then, they do not know the warrior's way. Its abilities or its limits.* Tugging Lilith after her, she turned toward the gate. And swallowed back a cry of joy.

Jachin leaned against the tethering post for the horses, chained hand and foot, his black head bowed. He stared at his feet, his face an ink-dark mask. He lived.

Kyrin's heart ached with a sudden stab. The one who taught her the sword must feel himself a betrayer of Ali and his house, though he could have done nothing even if he had been there. The dried blood on his head from a blow said he had tried.

Umar watched beside Jachin, his sword bare, his Hand lying around his feet, silent, tongues lolling. Kyrin glared at Umar. But Ali's bastard must have kept Jachin from death. She gave him the smallest dip of her head. He might not be completely against them. Or he merely followed the flow of power, though he was of Ali's blood. She tried to keep her lip from curling. *There* was a weakling.

The pack of salukis at Umar's feet turned their heads threateningly toward Cicero, who watched her quietly from his kennel. His manners did not suffer him to lift an ear in their direction.

Kyrin wet her lips. It was as useless to speak of Cicero to the wazir as it was to ask for Tae or Jachin. Her mouth firmed. She must not give Umar excuse to loose the beasts of his Hand.

Her old master's bodyguard looked at her without fear, without anger, and nudged Jachin with an elbow, not an unfriendly gesture. Jachin raised his head. His gaze went from her black earring to her bare ear—and his stony face relaxed.

Umar laid his hand on the saluki at his side, which growled. The glint in his eyes might be regret. It must be enough—to keep Jachin safe. Kyrin smiled thinly. Jachin's mouth turned up a bit, and then his head sagged.

Seliam cleared his throat behind Alaina, the rein of his readied camel in his hand. Alaina gave Tae a last kiss and walked to her camel, her sandals scuffing stone. Kyrin mounted Lilith, finding her seat among the bags.

Alaina's animal was much younger than desert-wise Lilith, and not used to the sands. So Sirius thought to ensure the dice he cast would not go astray before they reached his goal. If they tried to run, one beast was old, the other untried.

Kyrin glanced back. A guard in red and black guided Tae through the breezeway. Then they were gone.

Kyrin turned and nudged Lilith forward. *The Master of the stars is who he is. Then there is the beast of red and black, with fur of flame. I thought he was an apparition of Ali in the nights, hunting my will and the falcon. But my master is dead. And yet the tiger remains.* A desperate little laugh bubbled in her throat, pushing brittle tension ahead of it. The tiger stalked her, testing the edges of her mind. The terror of him tapped at her heart, tingled along her bones.

But she and the falcon *had* ridden him in the desert, together. Even if the tiger escaped the falcon, he must fall back from her mind's walls. She was older now, wise to his ways. When she was tired or angry he crept in, with despair in his wake.

"I will never leave you, nor forsake you." The words of the Master of the stars cleared her mind. All that remained to her was to do as she ought. Straightening her shoulders, Kyrin bound the kaffiyeh Seliam handed her about her head. The ends of the cord tapped her cheeks, bringing back the desert paths. So, she and Alaina would ride again concealed as men.

She remembered the desert raiders who captured Faisal, the peace she made with him in the sands. Saw again her arrow streaking into a Twilket assassin's chest. And the Twilket war against the Aneza that Tae forged into peace at the Oasis of Oaths, where he foiled yet another Twilket assassin at his own game. As she sought to outwit the wazir.

Tapping Lilith with her camel stick, Kyrin swung her head east, toward the stable gate, the rocky hills, and the Red Sea. Ali was dead, Tae captive. On her way home, she and Alaina might yet come to ruin. But the Master of the stars worked far more than she imagined.

6

Thine own friend. ~Proverbs 27:10

Seliam and Hadden rode at Kyrin's back, up the rough track out of the wadi. She ignored them. Alaina followed at her tail, leading the baggage camel with the rations, likely to keep her mind from Tae.

Rocky, grass-covered hills ringed them, sere in winter garments. Through the stable gate, Sirius's face was closed and watchful where he stared after them, his arms crossed.

Atop the first hill, Seliam and Hadden rode forward to flank Kyrin. She glanced at them. Seliam gazed wordlessly at the descent, and his mount picked its way ahead. He and Hadden led a spare beast apiece. Ali's house disappeared below the ridge behind.

Silent, they traveled at the camels' walking pace. The sun swung across the sky. Near winter or not, it was hotter away from the water that ran below Ali's house in the wadi. Riding out of the sharp, mountainous hills at last, they came to flats strewn with tufts of grass, clumps of thorn, wild olive, and tamarisk. They crossed small wadis along the way, most of them dry, covered with dead grass and bare shrubs. The brown stems thinned as soil turned to sandy gravel; fewer birds fluttered around them, and the animal tracks on the ground vanished among hard-baked pebbles.

Ahead, Seliam muttered with Hadden, and they looked over their shoulders. Seliam regarded her coldly, as if she had never held her blade from his throat. Kyrin shrugged. She could not muster anger for him, slave to the wazir as he was. There was other game in sight.

Hadden's glance was cautious. Kyrin knew he saw two young women, far from the women's quarters and out of place. One with healing hands, gold hair, and eyes green as woody moss, the other dark and angular, who wielded weapons with unnatural grace—and cast the evil eye. And he would do nothing to draw it. Hadden caught her return stare, winced, and looked over the ears of his horse with a mutter. He hastened his beast ahead. Kyrin turned her smile aside to the desert.

Hadden stirred up a fennec, its delicate fox-face comic. The fennec gazed at the four travelers a moment, its huge ears pricked, then melted into the desert's purple shadows. Three gazelle leapt light as dancers over the rocks and disappeared in the reddish orb of the sun on the hazy horizon.

Evening lengthened across the gravel expanse, bringing cold and the sharp, fresh scent of desert herbs. Kyrin breathed deep, dropped Lilith's rein, and lifted her arms, face to the sky. It had been so long. If Truthseeker were here she would cast her up to fly, to hunt before the sun winked out.

§

Seliam and Hadden pitched a quick night-camp near a great rock. Kyrin raised an eyebrow. From the look of what they had in their bags, they traveled light and quick as Bedouin on a raid. She dropped her and Alaina's baggage under a light cloth tied to four poles, which Seliam deemed sufficient shelter, and secured Lilith with a long thong tied from her back foot to a front pad. Lilith blinked her brown eyes, nibbled at Kyrin's arm, and lashed out at Alaina's camel. "Possessive, are you?" Kyrin rubbed her soft tan neck.

Seliam hobbled the horses between the cloth shelter and the rock, while Hadden kindled a fire on the desert side of camp. Rubbing down his beast with a handful of grass, Seliam kept his head up, watchful.

Kyrin eyed him, sighed, turned her back, and moved to the growing fire, where Alaina tended to the cooking. Hadden sank cross-legged on the far side, stretching out his fingers to the blaze. Seliam finished grooming his beast and moved to Hadden's horse.

Kyrin picked up a small water-skin from the ground by its leather strap, and Alaina cried, "Watch the water, Kyrin! We will have need of it."

Seliam looked round.

"Yes, you're right." Kyrin grimaced, swung the bottle, and set it aside. She picked up another skin. "Ah, tea!" Pulling the cork with a *shluupp,* she tilted the bag for a long swallow. With a half-mocking glance at Alaina, she offered the bag to Hadden, with a shrug. "It will spoil by the next sun."

Hadden's slim, muscular hand closed around the mouth of the bag, and he looked from her to Alaina in doubt. Well, if he didn't want it . . . Kyrin reached out a demanding hand. Hadden sniffed the bottle, eyed her over the rim, and then drank deep. Seliam came to the fire, his fingers drifting unobstrusively near his sword hilt.

The tea went round. By the time the rice and vegetable and lamb stew was ready, the guards swore it was the best tea they'd ever tasted.

"Yes, it is good." Alaina sprinkled extra herbs on her and Kyrin's food. "That tea is truly worthy of the caliph's court."

Hadden assented shyly, but Seliam just grunted, his eyes gleaming in the firelight. Kyrin swallowed her first bite of food before he would dip his fingers in his bowl. She smiled at him, wide and sincere, and received a silent glower in return. Her smile slid into a glare. There was no need for ill temper.

Alaina and Hadden went to their woven blankets first. The men had readied to sleep near the fire, between the shelter and the desert. At last Kyrin left Seliam to stand watch, facing the desert night with the last of the bottle of strong tea cradled in his arm.

Fully clothed against the creeping chill, she ducked under the cloth, lay down near Alaina, and tuned her ears to the night. Lilith sank to the ground with a sound of content to chew her cud. A cricket sang, ceased, and was answered by a friend. Others joined. Kyrin rolled over to face Alaina, growing more awake every moment.

Alaina's eyes opened. Hadden lay quiet. A horse stamped. Kyrin rolled over again.

The sands began not far from here. She wound her finger in a strand of hair, pulled it free. Coiled it again. If only Tae rested across from her, crisply telling her she'd lose that finger if an enemy caught her so entangled.

Long after she wearied of waiting, a sibilant snore threaded through the dark. In the fire, a dying ember fell and flared. It lit Seliam's slack face. His jaw moved, and he muttered in his throat. The tea worked—as did the herbs Alaina had added to their own bowls.

Alaina heard the snore too. She rose, rubbing her eyes. And walked quietly from the shelter into the starlight, disappearing behind a bush at the towering rock's edge. Kyrin held her breath, straining every muscle to listen and watch.

Their guards lay motionless on the earth beside the fiery eyes of the coals against the pale ashes.

Kyrin moved after Alaina toward the rock as quietly as she could. Her feet scrunched, gravel slid and whispered. Beyond Lilith, she moved to Seliam's horse on the south side.

It nickered softly, and she grabbed its nose and froze. There was no whisper of movement from Seliam, only her thundering heart. Her hand touched the packs.

What possessed Seliam to leave his bags on his beast? A captain of the caliph's guard would not forget to unburden his horse. No, he would not. Kyrin's breath quickened. He set a trap. But he did not expect the herbs. Or did he leave them to their escape? Or mayhap mount to hunt them down.

One hand deep in Seliam's left-most saddlebag, Kyrin touched a familiar cold length. The hair on her arms prickled, and she drew the falcon dagger slowly from the leather depths. Amber eyes reflected jet in the starlight. She reached in again and found a sword. Tae's blade. She huffed out a breath and stared at the weapons.

She'd suspected Seliam and Hadden carried them. Once they reached the ships, Sirius would not leave her and Alaina without means to protect themselves and his errand. Doubtless, Seliam was to leave the weapons with them. But Tae's sword . . . either Sirius meant to assure her that she would return Tae's blade to him when her task was done, or the wazir gave it as a further threat. Kyrin paused, her fingers tight on the chill metal. There were other saddlebags she must search.

Seliam's snore caught. A hand touched her shoulder. Kyrin jumped, and bared the falcon blade as she spun. Alaina skipped back.

Kyrin dropped the falcon on a quivering breath and scowled. She shoved Tae's sword into Alaina's arms, fumbled the falcon blade into her sash and moved to Hadden's animals. *Yes.* There were her and Alaina's staffs, tied beside her bow, with Tae's stick, all in a cloth-bound bundle slung below Hadden's saddle.

Kyrin's heart lifted. She knew the reach of her stick and ironwood staff, true friends to their cores. And her bow—the layered wood limbs and black horn tips were smooth, smelling of linseed oil. Her fingers tingled, rolling the limp, rough string. Now she could practice as her father said, with every rise of the sun.

"Let's take the horses," Alaina whispered, "they're faster and sure-footed in the hills."

"Yes. The camels will be fresh for the sands when we come back."

"Come back?"

"Sirius won't believe it either. Intelligent slaves would run to the coast. Only fools flee toward men they have robbed or enter the sands without a guide. And Tae is not a fool."

"Heh." Alaina bit off her laugh.

§

Kyrin fingered their guards' swords and watched Seliam turn over and Hadden sleeping hard. The thieves who once kidnapped Faisal had bound him in the desert, weaponless, to a dire fate. She dropped Hadden's weapon where she mounted his spare horse, but tucked Seliam's blade under her arm. She dropped the men's water bags on the ground and turned her mount after Alaina, the weary camels and horses tied behind her horse.

As they started back across the plain toward the hills there was no moon to betray them. Rocks, often mixed with sand, shushed beneath hoof and camel pad. Kyrin clung to the bay horse. Its muscles bunched and slid as the night blew past, riffling her hair. Its eyes were keen as a fox's; it never broke stride over the pitted, uneven ground.

They trotted a space over the empty plain, hiding any tracks they might leave in an ancient wadi that channeled a roaring, whiny wind through its dusty depths. Kyrin staked the camels in one of the sharp wadi curves and thrust Seliam's sword into the ground beside them.

They mounted and rode up out of the wadi, and Alaina's horse broke into a run, a dark wavering shadow drumming through the night. The air was spicy as frankincense; it beckoned with the cooling scent of hot rock, desert flowers, warm horse, and endless winds.

Kyrin leaned over her horse's neck with a wild grin, urging it after Alaina. Seliam would not catch them—even if he and Hadden woke and the camels had jerked loose from their tethers and found their way back. If only she could see Seliam's face when he woke to frost riming his blanket, to see all of them gone.

Sometime later, Kyrin wiped a pale streak of foam from the bay's neck. Her knuckles stung. She had dug too vigorously in Seliam's saddlebag after her falcon dagger. They would be blessed this night if she and Alaina came away with no greater hurt.

Her bay heaved a wet snort. "Stay a moment!" Kyrin called. Alaina pulled her horse to a walk, and Kyrin climbed down. Looping the bay's rope over her arm, she broke into a steady trot toward the black stone outcrop rising sharp against the stony plain ahead. It marked the path to Ali's wadi. Her cramped legs welcomed the change, but too soon her feet ached from plunging through deceitful shadows to slam onto hard sand.

She climbed back on the bay and kicked it to a trot, thrusting away thoughts of Nara and Tae. If they were caught before her plan bore fruit, they would be doomed to kneel under the sword for treachery. But only after hot metal rods hissed against their skin, leaving long charred marks to split at every agonized twist and turn. Kyrin found it hard to breathe. Her ploy *had* to work.

The black stone grew slowly in her vision, but at last they reached it. Beyond, the hills rose to the mountains, and passed on. Kyrin paused. Drawing her kaffiyeh closer, she rubbed the scar at her throat, the ridge of skin warm under her fingers. Their path split around a bare, rocky ridge with a single tamarisk at the top. "Alaina? When we passed this even', was the tamarisk tree on our left or the right?"

Alaina turned to face the desert, holding her hands out, seeking to remember how it had looked. "That side." She waved her right hand and turned back around. "If we keep the ridge on our left hand, we'll walk true."

Kyrin let out her breath. "My thanks."

The horses' hindquarters heaved upward on the slants, while they skidded at times on the rocky, dusty downslopes. Kyrin's knees and various other places ached. It had been far too long since she'd ridden. Subak horse stances did not train those muscles quite enough. Two ridges before Ali's wadi, she signaled Alaina. They slid down their horses' wet sides.

Kyrin's legs quivered, and she panted as she led the bay upward. Alaina walked steady enough. Kyrin rested her hand on the falcon blade. Nothing stirred on this side of the first dry ridge but scattered grass clumps in the gentle wind. It smelled of warm earth. They moved over the crest at a low spot, under another tamarisk.

Kyrin furrowed her brow, her thoughts fever swift. Nara had played her part, or the wazir's men would be waiting for them with bared blades. The warriors in red and black could lie in any shadow between them and the shepherd's hut at the top of Ali's wadi. She wished she had donned her leather body shielding. It would help against a stab in the back, or even from the front. The bamboo under the leather was strong and resilient.

She shivered. What did she think she could do against more than one warrior? A raised sword took her mother. If there were anyone lying in wait, there would be more than one. She would fail—and she and Alaina would die—as oath-breakers.

Kyrin gritted her teeth and pulled her sash tighter about the falcon dagger, sheathed against any betraying gleam. She'd faced Seliam's blade and won, and freed the captive falcon to ride her enemy's back . . . Fool—to open *that* door—the tiger blinked at her balefully. Kyrin slammed the door of her thought hard. How was the beast of her dreams stalking her now?

But she must see to the task at hand. Where they could all die. Yes, they could. Though the Master of the stars oversaw all, he did not take choice from men. And evil men chose to harm. She could ask the Master of the stars to help her fight for good, ask for his protection, and for success. He would give it, though mayhap not in the form she sought. But he was her father, and gave no evil gift. *Though he slay me . . .*

And Alaina was with her. Kyrin smiled. Her sister loved scribing, working with herbs, and composing verses more than she did the way of the warrior, but the dagger Tae had made her slept aslant in her sash. Leather thongs bound her stick to her thigh, ready to hand.

Kyrin stopped, her horse's rein over her arm, and strung her bow. It had been two years with only short-range targets. She did not trust her aim for a long shot. Her father's favored weapon would be her last defense, if her enemy was close.

She fastened the recurve bow to the bay's saddle and dug a charcoal stick she had taken from their desert fire out of her sash. Alaina's face and soft hair blackened quickly. When Kyrin finished, Alaina smudged her face.

The dark wood reeked of burning, of her godfather's keep, of death. It felt smooth as her mother's still, cold face. Kyrin's hand tightened on her weapon. The falcon's beak pricked her wrist.

A growling cough came over the whisper of grass and wind across stone. Kyrin froze. In the shadow of a bush, the tiger crouched above them on the hill slope, round ears pinned flat to his wide skull. His face wrinkled with a snarl. His lips twitched back over his teeth, and his tail was rigid. Kyrin's heart pounded. The tiger could *not* be there.

"Kyrin—?" Alaina turned her head carefully, her hand cool against Kyrin's cheek.

The tiger chuffed, uncertain. He cast back and forth, as if they were hidden from him. His breath fogged in the first grey light, and he sniffed the ground before his paws.

The stick jerked in Alaina's clenching fingers.

Kyrin pulled violently aside and crouched, the falcon ready, futile as it might be.

Stripes of flame licked the stalking hunter under the old starlight, his stripes dark red, as of dried blood. No falcon's scream rang down the wind. The tiger raised his head and his ears came up. Even as his eyes fastened on Kyrin, his heavy shoulders faded. The bush grew starker behind his thinning form. The grass blades quivered. He was gone as if he had never been.

Fly high, see far, stoop fast. Where was the queen of the air, the falcon who had driven him to the sand one wild night in the desert, taming him? But it was only a wraith of her heart that haunted her. Kyrin let out her breath. *Madness . . .* or her mind played tricks on her, as it so often did at the edge of sleep.

Alaina threw the charcoal stick into the grass. "The shadows move, in this hour, and trick the eye. I didn't see the sand fox until it turned to go."

What fear had *she* seen?

But they must go. Kyrin rolled her brown cloak and tied it around her middle. Her low voice rasped. "If the signal cloth is out, we'll need horses. I hope the wazir hasn't put Ali's mounts in the stables." The wind's cold fingers patted her face. First light glowed above the ridge behind them. "It's near Prime. After we find Tae, I'll get the horses. If trouble comes while I'm gone, yell." She did not mention what might prevent her answering. Ambush or capture, a blade wound or death. Her mouth flattened. If they saved Tae, that outcome was acceptable.

They moved with the horses at a quick walk, up the slope and down, over a dry thread of watercourse and up the last rocky side-hill. Kyrin crawled beside Alaina a few feet to the crest.

The north-south length of their ridge edged Ali's fields and the house, a long dim shadow above the wadi water curling below the outer garden's walls in its bed. Grey-green puffs of juniper and the bones of tamarisk and fig trees hid the outline of the house's courts and walls.

The breeze whispered and muttered but brought no news. No camel groaned, no sheep blatted. The orchard and near fields nestled at the head of the house, cloaked in dawn shadows.

The stones under Kyrin's hands were cold and edged. Near the top of the wadi lay the shepherd's hut, out of sight in a depression, many arrow-flights from the house. It was but one from where she and Alaina watched.

Kyrin backed below the crest then scrambled down the ridge to her horse's side. His warm, prickly rough hair rubbed her arm. If only they were about to ride to watch the dawn, and not run into danger. His interested whiffle wet her hand, and he cocked his ears, ready for her command.

Alaina's mare flipped her head as her sister mounted. Gripping her mane, Alaina turned a darkened face toward Kyrin in the grey. "Take care for yourself, Kyrin."

"You also." Crickets, a sleepy lark's call, the rustle and thud of shifting hooves were as loud in her ears as an army.

§

At the top of the valley the walls of the wadi drew together in a flat rise above the headwaters that concealed them from the house. They tied the beasts, and Alaina muttered, "Father, keep us." Kyrin echoed her silently.

Hidden just at the edge of the rise, Kyrin stared through sparse grass and studied the stony hill-cup and the roof of the lonely shepherd's hut below. Alaina touched her arm, pointing out a circuitous route that made the most of the slim cover.

In their endless crawl along the swell of the hill, Kyrin's knees came to know every stick and stone. It took long, precious moments to move behind the hut. Then to its back wall and press against the wood, panting. The sky was brightening, a few fluffy clouds aflame with gold.

Kyrin's mouth was dry, and she loosened her dagger in her sheath, while Alaina touched her own hilt and nodded. On her hands and toes, so close to the ground her chin scraped the earth, Kyrin eased along the base of the south wall, clutching her weapon. She peered around the corner, feeling vulnerable as a dawn-chilled lizard. Except that most fighters would not expect her at the bottom of the wall. Umar or his Hand would. On her flank, Alaina stepped lightly through the grass near the edge of the cup.

White flickered. Kyrin stopped. It moved noiseless near the bottom of the hut door. Was it the signal? Or the edge of Tae's thawb, or an enemy? She inched up a fingers-breadth. Another flash of movement. It *was* a white curtain. Kyrin pulled herself to a crouch. Freezing wind swirled, billowing the linen out with a soft snap. She dashed forward. Her back was against the wall beside the door. Her hand ached with her grip on the falcon. Under cover of the next gust, Alaina joined her, thudding into place on the opposite side.

All was silent within. Their eyes met briefly. They slid around the edges of the curtain together.

Eyes and ears straining, Kyrin stepped right, her blade warding against the dark. Her feet rustled, echoing. She held her breath. No sound of any but Alaina. The air smelled thick and cold, of senseless sheep and droppings. Where was Tae? The shadows did not hide him.

Outside, a footstep rattled a rock, whispered through grass. Kyrin spun, blind with the dimness. She blinked. The curtain flapped out again. It molded around a man. The dark figure carried a long blade. The tip peeped beneath the linen. No, two blades. He stepped onto the threshold—and dived in a lunging roll. He came up with his back against the far wall. One of his swords pressed in a deadly arc across Kyrin's stomach, holding her still, her breath choked in her throat. His other blade menaced Alaina.

"Tae?" Alaina's voice quavered.

"Daughter." His answer was breathless.

Kyrin sagged. Idiots. She was so eager to free Tae she forgot the first rule. Do not give the enemy advantage of sight or movement. They had been rattle-brained as sand-foxes cornered by Cicero. They should have torn the curtain down as they entered.

Tae straightened from his crouch. His blade dropped from Alaina's side, thumping to the floor. He grabbed at the doorpost.

"Tae!" Alaina kept him from toppling. "Where are you hurt?"

Kyrin grabbed Tae's other arm and rescued his second blade from the wood.

"Not . . . hurt," Tae said hoarsely. "Fools. We must go. Now."

Nara had been successful, bless her. He was here. But under the scent of Tae's sweat lingered a heavy, strange sweetness. Without a word, Kyrin left him stumbling from the hut on Alaina's arm, and ran. She crawled on her stomach over the top of the ridge, and half slid down. Ali's house lay silent. Feeling an Eagle mile from safety, Kyrin brought the horses up and made as quick a crossing of the ridgeline as she could.

She and Alaina helped Tae get a leg across the mare's withers. He gripped her mane but slumped along her neck. Kyrin leaned to check the girth. Tae's limp foot thumped her head.

Alaina shook him and whispered fiercely, "Tae!" Nothing. She shook him again, a frown on her face.

Kyrin reached up to help Alaina hold Tae on. He was limp as a rag, though he breathed. A saluki barked faintly from the stables. And Tae was ill.

Kyrin whirled. The falcon dagger sliced free the linen curtain, and she tied Tae on the mare with quick, hard jerks. He was not awake to argue. When she finished his breathing was still steady, steadier than her own. Alaina would have to loosen the cloth bonds if needed.

Her sister's forehead furrowed. "We *must* have fresh horses for the sands, burn it."

"Yes. Get on, and hold him."

Alaina obeyed, with a glaring frown of unhappiness, and Kyrin swung onto the bay and tugged on the horse's rein. They followed her over the edge of the dell and down.

As the bay moved from one clump of shrubs to another, Kyrin's nerves jumped with every crackle of a branch. She looked toward the house. Nothing stirred in the far-off courtyard or field. They gained the date palms at the edge of the orchard. Kyrin climbed down to slump against a tree. Concealed behind the late leaves of a plum, she turned her head. There were certainly no beasts in the pasture on their left. As she thought, the wazir would not risk them.

If she made her way around the back of the house, through the fields and ditches, there might be slaves yet at their tasks. They would have a guard.

So. It was to the stables. All the way around the front of the house. With no cover but the wall. She must watch the great gate, and the smaller one.

Before the stable entrance, the last curve of the court wall echoed with faint snores. Kyrin drew near, hand on her blade. Sirius Abdasir's man rested in the stable doorway, his head on his chest. Her mouth curled in a slight smile. He was as sound asleep as she wagered those in the house were. He deserved to reap the punishment he'd receive for neglecting his post, though he'd feel more rested than she'd like when he woke. Nara had doubtless eaten the stew, after the feasters finished, as instructed. Kyrin sighed. If she could only see the cook and Nimah once more. But it could not be. All slept.

She clamped her teeth on her lip and eased past the guard. When she opened the stable door, the household kennel was full of sleeping salukis. In the kennel across from it, rose a growl, a hum of threat.

One of Umar's savage Hand trod on its sleeping fellows, its fangs bared, almond eyes glaring near orange in the morning light. It knew her. Kyrin stopped, staring. It had not eaten, or the herbs that brought sleep had worn off. She dared not drive the falcon in its side or take its head with Tae's sword; it would not pay to nudge the wazir to think to loose the Hand on their trail.

Cicero. She wished Zoltan might have kept him, at least, from slumber. But his grey, whippy form did not appear, and his tongue did not warm her cold, sweating fingers. A horse stamped in its stall. Kyrin jumped, and shook her head. A door slammed near the breezeway. Kyrin rammed her dagger into its sheath, backed into the stable, and gripped the sword tighter.

No voices—yet. But no moment for extra water-bags from the storeroom. Breathing fast, she looped a rope around the first four necks the curious horses presented to her in the dim stable and retreated the way she came. A dismayed shout within the courts urged her on. She walked the horses around the house, into the trees, and swung up on the bay. Alaina waited for her, holding Tae with an arm across his chest, kicking the mare to join them.

They went quietly through the orchard and up the far side of Ali Ben Aidon's wadi. Out of earshot of the waking house, Kyrin urged the bay to a lope, and circled the wadi. She did not like following the path through the hills a third time, but she did not know another. Tae knew every track around, yet he did not wake. Under his hood his head bobbed, his strong arms hanging slack. Kyrin looked away, uneasy. Her mouth tight with effort, Alaina kicked her horse again. The beast was slow, bearing two. They dared not go faster. They needed their horses' endurance. The sun glanced over the mountains.

Kyrin turned around. She picked a twig from her cloak and held it to the light. She wished her path were as clear as the water-drops along its length. A crystalline world wound over the bark map, trails threading among moss mountains, bare stretches like sand between. Kyrin let out her breath.

Somewhere ahead in the seared sands, Faisal and his Twilkets took advantage of traders who fled Baghdad's taxes with their rich loads. The caliph's taxation gave Faisal vast incentive to trade and charge exorbitant tolls. She *hoped* he traded rather than pillaged. Her mouth twitched. Prince to his tribe, soon to be sheyk, her erstwhile enemy led successful raids, according to Kentar. It mattered not. Faisal—his name still reminded her of a fire sizzle—dared much. As did she.

Alaina drew her cloak closer and bent around Tae to catch her slipping rein. The morning sparkled across them in dew drops. It illumined both their strength and vulnerability. Kyrin waved Alaina past her and dropped back to check their trail. Nothing. They left the last steep wadi for gentler slopes.

Midday spread over the plain, with no sign of pursuit. Kyrin's tired frown relaxed. Hooves swung rhythmically, pounding the thirsty ground, blurring beneath her.

She twisted a strand of hair about her fist until it pulled. Tae and Alaina wouldn't let her travel the sands alone. Kyrin's faint smile faltered. It would be hard enough to convince them to let her go when the moment came. She would never gain the master's black sash in Subak from Tae—but he and Alaina could never be made surety against her again. *She* was the one who promised the wazir.

Would Sirius pursue them with his guard? Or muster men from Baghdad and every village, and send word to his shipmaster on the Red Sea? It would not change her path.

They must run for the desert, and make it through the mountain pass to the coast. Sirius had men everywhere, but the desert was vast. Beyond the hungry sands she would persuade Sirius's shipmaster of the truth. That she must go, and her friends must stay. She glanced up at the mountains. *Father, you are the one who must get us through.*

7

Flight

Thou dost lift me up to the wind
and cause me to ride . . . ~Job 30:22

Kyrin woke, falling.

She thumped onto a hard surface. The jolt bit off her scream. She rolled rapidly downward in a whirl of sand and earth and sky. At last she came to a stop. Breathless with confusion and relief, she swallowed. Blood lay bitter on her tongue.

Alaina shouted, and there was the thud of feet. Her sister slid toward her down a steep bank dotted with camel thorn.

Kyrin shook the spots from her vision and recoiled. Her nose was inches from the vicious thorns of a small acacia. A horse snorted above, and Alaina's mount crow-hopped into view, Tae jerking at the cloth that bound his hands to the saddle.

"I am well!" Kyrin made it to her feet, swaying.

"Are you hurt?" Breathless, Alaina grabbed her arm.

"No." Heat crept up her cheeks.

"Are you sure?"

"Yes." She'd fallen asleep. Kyrin ducked her head. *Twice a fool.*

There was a squeal above, followed by the thud of hooves on flesh.

Alaina paled, spinning. "Tae—we can't let the horses run with him!"

He was tied on. Kyrin scrambled for the bank, but Alaina outstripped her. When Kyrin reached the top of the rise, Alaina was unbinding Tae, her hands fumbling. Tae looked grey about the mouth.

Kyrin grabbed the twisted halter of her stamping bay. The beast calmed, and she loosed her waterskin, examining Tae without seeming to. He had been as scared as she. She swallowed, her mouth dry. "I am well, Tae," she said in a small voice.

"Are you?" He reached for the skin as she lifted it for him. His face was lined but alert, watchful. His mount jigged and threw up its head with a snort. Alaina freed the binding cloth from the saddle and set a hand on the horse's neck, speaking softly. It whuffled and put its nose in her shoulder.

Kyrin shrugged, with a deep breath. "It's naught but a few scratches."

"I've never heard you scream so." Tae searched her face, his dark almond eyes keen.

"I—fell asleep. Then, there was nothing to, well, to hold onto." Heat ran up her neck. "But what did Sirius do to you?"

"Nothing, beyond the first drugging. I pretended to be ill, took an herb to bring on sweat, and drank water." Tae waved his hand. "I wished to be rid of their potions. The herb left me weak, though it expelled their poison. They sent Nara to make me eat." His voice dried. "Nara clucked and fussed like I was her last chick. The wazir must hold me in some esteem." He looked at Kyrin. "I read your recipe to Nara. She smiled, and laughed as she left to create the dish, with two additions of my own. In the evening, Zoltan got me through the household as it slept, and up to the shepherds' hut. He left me hidden where I wished and returned to the house to share Nara's dish of charmed sleep. They will not draw Sirius's wrath." He grinned.

Kyrin nodded. If Seliam later suspected the cook at all, he would not dare speak, not after his own drugged sleep. He would be counted at fault.

Tae's brow furrowed. "I followed you into the hut to teach you to leave one to watch"—he glanced at Alaina—"and to know who and what you attack." He shook his head grimly. "One ambushing warrior could have killed you both."

"We had to get you out—" Kyrin bit her lip as Tae's face stilled, implacable. Alaina looked at her hands.

"That is no reason." Then Tae's voice softened. "Your blood was hot, but you learned." He slid from the horse and steadied himself against it, turning to put a hand on their shoulders. "You are my only daughters. Never will you wager yourselves against so many again."

Kyrin swallowed down a lump. She could still feel his blade pressed across her middle. Alaina nodded.

A twinkle grew in Tae's eyes. "Though I thank you for my life, you won't, or I will make you run beside your horses until you learn their wisdom, to run from nonsensical death."

Kyrin grinned wanly. They were forgiven, and warned.

Later as they ate, every date and bite of tough, salted meat was the sweeter and stronger since Tae rode with them. They broke their fast in the saddle, Alaina delicately picking dates out of her bag, while Tae tore at a twisted length of dried meat, jaw muscles bunching. It was good to see his strength return.

In early evening they drew near the wadi where Kyrin had hidden Seliam's camels. They spread out in caution. Would Seliam leap out of hiding? But there was no sign of him, and no dust of pursuit in sight. Alaina spotted the mustard hides of the surly beasts lying against the wadi rocks. They blent so well with the earth that a company of warriors could have passed them, unknowing. They gathered the camels and switched their saddles, checked their bags, water skins, and weapons.

Only then did they free the weary horses, with their sweat-darkened saddles. Kyrin flicked the bay's hindquarters with the flat of her sword. The mare stumbled away, nickering, full water skins tied tight to her back. The second horse followed. It would be good if the beasts searched out Hadden and Seliam soon, but not before she, Tae, and Alaina were in the sands, far away under the stars.

Kyrin rubbed Lilith's neck and tapped her with her camel stick. Lilith rocked to her feet, hindlegs first. Her patrician head lifted high, she complained of her unfair lot as Kyrin turned her head north and west. They *would* find their way.

Near dusk the broken gravel plain melted into bare dunes. At the edge of the shadowed expanse Tae stopped, and Alaina and Kyrin rode up beside him. Dune after red dune stretched out of sight.

The cheetah, the leopard, and the lion came not here. Hyenas and jackals found no sustenance. Even the vulture left anything that strayed into the waste to shrivel in the sun, alone. It was difficult not to urge Lilith to unwise haste. The only other life in this place were themselves and the baggage camel. They were mere specks, lost among endless grains of sand intent on swallowing them.

Soon they made hasty camp in the bottom of a depression surrounded by dunes. Wind rustled among the dune crests, and no one wished for a fire, though the night would become bone-chilling cold. Kyrin grimaced. Alaina's face and hands must burn from the harsh sun and wind as much as hers. After he kindled their small fire, Tae sat cross-legged beside the camels on the dune crest and watched the night, sipping at weak tea, the mint leaves soaked in his water ration. He swallowed the last of it and rose.

"Come, I would show you something, Kyrin."

Alaina glanced at them. When Tae said nothing, she turned away, busying herself washing his handleless cup and storing it in his bag. Wondering, Kyrin walked after Tae behind the nearest dune.

She returned weary and aching, striving to wrap her mind around a knowledge that shook her with its power. Tae had showed her the death touch. Truly the art of Subak had no end. Kyrin wrapped her necklace meditatively around her finger. Her hands now held death and life. Tae must judge she would soon have need of it. But he must have spoken to Alaina, for her sister had smiled at her as she rolled out her blanket near the fire. Though Kyrin did not understand why Tae taught the touch of death only to her, that must be enough. With a sigh, Kyrin sat down and wearily dug in her bag after a cloth to wipe her face.

They ate cold fruit and meat again, and Kyrin collapsed onto her rug, falling into uneasy sleep. By the stars high in the sky, Tae roused them around Matins' midnight bell. The patch of ground they occupied soon lay deserted. They rode on, eating as they felt the need.

The sun rose. Sweat-damp saddles rubbed every grain of sand into skin.

The second evening, despite years of Subak training, Kyrin fell when her feet touched the dark sand. Her inner laugh was wry. She was too tired to smile; she'd been on the rack, not a camel's back. Sometime later she slept despite the pain.

She came awake with something disgustingly cold and damp rooting in her ear. Something snuffled, nudged her again. Made an eager noise. A meat-eater's hot breath blasted her cheek. Kyrin lunged out of her blanket, the falcon blade in one hand, her sheath in the other. Tae grunted, slid his blade home, and sat up in his rug, no longer needing to conceal his readiness. "He followed you. Zoltan must have let him out."

Cicero whined joyously. His narrow head sought, seeking, eager tongue licking what he could reach of Kyrin. His tail whipped furiously. Alaina giggled from her watch-point, just below the crest of the nearest dune. With a gulp, Kyrin sank down to rub Cicero's head. She pulled his lop ears and held him close, gathering in his long body. "Good dog, good dog." A tear dripped on her hand and dampened his fur under her fingers. He did not object.

Alaina slid down the dune. "I wasn't hungry tonight. Here." She pressed a piece of cheese into Kyrin's hand. Cicero ate it in one snapping gulp and regarded Alaina hopefully. Tae reached over to stroke him. Soon Cicero slept, a warm contented curl of saluki in a half moon shape between Kyrin's elbow and hip.

The stars did not slow their march. When the bell at home would have called Uncle Ulf to Lauds, Kyrin was back in the saddle with her companions. Tae knew the paling night sky well and kept them on a straight course.

They covered a little over forty Eagle miles during the next day, keeping to the north-west caravan route to the Hejaz Mountains. Cicero often trotted ahead but kept them always in sight.

The waterskins grew alarmingly flat. They drank sips at each stop. Kyrin's sore lips cracked, and sand encrusted her body. Alaina and Tae's eyes darkened and their cheeks hollowed. Their world shrank to the small hope of a sip of water, the smell of sweat, sore places that rubbed, and thirsty, quiet nights where they slept huddled in their bishts against the increasing chill. Sun, moon, and stars passed overhead. They and their beasts became part of the sandy, windblown earth.

Early the fifth day they rode into an oasis of palms and a village encircled by a mud wall. It was a *caravanserai,* a stopping place for caravans. Inside the gate, trees grew interspersed among wells and houses of mud brick that seemed to have grown up around a single long stone building lying between broad, golden dunes.

Around the palm trunks and in the water channels, mounds of glossy green leaves nodded high as Kyrin's thigh. The plants bore yellow, trumpet-shaped flowers, and Kyrin eyed them. Her mother would have gathered a handful.

Tae haggled for crushed date pits for their camels with the old man in the door of the stone caravanserai, while Kyrin helped Alaina lead their beasts to the common water hole inside the low-walled court. Her dark hair was concealed under her dusty kaffiyeh, rolled around her head in the men's fashion. At Tae's call, Kyrin ducked her head and walked to the door of the caravanserai as if immensely weary. Without a word, she dropped coins for their fee into Tae's hand, who transferred it to their host's palm. Their old host cackled, "Blessed be thou of Allah!"

After guzzling water for a large part of the morning and eating a mound of crushed date pits apiece, the camels regained their vigor. They led them out of the caravanserai and rejoined Tae, who had declined to pay the evening fee, making it clear to their host that they were passing through on an errand for their merchant master.

They left without mishap. Tae decided to travel off the caravan route for a time, though still following its course. Their feet marked but for an instant the glory of the sands. They crossed majestic, silver-blue bands that fanned delicately along orange-red slopes, then came to whiter, lower sands, and beyond them, broad salt flats. Kyrin grinned.

Uncle Ulf would find it hard to believe her when she returned. He would give almost anything for inks of such colors for his scribe work. Surely he and her sister would find much to speak of. Kyrin glanced at Alaina. Swaying on her camel's back, she stared ahead, red-gold hair burnished copper in the sun where her kaffiyeh slid aside. She was both kind and strong. But Alaina could not come. Kyrin pushed back the thought. Alaina must stay with Tae, and Tae must write to the wazir of her progress on his errand in Britannia. Soon, Sirius must know she had kept her word. He would have no encouragement to send yet more men against them.

Interminable plains of gray gravel followed the bright sands. They watered again at Jabrin, a thriving caravanserai surrounded by dark palms and thick acacia, with a shallow well of sweet water. No one questioned them.

Ten sunrises after they fled into the desert, a flinty flat stretched before them to the horizon. The camels went swiftly on its lonely, hard surface.

Kyrin looked over her shoulder. She wished they had a moment to hunt, or at least to shoot her bow. But Sirius Abdasir searched for them, and he was not a man to give up his prey. Whether he meant to capture or kill, whether Umar's Hand or others stalked them, she must reach the ship quickly.

Sometime in the afternoon a cloud of locusts buzzed harshly toward them, a mass of whizzing yellow-gray bodies. Denizens of the migrating carpet alighted and crawled over Lilith, over Kyrin's bisht and kaffiyeh, and across the ground. Kyrin picked one off Lilith's neck and ate it, remembering Faisal's taste for them. The locust crunched, and she made a face—it tasted of vegetables. She preferred camel's milk. Lilith and the other camels ate them as fast as they could snuffle them up. Even Cicero snapped them down. In camp that night, Tae roasted some he had gathered.

"These are good." Alaina reached for another locust.

"They *are* better roasted," Kyrin admitted. "With butter, I may find a taste for them." Alaina smiled at her, and Kyrin looked down to hide her tears.

At last, the wilderness began to rise gently toward the west. They rode the edge of the great plateau for one day and a hand of suns as the stony land swelled beneath them into a huge scarp.

There was one gap in the eight-hundred-foot limestone ridge. The wadi pierced it, then wound through more desert on the other side, running toward the Hejaz Mountains and the pass to Jedda. The village oasis of Sulaiyal spread two miles along its length.

This was the only wadi with dependable pools between the rains. A small, dark bird with white cheeks and a bright yellow underside sang among the shrubs. Cicero dashed playfully after it. Lilith groaned hopefully, and Kyrin smiled to herself. Likely Lilith smelled water ahead. Alaina hummed. But Tae's eyes roved over the valley. Kyrin's sense of rest vanished. Sulaiyal would have watchers. And they would pass through it early.

The next morn, Kyrin was thankful for the mist that had risen. They rode around Sulaiyal in silence, Cicero trotting at Lilith's side. On the far side of the scarp, just as Kyrin's shoulders had loosened in relief that no men in red and black had stopped them, Tae pulled up short and drew his sword. The mist-deadened clip of horses' hooves echoed over the rocks behind them. Kyrin strung her bow, running hasty fingers over the string. It wasn't too wet.

Cicero raised his head—alert—ears pricked. He made no sound. The grey veils billowed, concealing, but also blinding.

A cheery, deep voice called, "Shaheena! Shaheena!" The echoes rang among the rocks.

Kyrin caught her breath. Alaina laughed with relief. "Faisal!"

Faisal and an Aneza warrior with a lance guided their mounts through the grey. Kentar followed, his old face wrinkled in a grin of greeting, and he moved before the others.

"My brother!" He clasped forearms with Tae.

Tae sheathed his sword. "Well, my friend, you are far from our master's errands. It may please you to know that since you left your appointed trading run with the Aneza, Sirius Abdasir has taken over our master's affairs." He sobered. "Ali Ben Aidon no longer owns any man in this world."

"We know. That is why we have come—" Kentar broke off as Faisal shouldered his horse up beside him. Prince Faisal had changed little. His thin-planed face was strong and well to look on. Kyrin's face heated. Still a quick, bold son of the desert, now he bore a light of joy, though something of sadness lurked behind his gaze. He looked at Kyrin quizzically. Her mouth dried.

He held out his hand, palm down, pointing at her in the Arabic way. "Sheyk Shahin heard whispers of your master's fate and of your journey. He sent word by Kentar. I thought on your path, and by the will of God, we have met. We, I—would not have you go without the gift of salt." His gaze was steady. He was not angry, no.

The tightness about his mouth might be wariness. They had last parted with hard words, though afterward messages and gifts had been given and accepted. Kyrin smiled. She wished she had pinned her bisht at her shoulder with the falcon he'd carved her. But she had deemed the brooch too precious for common wear. It lay in her neck-pouch with Shema's gift. But there was something different about Faisal. With the gift of salt he offered her peace. Had he no bread to go with it? It was customary to offer salt and bread. Did he have no wife? Her mouth twitched, and she hastily straightened her expression. It was too late for her heart to be his, for he was Allah's. But still, to know . . .

"Faisal." Alaina's voice was soft, as she eyed a roll of paper in her hand. She clenched her camel's rein tight and held the paper out with sudden decision. "Will you get this to Seliam Abdeel, of the wazir's household?"

Kyrin stiffened. Faisal stared at Alaina, assessing. His nostrils flared, and he cocked his head in wolfish curiosity.

Kyrin said nothing. Alaina knew what she was about. Doubtless the message was a treatise on the nature of betrayal, with choice words for a treacherous friend, now an enemy. Faisal leaned forward and took the paper. His long fingers touched Alaina's a moment. She paused a bare instant as she withdrew.

Faisal nodded, the tail of his turban dangling down his neck. For once it was clean. He still favored blue, rich as the fall sky.

Kyrin grinned suddenly. He *had* grown. Faisal smiled back at her, and that was all. They knew where they stood. She need not fear. He would tell Nara they were well thus far.

Tae had no message for Ali's household besides his thanks, and Faisal nodded again. They rode on, the older men in front, Alaina and Faisal riding side by side behind Kyrin, Cicero trailing them. Kyrin grinned and shook her head. That Faisal.

She twisted abruptly in her saddle. "Faisal, what *does* your name mean?"

"A wise judge. What did you think it meant?" He smiled crookedly.

Heat flooded her. "I always—it sounded like a fire sizzle, to me." Faisal stared at her a moment, then broke into laughter. He doubled over his saddle, and his horse arched his neck and lifted his tail, sidestepping. Cicero bounded up, mouth open in happiness. Tae and the others looked back with grins. With a last laughing snort, Faisal wiped his eyes. "You do not cease to take me unaware, Shaheena."

There was mischief in Kentar's sly smile at them. "You must watch that one. She may strike the prey or your heart. And the edge of her blade is sharp."

Kyrin stiffened. Kentar's words struck truer than he knew. She wished Faisal had not found her words so sharp, once. Though they were true.

Seeming not to hear, the prince glanced aside. "I see Cicero yet follows you."

"Yes."

"I am glad you are loosed from Ali." His voice was low.

"Yes. Thank you." This was only getting more difficult. Kyrin blurted, "How is Truthseeker?"

"Ah." Faisal studied the sky. "She is somewhere above, guarding." He raised his arm and pointed at a speck that turned slow spirals above them. "There. She is quick to warn, swift at hunting."

To him, that meant beautiful. "I am glad. And—I wish you well." Kyrin could not look at him as he urged his stallion closer beside her. Faisal's lean, tiger form made her throat tighten, and the old wondering rose to choke her. But it could never be. She swallowed past a dry throat and looked down.

Faisal reached out a brown finger and touched the leaping fish under her chin. Kyrin's skin prickled. She jerked her gaze to his. His face was serious. "Tae told me what brought you that scar. You should know. I am your God's now. Jesu rules with mercy and justice in the world of men, and in me." He smiled, raising his head with the old defiance. "Don't fear Sirius Abdasir, a mere wazir, Shaheena. Not with Jesu beside you."

Kyrin could not look away. His face held a tenderness she had not seen, a certainty of spirit—and the joy she had glimpsed. His growing, teasing smile held true laughter. Her answering smile widened. Faisal was truly alive—that was what she had sensed.

Now he was her brother, indeed. And she must go, and leave him, to find her father and Hamal. Her brow furrowed.

"It is well. May your task be fulfilled with the honor you bring to all you do."

"Yes." It was as if he knew her thought. She lifted her chin. She must leave them to danger, though less than the danger she must meet.

"The wind waits for none. See, the mist clears." Faisal whirled his black stallion. "Come, my brothers, the wind is not seen, but we must fly the swifter, and bear messages to our enemies!" His stallion dug its hooves into the ground and he galloped away with a laugh, molded along its back. Like a true prince of the desert, he loosed a wild yell along their trail.

Alaina raised her arm. "Ride swift, brother!"

Faisal lifted his arm in reply, glancing back at them.

Kentar gave them a farewell salute and followed, and a strip of blue fluttered from the Aneza's lance as he thundered after. The scar beneath Kyrin's necklace felt cold. Aloneness crushed her. Soon Tae and Alaina would be gone, and Cicero too.

The last mists disappeared under the sun, and Alaina grinned. "There's the Hejaz!"

The mountains looming beyond the hazy hills led north to Makkah and the seaport of Jedda, some twenty sunrises off. Kyrin's heart leapt a beat. Roughly one-fourth of their journey remained.

The most dangerous fourth, among men and cities, with her passage at the last, to gain on a ship the wazir had provided. And she had yet to tell Tae and Alaina they could not come.

They wound higher into the hills, split by wadis eroded deep by wind and infrequent rains. Grey-and-black sand and grav-el flats wearied them to squinting, the glare relieved near the mountains feet by low ash cones and mounds of sharp rock.

She'd rescued Faisal there long ago, somewhere among the calderas, from the raiders who robbed horses from Ali's caravan. Her heart pained her. Would she never see Faisal again? Would she even reach home? The wazir's reach was long, and his word was law.

They skirted the once-molten lava. As close to the trade route as they were, Tae wouldn't take chances with thieves hiding among them once again. But one night they and their beasts were too weary to go on, and they were forced to halt near a group of the tortured, dull black cones.

Kyrin stood first watch, and later slept uneasily, waking at every noise. The tiger walked in the shadows of her dreams. Next morning the camels were snappish and grumpy as she.

In the mountains they rested a little in the village of Taif then pushed on to Makkah, the pilgrim city, the center of trade in the barren peaks, starkly different from the more southern, greener ranges of the Hejaz. Kyrin drank in every detail. They slept outside the walls and clothed themselves carefully before entering the city at dawn.

Framed in the gateway against a pale, cloudless sky, Tae swayed into Makkah on his camel above the clamoring crowd, clad in a thawb and kaffiyeh of cream linen bound with a thick brown head cord, a long ago gift from Faisal. Concealed by his cloak of black wool, Tae's great sword hung at the side of his saddle. Alaina followed him in a dim brown robe that made her hard to distinguish from the city wall. She treasured it only because it didn't show dirt easily. Tied on her beast, her staff stretched from its shoulder to tail. Her dagger slanted boldly in her blue sash.

Kyrin urged Lilith past a donkey blocking her, and swatted its rump, her arm dwarfted by her wide, straw colored sleeve. The green bisht from Qadira wrapped her ironwood staff, her short stick, and her bow, unstrung and tied under her leg, tight against the saddle. From her maroon sash, the falcon dagger watched the passersby. Here, she could wear it openly, for Ali was gone, and Sirius could not say her nay.

Kyrin straightened her back. It ought to be seen here, for Makkah was likely as close as she would come to the weapon's birthplace, where the Damascus steel was forged. They were just days from Jedda. On any other occasion she would have loved to wander the crowded market, the souk, wide and busy under raised awnings. Filled with enticing scents of cloves and curry, the bright patterns of varying clothing, strange parts of animals cooked and raw, and many foods she'd never seen, the booths called to her eye and mind. Men and women of Egypt, Persia, Yemen, Anatolia, and Syria watched sharp-eyed as falcons over their booths in the great square. But the wazir also had eyes, ears, and hands in this place.

Umar, or a beggar wielding a dagger, might be more dangerous than a man of note, such as Jachin or Seliam. Or did the wazir think they stayed in the sands with the tribes Tae knew, finding refuge with Shahin of the Aneza or Faisal of the Twilkets? Kyrin shook her hair back, the edges of her kaffiyeh tapping her cheeks. The wazir did not know her mettle, or the others', but she could not count on what he might think. She was returning to her land. She was almost done with hiding.

It would make getting on the ship much easier if she knew Sirius meant to capture them alive. Somehow she must find out. Kyrin squeezed after Tae and Alaina down a central aisle between booths, sometimes nothing more than a rug spread with the seller's wares. On the other side of the souk she watched the hurrying crowd thronging the narrow streets in the early sun. There was no flash of red and black or the gleam of a lance. Cicero stayed close, tail solemn, offering no insult or interest to other salukis or the press of people. Kyrin glanced behind them, scouring the shadowed corners of streets and houses. There were guards, but none in the wazir's red and black. She frowned. They had not seen one. That was curious in itself.

They found their way to the far side of the city without mishap, unnoticed beyond the first glance by every important official they passed. Kyrin curled the end of Lilith's rein about her hand. She supposed desert travelers and those on pilgrimage were common as flies, still she distrusted it They left the noise and thick smells behind with Makkah's last gate and turned onto the road to Jedda. Kyrin sniffed. Was that the first brine of the sea, or only her thought of it?

They jogged over hills, softly blue-green with juniper, and descended from the mountains by easy stages. There were other travelers on the road through the afternoon. Nomad gypsies in bright red, green or yellow, and desert dwellers in more earthy shades. The richer merchants and sheyks often wore white and cream. Alaina stared, her head turning from side to side, her green eyes intent. Almost as if she looked for someone. She was greatly interested in the different styles and colors of dress, and kept Tae busy with questions. Kyrin smiled to herself. None would mistake Alaina's bold look for a woman's downcast glance.

She herself was more intrigued by the faces of Araby. A proud sheyk ignored her curious gaze then muttered behind her of insolent boys. A dusty herdsman twitched the lead of his camel and grinned up at her. A woman glanced at her and then again, sharply, lifting a henna-bright hand to her veil across her nose, as she hurried to the edge of the road with her husband to let them pass. She did not speak, though her knowing gaze was curious. What had given her away? Kyrin dipped her head slightly in thanks for the woman's silence. A man with a load on his back staggered past, sweating, and struggled on, his eyes blank with toil.

The olive trees grew thicker, and they passed families breaking evening bread under the leaves. The road widened, closer to Jedda. The city spread out along the horizon, a dark rope of buildings cradled by the flat gleam of the sea.

As evening drew on Kyrin's head ached, and dust gritted in her mouth. She was tired of the faces, the strain of hiding her hair, of watching every gesture, of unspeaking silence for fear her voice would give her away. Sirius would have men here in the seaport if nowhere else.

The sinking sun harried people outside the city on errands back into Jedda before the gate closed.

A short, stocky watchman stood beside the stone wall, next to a gate of polished, ancient juniper two times his height. He crossed his arms across his chest, a frown between his eyes. Kyrin's breath came faster. His slippered foot tapped the earth. She swallowed and straightened.

Ahead of her, Tae dismounted and strode toward the watchman. At the same moment two men in red and black, fully armed with dagger, sword, and lance, stepped through the gate behind the watchman and moved to either side of it. The watchman said, "Insha Allah, at last you come, lazy ones!"

Tae never paused. The watchman turned to him, his round-cheeked scowl assessing. "Name?"

Alaina's fingers were warm on Kyrin's arm. Her other hand rested on her staff, unthreatening but ready. Kyrin slid her grip from Lilith's rein to Alaina's hand, for her sister's comfort or her own, she was not sure. Lilith shifted, crushing their ankles between their camels' hairy sides. Kyrin smiled at Alaina and nudged Lilith closer to Tae. If it came to blows, Tae and Alaina must get away.

Tae's low voice murmured, reaching only the watchman's ear.

"Destination?" He grunted something at Tae's reply. Coin clinked into his hand, and the official pointed, directing them toward the docks. Through that arch and down the street.

Affecting disinterest with a lowly watchman's business, the wazir's men stared into the crowd. Tae thanked the watchman. They walked their beasts through the gate.

Alaina kept her gaze from the guards and followed the way indicated. Around the first corner, Kyrin let out her breath and they looked at each other. Tae simply nodded, the edges of his mouth turning up the slightest bit, and they went on.

No man sought to follow them, as far as Kyrin could tell. They turned right, then left, though one really needed only to follow the fish smell and the raucous seabirds. She glanced at Alaina. Had Sirius found them? Or did he wait for them to come to him, lurking on the ship as a tiger? Kyrin's mouth thinned. When she stepped into his web, he would find a hunter. But it was late to seek the ship this night.

Alaina yawned. Tae led them to the gate of a caravanserai on their right. Every wall was of thick stones. Pale, cream, and white-and-pink, some were deeply ridged, some looked almost soft. Within the court gate the archway to the house stood open to the evening, lamplight bright within. Another gate ten lengths to their left led into an adjacent court for the animals. Kyrin reached out to touch a fan-shaped rock. The sharp ridges rasped her fingers.

The host stood beside his door. His wide chest puffed out below his square head and shoulders. In a white robe and turban, with crisp, clean sandals and a dagger sprouting formidable, odd, and elegant from his camel-leather belt, he rumbled, "The day has been good. Enter, blessed of Allah!"

Kyrin smothered her laugh with a cough. Tae paid him, and the man motioned them in with a beaming smile that belied his show of strength. Cicero's claws clicked on the floor at Kyrin's side as he walked, his head up, nose busy. Alaina inquired of a servant after their room and went to rid their beds of pests, while Kyrin followed Tae back out to the second court to settle Lilith and the other camels.

Tae drew water from the well in the middle of the court and poured buckets into the trough until they were satisfied, then they tethered the beasts and tossed them a few date-pit cakes. The court was full of bedded down camels, their masters hurrying to finish and get within the squat caravanserai to their own suppers and the gossip of local news.

On one side of the courtyard, fires crackled and popped in front of two tents. The riders of the desert preferred to sleep outside the stone roof. The rich sweet of cardamom tea and milk drifted around Kyrin with the quiet talk of men at peace and the crunching of contented camels.

Tae and Kyrin walked slowly across the caravanserai court. Tae nodded to the night guards who'd appeared beside the outer gate. They passed between two more posted at the house door. In the main room inside, Kyrin touched Tae's arm. "Tae . . ."

His steps never pausing, he clenched his fingers into a fist, the hand signal for "stop." She closed her mouth; he wished to speak later, when they were alone. A youngster directed them down a passage with doors on either side, to the last room on the left.

Inside, Alaina swept up a last pile of dust and used straw. Arranged around the walls, their new pallets were pungent and fluffed. Strewn herbs against biters peeped from within their spread rugs. The open window freshened the warm air, and the last ray of the sun burned past the horizon.

Tae stopped and stared out the window, tapping his chin, brow furrowed. Kyrin sighed silently. The words she must say need not be faced till the morn. Best not to disturb him.

She took out the dust heap for Alaina, then sank on her pallet with a sigh. Her neck was tight and her legs sore. The glow in the window overwhelmed the flame of the lamp Alaina lighted.

The growing coolness of night felt wonderful. Kyrin kicked off her sandals and washed her face and feet after Alaina.

They would eat at a table. A table where Ali would not drum his fingers and bark at them. What would they eat? Honey cakes with almonds and cinnamon, or hummingbird tongues, or other delicacies? Kyrin grimaced. Let the beautiful airy creatures keep their tongues. There was one thing she had not tasted in this land.

Ali had never let her try the tea from the East, near Tae's land. She fingered the coin from Sirius's bag that she had put in her sash. She would order tea for all of them, and the best dishes the caravanserai boasted. They would have a feast to remember.

"When the sun rises, we'll see if the ship is here yet," Tae said easily. "But this night I desire we eat to our heart's content." He kept his back to them, watching the night. He spoke as if they often stopped at such caravanserais and ate and slept and moved on.

Kyrin touched Alaina's shoulder. "What would you have?"

"Shall we have curried lamb and rice? And I've wanted a melon for ever so long."

"And sweet pork with lemon, and their best fish. It has been an age since I tasted fish," Tae added.

"We shall have it all." Kyrin smiled at them and tucked her arm around Cicero's neck, drawing him closer, wondering if they had any baked sweet with apples.

8

Persuasion

I am a stranger in the earth. ~Psalm 119:19

Kyrin rose with Alaina before first light, slipped on her thawb, and went down to tea, goat's milk, cheese, and flatbread. Near the half-circle of men gathered about the communal breakfast dish of rice, Kyrin forced bread and cheese down her dry throat.

Tae bent over a dark-skinned man sitting cross-legged in the corner with a lamp beside him, smoking a long pipe with relish. His clothes were worn and patched, his brown-grey hair and beard long, but trimmed.

Tae said something and the man's blue eyes gleamed. He nodded, beard jutting, and rose. His pointed felt slippers whispered as he passed Kyrin on his way to the door. His turban cleared the lintel by a hair, and he stepped out under the stars. Kyrin eyed his brisk back. An Arab with blue eyes?

Tae looked after him a moment, then came to sit by her.

At this distance, the men would not notice her voice over the low hum of theirs. "What did you say to him?"

Tae grinned. "I sent him to look for Sirius's ship. He'll find the *Sabra* if she's in port. I offered coin for a little asking around of her errand and of the men aboard her. What a man thinks of his master tells much about both."

Kyrin gave a short laugh, and a shorter smile. Trust Tae to know his ground for any coming conflict. Tae grinned and left. Alaina sat beside Kyrin, quiet, idly playing with her eating dagger.

Kyrin chewed her bread. She still found it hard to swallow. Alaina. What would she do without her to watch her back? But Tae would need her. Together they would pass anywhere in this land as a hakeem and his apprentice. She would not draw harm to them. Kyrin's mouth tightened.

Sirius would not find her companions caught in his web, to suck from them every vestige of Tae's dangerous knowledge and Alaina's skill of needle, pen, and staff. To keep them, or sell them in the caliph's court to the highest bidder, or give them to Umar's Hand.

Alaina laid her dagger gently down in the middle of the empty dish in her lap. She looked up. Her green eyes were dark. "I know." Her lip trembled. "I know you want to go alone, Kyrin. And I will stay with Tae, as you wish. Until the wazir lifts Umar's Hand from our trail or you find Hamal and send word. The pride of"—she looked aside at the eating men and dropped her voice—"the one who hunts us, will not let Tae leave these shores alive." Tears stood in her eyes. "If you find my mother or my brothers, tell them I love them." She swallowed and the tears ran down her pale cheeks. "Tell them why I cannot come. I—we will come to you. When I can."

"Oh, Alaina." Kyrin's throat closed up. She dared not take her sister's hands. "I will find them, and I will tell them of my faithful sister, who is theirs also." She leaned forward. "You and Tae will evade our pursuers until I find Hamal." Her voice was husky. "But don't tell Tae I'm going alone, just yet." She felt she would never smile again. "I thought we'd go home together. But blades do not frighten me now, and you are far more than a scribe, with more to lose to the caliph. If the Master of the stars wills it, we will meet again." The falcon blade was cold under her hand.

I am sure he wills it. He would not separate us. I will find my father and Hamal then Alaina and Tae will come. They will be safe in Cierheld, and what a band of mercenaries Tae will train for Father! Surely Cernalt and armsmaster Nith will love him well. Mayhap we will train together, and I will earn the black sash. Tae could go with riches to Huen. And Alaina will stay with me always. She almost smiled. Alaina nodded once, sober.

In their room they gathered their gear and weapons.

"The camels are ready." Tae tossed their bishts to them, while Cicero pounced playfully at their feet. In the main room, Tae bid their host farewell, and together they stepped under the arch.

In the beasts' court Lilith, faithful Lilith, lifted her fuzzy tan head, her dark eyes mournful. Ready for their last journey. And then the *Sabra.*

What manner of man was the shipmaster? One such as Ali, who loved power and pain, or one such as slavemaster Kef, who cared for his vessel but little for the affairs of others, far less the slaves he carried?

§

The sun warmed Kyrin's face. She peered around the corner of an old, broken building, her ironwood staff in her hand. Dead fish and garbage crowded the narrow street before her. It touched a wide cross-street, revealing stone flags and the sun gleaming on the waves beyond. In the shadow of the last building sat her quarry, his back against the limestone wall. Blue-eyed Kaish from the caravanserai rested, his legs drawn up under his dirt-colored thawb, his head on his knees, skinny arms wrapped around his legs. Kyrin glanced past him. Nothing but the noise of unseen seabirds and seamen and ship's doings.

She gave herself a small shake and walked toward the sleeper. Tae and Alaina were somewhere near about. Sea air whipped away the stink of fish and batted a bit of hair fallen from her turban against her cheek. Sniffing, she breathed deep. She had missed the bracing smell of salt, memories of her godfather, and of Britannia's many walls..

A loud snore reached her. Kyrin grinned. She could assume she'd been heard. Out of the man's reach she stopped and leaned on her staff. "Kaish."

He raised his head with a soft snort. Bleared blue eyes stared.

"Tae sends word." She waited.

Interest animated Kaish. He glanced both ways then up at her, and his lean neck bobbed with his swallow. Bobbing . . . bobbing like a lean form in a boat below Ali's slave ship in Gaza, selling stinking fish and sweet oranges long ago . . . It might mean nothing. Kyrin bit her lip. The man lived by the sea and went where his trade took him. But where else had she seen those eyes?

Kaish pursed his mouth, careful to shape the word. "Kyrin?"

"Kyrin Cieri is my name."

Kaish's turban lurched as he got to his feet. "The *Sabra* is ready. You will find her there." He pointed beyond the visible stretch of stone and blue-green sea. Far out, small whitecaps whipped up. "But the most illustrious *Sabra* does not depart." His blue eyes stared keenly into her face.

Kyrin smiled, as if she did not fret over each moment in the open so near Sirius's vessel. "Be assured, I mean peace. I travel on her. Tae wishes to know if she is—honorable." She held out her palm with two coins. With a gap-toothed smile, Kaish closed his creased, leathery hand about her offering.

"Servant of Allah, she is, with much honor," he said earnestly, his teeth gleaming. He bowed. Feet shushed on stone behind

Kyrin. She spun. Tae and Alaina strode toward them, Cicero at Alaina's heels.

"Kaish . . ." She turned back. The street was empty. "Well." Kyrin frowned, thoughtful.

"The *Sabra*?" Tae stopped beside her.

"Kaish says she waits. And has much honor."

"Ah. Let us watch a little."

Alaina and Kyrin followed Tae toward the clean breeze at the street's mouth. The worn stone of the quayside stretched away from them on each hand. Shipmasters and bargaining merchants strode back and forth near docked vessels, yelling orders or haggling. Artisans, sailors, and barebacked slaves toiled about their work. Some bore loads of goods or tack and were sheened with sweat.

To their right floated three ships. Two were berthed together. Fifty yards farther the *Sabra* was moored, an empty stretch of water on either side. She rode low, her hatches closed at both ends of the deck. The sails flapped, waiting to be hauled tight to catch the wind.

A sailor walked toward the shipmaster's quarters near the middle of the vessel, where a guard stood beside the door. A dark Arab with close-curled hair and a bull neck stepped from the low quarters to speak briefly with the guard and glance at the approaching sailor. He shook his head at their reply to his query, threw up his hands, and vanished inside.

Tae leaned back against the wall, his eyes moving about in lazy interest. Thieves, fishermen, tradesmen, women, and beggars moved past. They did not give a second glance to the three Arabs meditating on the shipping.

Kyrin twisted her fingers around her staff. How could she convince Tae to let her go?

Cicero put his nose in her hand, and she rubbed his head. "It looks well enough—"

Alaina grabbed her arm. "No, there! Tae, that man in front of the drinking house, and the other on the left by the fruit seller's, and that one mending his net on the quay: they watch everyone who passes."

Alaina leaned forward, clutching Kyrin by the arm as if she could keep her force of will. "The one in the middle with a fishnet, he has a warrior's marks. His sun-bleached hair is braided, there's a double-bitted axe at his feet and a smaller one in his belt. Kyrin, he comes from the wolfships!" The man bent over his net after another sharp glance about. Alaina's brows met above her green eyes. "You cannot go!"

Tae glanced at Alaina quizzically then at Kyrin.

Kyrin's breath came short. "So? He will do nothing if he knows I obey Sirius's word."

Tae cleared his throat. "Move back." Down the side street once again they stopped. Tae turned to Kyrin. "I know," he said simply. "You wish to protect us—" The impassivity of his face was marred by the deep wrinkles about his mouth.

Kyrin gripped his arm. "Please, Tae. I must go alone. The wazir will have you taken to the caliph's palace—or killed. He will hold you as a threat over me. And what of Alaina in his house or the caliph's court? But if you are free, you are a threat to the wazir if he thinks to do me ill. So he will think twice about my harm, since I seek only to fulfill my oath and find Hamal. I will send Hamal back, as I swore. Then you will be free. We will be free. And I will live as first daughter of Cierheld again. You and Alaina can come to Britannia, or"—her voice dropped—"you could go to Huen."

Tae studied her, silent. She bit her lip and did not look away. She had to go, with only herself to blame if things went wrong.

He sighed. "How will Alaina fare in this land, hunted beside me?"

"As a hakeem traveling with your apprentice, all will welcome you into their house or tent, and none more so than Prince Faisal. And she asks me to take word home for her. And I—you will get letters from me about how I fare with Hamal, to take to the wazir if you think fit, if the others go astray."

"All right, daughter. It was my thought to go, but I do not know your land. That you go is the better choice." His voice was low.

Kyrin gulped and stared at him. Tae smiled, wry. "What, my daughter? You did not think me so shortsighted as to put all of us in the wazir's hand at once?" He grinned lopsidedly.

"I—" Kyrin laughed. She sobered and held out her staff. "My father, keep this. You may have need of it. I will have one of oak where I go." Tae gripped it, and she reached for him. They held each other tight, and Kyrin whispered, "You've taught me everything. I will see you again."

Tae pulled back and waggled the staff at her. "We may come to you. Never forget the Master of the stars. Begin every task with him. End all things with his counsel."

"I won't—I will, that is, he won't let me forget. And I will learn well what you showed me in the desert." Kyrin stumbled over her words. Alaina watched her, mouth tight.

"Yes." Tae laid his hand on Cicero's head. Cicero licked his fingers. His brown eyes on her were deep.

Kyrin could not swallow. A ship was no place for Cicero. The food would be bad, the journey long. He needed wide open spaces, the wind singing past his ears, and a stooping falcon to flush game for his hunting. Only the falcon blade went with her.

Cicero strained against the thong about his neck, ears up, a whine in his throat. Kyrin knelt and put her arms about him. He licked her face and growled deep in his throat with joy. Her father had many hounds, but they would not be Cicero. He licked tears from her chin with a swipe of his tongue.

At last Kyrin rose and Alaina hugged her till her shoulders creaked. "Kyrin—" she choked, and stepped back, her hands darting at her in a last dance of Subak. Kyrin returned Alaina's light strikes, her eyes painfully dry, her heart twisting. They whirled and stepped and struck, their low laughter echoing through the street, bittersweet.

Kyrin gently caught Alaina's last blow between her hands and bent her sister's arm, sliding behind her shoulder. Alaina's mouth pinched. She was probably biting her tongue to keep from saying she would go, burn the wazir and the caliph.

Kyrin released her with a grin. Tae watched them. She etched his smile in her mind, staring at them, her breath caught inside.

Then she turned away, walking fast. Her feet on the quay were the crash of ocean breakers. She forced her head up against the searching eyes of the men near the shops. They glanced at her and away, then their attention fastened on her as she neared the *Sabra.*

The man with the net was staring at a knot in his large hands, heavy brow furrowed. Kyrin walked closer. "Sir—" She pulled her kaffiyeh free. Her hair fell about her face, hiding the jet earring.

His eyes were the sharp color of the sea; his thick hair gleamed. With a sudden curse he leaped back, out of reach. She grasped a coil of his mending line, the heavy knotted end swinging. He looked sharply to either side and his fingers edged toward his axe.

"No—" Kyrin held out her hand. A saluki barked somewhere behind. *Don't, don't loose Cicero!*

The man stood unmoving his frame coiled and ready. This close she could see his beard was also braided into hand-span plaits. They would give an excellent grip.

Kyrin lowered the rope slowly. She might not need it. "Please, I wish to speak to the *Sabra's* shipmaster. I need passage. By order of Sirius Abdasir, wazir to the caliph."

"Ah." The warrior looked her up and down and dropped his hand from his weapon.

"I am Kyrin Cieri—" Feet pounded behind her. Kyrin tightened her grip on the rope and kept her gaze on the warrior. The footsteps spread out at her back, accompanied by heavy breathing. The men Alaina had spotted had blocked her escape.

No matter. She did not seek it. Kyrin shrugged, her shoulders tense.

The net mender said a harsh word in a guttural voice, and protest broke out at Kyrin's back. The warrior thrust his chin out and bellowed, his eyes gimlets, and touched his axe. Kyrin's ears rang as she listened for Cicero and watched the giant before her. He would tense if Tae or Alaina approached behind her. The quay around them went quiet. Gulls cried; nothing else moved. Then feet thumped wood, and the men stalked past Kyrin toward the ship, muttering. Quayside movement sputtered up again, and the net warrior jerked a thumb over his shoulder.

"There is the *Sabra.* Shipmaster Heber waits for you."

"My thanks." Kyrin dropped the rope and worked her fingers. Thanks to the Master of the stars, Tae kept Alaina and Cicero back. She twisted her hair up under her kaffiyeh and curled both into a turban again, jamming on the head-cord to hold it. She dared not look behind her.

The plank that led aboard the *Sabra* swayed beneath her. The warrior followed close, his net slung over his shoulder. He smelled of salt, sweat, and fish and was a head and shoulders taller than she. Two of her would stretch across his broad chest.

The plank spanned infinity. Kyrin at last stepped down on the *Sabra's* deck. She braced against the slight heave under her feet. Lean, sun-browned men near the mast stared at her with various degrees of intensity.

A thick-browed, dark haired man stood a little before his men and the shipmaster's quarters, arms crossed over his chest. It seemed his usual pose. Kyrin bowed.

"Greetings, shipmaster Heber. I am Kyrin Cieri, and I come from the wazir Sirius Abdasir, on his errand. Do you know of it?"

Heber rocked back on his heels, his gaze narrow. "Was is not to be two on this errand? My ears have heard of horses raided. And of an escaped slave, a hakeem, taken from my master's hand."

Straight to the attack.

"My sister has other matters she must attend to." Kyrin ignored Heber's insult to Tae. "The wazir's horses I loosed to find their way home. I will not keep your vessel longer, shipmaster, but be about the wazir's errand if you deem the wind and tide favor us."

Heber's thick brows drew down. Would he order one of her thieving hands cut off? The hand-axe in the wolfship warrior's belt looked sharp and well-tended enough.

The shipmaster tilted his head, and the sailors scattered. "Very well." Heber yelled, "Boy!" A slight figure popped up beside Kyrin, noiseless. Her hand went to the falcon.

The boy piped, "Yes, my master?" His ears were ringless beside a mass of curly black hair. He looked to have a few summers less than she, with an alert gaze, round features, and an impish snub nose.

Heber said briskly, "Stow her goods." He glanced at her ready weapon hand with scorn, and disappeared into his quarters.

Kyrin dropped her hand. It seemed they were to sail without a fight to force Tae and Alaina out of hiding. She pointed toward the far side of the quay, seemingly deserted but for her things at the corner of Kaish's street. "See there, my pack in the street. Bring the things beside it too."

The boy dashed off and returned with her pack and bow. She had not seen Alaina and Tae leave their hiding place behind Kaish's street corner. They would take care that none from the ship should find them. As it should be.

On a deep breath of sea air, Kyrin held her father in her inner eye and followed the boy to a hatch the wolfship warrior lifted, then down a rope ladder to the hold.

Shipmaster Heber had prepared her a space among the goods. It would be lightless and cramped when the hatch was closed, and smelled of bilge water and the *Sabra's* varied cargoes. Kyrin smoothed the full sacks stacked around her bed-place. The sack walls surrounded her bed on three sides. The narrow walkway on the fourth side ran across haphazard aisles between dimly seen goods to the foot of another ladder at the far end of the ship, where the sailors slept. This cargo was sweet and sticky. She was to sleep beside dried dates. A corner of her mouth turned up. At least it was not grain. The boy shifted his feet, staring at her.

Kyrin set down her pack, heavier than it had been, and unfastened Faisal's falcon brooch from the shoulder of her bisht. She spread the cloak over the rough, raised bed-place of wood. In her sash, the falcon dagger gleamed in the light of the hatch, and her stick lay solid against her ribs. The boy made a small sound, his eyes on her weapons.

Kyrin caught back her smile, and he lowered his gaze quickly. So. The falcon dagger and the stick Tae had carved her were foreign to him. Her thawb and desert cloak were simple, but her weapons rivaled those of a rich warrior. She supposed she was a riddle indeed. The jet earring glimmered in her ear, and her black, horn-laminated bow of the northern Steppes nomads rested against the wall of sacks. This bow would kill a hart easily, or a man. Tae had gotten it for her as her arms strengthened, practicing in Ali's old garden.

"What's your name?"

"Ebrahim," the youngster said, his eyes straight ahead. His hand curled into a fist, shaking slightly.

"Put this with the bow, Ebrahim." She pulled the falcon blade from her sash and held it out. Doubt darkened his face as he eyed her. At last he grasped the blade and obeyed. She set out the rest of her gear, emptying her pack. Then she froze.

Tae's waterproofed scrip lay at the bottom. She pulled it out. Under the proofed material was a complete copy of the Vulgate that Alaina had finished. Kyrin slid it out, smoothing the leather binding. She closed her eyes. Beyond precious, it smelled of camel-dung smoke, Alaina's rose water, and Tae. After their master Ali's execution, Tae had somehow taken it from under Sirius's nose. The Vulgate was for her people in her tongue, as Alaina would wish.

"Mistress, may I get you bread and meat?"

Kyrin stiffened and opened her eyes. "No, I have eaten. And call me Kyrin." She smiled quickly. Ebrahim blinked and grinned, his small teeth perfect.

He disappeared up the ladder but left the hatch open. Kyrin walked back to the hatch and lifted her face to the sun and welcome air. So, she wasn't a prisoner.

Heber's vessel would travel up the Red Sea. She would journey overland to Gaza, and reach the ocean that touched Britannia's shore at last. She must find time to practice on the *Sabra.*

There were shouts and thuds above as Heber's men readied the *Sabra's* sails. Kyrin quelled a shiver, remembering Tae's voice, the tears on Alaina's face. The warmth of Cicero's tongue. She picked up the falcon and dropped the dagger inside her thawb and made herself smile. Heber had sent no one ashore after Tae and Alaina.

§

In the middle of the *Sabra's* third day at sea, a storm hit. Kyrin took her turn bailing water out of the hold and ate a cold dinner. When the morn dispersed the clouds, the far shore was slipping past. She climbed on deck and lay on the wood in the warmth. The wolfship warrior watched her, saying nothing.

Kyrin smiled at the sky and did not break the silence. After the sun warmed her to a light sweat, she rose, went below, and returned in Mey's warm black Aneza trousers and thawb, bound by her white sash. Faisal's falcon brooch rested over her heart.

It brought closer those she had left behind. The falcon bumped beneath her thawb. The sailors' laughter and banter rose around Kyrin as she scratched at places the biters had gotten and hung her damp cloak and thawb on the rail. While they steamed their way toward dryness, she went to speak to Heber.

She almost tripped over Ebrahim when she stepped back outside Heber's door, and the sailors' gazes followed her. Kyrin scowled at Ebrahim's guilty face. He must have had a tale to tell of her. Her lips twitched at the cautious distance he kept. "Come. I have need of one who knows things he ought not and speaks of them."

Ebrahim shuffled after her into the hold, staring at his feet. Several of the men followed, picking up a sack here, shifting a jar there.

"So, the shipmaster says it's to be done." Kyrin smiled at them, took a large bundle of herbs from her pack, and sent Ebrahim with it to the sailors' end of the hold. The sailors lingered in the aisle, and a prickle went up her back. Then the wolfship warrior stepped off the ladder.

The men moved immediately to the date sacks at the top of the stacks, lifting them aside. The warrior approached Kyrin and eyed her bow, still in its place. The *Sabra's* men looked beneath the sacks they moved. For dampness? No. If he had come to oversee Heber's order, he would not find it in the boxes and bags about. He lifted one and looked straight at her.

Kyrin shifted back a step and stared. Swords, bows, and quivers of arrows lay beneath the top bags, as far from the damp hull as possible. Waterproofed wood boxes that they dragged from the aisle contained daggers, spices, and rolls of rich cloth carefully packed in rows.

With little talking among themselves, the men sat where they could, stood where they could not, and began to oil the weapons and inspect the goods. Kyrin was glad for the wall of dates looming at her back.

She sat on the edge of her bed, watching, for she had no room to leave. The men shot glances at her bow and sword in the corner then at her. The warrior took a seat opposite her, still silent. Kyrin raised a brow and waited. Best to take the high ground, here. No one said anything. So she reached for a blade and an oil rag from the warrior's supply at his side. Even to her it was a restless movement. He might mean to question her for Sirius Abdasir. But the wolfship warrior seemed captivated by the glowing grain of the wood grip in his hands, the gleam of oil, and a good weapon's edge. Kyrin's mouth quirked. It could be worse. She picked up a bow, oiled and inspected the limbs, then paused, frowning. These bow limbs were straight.

"It's the shipmaster's orders!" Ebrahim cried indignantly at the far end of the hold. Kyrin raised her head. Another voice protested, "By Allah, let the biters feast on my flesh. She carries the evil eye. Have you not seen . . ."

There. Behind the ladder, his chin thrust out, Ebrahim faced a sailor who blocked the boy from his mat.

With a tempered rumble, the wolfship warrior stood. "It is rosemary herb. It will drive the biters farther from your back than they have ever gone, Sulah." He jerked his chin at Kyrin. "She brought the herb sprigs to shipmaster Heber for his leave."

"She cannot make her peace with biters who also take flesh of the pure servants of Allah?" The sailor's mournful brown eyes were anxious.

Kyrin straightened, then shrugged slightly. They had seen all of her weapons and her errand she would give them. Her lips firmed. Alaina had given her the rosemary for her sleeping place during her journey. At least the wolfship warrior seemed willing to give a word on her behalf. The men must make their own decisions whether she was evil or no.

She set down the bow, and arching a brow in question, fingered a box of goods at her feet and the weapons it concealed. She had never been so forward, but there was no one to speak for her. Now she must make her own way. She did not take back her silent question.

The warrior raised a hand to his pale beard, his bushy brows drawing together. "Ah, that's a ransom. For the caliph's need."

Kyrin did not doubt he knew of her errand and what the need was. She nodded.The wazir kept his word.

§

Night descended. The stars enclosed the *Sabra* in the heavens. The anxious sailor was at the *Sabra's* rudder, Ebrahim beside him. A shadow slipped from the hatch.

The sailor turned as the feet of the woman of the East whispered across the deck, her black-clad form shadow on shadow except for the white of her sash. "Shipmaster Heber said I could come up after nightfall." Her direct voice did not hesitate.

"Yes . . . mistress. Our master has said so." With his elbow, the rudder-man nudged Ebrahim, who trotted toward the sailors' hatch. The wolfship warrior had wanted to know if she moved.

The woman still stared at him. The sailor licked his lips and clutched the blue bead in his hand. His lamp was low on oil, but Ebrahim would return with more soon. She could not draw the eye of evil so quickly, and he held blue to fend it off.

"My thanks." The woman turned and walked to the stern.

The rudder-man shuddered, sweat cold on his face with the night. Did she catch him staring at her ear? She had the whole voyage if she wished to cast ill will on them . . . He had heard it said that Ali Ben Aidon bore no children to the day of his death, and she had been his slave.

The woman sank to the deck and bent in a series of strange ways that nothing human with the blessing of Allah could attain. He gulped. She had spun into motion.

She glided over the wood deck, kicking and striking the air in a violent dance. Mayhap she dealt with djinn. He held his breath. Drawn steel whispered.

He drew back further against the rudder, and a pale gleam flickered in harmony with her shadow. After long moments the dagger slid back into its sheath. She pattered toward him. The lamp he lifted shone on her face and sweat-dark hair that clung to her neck. She wore nothing over her hair. The evil eye winked. Her eyes gleamed as black. Large, dark, and fathomless.

Were they set on his obedience, watchful, or planning his destruction? If he brought news to the one who paid for it before the wolfship warrior did, gold might be his, but also misfortune, if she began to walk in the wazir's favor again.

"I thank you." She bowed and disappeared down the hatch. The rudder-man fingered his ear and let out his breath. The way she used her blade was strange, but each shadow-blow had found its mark. He would leave her to the wazir and his watcher. No gold was worth the evil eye.

Neither of them saw the wolfship warrior draw his head below the level of the deck as Kyrin moved toward the hatch.

§

The morning the *Sabra* sailed into the Gulf of Aqaba was clear and warm, without the lingering chill of the sands or storm. The water sparkled between the vessel and the quay as Kyrin disembarked, clad in her Arab thawb and cloak again. Water creatures swam in the clear water, a myriad jewels below the surface.

Near the rail, Ebrahim waved. Kyrin had showed him several ways to throw a man thrice his size. She sighed. The wolfship warrior strode behind her, his double-bladed axe strapped across his back.

He reminded Kyrin of her father's mercenaries. Lord Dain hired good men with straight tongues, descendants of invaders or no. And he gave them land when they retired, trained them in a trade, or let them go if they wished it.

The wolfship warrior said nothing, his mane tamed this morn by a thong. He frowned every time his gaze touched her fish necklace. Kyrin fingered it.

She wore the carved fish of gleaming rainbow shell that her father might know her easier by his gift, shaped by his hand. But Hamal—where was this Cedsel? Taught well how to read and write, and with the appeal of his sun-kissed skin, surely Hamal must serve someone in a high position in Britannia. Unless he was dead. Kyrin bit her lip. Slavers could be unpredictable.

They took the mounts the wazir had provided ashore, and rode in silence. The overland way was long, rocky, and dry. The wolfship warrior kept his head up, his muscled body agile in the saddle, but he was the wazir's man. Kyrin squashed her longing for Cicero, riding before her saddle, watchful and eager. *He* never watched her with anything in his heart but love. They reached the *Howler* after the sun sank, and walked up the loading plank.

Sailors were unloading a nearby ship by torchlight. They milled below the *Howler's* rail, calling to each other, laughing or griping. Kyrin blinked hard, weary to the bone. They reminded her of stern Kentar, of Jachin's rolling laugh, Zoltan's sly grin, and Nimah's dancing feet. Tae's hand on her shoulder and Alaina's understanding touch were close, as were their merciless blows in Subak training. She could almost see Nara step out of the shadows with a platter of her honey-almond cakes.

The wolfship warrior coughed behind Kyrin. The men looked up and quieted. Kyrin dragged her pack across the deck after the warrior, who followed a sailor. Sirius's wolfship warrior would sleep on deck. He'd never told her his name. With first light he'd leave her to peace and the sea. The sea and home.

Kyrin closed her hand about her necklace; she found it hard to breathe. There was no Alaina to warm her back, to whisper to of the bright sea-creatures she'd seen. Her sister would want to draw them in her book of herb sketches. *But we look at the same stars. And the warrior will leave with the morn.*

9

Bargains

Give an answer to every man
who asks a reason of the hope . . . in you. ~1 Peter 3:15

Kyrin collapsed on the mat the shipmaster had provided, with a perfunctory sniff at the air. Her bed was not near grain. Sirius Abdasir missed nothing. That did not bode well for Alaina and Tae. She struggled with fear as her eyes closed.

Later, Kyrin woke. Unease held her tense. Blackness.

Wood flexed and groaned. The *Sabra,* and Heber . . . no, this was the *Howler.* What was the shipmaster's name? She had been so weary when they boarded she did not remember.

No sliver of light. Where was the hatch? Her breath rustled in and out.

Kyrin sat up and stretched her arm in front of her, feeling about. A wood wall rose a hand-span from her back and her weapons lay between, but there was nothing else. She stood and swept her arm over her head. No low roof or dangling ladder. Nothing. She swallowed hard.

She stepped forward, feet sliding across the floor purposefully. Seven paces and wood brushed her fingertips again. Fifteen tentative paces along that wall she met another. Back in the middle of the room, a draft stirred her hair, but not a scrap of light broke the dark to hint at a hatch.

Her nose twitched. An old odor—that was why the sweat broke over her. That smell . . . rank human pain-sweat and filth. Ali's vessel—and slaves. Kyrin clutched the falcon dagger. A low growl rumbled behind her.

She whirled, saw nothing, heard nothing. And dragged in a sobbing breath, trembling, shoving back a vision of herself in chains. *Jesu!*

Her heart hammered and cold spread through her. She closed her eyes, forced in a deep breath, held it, and pushed it out with the cold. The Master of all was here. The chains were not. No cold metal grated against her ankles. Fear yammered and roared. The tiger had brought her to the deck by those chains. . . no. *I will never leave you nor forsake you.* The chains were broken, the falcon freed. The bright door of the Master of the stars's word slammed truth between them. She made another circuit of the room. She had not missed a ladder. Back on her mat, she froze at another moan. Silence. It must be the motion of the *Howler,* and old wood noises.

Kyrin beat the falcon's bronze head against the wall. "You, up there!" It came out more of a broken scream. Feet thundered above; she did not stop. There was nothing left but to call out and discover what they meant to do.

A heavy tread paused, and a hatch opened in the planks above with a squawk. Kyrin raised her face to a rush of briny air. A man's bulk loomed against the colorless morning. *Fool*—why did she ever trust the wazir's man and descend into this rat's trap? Did Sirius's orders include keeping her prisoner in the dark until she came to Britannia's shore? *It is only dark, only stench.*

"Eh, what's the noise about?" Sirius's warrior growled. He squinted past her, his axe in his hand.

"I couldn't find the ladder. I'm sorry. But I see it at your feet." Kyrin's heart tried to squeeze from its place. She motioned at two rings in the floor near her own. "I'll make it fast."

The ladder uncoiled and thumped down. The warrior watched her tie the rope ends expertly to the rings, one eyebrow arched at her fumbling fingers. She climbed up the first rungs shakily, glaring at him. The sky spread wider around her, like her smile of relief.

The wolfship warrior hoisted her the last few feet with a strong pull on her arm. "Be careful of the shipmaster. He has less of the wisdom of Allah than shipmaster Heber."

Kyrin stared. Why did he speak so much of a sudden? What *was* his name? "You—you are of the wolfships," she stammered.

"And *you* are a White Christer. The wazir chose a White Christer for his need." The wolfship warrior grimaced at her fish necklace and his lip curled. "You, such a warrior as you are, follow *Jesu?* He let his life be taken by those without justice." His steely eyes challenged her.

What had antagonized him? Kyrin opened her mouth, but the warrior continued sternly,

"Since he came to life—according to the black-robes—I've seen many like you die without his favor. And their prayers were long and offered with everything in their hearts. *Odin* fights for what is his."

"Perhaps you don't know what Jesu fought." Kyrin worked the words around her stiff tongue. She was thirsty. The wolf-men weren't known for even tempers, but what had set him on edge? This was the first time he'd said more than a few words to her. She rubbed her mouth with her hand and sighed. "He fought the evil one's hold over us, paid for our wrongdoing, and lifted us from death. *That* was what he fought to do. His death *was* unjust, but he brought justice by it." Couldn't the warrior have let her eat first? Her stomach was growling.

The warrior stared at her, silent again. Maybe he was under the wazir's orders to speak little with her. Glaring, he growled under his breath and re-slung his axe. He *was* prickly.

It mattered not, he had loosed her tongue. "The White Christ was the only one who *could* defeat what we cannot. With his white heart and his red blood, he paid my wergild. He owns me now as his adopted blood-kin." Kyrin found herself smiling, and blinked. That poetic rush belonged in Alaina's mouth, and not hers. But now—her mind was empty. Wry laughter bubbled in her, and she let the silence rest with the one who loosed her heart.

"You lie. You have no scars; life and death have not stared *you* in the face." The warrior turned toward the sea, beard bristling.

Kyrin wanted to laugh or cry. "No." The salt water and blue sky was eclipsed in her mind's eye by blood, darkness, and slavery. Ali's execution, Tae and Alaina's danger, Sirius's oath, her own. And beckoning freedom. Memories held her wordless. She moved to the rail. The heaving side of a wave reflected the blue heavens, swaddled in a veil of pink-white clouds. It shattered against the ship's side.

"You do not defend your word, if it has honor. Does fear cramp your bowels?"

Kyrin turned, her cheeks heating, fists clenching. The warrior shifted his balance, leaning a little, his weight on the balls of his feet. Waiting.

"No. I *have* felt pain, though I love it as little as any man." Her words were short as crossbow bolts. "As for honor—true words keep their own honor. They do not need my blade or my body to defend them. Wisdom is borne out by her children."

He frowned.

Her growing smile edged up on one side. "I will not fight you. That way, I might convince your head, but not your heart."

"Hah!" The wolfship warrior's eyes crinkled with amusement and he slapped his axe haft, shaking with laughter as his gaze traveled over her again. He stopped, with a meditative stroke of his beard. His eye was sharp, but the anger was gone.

She felt exposed under his gaze, though it held no dishonor. Kyrin raised one hand to her scar and the other to her head. She had hidden her hair before boarding; had the kaffiyeh slipped?

He grunted and gestured at her thawb. "You wear a man's robes. If you'd be a stripling on this vessel, with so many so close, you'd best get below and make yourself more like a man."

She flushed, and he looked away. "The voyage is long. I owe the wazir wergild. I'm the *Howler's* Blessing, call me Hyl. I've been with her since she first rode the wave. See that you speak little with the others, for my master's sake."

So he was not leaving, as if he could, out of sight of port as they were.

"And never back down from a chance to use that stick at your side again," Hyl growled. "Unless you wish to be thought weak."

"I give place to no one, save you, on some things." Kyrin looked at him sidelong.

Hyl snorted and shook his head, muttering as he turned away, "White Christer snotling."

Kyrin retreated to the hold. So Hyl had ridden all the way to the *Sabra* to be her escort to Britannia. How much farther did the wazir command him to follow her? Her lips firmed. Her people would kill him unless he had blood-kin in her land. His raiding kin were not unknown there. She must make him stay on the *Howler.*

She frowned down at her thawb. Hyl spoke true. Aboard ship she could no longer trust to her flowing robes alone to conceal her. But that slave stink meant the *Howler* had carried slaves, though it might be long ago. It was a common horror. She cocked her head and sniffed. Nothing but pitch, sea-smell, and fish.

Hyl had cracked the hatch, so a little light slipped through. Kyrin disrobed and wrapped her chest flat with a bit of her extra linen. In her thawb again, she twisted her kaffiyeh into a turban with a grimace. Her disguise also meant less washing. She'd smell like a slave soon enough, if the winter storms did not wash her. Might she get away with using the herbs to keep herself a little fresher, the leaves now dry and crumbling? Since she'd said she was a hakeem's apprentice, it would not be unexpected.

Finished, Kyrin climbed the ladder. Leaning his bulk against the rail, Hyl nodded, grinning approval. "I might teach you a bit of the axe, whelp!"

§

Kyrin kept out of sight except for her nightly practice, avoiding the crew. Hyl told them she was an assassin on the wazir's errand. Knowledge of poisons fit with the healer's art.

His axe proved too heavy for her, though Hyl admired her dagger work. None spoke to her but Hyl. He had been captured when he was fifteen summers and his wolfship attacked the *Howler* on her first sea trial. He became a good luck symbol in shipmaster Ragad's eyes. An expert seaman, Hyl loved the sea, and used the art of tacking into the wind with the lateen sail of the Mediterranean. He had heard little of Britannia but whispers of constant infighting among the lords. He growled, "Your king must be weak."

A month dragged into two. Yet another storm played with the *Howler*. Kyrin rubbed a drip from her nose. If she tasted another bit of moldy barley bread or salted meat or if the squealing, tortured ship made her cringe again, she'd hit something. She stretched her legs and groaned. She had taken as much of a battering as the *Howler.* No doubt her skin was blue in places. That night the waves denied her the deck as her practicing ground, so she did what she could in her five-by-fifteen paces.

In the morn, unable to read the Vulgate for the gloom and the continuing wet, she huddled in her damp clothes on her mat, bracing against the *Howler's* sweeping dips and steep, upward surges. Spray soaked everything; the very air seemed suspended water. *For in thee the orphan finds mercy.* Next day the coast was in sight as darkness fell, a mercy indeed.

After they traveled up the Humber it would be a matter of days to Cierheld, and then to find Hamal . . . Kyrin sighed and then scowled. The wazir ought to save his own kin, and Hamal ought not to have fallen in with slavers.

She swallowed against an increasing tickle in her raw throat. It had grown despite her generous use of her dwindling supply of powdered myrrh Tae had packed for her. Had he and Alaina managed to evade the wazir's Hand, with Cicero and Faisal? Had Sirius trapped them in his web of men? She rolled over and did her best to soothe her stomach and ignore the swell, and fell into dark dreams she could not remember.

Kyrin opened her eyes to the thump of feet overhead. The *Howler* was almost still. The hatch groaned open, and foggy air poured in. It smelled of muck earth and fish—and eels. Gulls called. Britannia.

"Come up, come up!" Hyl rumbled, his long braids dangling, his figure dark against the grey.

Kyrin got to her feet, her skin tingling and hot. She shivered as the mist curled around her and pulled her bisht close. No, she must call it a cloak now. She must recall her mother tongue. She smiled, caressed the falcon dagger, and slid the blade through her sash. *Father . . .* Her sore throat tightened. What would he think of her knowledge of the death touch and Subak? Her training in the sword?

Jachin's lighter swordwork differed from the heavy blade her father used. And her embroidery, when she attempted a gift for Shema, had tangled on the underside, the thread-stitching of a rosy apricot identifiable only by generous imagination. It could have been a sun, a harvest moon in the mist, a coin. She did not have the foremost of women's skills, but he might forgive her that.

She fingered the falcon's head, the hunter's cool jet eye, and climbed the ladder. Would her father wish her mother's dagger at his side? She would like to see it with him, yet she would miss it in her hand. The falcon had given her its courage and still called her on. Kyrin shrugged. She could do without the blade if she must. It would be nearby.

At the least, Lord Dain Cieri would know she had not forgotten his teaching with the bow. She had practiced, and would every morn to master what she'd promised. Till she could hit an ash leaf at a hundred and fifty paces. That was equal to a larger target at two hundred. She was well on her way to achieving it, since Tae continued the training her father began.

Her father had taught her the steady hand, the breath taken and held, the hiss of his black feathered shafts as they thudded into the center of a round straw target in a pattern covered by her palm, her own shorter, lighter shafts whisking in beside them. That time could never be taken from her, whatever came.

Kyrin closed her eyes and lifted her face to the salt breeze. The *Howler* wended many Eagle miles up the Humber estuary, the men quiet, searching the early spring fog for sand bars. Eels lived in the peat-dark waters below the banks of pale mist. Their sharp teeth reminded Kyrin of Ali's predatory grin, their mire-dark skin of the time of Shema's death—and the red tree dropping its leaves one by one in the Blue Flower room. The Blue Flower room would be empty now, Ali's great chair gone, unless the wazir took the remnants of the house of Ali Ben Aidon under his protection.

Umar would look after himself. She hoped Jachin and Qadira yet oversaw the rest of the household. Had the dais she so often fought Alaina on been removed to reveal Shema's blue mosaic flower? Did Nimah clean those bright stones? She might well have taken the figure of Huen from their quarters that Tae made as a sign of his oath of fidelity between them. They had not seen it when they packed, overseen by the wazir's guard so closely. Kyrin shivered violently, cold.

Lord, keep them all. And guard me on my errand. And my father. May I see him soon. There was sweat on her lip when she wiped her face. She hunched into her cloak.

The fog melted about the midday Sext bell, and the sun fell toward evening. Passing the marsh on one side of them, a low, brown-green line across the wide water, Ragad navigated the ever-treacherous sandbars without mishap. The *Howler* berthed at a town near where the Ouse emptied into the Humber. The shipmaster shouted, and a sailor tied the *Howler* to the dock where seagulls rose, shrieking.

On deck beside Hyl, Kyrin's hands were icy as the harbormaster stumped along the dock toward them. She tucked her hands under her arms and forced a smile, shifting her feet against the damp cold that bit deep. No one had discovered she was not a man. She would soon see the last of the *Howler* until she returned with Hamal, to transfer the ransom payment. It was best to travel to Cierheld without the ransom price. Such riches would cause too much talk, with increased risk of raiding lords that Ragad spoke of. And her father would find quick use for the weapons himself, if he could pay Hamal's ransom in coin instead. And there were always common thieves.

The harbormaster clumped onto the *Howler.* His quick gaze stopped at Ragad. "I see you come in peace. What do you trade?" His voice was rough but civil.

Ragad bowed slightly, with a graceful gesture. "Your estimable servant in the employ of the caliph, blessed be he, brings dates and other fair delicacies from the land of the sun . . ."

Kyrin turned from them and eyed the busy port beyond the harbormaster, ignoring Ragad's attempt to ingratiate himself.

Fishers, local traders, and a few merchant ships from across the channel clogged the slips between wood walks that were sturdily roped atop tree-trunk pilings. Men cleaned nets, hauled goods, and ordered cargo loaded and unloaded. Their shouts were music to her ears—the tongue of her people, almost harsh but clean and clear beside the shipmaster's language, changable as the prevailing wind.

She drew a breath of damp cold and grinned, forgetting her thick head. Despite the evening chill, the air held the feel of first planting time. The willows on the far side of the town held the green haze of beginning leaf. She did not care if she did not hear the smooth tongue of the wazir of Araby ever again.

She nudged the pack at her feet. Her bundle held her stick, her black tunic—she must not call it a thawb now, and her black Persian trousers rolled around Shema's armlet and her neck pouch, empty herb packets, and other needful things such as her firestones. Kyrin checked that her kaffiyeh concealed her hair and the fish necklace her scar. The harbormaster had not looked at the Arab youth on Ragad's deck twice. She held her bow in her hand, the falcon ready to her grasp.

Behind her, Hyl cleared his throat. He said low, "You carry the weapons of a warrior. Yet the White Christ must prove himself, and you, in battle. May your tongue be true, concerning Hamal." He crossed his massive arms over his chest and glowered at her.

He meant true also in justice, bravery, and loyalty. "Well brother, I am sure the White Christ will prove me, and himself. Only it may not be the battle you think."

"When the ravens gather, then power will be seen."

Kyrin's teeth chattered and she ducked her head on another shiver. She could never convince him, and her head ached. But she must speak of her road. "Hyl, I must go alone. You, you would draw swords down upon us and the wazir's name. This is my land, and my people in the hills. You are a wolfship raider in their eyes, but I can go safely as a wanderer.

"My father, Lord Dain Cieri, commands many men. He will pay Hamal's wergild in coin to this Cedsel and come for the weapons"—she pointed to the hold below—"in repayment. I will bring him and Hamal to you." She waited, her grip tightening on her bow.

Hyl grunted and his shrewd gaze held her. "It is well," he said at last. "The blade must have freedom to kill with skill. But I will see your face before the end of summer or I will come to Cierheld as the Hand of the wazir." He gestured at the *Howler's* men, moving diligently about their tasks. "Bring the wazir's nephew or proof of his spilled blood. The wazir will pay for his vengeance, if he is dead." He frowned and growled, "If you act falsely, you will die—by my axe. Your hakeem and your sister by Umar's Hand. The wazir has spoken."

Kyrin gritted, "I am not false. Will the wazir never learn that?" Then she stared into his cold sea eyes and sighed and nodded. "It will be as you say. But make you sure it is not another's will that keeps me from my word. I do not leave those of my blood to death." She picked up her pack, slung it over her shoulder, and turned away. Her body convulsed in an aching sneeze, hammering her skull yet harder. She wiped her nose, and padded down the plank. Her feet whispered onto the dock, where she glanced back.

Ragad gripped the harbormaster's forearm in friendly accord and motioned him toward the hold, speaking of his wares, his gestures animated. She was beneath their notice. Hyl stood, looking after her. With his threats, the wolfship warrior only sought to serve the one who held his life debt. Kyrin lifted her arm in farewell, and Hyl raised his in return.

She touched Britannia's soil, and it did not feel real. Would she see anyone she knew in the town? It was not likely. It had been too long. Her father would be preparing the fields at Cierheld. How Esther would laugh in her delicate tinkling way and tilt her chin in scorn if she saw Kyrin in Arab robes. Not that she would know her.

Kyrin shook her head. Three springs ago they were children. Since then, Subak had given her grace, and the language of Araby had rubbed onto her tongue more than she wished. Add a little dusky walnut to her skin, and her mother would look at her twice. *Mother.*

Her mouth suddenly trembled. The smell of mud and willow, grass and smoke from wattle chimneys brought it back. The fall of her godfather's stronghold, after her last sight of her father and his men on the road to York. But this hour was not then.

Kyrin shivered again and walked slowly into the town, searching among a jumble of shops pinched together along the streets for an herbalist. She found that the only herb-woman in town had gone into the hills to help a family in need.

The soap maker beside her shop didn't know when she'd return. "An I say," she said stolidly, "I don' know where the family lives. And no, again, you canna' leave that foreign coin for her herbs. I don' know the worth of it. I have walnut juice for what you're wantin', but naught else. There you are." She gave a pottery bottle into Kyrin's hand. "Come back with the sun, now, for Elsie'll be here then, mind you."

Kyrin shuffled miserably down more thin streets. The mist rose and turned to cold rain. Near the gate of the ancient Eagles' Ermine street out of town, she made her way to an inn, and paid for a good room above stairs. The dark, smoky common room that smelled of old food, ale, and worse, with a reed-thatched wooden roof, appeared squalid after Ali's clean stone house. But for two days after she did not stir from her room. Her fever rose in the night. Over the hours marked by the bells of Matins, Terce, Sext, and Nones, endless warriors hacked with red-edged blades at falcons that screamed for mercy. For another coin, the innkeep kept her supplied with water and broth and mint tea, which she drank when she was aware. Strangely, the tiger did not enter her blurred dreams.

The third morning Kyrin woke with a clear head. She reached for the water jug at the head of her pallet and her arm shook with weakness. The call of seabirds poured through the high, cracked shutters of her small window. No smell of fish, only the open ocean.

A thunderous knock shook the room's oak door. Kyrin almost dropped the pitcher, and hastily set it down. The door slammed open, thudding against the wall, giving her no time to call greeting. She looked blankly at Ragad.

His face was as red as his bloodshot eyes, and his kaffiyeh brushed the lintel. "I come to trade in our master's name, peace be upon him, and what do I hear?" He stepped forward, his brow dark. "One from the land of sun and sand lies alone, with a dark ring in his ear." He spat. "Fools, not to know the eye of evil. What do you do here?" He stared at her accusingly.

"I'm ill," Kyrin croaked, hugging her greasy wool blanket closer. The damp draft from the door made her shiver.

"You should be on the wazir's errand!"

"I—I'll soon leave—"

"Up, treacherous one," the shipmaster growled.

Rising on her elbow, Kyrin slid her hand beneath her pillow for the falcon blade she'd laid there against rats. She hadn't thought to need it against rats on two legs; the innkeep had seemed a dependable sort. But there was nothing he could do now against his word flying about the docks, of a sick stranger with enough coin for a good room. One who did not drink with the rest, when the innkeep offered.

"Shipmaster Ragad," she strengthened her voice, "I will go when I won't fall to robbers or the road, which will not help Hamal. The wazir is known for his wisdom in such matters."

Ragad opened his mouth then shut it with a snap. "Hummph!"

"Judge what I say. Is it not better so?"

"I will wait and and watch. As does the wazir's hand!" He glared at her, whirled and stomped out. Kyrin gave a long sigh and lay back. She rolled over and soon sank into dreamless sleep.

With the next sun Kyrin felt quite strong enough to bathe and afterward gathered her gear. Down in the inn's common room, Ragad bartered with a man in a clean-cut brown tunic, with a sigil on the breast. Kyrin's gaze slid across it and then back. It was an orange flaring torch on a black background. The colors of flame and night. Uneasiness stirred her feet.

Ragad said smoothly, "Your lord Mornoth will savor these finest sun-fruits: dates so light and sweet the very scent of them takes you to the Holy Land. They will be the wonder of his feast . . ." A ring of keys hung from the man's belt. A steward. Kyrin pitied his chances against Ragad's persuasive patter. The wazir's shipmaster stood to make much, as master of the first tradeships of spring. Other men waited their turn in a line, facing him across the table where he'd spread samples of his trade goods.

Ragad pretended not to notice her as she paid the innkeep, but she felt his eyes on her back. The other guests stared openly. Sitting at table over his bowl of porridge, a child pointed at Kyrin's turban and said to his mother, "Where is *he* from? Is that another barbarian?"

His mother ducked her head over his honey curls. "Hush, Dyrn. That one is from the East, the land of the holy family."

Kyrin nodded to the two, took a wooden bowl from the innkeep, walked past Ragad without a word, and stepped outside to eat her porridge in peace. She did not see Hyl, as she had more than half expected. There were no prayer rugs, and no Umar bowing toward Makkah in the stone paved street. A church bell rang Prime. She smiled and drew in a breath of salt and mist that tingled in her nose with cold.

She was not as strong as she wished, but she didn't want another run-in with Ragad. The harbor lay on her right. On her left the green valleys and majestic woods beyond the mist and the Humber called to her. Home felt so close she could taste it, in the warm oaken bowl in her hand, the child at the table, the imperious bell of the church. This morn she must keep an easy pace, if she could hold herself back from running. If he meant to follow, Ragad would have to catch her. Her mouth twisted wryly. Her legs would probably change her mind all too soon.

Porridge finished, her bowl handed to the help inside, Kyrin laid her pack on her shoulder and left the inn, followed by many stares along the narrow, stinking street. At the edge of town, just before where she would cross the river toward the ancient Eagles' inland road, she stopped at a tailor's, with a wary eye about, and dug into her sash for local coin of gold and silver that she'd exchanged at the inn.

She bought used hose as grey as a falcon's feather, and a soft undershirt. A green tunic, not too stained; long brown breeches and a belt; boots of dark leather; and a grey-green wool cloak and cap that would blend with the woods. In one dark corner of the shop she found a flask for water.

In a metalworker's shop beside the tailor's, she acquired a worn but strong mail shirt of iron rings, sewn on leather. She was careful not to let the metalworker know she had gold; his eyes lit too bright over her silver. Though news would spread soon enough if the innkeep did not keep his own counsel about their exchange. Pursing her lips, Kyrin told herself she'd switch the gold to her neck pouch later, or her boot. She was glad no one knew her road. Not yet.

Necessaries purchased, she made her way back into the middle of town for the herbs she wanted from the herbalist, and asked the woman for news of the roads.

Elsie dried her work worn hands on her apron, her breath steaming as she spoke. "Travel's been peaceful for the last moon. But I've never heard of a Lord Dain Cieri or a Father Ulf. They must be from other parts. Mayhap up north, like."

This was the border between the southlands and the northlands, and more southlander trade flowed here than came from the mountains and the high dales. Neither southlander nor northlander took much note of the other, unless it was to take each other's coin. Kyrin shrugged and left her with a smile of thanks.

None seemed to care when Kyrin passed the metalworker and the tailor's shop a second time on her way from the inner streets to the edge of town and the inland road. Though determined footpads might yet lie in wait. For there had been few armsmen in the streets, and fewer farmers. The colors the armsmen bore were the same as the steward wore in the inn. Brown, with a flame in the night. She turned away.

Not far outside the gate, Kyrin moved into the trees and changed in a thick alder copse. In her new soft shirt, hose and trousers, with her desert clothes at her feet, she knocked the worst of the dirt from the mail. It needed a proper polish. She wriggled into it, pulling it over her shirt. The mail had been made for a child, a dirty youngling who evidently cared naught for his things. Doubtless some lord's son. She wrinkled her nose, then donned the green over-tunic and the cloak. They fit her well, as best she could tell without a mirror.

Her lips twitched. No lord's son would seek *her* hand. A woman who could read, write, speak the language of the East, and wield a sword—when she could borrow or buy one. Kyrin fingered the green, brown, and grey wool of the cloak around her shoulders. Warmer than her Araby cloak, its ill-dyed, patchy craftsmanship broke up the outline of her form. It would conceal her better yet when spring burst into full glory.

She twisted her hair and tucked it under the cap, which fit tightly around her ears. Leaving the chin ties loose, she curled the earflaps up. Nothing must interfere with her hearing.

The cloak hood fit over the cap, and her ears warmed quickly. Kyrin dug in her pack, and donned Tae's leather-and-bamboo arm and leg shields. Defense against thieves began with confidence. Strengthened by clean dress, a necklace of shell and wood not rich enough to draw itching fingers, and a stride that told all comers here was one who knew how to use the weapon she carried, that was a start.

She did need a weapon she could carry openly. A staff would do perfectly. Not the thick quarterstave of the armsman, but the more slender staff of Tae's people, better suited to her strength of arm, with the advantage of limber quickness. There were plenty of oak and ash saplings at hand to shape into a sturdy length. She touched the bark of the nearest sapling, fingered the soft buds. Real trees, not the scrawny, thorny ones of the Araby sands.

Kyrin cut herself an ash staff with her eating dagger, which the metalworker had thrown in with her purchase of the mail. It was hard enough work cutting the soft, limber wood. She gladly left the tougher oak for a later moment when she had an axe. The ash sap was slightly sticky.

If only Alaina walked with her now; they could face off a dozen men. Kyrin grinned; she almost felt strong as ever. Tae's steady voice whispered in the back of her mind.

The touch of death is for none other than your hands. Do you hear me, my daughter? Alaina I will teach when her heart can bear that burden. You go into peril. The death touch is for greatest need.

Remember: Subak for your life, for the life of your people, for your land, and for the one who created you.

Kyrin whispered, "Subak for the man who will bring harm." Her lips flattened. Britannia was in her bones in a way Araby was not, however majestic. Any thief who did aught to keep her from Cierheld deserved what thumps they got. She was back.

10

Travels

I am poor and needy;
yet the Lord thinketh upon me. ~Psalm 40:17

Her bow across her back, her short stick thrust through her belt, Kyrin was ready. Beneath a small store of bread, cheese, and dried fruit in the top of her pack, her black Persian tunic and trousers and her Araby robes hid the falcon blade. At the bottom of her pack rested the Vulgate.

Staff in hand, she followed the Eagles' stone cart road that ran up along the sides of the valley to avoid the misty, reedy marshes of the lowland about the river mouths. The great Ouse bound the rivers together, as a skeletal wrist joined fingerling streams. The thumb of the Trent pointed south. Lord Dain Cieri held lands in the high dales up along the third river.

She might make it to the edge of the hills in less than a hand of days, if her legs gained strength as they ought. If only she'd had enough money for a horse. She blew out a breath. *Mother, I'm coming home, following your falcon.* The sweet, rising scent of sycamores and oaks would be strong about Cierheld in summer. She would never serve a table there, but sit at the high table and be served. A desert ant of unease crawled down her back.

First daughter of Cieri, she had come home from slavery a warrior. What of Esther, Myrna, and Celine? Did they hold memories of her? Did Celine hunt in the woods with hawk and horse, astride, as she had? Surely Esther possessed a lord, and enjoyed his lands. Did they have children of their own? Seasons had passed, bringing change at court and among the lords, including her father and Cierheld. She wondered who held standing among the strongholds and at court. At the yearly feasts, did Myrna yet follow at Esther's heels? Would any of them welcome her besides her father? But she was what she was. She had not returned from slavery to be enslaved again. She was home, and she must step into her place as first daughter of Cieri. Kyrin raised her fingers to her hair, twisted under a strand strayed from her cap. But the road was no place for woolgathering. She must keep alert. She held her breath a moment. Nothing but bird calls disturbed the quiet wind through the trees.

So many birds, so different than those in Araby. In feathers far less bright than the green bee-eater or purple sunbird, a dainty robin lifted its beak, its bright breast swelling. It sang its heart to the sky, so clear and sweet. It felt as if she could reach out and touch the hills that lay before her, lush in her mind's eye. Her land was smaller than she remembered, and wet after the vast, hot sands and towering rock mountains of Araby. Yet her heart sang with the robin. Northumbria, and her people.

The road rose slowly, paralleling flat-topped hills with winter-dark grass and shrubs growing on their earthy sides. Across the valley, more of the same hills were patchy with fog. Kyrin rubbed her green ash staff with her thumb. The old Eagle stronghold of York lay three hands of miles north where, before Ali's raid and her capture, her father had waved good-bye on his way to the fair to bargain for steel.

Beech, oak, and ash rose around stone fences that protected farm fields on either side of the rutted road. Grass grew between the marks of carts and wagons. She paused beneath a large oak and pushed her hood back, breathing in the greenness and the mossy tree's sweet-sharp scent. The wide oak's trunk was clad in rough white bark, its lofty, spreading crown upholding a wealth of swollen buds and tiny, yellow-green leaves. It reminded her of her name-day circlet of bluebells, the day she came of age. Esther struck at her that day, and through her, at Cierheld. But that day was not this. Kyrin walked on, swatting at grass with her staff. Esther would find her changed, able now to take a poker from her with ease, to defend herself if need be.

Just after midday, Kyrin left the road for a path that branched along the bottom of a rolling valley. The land flattened into thickening forest, and grey damp pervaded the air and the ground. The butt of her staff splatted mud in the road. Like pillars, chill, mossy trunks upheld the near-naked forest, branches grotesque and menacing as tangled insect legs in the fog. Then the sun carved a stray white hole for itself, illuminating bracken and streaming across her path. Kyrin reveled in a bright spangle of jewel-green moss that blanketed a log, in a scattering of crocus, water-pearls glistening on their petals. A snort came from her right, and the dull *clunk* of a struck log, followed by rooting snuffles and a squeal. Kyrin stopped short.

Wild pig. And she was on foot, without a boar spear. She glanced about for the nearest climbable tree, then stared back at the bracken as it stirred.

A piglet with faint stripes on its grey-brown sides trotted across the path toward a patch of purple crocus. Kyrin dropped her staff quietly, eased her bow off her shoulder and an arrow from her quiver, looking for the moving bracken that might signal a larger beast. A deep, angry squeal rang from concealment behind the piglet, and it spun and darted back among the fronds. A boar. And she was not likely to make the nearest tree.

Kyrin eased her stiff, cold fingers around the arrow, nocking it. A scuffle and another squeal, a commanding grunt. The fronds swayed—away from her. The scuffling and squeals faded, leaving the scent of crushed ramsons, the garlicky smell strong.

Kyrin let out her breath. Thank the Master of the stars the pig didn't get protective. She stifled a laugh, half of relief. Ramsons might even help her fever. Or mayhap it was the mist closing in again that made her bones ache so.

Shaking her head, she re-slung her bow and dug a bundle of the ramsons with their white roots from the soft leaf mold with the end of her staff, careful not to crush the delicate bluebells growing among them. Chewing on the hot herb as she moved on, she came to a small house, thatched with bracken, with a lean-to at the back.

The man in the yard glanced at her warily, wiped his hands on a grimy tunic, and strode toward the lean-to and his cow. The beast swished its tail as he passed within without greeting. Kyrin's greeting died in her throat. She frowned.

A woman's voice rose inside the house, and a child burst out the door. Kyrin smiled at him, and he darted back inside, screaming, "Tha's a man, a man!" The woman cracked open the door and peered around it, her face pinched. Her lips thinned, she pulled the child inside, and the door slammed. Kyrin stared a moment, then with a shrug she took a better grip on her staff and walked on, the ache creeping up her legs.

As one who dealt with mercenaries, her father did not abide filth of mind or manner in his stronghold, or let his men inspire unjust fear by word or weapon. They had no wish to, when they were brothers, and more often than not destined to become family, mixing with those of Cierheld blood. Why was the freeman's family so watchful and inhospitable? But this was not her father's land. Though she did not carry a sword, she had best be wary.

At the thought of Jachin's night-dark skin against his pale flowing robes and turban, his sword high, strong face set in the battle-frown, Kyrin laughed softly. If the freeman had seen *him,* he would be running for the woods, his wife and son screaming behind him.

Kyrin shook her head again and sat down on a nearby rock. She ached. A stream crossed the cart tracks ahead. A coal-bright butterfly searched out a bluebell in the rich grass, the flower poking through brown leaves that dampened her shoes. Kyrin shifted her foot, wondering how her skill, or lack of it, would be tested at Cierheld. She had never trained with spears: boar-spear, lance, or otherwise. With a dagger, a staff, or hand to hand, she might best most of her father's men.

And at fifty arrow-lengths, her arrows flew as she willed them most of the time. But among the strongholds, the bow was most often a hunter's tool, not a warrior's weapon. She had seen none other use a great bow as her father had, practicing for war. She'd heard that the men of the inland mountains and the green west beyond used great longbows near tall as themselves. That must be where he'd learned it. If her father's mouth twitched at her short bow, even in kind amusement, she'd show him how it could shoot from horseback, strike a man far away. But he might think of that before he laughed. Lord Dain did not miss much, and he'd never thought her a fool. Kyrin touched the recurve limbs of the bow over her shoulder. He might know it came from the Steppes riders of the East.

It would shoot two hundred and fifty arrow-lengths, with her draw, but she could only hit an ash leaf nine out of ten times at fifty. She needed to be able to hit a sycamore leaf at a hundred, and a man at a hundred fifty, to keep her promise. If her father asked her to shoot, and she could not please him . . . Such thoughts stalked her from the wet, the misty greyness, the chill. Regardless, she'd never be good at embroidery. Maybe spinning? It did not take such minute, frustrating stitches; only attention to keep the thread-feeding even, and spin and spin.

Kyrin sighed and rose. Her legs were limp as eels, and she had far to go. She shook herself. *Enough. Father will be glad to see me, and I him, no matter my skill with his favored weapon.* She dashed away an errant tear, swung her arms, and blew a few darts of steaming breath about her, like a dragon, into the mist. The clear, wild moorland loomed above her. She eyed stag tracks across the muddy path. A hare peeped from a hazel and alder thicket at the meadow edge, and his brethren gave thumping alarm. Spring was pushing into the world everywhere. The sun strengthened, and the fog wisped away against dripping trunks and new leaves.

Sometime after Sext, Kyrin sat on a hillside rock with her back to a tree where she could watch the path from concealment and eat her bread and cheese. Stretching out her tired legs, she worked over her mail. Glancing at the path often, she rubbed at the rust spots with an oiled cloth she had gotten from the innkeep with her food.

The sun warmed her back and her aches withdrew. It was so warm and quiet. She paused to lean back a moment.

Later, Kyrin awoke in alarm in the cold shadow of the rock. Anyone could have stolen her things, or worse. But at least she was rested. She set off with a determined step. The Ouse flowed behind her, as she wended deeper and higher into the hills.

Near dusk she forded a second river, and sometimes traveled on and sometimes off the path. Once a stocky shepherd approached her, cautious, his charges baaing around him, his crook held ready. She asked where a traveler might rest, and he said, "Weel, lad, it's late, and tha's a stranger." His weathered eyes bored into her. Kyrin forced herself not to drop her gaze. "But tis' no safe without. Tha's raiders about. Tha's a hermit up the way tha'll give thee night-shelter."

"I thank you, good sir." She tugged vaguely at her cap. "Can you tell me ought of Cierheld? Surely Lord Dain Cieri guards his lands against such raiders?"

"Oho, that one? Tha' lord keeps close to his walls. And when he does go after tha' sneakin' weasels, he'll na be tellin' me. He'll pounce, and they'll be dyin' neath the shadow of his men, the Holy One bless 'em. Though, mind ye, the land hereabout is Lord Jorn's."

"Well then, I thank you." Kyrin followed the rocky path upward, smiling despite her growing lack of breath. Her father kept Cierheld, and the shepherd didn't pierce her disguise.

She ate the hermit's simple fare and slept near the remains of his winter woodpile. Next night, in the foothills, she supped with a widow on the edge of a hamlet when everyone else in the village turned away, avoiding her glance. The old woman gestured her to follow and led her to a clearing, separated from the rest of the houses by a screen of trees. Her hut was well tended, the door that thumped shut well-made.

Large-boned, her body was as bent as a wind-resisting willow, her dark hair long and silvered. The old woman muttered about lads wet behind the ears, always a hungerin'. "There, sit by the fire. There'll be porridge in a bit. So you say ye're on yer way to Cierheld, are ye? I've heard the lord's a passing hard man, since the killing, and he took that sun-hair in. What do you want with Lord Dain?"

Kyrin gratefully sank onto the worn hearthstone. "I—"

The woman clucked. "You'll be wanting to join him, won't ye, to fight beside the lord? Well, he's fair, though hard. I'd wish he owned fields about here, 'stead of the lord we got, then there'd not be cows and pigs gone in the night, and women got with child through no fault of theirs but planting the fields while the men is huntin' the godless thieves."

Kyrin frowned. "Why doesn't the king—"

She snorted. "King? We have na king. The one who calls hisself so is ailin', and his men be not much better than those they come to judge—though don't tell aught old Margye breathed so. The south lords are a pack of wolves nippin' round our flanks. But for a few north lords like your Lord Dain Cieri, things be worse here. Tis' true, my Lord Jorn does as he can, but he's got troubles of his own."

Kyrin stared at her, her stomach twisting. "I'll not breathe a word, mother. And I'll do what I can, what little that may be." She eased the stick in her belt to a comfortable place, and slid back her hood, with a shiver for the welcome heat.

It was Margye's turn to stare. "You're not from these parts. Look at ye, huddling close to them flames. An that bow, an the way ye talk . . ." She peered closer and grunted. "Though ye've got hill blood, with tha' thin face an witchy eyes. An tha' black ring in yer ear, now, and ye're so brown. You won't go takin' my Mekkie's milk in the night, will ye?" She frowned.

Kyrin straightened. "No. I was a slave far from here, when the earring was forced on me. I follow this one . . ." She fingered the fish at her throat and turned it till it glowed in the light of the hearth.

"Ahh, bless you. The Christ is one to follow—if you're gentle like." Margye sat with a sigh on the stool before the fire and stirred the steaming pot, smelling of fish and herbs.

"Mother, he's the only one for any to follow. Because what he says is true. He's led me home—the Master of the stars."

"Tha's strange words. As if you speak to him much."

"I do, mother." Kyrin stopped to sneeze and her neck prickled. She sniffed and rubbed her nose. "And he's kept me from much harm."

Margye cocked her head and hummed, her dark eyes sharp. "Bless you, tha's a strange lad, though I think my Mekkie will take no harm from ye." She cackled a good-humored laugh. "A good thing, as she's the last goat among us, an the babes need summat." She reached for a bowl, and Kyrin saw the last two fingers on her left hand had curled and grown into her palm after some injury, long healed. In the flickering light her seamed brown skin glistened like a knot of wood . . . and her mother's hand.

Kyrin throat closed, and she stiffened against a rising fear. Her godfather's stronghold, the tower room, the fire in the yard, the wave of raiders, and her mother's gasp after the *thunk* of the blade. Sliding, sliding down the stone wall, the feel of her mother's arms, her back protecting Kyrin, the smell of chives and lavender . . .

Margye's face softened and she patted Kyrin's knee. "There, lad, eat up. It'll put heart in ye. We need ye strong if ye're goin' to fight the likes of our wolves."

Kyrin drew a breath, dashed her eyes dry with her sleeve, and ate. The widow watched between bites from her own bowl. The barley and lentil stew had no meat but fish, with plentiful bay and sage and butter.

Kyrin scowled; her thoughts were thick cobwebs. How to ask about the "sun-hair" taken in, mayhap a wife, that Margye spoke of? A man would not ask such a question. She felt heavy and hot, but there were no windows. A loom stood in the corner, dusty, the naked frame broken, the warp as threadbare as the woman's ankle-length linen tunic.

After the meal, Kyrin refused Margye's pallet in the one-room cottage. "No, lady. Though I thank you. My bones take to the earth easier than yours."

She bedded down in the hay shed against the house, near Mekkie, the black, white, and brown goat. Thankfully, the hay was not the kind that swelled her face and did not add to the misery of her headache. Kyrin rolled herself deep in it.

When the rooster woke her with the sun, tree shadows lay across Margye's small clearing. Kyrin tossed meadow hay to the goat and watered it and the chickens pecking around the yard. Robins and blackbirds sang. Her throat scratched when she swallowed a dipper of water from the widow's bucket she lugged from the nearby stream. Her fingers whitened on the wood handle. She had no more myrrh, and despite Margye's kindness her strength waned. She needed to reach Cierheld and her father.

They broke their fast on milk and oat porridge. Kyrin gathered her things and ducked outside. She left Shema's armlet of pearls-and-shell under the wood bowl she cleaned and left upside down on Margye's hearth to dry. She had plenty of gold and silver for her needs, and the Master of the stars smiled at the coin put to good use. She rather thought Shema and her mother smiled, too.

Outside, Margye said, "Lord Dain's dale lies tha' way, through the woods, an' you know. God bless ye!"

"And you, mother!" Kyrin lifted her staff in salute, a lump in her throat. She turned away, and the clearing was soon out of sight.

The sun moved across the heavens, and at the third river she turned northeast.

A bank of clouds advanced ahead. Kyrin walked down a heather-topped ridge, bathed in afternoon light, her calves burning. There would be rain before long. But she should find an inn in the large village that straggled about the foot of the small hill before her, where many paths crossed. She rubbed her tight forehead against the ache there, frowning.

By the shadows, the bells for Nones had rung some little time past. Had she gotten turned around in the woods? There should have been one day of steep going to reach her valley, then another two up the river in its bottom to Cierheld. But with the way her legs trembled, it might be three or four days.

Fever-sweat burned under her fingers and prickled her neck and back. The ramsons hadn't been enough. Soon she'd be shivering with more than aches.

The village looked cleaner than the port on the Humber. As she approached it seemed more hospitable, for rain had swept the canted streets, and laughs sounded here and there from open doorways. Margye recommended the village inns, and she was going no farther this night. Kyrin turned down a side way and her nose wrinkled.

Waste from the thin houses looming tall on both sides was scattered about the twisting, muddy street. Near the far end, the houses dwindled to low huts where the road widened. There the Brewmaster inn, according to its sign, raised its two-story head between squatting houses and huts on its side of the street. A lane dividing it from more huts on the street beyond. The long inn-front was crammed with shuttered windows, like a mouth missing teeth. The street's worn cobbles gave way to a dirt yard. Lamplight streamed across them from the inn's large door and windows.

As Kyrin hurried toward it with relief, the door of a hut across from the Brewmaster burst open. A woman tumbled out. Her shapeless tunic fluttered, and she shrieked as she hit the dirty cobbles.

11

Accused

A spirit of divination. ~Acts 16:16

A heavily muscled man strode after the woman, a horn of ale in his hand. His flaxen hair hung to his shoulders. Four other men spread out around them with catcalls and laughter.

The weasel on the leader's right was rake-thin, his shadow long and cold. Beside him danced a man with a homely face, and over his shoulder a wood-cutting axe as long as his nose. Their burly, red-haired companion opposite held a staff, and next to him a fat man sported a long dagger in his belt.

Towering over the woman, the flaxen-haired man roared at her, "By Thor, woman, keep your wandering, witchy eye to yerself, then!" He kicked her savagely, rolling her toward the middle of the street. "Your witching ways changed my dice so the throw fell ill!" He tipped his pale head back, drained his ale, and spat. His face glistened with sweat around his long mustache as he circled her in the last of the sun. "I'll have another, more comely than ye. But you'll not shame Thorgil Axen and take naught for it!" He tossed his ale horn aside and reached for her.

"No!" she cried, "I didn't, I swear by the Holy—" He drew back his foot in a calculated movement and drove it into her side between her hip and ribs. The woman screamed and curled away from him, retching. As Thorgil grabbed her by the neck, her brown hair straggled into the dirt, and she tried desperately to shield herself with her arms. Her body flopped as he shook her to and fro. She plucked feebly at his hands.

Kyrin gripped her staff. Onlookers in the street surged forward. Men stood in doors, and women and children peered from windows. No one with the air of the village reeve stepped from the Brewmaster or strode down the street with a frown. Kyrin huffed out a hard breath, pulled her hood low, and belted up her cloak with one quick pull.

She darted between servants and shop owners, striving to reach the woman before the crowd packed. The woman sobbed piteously, "Mercy! Have mercy!" Some of them laughed.

Heat burned through Kyrin. She elbowed a large midriff and swatted at shoulders and shins with her ash staff. Indignant yelps followed her rush. She broke free of the press behind Thorgil.

Silently, she whipped her staff down across his thick neck, vulnerable where he leaned over to grip the woman by her hair. Thorgil jerked and fell to his knees. Kyrin kicked him in the head.

He dropped, rolled over, rising too late. She thrust the end of the green ash into his stomach and propelled him spread-eagled onto the cobbles. Spinning around him as he shook his head, dazed, Kyrin moved toward the thin man. The weasel stepped forward, fists ready. Her staff whistled into his knee then up to strike his temple as he leaned forward with a cry. He crumpled.

Darting around the moaning woman toward Kyrin, the fat man yelled in a slurred voice, drawing his dagger. She smacked his ankles to disrupt his balance then flipped her staff up level, bracing herself. He ran into the end and halted, eyes bulging, then stumbled aside with a breathless groan, clutching his stomach. The limber ash struck the base of his skull, and he fell in a boneless heap.

A lunging step rasped on stone beside Kyrin as the burly man raised his oaken quarterstaff, his red hair askew. Kyrin thrust her weapon straight left, across her body. Planting itself under his breastbone, the ash stopped him like a brick wall. Choking for breath, he lifted his stave again, and her flicked against his wrist. His weapon flew from his hand. Instantly, Kyrin pivoted and with a grunt of effort, she smashed his collarbone then punched the tip of her staff into his throat. Not too hard—she didn't want to kill him. Clutching his neck, he gurgled on the ground, his weapon yards away, near the hut he'd come from. The smell of raw hides hung around him. A tanner.

Kyrin rubbed her nose, breathing hard. She'd always hated the tanner's yard. A shiver shuddered through her, driving the ache to split her head. She tried to smooth her grimace, swayed, and swallowed sour bile. The crowd watched, transfixed.

The axe-man who stood between the inn and the motionless woman closed his gawking mouth. He leaped for Kyrin in the building's shadow, and wavered into two figures, both with axes high, descending with a furious scream. She blinked him into one attacker, and the ache stabbed her eyes. A child wailed.

This fight must end soon. Kyrin slid back and faked a blow at the axe-man's head. He shifted his weapon in reflex to block the wood, and she flipped the opposite end up between his legs. He doubled over. She drew back again and swung, short and hard. He crashed to the ground on top of his axeblade, his feet tangling with the woman's. Blood bloomed along his arm.

The man dropped the axe and grabbed the long gash, and Kyrin aimed a second stroke for his temple. He twisted to face her, so she caught him across the forehead. He shook off what should have been a knock-out blow, his hair black against his white face. It must end now or she'd be on the cobbles. To her right, Thorgil rose from the street with a scrape of leather shoes and a growl. Kyrin spun, anger clearing her vision.

Thorgil scrambled around the woman and ploughed into the crowd. His bleeding companion staggered up and followed, cradling his arm.

Everywhere there were staring faces and open mouths and silence in the sun's last light. None raised a hand to her. It was as well they did not, when they should have taken a hand earlier. Kyrin snorted. Hooking her toe under the axe-haft, she snapped out her leg. The axe sailed high, past the woman, and landed near the Brewmaster with a *kathump.*

Among the villagers, Thorgil startled and looked back. Kyrin glared. He dropped his gaze, and she leaned on her staff. Her lungs and legs burned. Her sight wavered. She blinked it clear.

Oldsters looked at her sidelong, others frowned. Some of the younger faces shone with awe and eagerness. At the back of the crowd, Thorgil chewed his mustache and spat noisily, dragging an arm across his face.

In a moment, Kyrin seized the limp woman under the arms and dragged her toward the wall of the nearest house across the street from the Brewmaster. The crowd thinned to let them through. Kyrin propped her burden against the wall. At the sound of a raspy breath, warm against her face, her heart jerked in relief. A patch of sparse grass struggled through the mud around their feet, red-gold with evening.

A foot scuffed. Kyrin straightened and snarled at the villagers who surged hesitantly forward, muttering. She leveled her staff as her mind traced her left hand's path to her common dagger, her right to her short stick. Her cloak tugged free of her belt where she'd stuffed it. It belled out on a gust of wind. Wind that carried rain behind it. Kyrin squinted. The wind had also carried something else.

In the dusk, two men stood near the end of her wall, nearer than the half-fearful villagers. Hooded cassocks of black over long tunics of equally black linen eased them into the shadows of growing night. The long, stern features and raised, bony hand of the tallest monk drew reverential bows and shuffling obedience as the crowd pressed back toward the inn. The younger monk behind his brother hesitated. His narrowed eyes never left Kyrin. Despite the spareness of youth or monastic life, his strong-boned frame held power and an easy way of moving, attested by sleeves rolled above his elbows and capable shoulders.

Kyrin frowned. Benedictines, like Uncle Ulf. She wished they had no part in this.

Someone in the crowd yelled, "Justice! Justice! Obstructer!" And she wished for the falcon's solid grace in her hand, but she'd make do with her bread blade and her short stick. Not that any weapon could stop this tide if it turned.

A clod of dirt struck her leg. She lifted her chin. "Come on then!" She was ill with pain, the woman's pain, and her throbbing head. Sickness welled in her, deepened ten-fold by the appetite of the open mouths around her for wrongful violence and blood. Her mouth drew flat. The woman's other attackers had disappeared except for Thorgil, who'd crept back for his henchman's axe. Or was it his own?

"'E saved the witch!" Thorgil cried in a deep voice, pointing at her. The monks approached as the others closed in.

She would move the crowd before she fell. Kyrin leaned into what forward shuffle she could manage, and her staff hummed in a wide arc.

"Stop!" The thin one raised his hand again. The red-haired monk backed a step and then flushed. Kyrin's mouth curled as she halted. They belonged to Uncle Ulf's monastic order, but not his mettle.

"I am Father Ulf."

Kyrin's breath stopped and the staff in her hands jerked. She opened her mouth helplessly.

"Ah, I see you've heard of me." The taller monk's satisfied smile hardened. "No one stands against justice, impudent boy! Why do you defend the devil's tool, a woman sunk in mire, who returns to her natural flesh?" Uncle Ulf's voice was heavy and cold. He was thinner, and the shadow of his garb cloaked his face, even as it made his frame taller than she remembered.

Thorgil glared at Kyrin and glanced at Uncle Ulf. "Did you see his fell arts, Father? Na' one can do the like! That one's witch-kind!"

Kyrin turned her gaze to Thorgil, dispassionate. "Stay back, if you value your skin."

Father Ulf shifted his grip on the silver cross in his hand, and retreated two steps for the one he had taken. His mouth thinned as he colored. Kyrin's stomach sank. He was her uncle and Father Ulf, and yet she did not know him.

§

Brother Rolf glanced at Thorgil, who backed away from the straight gaze of the strange warrior who had beaten him and four others, albeit at various stages of drunkenness. If he didn't do something, the white-faced woodcutter would see that all his brothers at Jornhold and the surrounding area got rotten wood next winter.

The young defender's hood blew back in the wind, herald of the coming storm. It took his cap with it. As Father Ulf retreated, Brother Rolf took a cautious step closer. Long dark hair fell, tousled from hard travel, tugged by the strengthening wind across a curving, slender frame.

At Rolf's shoulder, a villager gasped, leaving the reek of onion in his nose. The warrior's dark-eyed regard turned to Rolf. Her steady eyes blazed amber dark in her thin face.

The black tip of the bow above her shoulder curved, the other end likewise, resting at her hip. The weapon was no longer than a child's. Could it possibly be one of the Nomad horse bows? And her quarterstaff was fresh ash. No, it was thinner than any quarterstave he'd seen. Brother Rolf shook his head; to get rid of his neighbor's onion or his growing respect, he didn't know. A foreigner, yet a woman who knew the staff so well? If the king or one of the lords had aught to do with this, the people of the village could be in trouble. He opened his mouth, grim. "What are you—"

Her weapons rose with a jerk, and Rolf paused. She would fight for the limp body behind her. His mouth twitched in approval.

Father Ulf threw up his arm, all the authority of his office in his voice. "Stop!"

Her cloak rumpled and dirty, the warrior stared between them. Drained of color, her face was carved of sharp stone, of pain. A tap might shatter her, or she might take a hundred blows. She swayed.

He laid a hand on Father Ulf's arm. "She doesn't know us from Adam. Ask her to bring the woman to the infirmary. She looks as if she has need of physic herself."

Father Ulf shook him off and raised his voice. "Who are you, woman? I ask again, why do you stop God's punishment?"

§

Kyrin looked at him, anger and sadness choking her. "I heard something from Thorgil of a witchy eye. And you speak of punishment? For the way God created her?"

"You are a stranger here," Uncle Ulf said, his voice sharp as a blade. "Why do you interfere?"

His brother winced. A spark of life there. Kyrin drew another breath. "If you do it unto the least of these . . .'"

Brother Rolf nodded, but Father Ulf, as if straining to hear her, leaned closer in mockery. Kyrin's breath shook her body. She coughed, and her chest hurt. Her voice rose thin. "I cannot throw the first stone. I too am a sinner. And I have heard no lawful judgment against her. It's a matter for the reeve, or your prior." The men in the crowd looked at each other.

Father Ulf pursed his lips and his eyebrows rose. "Best come to our humble infirmary, then, where we can care for you, and debate this 'lawful judgement.'" He lifted his voice. "You may stay in sanctuary until the prior can settle this."

"Are you certain, Uncle Ulf?" Kyrin asked softly.

He seemed struck to stone. And then the breath went out of him. "Not Willa—"

"It's Kyrin, Uncle."

"You, here! It is as if the hand of God—"

"Yes. He sent me home." Kyrin waited. Her uncle moved not.

She wanted to run into his arms, but his gaze locked on the ring in her ear, traveled over her garb and weapons, then came back to her face. "Why do you travel so?" He leaned forward, hungrily awaiting her answer. Kyrin shivered hard.

"I had no one, and it was necessary to dress so, and carry weapons, with the wolves on our roads. If—will you come with me to Cierheld?"

Uncle Ulf said nothing. Was there an obstacle she knew nothing of, or was he that ashamed of her trousers?

"I may not leave my monastery except for need."

Surely family help counted as need?

His voice rose proudly. "I am on pilgrimage before I become an anchorite to Bolton church, walled in from the world . . . from my lost Willa." He grimaced as if at the taste of something foul. "You are hers in name, but your father's in blood. That is clear. You follow his path, and are none of mine."

"You have fallen out with my father?"

"Fallen out? He has turned heretic. It will be proven."

Kyrin stared at Uncle Ulf. She would not cry. He had crowned her on her name day, Cierheld's first daughter. She would show him how his blood could be strong.

A few raindrops spattered down on the rushing fresh wind, and men and women turned toward the inn and their houses. A child's protest drew farther away. "But father, I want to see—"

Kyrin cleared her throat. "I hear you, Uncle. Mayhap I may speak with you on a better day."

"If God wills." His smile held something that made her stomach sink. "For now, I care only for my road. Fare you well, *first daughter.*" It was a curse.

"Go with God." Her lips were numb. Kyrin slid her eating dagger into its sheath, pulled up her hood, and shrugged to resettle her bow.

Uncle Ulf stared into the gathering dark, and his companion eyed the good father with his mouth open then shut it.

Kyrin drew a breath against pain. The woman must not get wet. They both needed warmth for the night. If she paid the host of the Brewmaster well, would he take them? She leaned her staff against the wall and knelt beside the woman.

The red-haired monk stepped forward, but Kyrin ignored him and slid the woman up to her shoulder with a gasping heave, bending under her weight.

Clattering hooves brought her around fast, the woman's feet swinging. In the street, six armsmen reined their mounts to a walk. Kyrin dropped her shoulder and let the woman down, overbalanced, and fought not to fall on top of her.

The foremost rider halted his horse and removed his simple helmet to the crook of his arm, drawing his sword to rest it across his saddlebow. Ready for peace or a fight, he let the few left standing before the inn know the same.

Kyrin sighed. Here was the reeve at last, or his equal, doubtless trained as an armsman. The close links of his chainmail shone with care even in the dusk. The reeve kept his distance, safe from any move she might make, yet close enough to attack. An armsman as well trained at her father's, then. His five spearmen sported every type of armor from boiled leather to leather and sewn-on platelets. Costly, such mail was.

She leaned against the wall and returned the reeve's thoughtful stare. She kept her hand from her staff.

Father Ulf went to murmur in his ear. The man lifted his head with a grimace of distaste and waved Father Ulf back.

Kyrin waited.

"You fight differently with the quarterstaff." The reeve glanced at her hair and her mail under her damp, clinging tunic. "You're a woman, are you not? What is your name?"

"Kyrin, my lord." That should answer both questions, since Uncle Ulf had not enlightened him. He concealed her full name, for shame or reasons of his own.

"What do you here?"

"I'm passing on my way to the mountains."

"What do you want with the whore?" The reeve gestured at the woman at Kyrin's feet in sharp dismissal.

"Before I answer, I'd know who you are, lord," Kyrin said, quiet and courteous. "Not all dangers are met on the road."

"I'm Lord Jorn's shire reeve, and these are my watchmen. Disturbances and strangers fall to my lot. As for what I require,

I will know more of your errand, which the good Father does not know much of."

At least the reeve didn't take offence at her being a woman dressed as a man, but only for breaking his peace.

"You're not mad, are you?" The reeve asked suddenly.

Kyrin choked back a laugh. "No."

§

The shire reeve sighed.

"No," she said, with an amused sound. She did not speak as a peasant. Sweat dripped from her smudged nose. Though she did not look the otherworldly danger Father Ulf claimed her to be, she was slim with the grace of a hunting falcon, and something about her mirrored its wild beauty. But his men hemmed her against the wall, witch or warrior, caging her well enough. He shrugged.

The last of the sun before the storm caught the flash of her small smile as she looked up. And the danger in her prickled along his spine. She did not fear him. At all. He straightened with the shock of it, staring, his hand tightening on his sword. His men stiffened.

She crouched slightly. Clearly, she respected him and his sword-arm, yet fear of his attack or judgment did not reach her. She only noted his seat and stirrup, the better to flick him out of his saddle. Father Ulf was right, he reflected grimly. This one was a matter for Lord Bergrin.

§

Uncle Ulf took his leave of the reeve and turned away from Kyrin. He did not even glance at the woman at her feet. He was not the uncle she had left.

His brother monk followed, with a wordless glance over his shoulder: part compassionate, part troubled, and part annoyed, as if she were a puzzle he wished had not been put before him. Kyrin shrugged inwardly, weary to her bones.

The shire reeve raised his hand, and one of his men trotted away. He turned his mount and beckoned to her. "Come. Lord Jorn welcomes fighters and wishes to see all such who pass through his lands. He gives lodging and food for a night."

It might be safer than the Brewmaster, but she could not count on that. Better a back door—as Father always said. She was like him, in that. It warmed her. Kyrin straightened. "I'm ill—"

"Of what matter is that?"

Kyrin did not have time to answer, for the lord himself arrived at an easy trot from where he watched between house and inn, his mount's hooves ringing. Deserted by the sun, still the lean lord's hair glowed like wet ash in the dusk. The armsman escorting him carried a pennant with his house sigil. If she could judge by the armsman's dour glare and his pointed look, no doubt the green field with something darker hidden by the limp folds was an important sigil.

Lord Jorn sat his equally pale Arab as if born a part of the graceful, stamping beast. His orange surcoat under polished ring mail stretched around slender, strong shoulders. *Orange. An orange surcoat, and might that be a green field? Esther's feast—and Bergrin—who teased me. Lord* Bergrin *Jorn.* Kyrin's breath caught in her throat, and she stiffened her legs against a wave of weakness. With her slow wits she had not put the two names together. Or the name with the man. He had been a young lord when she saw him last, and she but a girl. His father had been Lord Jorn, then.

Wonders never cease. Myrna's brother. Has he changed for good or ill? Uncle Ulf left her to him. Curious.

Bergrin said softly, "Why do you refuse my hall?" *He* sounded curious, his eyes gimlets in the gloom.

Was *he* mad? Kyrin wanted to drop in a heap and cry. She lifted her chin. "I mean no ill will, but I must lodge at the Brewmaster. I've a fever." He could take that how he wanted. She was not ready to face him, or Myrna. They would find her too changed, unwomanly, wild, and she was sick and her wits were sleeping. She reached for the cool strength of the falcon at her side. No, the blade was in her pack.

"Hmm." Bergrin stroked his chin, mocking. "You don't trust me? What is your name?"

What standing had Lord Bergrin with her father now? Had he helped the lord of Cierheld when her mother fell, or turned away from her father's need, when some cried heretic?

"What is your name?"

She was slipping indeed. "Kyrin. I'm a stranger here." She bowed her head. Her name sounded as those of Araby said it: Keerun. Years agone, she'd spoken of training his hawk, counseling him to let his wild-caught bird go, for a chick to come. And come freely, bound by choice to hunt from his hand.

"One name?" He cocked a brow. "It will do—for now."

He did not know her. What game did he play with the fighting men about these lands, wanting to appraise them? Did he seek to trap a spy, or gather news? It was best to know the currents. Then she must find her father, and Hamal.

Lord Jorn leaned forward. "So, tell me, you think me more dangerous than that—pack of villagers?" He waved his arm in the direction of the inn.

Kyrin stifled a short laugh. Bergrin had always hunted for words. He had not Alaina's way with them. But wordplay was a danger she was too foggy to keep up with. And she could not bear his laughter again, not now. He had not been close enough to hear her and Father Ulf, but he was dangerous. She must not break. "Yes, my lord. You are dangerous as any warrior."

"More apt to bring you harm than attacking five men over an outcast? Yes, lady, I saw."

Lady? Her stomach clenched. If he would only let her be.

Bergrin waited, pale head tilted, shining redly in a torch his armsman lit by a coal a boy brought glowing from the inn.

"I had to protect her," Kyrin said after a moment. Why did Bergrin care? He never had before . . . her mind was wandering.

Lord Jorn stared at her. "Very strange," he murmured. "I bid you take my bread and salt. I swear you won't take harm from me or mine."

Kyrin bowed her head again, hiding her tight mouth. She could do nothing else. But she must ask—

Lord Bergrin lifted his reins. It took Kyrin a moment to remember the old words and fashion them, her mouth quivering. "My lord, I crave a boon!"

"Not granted," Lord Bergrin Jorn barked, turning in his saddle with a frown, "If it concerns your refusal."

"Lord Jorn, I beg you, care for this woman as my companion." Kyrin kept her voice even with effort, as her blood settled from the fight and the revelation of Uncle Ulf.

Bergrin glared, as if she'd asked for coin. At last he grunted, "Very well." He nudged his horse on, shaking his head. His shire reeve joined him, leaning to speak in his lord's ear.

Kyrin heaved the unconscious woman over her shoulder again. Her bow slid down her arm, caught inside her elbow, and thumped her leg with every step. She wouldn't give her weapons up. If she fell in the mud, a rider would have to carry them, two women, her pack, and all her weapons. She almost laughed. She never thought that they might fear her anger and their lord's ensuing displeasure.

The men closed in around them. *Heartless they are, twin to the tiger.*

12

Suspicions

They gather . . . against the soul . . .
and condemn the innocent. ~Psalm 94:21

Their journey through the dark began. Kyrin took a breath, balancing the woman over her shoulder, rain misting in her face. Blessedly, her vision did not waver as she strode forward. Her legs did.

After a bit, one of the men led a horse to her and helped her hoist the woman onto the saddle pad then he mounted and rode to report to Lord Jorn. After Kyrin gained the saddle she slung her bow across her back. Three of the reeve's armsmen fell in behind her. None of them spoke.

Was she so repulsive, or did they not wish to associate with an outcast, or perhaps they were ordered to keep their distance? Shoving away the nagging thoughts, she wrinkled her nose at the odor of wet wool, ale, and things she didn't care to name that rose from the woman's clothes. Kyrin smiled wryly; she herself smelled none too sweet.

Houses and streets faded into a gloomy tunnel of darkness and rain, squelching mud and vague trees that passed at the edge of torchlight. Kyrin's scalp prickled on a wave of heat then she gritted her teeth against chattering cold. She clamped quivering legs around her horse's warm, soaked sides.

The torch at the head of the column flickered, interrupted by wind and the shapes of men. The leather shirt of the man in front of Kyrin was a blur she followed like a beacon. The woman rode, slumped bonelessly before Kyrin, who held her in the saddle. Her limp hands bumped Kyrin's legs.

Several miles later, her back and arms stiff as wood, Kyrin rode after the shire reeve inside the log palisade of Jornhold. They halted before a small, squat building in the yard. The door faced roughly west.

In the stronghold watchman's hand the flame of a torch spat in the rain. "Get down," the reeve said.

Kyrin waited a breath, then slid down and took the woman's limp weight, not making sense of more than the vague loom of a stronghold hall and a barracks on her right, while a few smaller buildings straggled beyond the isolated one they'd stopped in front of. At the shire reeve's gesture, Kyrin steadied her legs and walked forward, bent almost double under the woman. The thick logs and split-shake roof would keep out the wet—and keep secure anyone inside. Kyrin shrugged inwardly. On a night like this, she might die outside, let alone the injured woman.

Her foot caught on the grey weathered sill of the doorway and she fell painfully on her elbows, sprawling painfully half across the woman as she tried to keep her head from hitting the hard wood floor. For a moment Kyrin didn't care she was down.

A candle guttered on a stool on her left, and the corners of the room were dark. Was that a bed on the right, and a skin floor-covering before her? If she could lie where she was, just close her eyes until the darkness and the candle stopped spinning, until her elbows decided they weren't spears boring into her arms. There was a muffled laugh behind her.

Kyrin stiffened and dragged her feet over the sill, sliding over the woman, then she rolled. *Fool.* The bow—the tips would break—Kyrin spun swiftly to her side, closing her eyes against the dizziness. She'd heard nothing crack. At least she hadn't fallen on her charge.

Kyrin frowned. The ox hide beneath her smelled clean and dry. Opening her eyes to stare at the brown-black hide, for a moment she needn't raise her face to the amusement of the men.

The woman moaned. Kyrin sat up swiftly then grabbed her head. It *would* split soon. She rested a shaking hand on the woman's damp shoulder. "It's all right, you're safe." The woman's eyes did not open. Her face was pale.

Lord Bergrin leaned inside the door, unsmiling. "You're weary; anything you need, my man at the door will get you." Water dripped down his cheeks and around his clean-shaven mouth. His voice jarred against her, a force in itself, though his words were not loud and could not be called discourteous. The draggled, ashen tips of his hair brushed his shoulders, and the color of his eyes reminded her of ferns and earth. He turned, his wet cloak slapping against his legs, and Kyrin sighed, no longer caught in his intense stare. What did he want with strange warriors who passed through his lands? What did he want with her?

The door whispered shut and the planed oak half-poles shuddered as an outside bar thudded down. Released from watchfulness at last, Kyrin hitched in a breath and hugged her knees. For long moments she fought her shuddering muscles and clicking teeth, breathing slow and deep through waves of fever. The candle wavered; shadows grew and stretched, watching her with fiery eyes. Tiger's eyes. There were others.

She glanced up from her muddy boots. Father Ulf's hard gaze peered at her from a corner beyond the candle flame. Kyrin set her jaw and did not blink. His gaze that wished her ill disappeared into two knots of wood, his dark cloak and hood becoming the looping grain again. She sighed.

The mind and heart played tricks. And there were spirits in the world. There was also one who ruled all hearts and spirits. And her mind. *Be with me.*

Kyrin eased herself to her knees. She was breathing a little better. Maybe staring her uncle back into the wood had helped.

She wrestled the woman onto the ox skin to pull her to the bed, and realized she was slight and younger than she'd thought. She felt her limbs for broken bones, and hoped their awkward fall over the sill hadn't added too many bruises. Kyrin smoothed the thin, straight brown hair. At the touch, her soft features distored by a frown, the young woman turned her head with a slurred mutter. Fever. With a frown, Kyrin rose and thumped on the door. It opened.

A gray-haired man in a leather jerkin with a woolen hood over a linen tunic kept a sturdy hand on the door, as if it might turn insubstantial or whisk out of his grasp. He dipped his close-clipped head, his careful eyes never leaving her. An armsman—no other would be so alert, though he bore no visible arms but a dagger in his belt.

"My lord," Kyrin said, bowing, "I need a pot of boiling water and clean cloths and a bucket, if you would."

He raised a brow slightly at her courteous address. "For what purpose? I'm sorry, lady, but it's my lord's orders."

"To wash our hurts." Her laugh was thin. "I wouldn't get far even if I did manage to hit your skull with the bucket." Couldn't he see their fever-sweat? It pricked her back and brow.

"I'll bring it. Would you eat, lady?" His level, steel gaze declared he wouldn't cause her trouble if she caused him none. Bergrin had been truthful, in that.

"Yes, with my thanks, sir." The armsman relaxed at the "sir," and before he had to ask, she moved away from the door, picking up the candle. The door closed and the bar grated home.

Kyrin sighed. "Ah well, barred doors do not stop the Master of the stars." She looked down—and the young woman's wide gaze was locked on her, still as a rabbit's on a snake.

One of her eyes was dark as a black peat bog. Her other eye, sky-blue and beautiful as any woman's, sought focus, wandering aside. It was not the cloudy blue of hurt. She had been born with a wandering eye. Kyrin glanced at the candle in her hand and down again.

The woman whimpered. She bore new-worn lines of pain in her face and a shrinking gaze, wiser to the world's ill, that stared at Kyrin past a straight, feminine nose. Her generous mouth trembled as she clamped her lips.

"Easy, easy." Kyrin touched her shoulder gently. "Lie still. I'll not harm you. My name is Kyrin." She paused. "I'm a guest of a sort, of your Lord Bergrin Jorn. I thought you would find being here with me less hard than on the street, though we appear to be locked in. I don't know your name—"

The young woman opened her mouth, glanced at Kyrin, and froze. Kyrin did not drop her gaze. She continued softly, "The ruler of this world makes many strange and beautiful things. My eyes are not, well, not like others' either. I do not find you evil."

Wild hope replaced shock, flickering across the woman's face. She lunged to her knees, reaching. Kyrin fell back in startlement, tripped over her pack, and sat down hard. She caught back a groan at the stabbing pain behind her eyes. The woman grabbed her ankles.

Kyrin did not move, dizzy again, not sure if she meant ill, but afraid to strike amiss. Neither of them needed more hurts. If she just held still . . .

Tears ran in glittering tracks down the young woman's pale cheeks. "Help me. I *won't* sell myself! Cere, my good man, he's gone. But I'll die before I serve Thorgil or any man so! I serve meat and ale and naught else!" Her voice rose, strained and near breathless.

Kyrin stared at her. She struggled for words. Thorgil wasn't here. And she'd told the woman she was also a prisoner. The woman's eyelids fluttered and she slumped across Kyrin's shins. "Lady?" She did not stir.

Kyrin put the candle aside, guarding against the hot wax as her hand shook. How had it not burned her when she tripped over her pack? At least Thorgil could not bother them here. Leaning forward to touch an unresponsive shoulder, Kyrin smelled their sweat and dirt and blood. Worse, she was running out of strength. One last task then she could rest. Her head whirled.

As she struggled to move the woman up onto the bed near the hearth, their guard knocked. "Come."

The armsman entered. He waved her back against the wall and set a steaming pot, a bucket of water, the cloths, and a covered basket in a neat row on the small hearth near the head of the bed, at the end of the room. He glanced at the woman then bowed to Kyrin.

She smiled at him gratefully. He didn't *have* to carry the supplies inside. She asked him for wood. When it arrived in a generous bundle, she paused, holding the pot of coals in front of her, which she had forgotten to ask for but he brought anyway. "What is your name?"

"I am Pellam, lady. God keep you." He nodded. She inclined her head, and the door closed.

Kyrin took off her wet cloak and laid it near the hearth, started the fire, and stripped off the woman's patched garments, or rather caught them when they fell off after a cautious tug—and gazed at her in shock. Every rib jutted under her pale skin.

Kyrin winced as she found bruises old and new, laced across arms, ribs, and legs. She bit her lip.

Those scratches and gashes needed cleaning. Dirt in wounds brought sickness. She shrugged. She might as well clean off the entire layer of grime that covered the woman from head to toe.

She threw the rags of the woman's once-white chemise and linen tunic in the fire and stood before the warm flames a moment, wishing for extra fingers to hold her nose. A smile tugged at her mouth. As Alaina said, she couldn't stand smelling like a caged baboon. She'd come to relish the clean habits of Ali's household.

After cleaning the woman as best she could without a tub or barrel, Kyrin crushed the last of the old herbalist's heal-all and dropped it into the steaming pot on the fire. It steeped, its light, wholesome sweetness filling the air. Kyrin soaked a cloth in the brew and cleaned the woman's wounds, thankful none needed bandaging, and that the woman slept through her ministrations.

Afterward, Kyrin curled under her cloak on the floor, shivering again. Her bones were ice, but her skin burned. She reached into her pack, took out the falcon blade and slid it close to her side, then pulled the pack under her head with a groan. She stared upward at the roof beams in the interplay of firelight and shadow.

The Master of the stars did what was best, but it didn't change the lonely hurt that burrowed inside her like a worm, deeper than the cough in her throat. Somehow she'd thought to see her father at the dock. Kyrin huddled on her side and a wave of tears drowned her. What dark thing did Bergrin want from her? She needed an onion poultice and garlic, among other things. But she was too weak to summon Pellam now. Better to wait for the morn.

She could hope she reached her father in a seven-day. But who would help the woman? And she must find Hamal soon, or the wazir would succeed in hunting down Tae and Alaina. Was her father even at Cierheld? If she could just get news of him, or send a message . . . but she could not tell Lord Bergrin who she was, for she did not know how he stood with her father and Cierheld stronghold. And Myrna—

Would Myrna remember her, Lord Cieri's daughter, who loved horses, falcons, and the open sky? Could she reconcile that lost girl with a woman who could swing a sword at need, who loved the fighting art of Subak, and rode in the hunt astride? Could she accept the foreign tongue and odd ways that girl learned as a slave? Kyrin shifted her shoulder on the hard wood. As for her ability to kill—no one must know of the death touch. And no one would, unless it was the last thing they felt on this earth.

But she was not so different from those of her blood who had gone before her. Not so different. Warriors and warrior-women, all who could kill with a staff or sword or weapon of choice. Subak simply leaned less on brute force, combining precision with the hands and feet applied to vulnerable points on the body—and used weapons if they were available. She'd had a good teacher, the best, her second father. With a prayer on her lips for Tae and Alaina, Kyrin slipped into uneasy sleep.

The tiger loomed over her, his great paws on either side of her shoulders. His claws kneaded, kneaded the wood, his forelimbs thick as her legs. He watched her as no animal should have the power to do. Green-gold eyes unblinking, he glared into hers. His breath thrummed in and out against her face. He would trap her far from help, far from the falcon blade—he turned his head, staring into the dark, and the silver collar about his neck slid across orange and black fur. Caged in silver, alone and sad, their round eyes of jet stared her. Falcons without wings. The tiger's head swung back—he came for her.

Kyrin sat up with a shuddering gasp. Heart pounding, she scrabbled for the falcon dagger. A dark form leaned over her, part of her nightmare, a black eye and a blue one staring down at her. Kyrin whipped her dagger before her, and the pale human face drew back with a sharp breath.

Kyrin gathered herself while her fellow captive pulled Kyrin's black bisht closer around her and retreated to the bed.

Humph. Kyrin grimaced and let her head back down on the floor. Esther would glare at her for such a slip of speech, using Araby's word for a cloak, in her own land, no less. *Bisht.* Lord Bergrin seemed less sure of himself these days. Was Esther? Or was she still as proud of her princess bearing, of empty conversation, and her pursuit of lords' sons?

Her thumping heart would not let her sleep now. *Father, keep us this day. Go before our way.* The room was cold and dim with morning that peeped under the eaves. The door was still shut, and probably barred. Kyrin sat up, slid the falcon dagger under her pack, and rubbed her face.

"You were crying out," the woman whispered. "Are you—well?" She reached toward Kyrin then pulled her hand back.

"I'm well enough." Kyrin's voice croaked. She tugged at her damp cloak, tangled around her legs. "Just a fever."

The woman rose and crouched next to Kyrin's leather boots and unwound the cloak, which had snagged on one. Her eyes widened at Kyrin's shin and knee guards of padded cane, her gaze rose to the gleam of mail peeping from the neck of her tunic. The woman dropped her gaze. Her breath came fast, and she scuttled back.

Kyrin cleared her throat. "I'm Kyrin. What is your name?"

"I'm Nell—Nell Trinley, yes." Nell fell silent, her generous mouth tense, not missing the omission of Kyrin's last name.

"Nell, you're welcome to my bread and my salt," Kyrin said formally. She smiled. "Pellam will have food for us soon, I think."

"My thanks." A small smile flashed across Nell's face and was gone, a doubtful mouse into the hay. "Thorgil—and the others. What happened?"

Kyrin got slowly to her feet. "I thumped them well with my staff, and they decided to leave you alone." Nell did not need the burden of Lord Jorn and the monks' interest. She said nothing.

Hope rose in Kyrin as she took a step. Her stiff legs were not as weak as she thought they would be, and she did not feel cold. Maybe the fever had gone.

Quiet thoughts passed behind Nell's eyes as she looked Kyrin over from head to toe.

Kyrin's cheeks heated. She coughed and it hurt. Mayhap Nell needed herbs also. She took a slow breath. "Well, are you dizzy or numb or pained anywhere, Nell? You took some blows. Does anything hurt when you breathe?"

"My side hurts, as I think it would after last night, but nothing over much."

"That's good." Kyrin walked over to the necessity bucket Pellam had brought, rubbing her forehead. The dull ache grew. The king was ill and raiders stalked the land, while Nell was an unknown piece on the board, to say nothing of Lord Bergrin Jorn.

Would Pellam get her the herbs? She must get better, must get to her father and Hamal. Kyrin found herself twisting a strand of hair while a despairing laugh bubbled up with a flood of tears. She choked them back hard. What was wrong with her? This was the Master of the stars's day, and his to provide for.

While Nell politely turned her back, Kyrin finished her morning business.

When her rumbling stomach decided her on something to eat, she knocked on the door, once again on the wrong side of it. "Pellam?"

When he returned with her request, she and Nell dug into a feast for a king. Hot porridge, bread, cheese, and cold roast ox. At last Kyrin asked him for more buckets of hot water. "As hot as you can get it, and a half barrel to put it in."

"Is there trouble?" A frown grew between Pellam's bushy grey brows.

She looked down. She needed a bath before she saw a healer. "It's for washing. I used the other for Nell, last night."

Pellam looked mystified but fetched the water, and kept his thoughts to himself. After his sixth trip across the yard with the buckets, in addition to what she heated over their fire, Kyrin blessed him silently. She kept her ears open for approaching footsteps over the morning noise of someone axing wood outside. She almost trusted Pellam to guard their privacy as she bathed. Pigs and cows asked for morning scraps and milking, chickens clucked, voices called over the scrape and thud of weapons practice. There was no sound of feet or voices near their door. She almost trusted Pellam to guard their privacy.

Pellam was a rather long name, rather formal, she mused, more like the name of a servant Esther Govannon would keep in her retinue. Not that Esther would often call a servant, even an armsman, by name. Would Jorn's armsman mind if she called him Pel? His steady gaze reminded her of old Cernalt. Faithful Cernalt. Did the steady armsman yet guard her father's side?

The hot water stung, but the heat and freshness of the dried mint she'd sprinkled in melted the knots in her legs and back, and eased her chest. "Nell, do you know if Lord Jorn's armsmen stay in the hall, or sleep elsewhere?"

Nell lifted her head.

There was a confused thud of feet and voices outside. Pellam yelled, "Open up the gate, clod!"

Listening, Nell said, "Lord Jorn must return from an early hunt." Kyrin looked hurriedly about for something to dry with, and Nell said softly, "I think they will eat, first. As for the armsmen, we're near the barracks. Lord Jorn has been hiring every warrior who will join him. Mayhap to strengthen himself against raiders or another lord. I know not."

"Ah." Nell certainly thought for herself. "Have you ever been in Lord Jorn's stronghold before, Nell?"

"No, but he is a good lord—when he is not pressed. My husband Cere cut wood for his winter store, and he has always—he always said so."

"Well." Kyrin washed herself once more, skin tingling with mint, and climbed out. Drying herself with her cloak, she donned her tunic, comb in hand. "Do you want a bath? It's still warm."

"Just my hair. I'm well enough." Nell scooted down the bed to make room for Kyrin, with her first real smile.

Kyrin was glad to see Nell breathed freely, after Thorgil's kicks. Bending to bathe would probably hurt. Kyrin combed her wet hair, eyeing the cleanest corner of her cloak with a grimace. She must wash it too, when she had a chance. But she would need her fresh green cloak for later. Her hair must dry as it could. There was a more pressing matter. "Nell, what were you asking me last night—when you grabbed my feet?"

Her wet head over the tub, Nell turned strawberry red. "You must pardon me. I thought you a holy woman."

"Oh." The red and blue embroidered cross. Kyrin touched the neck pouch at her throat. "You mean, a pilgrim from the Holy Land? No, I'm not. But—"

Nell rushed on, words tumbling. "Father Ulf says a convent is the place for me, or that I must marry again. He wants me gone. He—finds me a part of the world hard to resist." Nell scrubbed her scalp furiously, wrung her hair out, and wound it up. "I avoid him as I can."

So, she had heard something, had not been completely unconscious. She sat, knotting her hands in Kyrin's black cloak, as if taking courage from it.

"Thorgil will not rest, he never liked Cere, and I know I can't go with you—but I won't be a bed-thing. Mayhap Lord Jorn will find me a place. I have nowhere else." Her voice dropped, bitter. "If Father Ulf does not find a way to drive me out, or into a convent."

"He will not." Kyrin's mind firmed. "I'm not a nun, nor a pilgrim, but Nell, I have the Holy Book, and I'll teach you to read it."

"To read? But I may not be able to stay with—"

"You could be my companion." Kyrin grinned. "I think you were sent to me, for I find I have need of one with me on my road. And you need never come back here. Yes, we will teach you to read."

Nell's mouth opened. Her face glowed with hope, "Me? *Me*? Why would you—nothing comes without cost! And you, you are not as other women." She shifted, then straightened in quiet dignity. "You do not need a handmaiden. I have nothing you could want. What do *you* seek?"

Still distrustful, and little wonder. Kyrin dug down to the bottom of her pack she had set by the bed and withdrew the plain, curved dagger she'd worn in Ali's house. She extended the haft to Nell. Nell looked at her, her blue eye casting warily, the black steady on Kyrin.

Kyrin waggled the blade. "Here, take it." She shoved it into Nell's hands.

"I might stab you, you know, on the road. One such as I. So Father Ulf would say, though I was raised as a novice near his monastery." Nell's fingers tightened around the wood.

"Ulf. Umm, yes. He says much. Make sure I'm asleep, or you won't get far." Smiling, Kyrin rose. In one swift motion she was beside Nell, twisting the dagger out of her hands without effort. In less than a blink her back was against the wall, the dagger warding, a laugh in her throat.

Nell stared, eyes wide. "*That's* why Lord Jorn wants you."

"Yes." Kyrin sobered.

"I have never seen the like." Nell swallowed, hands rigid on Kyrin's black desert cloak. "What did you truly do to Thorgil and his men?"

"I taught them to respect a staff and the law of common courtesy. I like to think they will not harm a woman or a stranger again without looking twice. But I think that is too much to ask, from such as they." Kyrin's mouth twitched. She felt strangely lighthearted.

A line between her brows, Nell eyed the cloak around her cautiously. She glanced from Kyrin's odd bits of gear scattered about to her pack and bow. "Where are you from?"

Kyrin returned the dagger and Nell laid it in her lap carefully.

It was much harder to get the first word out than snatch a blade. Kyrin clenched her hands. It was a risk she must take. "I was born a lord's daughter, but I have been a slave in Araby. There are things I must do, before I tell you of which hold I am. I *can* tell you I mean no man ill in my land—besides slavers, and those who would hurt another without cause. Presently, I travel to Cierheld." She swallowed.

"If I become your handmaiden, your companion, you go to Cierheld?"

"Yes." Kyrin looked at her rather anxiously. She wished she had asked where Uncle Ulf went on pilgrimage, and wished for Tae or Alaina's voice outside the door. Were they well, walking the Araby sands beside Faisal? Not for long, if she did not find Hamal.

"I have heard good of Cierheld, and of their great sorrow, years ago. I wonder if it is soon to be healed?" Nell glanced at Kyrin, who said nothing. "I will think on your words." Nell bent her head.

Kyrin left her to her thoughts. The flames flickered hungrily in the hearth, and she was near as hungry. A good sign.

Nell rose, only to pace to the door and back. Kyrin's hair dried, and she rubbed the stiffness from her sore legs after giving Nell her spare black garments to go with the cloak. Nell smoothed the embroidered falcon on the tunic's breast, silent. She did not seem to mind that her undertunic and kirtle had been burned.

When the sun was high, by the bright sun shafts that leaked under the eaves, Pellam came with food again, and left. He could tell Kyrin nothing. Why did Lord Bergrin not come? She could do nothing unless she learned what he wished of her, and why.

Nell napped, and early afternoon dragged. The room grew hot and stuffy. Kyrin's aches returned ten-fold. She lay down on the ox skin, her eyes roving over every inch of the wood walls, the roof beams, and the thatch. That was a possible way out if she needed one. But it would take risky noise and effort, digging through thatch, and Pel had many men at his call.

The door shook under a heavy fist. Startled, Kyrin got to her feet. Pel thrust the door open to the limit of its hinges. She squinted. Pel's blue, white-trimmed tunic flashed in the rays of the lowering sun. Not a lowly armsman, no indeed.

Nell rose, graceful in her black tunic and trousers, with the womanly curves Kyrin had never possessed.

"Lord Bergrin Jorn, the protector," Pellam announced proudly, back straight, his grey eyes fixed on his lord.

Kyrin bowed, and Nell slipped up behind her shoulder.

Bergrin strode over the sill, taking in Kyrin, her pack, the room, and Nell in one sweeping glance. Nell dipped a curtsey. Her face was red, but she kept her head up.

Bergrin bowed, returning their courtesy, and eyed the buckets and dirty cloths and clothing in a heap beside the fireplace. He nodded, with satisfaction, Kyrin thought, and turned to her.

"You are well?" His scrutiny was brief and searching, then his hazel gaze slid around her.

Kyrin swallowed. "I wish to consult a healer. The fever was gone this morn, but it comes and goes as it has this past five-day." Kyrin swallowed.

Bergrin's gaze snapped back to her. "You have a clever tongue to head off my purpose. But I'll have Jordan see you. Is all else to your satisfaction?"

"But for this prison, my lord." Something cold, sharp, and shadowed in his abrupt glance made Kyrin sure she'd better not change his opinion of her mettle. He looked rather like one of the fey of legend, with his near-white hair and pale skin, and his quick, precise movements. A cornered fey, one taking whatever weapon came to hand. She could not let him corner her. "What is your purpose, my lord?"

"It is well," he said, "you are welcome here, and Nell Trinley." He eyed Nell.

Kyrin flushed. Ever fair-speaking, Bergrin Jorn, who smiled even as his treacherous hand drove a blade of words deep. As always, a lord's son.

Startled, Nell met his gaze. "My lord."

Kyrin repressed the hot words that sprang to her tongue. Nell *was* distracting. Nell's hip-length hair was warm as silken honey, the skin of her white wrists milky between bruises. and her cheeks blossomed with pink under the lord's scrutiny. The livid marks of Thorgil's fingers and her blue eye were her only blemishes. Lord Bergrin's mouth curved in unconscious approval. He smiled.

Nell stiffened as Lord Bergrin opened his mouth, about to cede ground. And a sudden shiver rattled Kyrin's teeth. *Not now.* The wave of cold heat came again.

Bergrin's pale brows almost met. His mouth twisted. Then his face smoothed as he glanced at Nell. "Rest now. In the morn I will see you again." He turned toward the door.

"But my lord—" Kyrin protested.

"You stay!" Bergrin snapped, whirling around.

Kyrin stepped forward and glared back. He gave way before the simple surprise of it. "Why am I a prisoner here, my lord?" If she must stay she would hear the reason why. The lord of Jorn hesitated. Kyrin's mouth tightened. Bergrin never could answer a simple question.

"You'll be useful to me, in an honorable way."

She'd heard that concerning Hamal. The stubborn know-it-all.

"When you're well, I will tell you, lady. Now rest, and I will send the healer." Lord Bergrin looked at Pellam. "See to it Jordan comes as soon as he can."

"Yes, my lord." The armsman bowed, carefully not looking at Kyrin. Lord Jorn stalked out, back straight, his face cold.

Oaf. Kyrin wanted to stamp her foot. So, ill-mannered Lord Bergrin thought he knew what she needed, did he, when he'd seen her but a few moments? And never listened?

Later, she lay under her cloak, wretched. Old Jordan prescribed healing remedies, of herbs whose names she remembered but not their use, and she drank his bitter concoctions. Her teeth chattered in spite of her clenched jaw. She wished for dark and quiet, the light of the fire split her skull.

The stars shone outside when Pellam opened the door again. She'd not called him Pel yet . . . On fire within and without, Kyrin ate nothing and passed into a desert place of heat and pain.

Her nemesis followed, circling, his paws soundless, the dunes hot and silent.

I left him! Kyrin wailed, small in the darkness. She gathered herself and turned to face her enemy. *Why do you follow me?*

The tiger looked through her, his eyes glowing green with the fire of his knowledge. A horrible pleasure rasped in his throat. Then his sinuous length faded. The falcon did not come. The dream dimmed to grey nothing.

Other dreams came. At times Kyrin clung to gentle hands, and other times she fought iron chains that ringed her ankles and neck. Her eyes burned, they were so hot. As searing as the falcons's eyes, burning, burning her spirit from the silver collar whirling before her. Kyrin leaned closer. Were the falcons angry—no, only her face reflected in those jet depths of swift understanding, her likeness twisted. There was Bergrin, laughing at her earnest awkwardness, Esther simpering at her love of the hunt and unwomanly things, and Celine and Myrna giggling over her unwomanly garb.

Kyrin woke and turned her head. Her eyes did not burn. Cool, damp dawn streamed in the open door.

"Water." Her voice cracked. What would Tae say this time to make her laugh?

There was a short cry, and Nell sprang to her side and held a cup to her mouth.

Nell, not Tae. She was not in Ali's house. Cold water lapped over the rim of the cup and eased Kyrin's dry throat. She was in Britannia.

"How do you feel?" Nell looked different in a woman's graceful kirtle, back-lit by the cheerful fire, her smile wide.

"Like a dry reed. Like I could eat a sheep," Kyrin managed. The tiger, the laughter, Esther—she shoved them away. Bergrin must not know who she was, not until she saw her father.

Nell gave her another drink and brushed away a trickle that slid down her chin. Kyrin smiled, and there was gentle warmth in Nell's brown eye and blue. She was like Alaina, true and kind.

Kyrin suddenly wanted to cry, and looked at her hands on the coverlet.

Nell gave her another cup of broth, then turned Kyrin out of bed to lay down fresh, springy heather. When she finished with her, Kyrin lay cocooned in a dry blanket on a fragrant bed, and fell asleep. By next sunrise she wobbled about, gaining strength. One thing had changed.

Their door now stood open, and Kyrin watched the activity in the yard between the hall and the barracks, where armsmen trained continuously. Mounts were trained as well, dogs waited in the kennel to be called to the hunt, and chickens pecked about the garden wall that flanked the side of Lord Jorn's great hall.

It stood two storys high, two short bow shots from their prison. The great door at the hall's end faced them, framed by tree trunks, and buttressed by grey native stone, close mortared. The top story seemed to be living quarters, with no visible windows. Kyrin never saw Myrna about the yard. The cook poked his head out the side door this morn to yell at some serving women to hurry up with the cream. Crocuses were out in force in the sunny spots, and the birds sang. The trees continued to leaf.

Three morns later, Kyrin was well enough to laugh with Nell as they broke their fast with bread and cheese and fruit.

Footsteps and hooves thudded dully around the corner and Lord Bergrin emerged.

His pale Arab whinnied and threw up his head. Patiently, Bergrin pulled his head down, the beast's blue barding resplendent against his white coat. Kyrin swallowed the last of her bread.

Behind him, Pel held the leads of three others. A sturdy gray, a lady's piebald mare, and a bay. Kyrin choked over the bread. The bay was a warhorse.

13

Defenses

There is a friend . . . who sticketh closer than a brother.
~Proverbs. 18:24

Lord Bergrin held Kyrin's foot for her while she mounted the blood bay, sharply watching her mount with ease, the flex of his jaw and his glare daring her to speak. Kyrin said nothing and stared straight ahead, quietly restraining the horse with foot and rein. She could be patient.

With a stolid, gentle grip, Pel assisted Nell onto the piebald mare. Nell stroked the horse's neck with an awed smile, and her fingers whitened in its mane.

Pel held the Arab for Bergrin, then mounted and followed them on his sturdy grey. Nell's piebald broke into a trot, passing Lord Bergrin Jorn on the way to the gate. Nell held the reins helplessly, her eyes wide. The lord of Jornhold did not call her back, but kicked his Arab into a trot and caught up Nell's rein and fastened it to his mount's saddle. He called to Kyrin, "Walk with me, warrior."

Kyrin nudged the bay up beside him.

"So you are silent at last?"

Warhorse or no, the bay answered her well. Kyrin patted his neck, her lips tight as he danced under her tense body. Smiling slightly, Bergrin said nothing further. Kyrin took the opportunity to examine his lands. The valley was wide and lush, the hills rolling, with plenty of forest and fertile ground to judge by the oxen in the fields and men with sacks of seed on their hips, following the furrows of diligent ploughs.

Eight Eagle miles down the dale's winding track they entered the village. It was built on a circular plan, extending up the side of a hill. Two main roads formed a cross within the circle, the northwest track leading to Bergrin's hold, behind her. Kyrin looked up the road, noting where she had come into the village along a smaller, south-west road to encounter Thorgil and Uncle Ulf. She glanced at Nell, who seemed undisturbed by memories.

Kyrin followed Bergrin southeast, past guilds and crafter's houses. They and the more prosperous villagers lived in two story houses of wood and stone, closer to the shire reeve's simple keep with its armsmen's quarters. The rest lived in one-room, thatched dwellings dotted about the grassy shoulders of the hill. None of the people bustling along the road gave Kyrin more than a glance. They knuckled their foreheads to Lord Bergrin, and all eyes followed him. Some faces held question or unease, others devotion.

The cavalcade passed three women, who whispered behind their hands, their white linen caps bobbing. The raven-haired one's voice came sharply to Kyrin's ears. "Nell Trinley thinks herself come up in the world, does she? And settin' her cap at our lord?" The pleasantly plump one added, "I always said that man of hers was no good . . ."

Nell's head drooped, and her cheeks flushed. Kyrin pulled the bay back beside her, eyeing the women askance. Bergrin turned in his saddle. There were tears on Nell's face. He urged his Arab to a faster pace, kicking up dirt, leaving the women behind. One of them lifted her hands to her hips in indignation. "Well I like that!"

It was well done, maybe the only thing Bergrin had ever done well. Kyrin eyed him. There were depths of purpose here that needed plumbed, to use Hyl's words.

She stiffened warily as Lord Bergrin Jorn led them to the Brewmaster Inn. They rounded the front corner and clopped into a lane that led to the rear. Between the back of the inn and a thatched stable with three arches across the lane from the main establishment, was a large circle of beaten earth bounded by weathered stones two feet high. Seats and benches were set around it.

Two boys wrestled in the ring, one curly-haired. When they noticed the lord's approach they yelled with excitement, stopped their play, and ran across the lane and inside the Brewmaster. A man rose from a bench tilted against the inn wall. His huge hands gripped his seat to let the front legs gently down as he stood. A couple of minor scars pulled and pocked his face, and his nose had been flattened, in spite of which his smooth-shaven grin had the appeal of good nature. He resembled a red-haired bear. He walked toward them easily.

Kyrin expected Bergrin to hail him or the innkeep. The lord said nothing. The man passed him without a word, only a telling glance. He stopped at Kyrin's side.

She nodded courteously and waited. He cocked his head and looked her over. Then with a wide smile he slapped the bay's shoulder. The warhorse flinched, shifting beneath Kyrin. "Just give me a trial, lass, I won't hurt ye, just run ye off!" His laugh boomed between the inn and the stables.

Kyrin calmed the bay, frowning. He wasn't drunk, though evidently he wasn't the innkeep. The man drew himself up, and his shock of hair burned in the sun like flames while she looked at him in doubt.

"I'm Hal." His grin faded in growing puzzlement as he looked at her. "I've said truth. My name is Hal Loring."

Evidently he expected her to know it. He resembled a friendly, brown-eyed bear, yet a bear all the same. With the same dangers of strength and speed, and far more wit. Kyrin pulled in air. Was this Lord Jorn's way to get her to speak of herself and her errand? She did not think much of it. She bowed slightly over the reins in her hands in apology. "I am sorry, Hal, but I do not know of what you speak."

Hal faced Bergrin sharply. "You didn't tell her?"

Lord Jorn's voice was cold and measured. "No, I did not. Is not this moment enough?" Anger snapped in his eyes.

Hal sighed and held up a wide hand to Kyrin. "Step down, lass, and I'll explain."

"Just a moment, good sir." Kyrin tightened her grip and stared at Bergrin. "Is this my honorable purpose, Lord Jorn, which you would not tell me of before? An arranged fight?"

Bergrin's mouth curved, smug and untouchable. "Yes. You'll fight Hal for me. For his gold. I will reward you well."

Kyrin's knees tightened, and the bay sidestepped.

"It won't be a hurting match, to cripple," Hal put in anxiously, "just friendly like."

Kyrin looked from his scarred face to Lord Bergrin, and her mouth tightened, heat rising in her belly. The lord of Jornhold took much for granted. "You want me to fight him for *coin*?" she burst out. "For a gamble? You're witless as a loon! He's a warrior, and I fight for need and naught else!"

"Please!" begged Hal, grabbing her horse's uneasy head. The bay snorted and snapped at Bergrin's Arab.

Before Kyrin could say a word in reply, Bergrin spurred forward. His cheeks were pale, and his eyes glittered. His blade whispered from its sheath. He set the point below Kyrin's breast, his arm braced to drive it home.

The hair rose on her arms. He was in deadly earnest. Carefully, she moved her hands down to her pommel. Past the shining blade, Bergrin's gaze was threaded with anger, something dark and brittle lurking behind it. The muscles of his jaw stood out, working. Now they came to it.

"You have another reason than gold, my lord. What is it?"

Bergrin's blade wavered then pressed harder. Kyrin held still against the prick, willing the bay not to move.

"My sister is ill. I must have gold—for medicine." His words were hoarse.

Kyrin eyed the rich browband, breast collar, and saddle pad of his Arab. Though Bergrin himself *did* wear simple linen and a woolen cloak. Not the orange silk surcoat and mail she had first seen him in. She frowned. Hal wisely did not move.

Bergrin noted Kyrin's gaze on his horse and grated, "These trappings keep Lord Keffer"—he tilted his head toward the north—"and others, uncertain of my resources. Nidfael Keffer, part of that Southland scum, has wanted a piece of Jornhold since my father passed."

Behind Bergrin, clinging to her mare, Nell held the dagger Kyrin had given her behind her thigh, out of Hal's sight. Kyrin shook her head slowly, as if looking from side to side. *Don't try it.*

She didn't much care what trouble Bergrin had brought himself, but Myrna, sick? Kyrin swallowed. Sympathy and suspicion tangled in her. Her mouth flattened. She did not move a muscle.

"But if you will not fight—" Lord Bergrin eyed his blade and lowered it with a bitter twist of his mouth. A brush of red flitted across his cheekbones. Averting his face, he nudged his Arab back, dragging Nell and the piebald aside.

Nell's instruction could not begin too soon, but Myrna . . . she must do what she could. "Very well."

Bergrin spun the Arab and shifted in his saddle to peer in Kyrin's face. "You are certain?" Hope lit his eyes, and distrust.

Kyrin dismounted and looked up at Hal, towering over her. "I hope this isn't a wrestling bout."

Lord Jorn smothered a sudden laugh, and Hal looked aggrieved. "Certainly not."

"Well then." Kyrin smiled. And nodded cheerfully at Nell, who slid her weapon hand behind a fold of her skirt. "What weapons do we use, sir? Give me a staff, and I'll beat you from here to doom. If we fight without weapons, I'm trained in a way you have never seen."

Hal grunted thoughtfully.

A thin voice piped up behind him, "Do both! Do both!" The curly-headed boy from the arena hopped up and down in hopeful glee.

Kyrin could not help her smile. "I'm willing," she said. "You, Hal?"

Hal pretended to ponder, and the boy hung on his arm, brown eyes wide, pleading. Hal grinned, and the boy raised his fists and cried, "Yes!"

Hal ruffled his rye-brown curls. "Get on with you, sprat."

"Yay, Uncle Hal!" The youngster ran back inside the inn, shouting, "Uncle Hal is going to win the wager again!"

Kyrin sent a sharp look Hal's way. Hal grinned, embarrassed. "I let him come. I thought he might help Lord Jorn's warrior if that warrior needed encouragement. Now he's got me in trouble with a quarter-staff fighter." His smile was whimsical and shrewd. "You bested six of 'em, didn't you? But they didn't know you were coming. I do."

§

Four days later, Kyrin inspected the fighting ring behind the inn. She had not enlightened Hal that she did not use a quarterstave, precisely. The sky was a span of turquoise, and the sun lightened the frosty air. The ground was hard as iron under her boots, the weather having taken a turn. All the better for a bout. Her green tunic and brown trousers were barely warm enough, and the cross-gartered gray hose itched. She scratched her calf and scuffed at the ground with the toe of her boot.

It was clay, and fair footing unless it rained after Nones. She could hear the bells here, unlike Jornhold, which was too far from the village. She cocked her head at the sky. At the third quarter, the sun would swing low enough to be an advantage or disadvantage, depending on the direction faced. A little practice would go well.

Kyrin shuffled forward and back, side to side, jumped and kicked, spun and rolled. Straw sparkled in her dusty braid hanging over her shoulder. At last, breathless and sweaty, she brushed off and walked back to the bay horse, satisfied. She had proven the ground well enough, and she hoped Hal, surely watching, believed he had an edge on what she might try. Her smile was sharp.

Back in Jornhold before her quarters, Kyrin showed Nell how to rouse her with quick upward knuckle strokes along her spine if she were knocked senseless. And she stretched thoroughly, striking at the air. She whirled and darted, her breath hissing out with the fluid force in every blow of her latest Subak form that Tae had been teaching her. Bergrin's armsmen watched, fascinated.

Awe spread over Nell's face.

Kyrin finished and sat with a huffing pant beside her in the doorway. "It's not like that in a real fight, you know. It's confusion and fear, and moving well and faster in spite of it. If you ever watch a real master of Subak you'll see the difference. My second father, Tae Chisun, now there is one you should watch."

"You're going to teach me—that?" Nell shivered, her blue eye as bright as her dancing, rapt black orb. "I will not fear the likes of Thorgil anymore!"

Kyrin sobered. "Oh Nell, just—pray you never face anyone over a blade. But if you do, a staff, even a short stick can well save you, by God's grace."

§

Nell sat on a stone in the front row of the arena. Here and there the shire reeve and his men stood, watchful. Staff in hand, Kyrin faced Hal. Their shadows stretched west, to the feet of the gathered crowd.

Their staves tapped once in salute, wrist-thick oak against slender ash. Then they struck, rattling to a sharp, blood stirring crescendo.

Kyrin's ash staff bent under the assault of Hal's heavier oak, and some of those behind Nell booed.

Their catcalls turned to muttered astonishment. Kyrin waded into Hal's attack, deflecting his weapon by fingersbreadths. He fell back from her rapping, stinging blows to his hands and shins. The warrior caught himself, feinted low, and flipped his staff around. But partially deflected, the oak thumped Kyrin's head. She fell, and the gathering shouted. She scrambled to reach her feet, but Hal's rain of blows kept her down.

Kyrin whirled onto her back, fending him off furiously with her staff. At the first chance, she rolled up again and thrust at Hal's head on a deceptive angle. The end of her staff slid toward his eyes like a snake, and he pulled violently back. Nell let out her breath and heard a few boos on Hal's account.

Kyrin lashed out, striking Hal's feet and legs in lightning succession. Then her staff-butt seemed to dance across the warrior's middle in three rapid thrusts, in a pattern Nell had never seen. Hal staggered. His oak weapon dropped from his hands. The crowd roared.

Hal stared wide-eyed at his wavering legs. Somewhere behind Nell rose the cry, "Witch!" Kyrin laid her stick on the ground and beckoned. Hal raised his head, wonder and fear in his eyes, took a wobbly step, and pitched forward. Kyrin caught him, yielding to his weight, and lowered him to the ground gently.

She propped him to sitting, his legs stretched before him, and knelt to slide her knuckles briskly up his back on both sides of his spine. Hal's lolling head shook groggily.

"Better?" Nell barely heard Kyrin's voice over a storm of clapping and boos. Nell rose from her seat to peer around the cursing man in front of her.

Hal nodded, blinking. "What under heaven did you do?" The crowd quieted, heads craning as if they also wanted to hear.

"Disturbed the body's humors, and just restored the flow, more or less," Kyrin said between pants.

"I . . . see." Hal shook his head like a bear full of winter's sleep.

In relief, Nell sniffed at the wine-sweet cold air in deep, satisfied delight. She hugged her arms tight. The warrior was all right, and Kyrin had won the first bout.

Nell sobered a little. It was uncanny, the way Hal had dropped. Even he was surprised by his weakness. That pattern of blows had been curiously precise.

Men and women shouted to each other amid impatient growls and ribald encouragement that heated the chill, golden afternoon. The villagers were eager for the bare-handed struggle, where surely their warrior would fare better. With a heave, Hal got his feet, using Kyrin to rise and almost toppling her over. She counter balanced, stepped back, and bowed to him.

Hal glared at Kyrin from under red brows. "Are you ready?" His fierce hair was awry, not as thin on top as Father Ulf's, tonsured long ago. Kyrin had reason to beware Hal's grip.

Nell grinned, and licked suddenly dry lips. He was not Father Ulf, but trained as a warrior, and the more honest for it. Hal's arms were truly a bear's under the tunic he wore, in deference to Kyrin's being forced to wear the same for modesty's sake. No unfair advantage of oil made *his* bare torso slippery as a greased pig. The contest would be fair that way. But there was no room for a mistake. Nell picked at the hem of her sleeve nervously. Once in those arms Kyrin would have short shrift.

Hal took the age-old fistfighter position, and Kyrin's hands rose to guard her head. Arms up, her elbows near touched before her nose and her shoulders hunched.

"Hah! There the beetle raises its feeble grip!"

Nell thought that the tanner's voice, as ugly as the pits of his trade. Laughter broke out. From the other side of the arena, the shire reeve lifted a hand, and one of his men eased watchfully into the crowd. Nell forced herself to grip her rock and hold her place in the press that threatened to tumble her away.

The shrill treble of Hal's nephew rose over the heaving sea of bodies, and Nell turned her head. "Go, Uncle Hal!" The boy strained to wriggle past a wall of men in front of him. They elbowed him back.

"Quick!" Nell gestured to her seat. A wide grin on his thin, freckled face, the boy slid between the legs of those caught up in the spectacle and crawled up on her ringside stone. Nell looked around the crowd and did not see the tanner. But if he was about,

Thorgil lurked there also. She pulled her cloak tighter about her. But the reeve would keep order, and she had the dagger.

The crowd yelled in delight, and Nell swung back around. Kyrin could take care of Thorgil if the reeve did not. That is, if Hal did not best her first.

Hal swung, fast and hard. Kyrin skipped aside quicker than thought. Nell made nothing of the next flurry of blows then bit her lip. Hal's straight jab connected with Kyrin's shoulder, shaking her to her toes, and the slamming force of his right cross surged for Kyrin's face.

She ducked far down—and in, and up—inside his blows. She spun. Her leg swept out in a reaping motion and she jerked on his arm and shoulder. Off-balance, Hal took a step to avoid falling. Kyrin followed him closely. She gave a quick jab, then a right cross, a hook—and an uppercut with all the strength of her small form surging up from the earth.

Nell winced. But instead of Hal's granite jaw, Kyrin's fists struck his softer neck and belly. The *thunk* of her blows against his flesh reverberated in the silence of the audience's surprise. Hal shook himself, his thick neck reddening. They circled.

He crouched and rushed, huge arms spread crablike. Nell caught her breath. Hal closed, and closed—until Kyrin slapped her hands on the back of his neck and shoved downward, legs spraddled as she drove him to earth like a felled tree.

Hal's breath burst from him as he crashed down. Kyrin instantly changed position, spinning from in front of him to drop atop his back as he struggled for his knees. Her legs snapped in, curling about his ribs, tight to him as a crab's shell. She reached around his neck. Gripping her opposite hand, she pulled back.

Hal reached for her choking arm and pried desperately at her hand. He got it loose—but somehow her other arm had slid tight under his chin in its place. She gripped her tunic at her shoulder like an eel, and anchored her hold.

Hal's face was on fire, and Nell stopped breathing. How could Kyrin hold against that bull neck?

Kyrin slid her tightening grip across the back of Hal's head. She anchored a second time and arched her back. Hal gave a mighty buck against her cinched chokehold, which Kyrin grimly rode out, and a weaker attempt. Then the warrior dropped to the dirt, a loose sack. Three moments of time, and he was senseless. Everyone stared.

Nell let out a short breath, wound tight as a lute string. Kyrin rose, stumbled a step, breathing hard. Hal lay where he'd fallen. Nell leaned forward. He wasn't dead, Kyrin would not—

With a cry, Hal's nephew slid down the rock toward his uncle, lying in the arena in the gold of the falling sun. Nell reached out, snagged the boy's arm, and reeled him back. "Shh, it's all right. I'm sure it's all right." The boy's gaze darted from her to his uncle to Kyrin, his dark eyes worried.

"I told you so!" cried one voice, and another "That's impossible!" "What now?" Others stamped and cheered.

Kyrin ignored the chaos her second victory provoked and moved to prop up her opponent cross-legged once again, his hands in his lap. A brisk back rub later, he raised his head and blearily swiped at his eyes. Nell sighed.

Hal grimaced and rested his forehead in his hand. "Truly, you've skills I've never seen. My head aches." He squinted at Kyrin soberly. "What country teaches its warriors to use so little strength to choke the breath and blood from a man?"

"My master taught me the way of the warrior, of the Land of the Morning Calm in the East."

"What will you take to show me such a secret? A tanned hide, a new cloak? Silver, gold? That sneaking arm across the throat—loosing the goose from the net, knowing it will be caught by the snake on the other side—that is something I have not seen."

Kyrin shifted, flushing. "I am sorry. I may not teach that—but I can show you other things."

Hal eyed her, his shrewd gaze unable to hide his eagerness. "Which are the best things, and when can we begin?"

"Come to Jornhold on the morrow, after the Prime bell, at dawn." Kyrin grinned. "As for 'the best things,' it depends on who you fight. There are various tactics. A fistfighter is susceptible to kicks and takedowns. A bow is best against some weapons and attacks, and a blade or a stick can do much. That's a beginning. For a wrestler who rushes in—there are various pitfalls." Her smile turned impish.

"Hmm. You saw my fist and quarterstaff work. Will you teach me what you know of those also?" Hal was near pleading.

"Yes."

Hal scratched his head, a pleased grin on his face.

"Good." The word of approval rose at Nell's shoulder. Lord Jorn stalked past her. Kyrin rose to meet him, and Nell stepped back, blushing. She had not the ears of a fox as Kyrin had. People were always taking her unaware.

Lord Jorn hesitated then grasped Kyrin's hands, streaked with sweat and dust, and pressed them between his own. "You have my thanks, and my sister's."

Kyrin gave Bergrin a little bow and used the movement to pull her hands free. The lord of Jornhold dipped his head to Hal, then turned to the crowd, which let out a rousing "Huzzah!" as he grinned broadly at Kyrin. Someone near the far end of the lane called, "Unholy power! Witch!"

Bergrin did not bat an eye in the direction of the tanner and Thorgil beside him, who shook an angry fist. The lord of

Jornhold raised Kyrin's arm. "This warrior is the clear victor!" Nell smiled, and her yell of approval joined those around her.

Not everyone was happy about the outcome of the contest. Some cheered, some frowned, some stared in doubt. Nell heard a whisper, "How could a woman do such?" The silence grew as uneasiness spread.

Red crept up Kyrin's face.

"Aye, look to the ring in her ear! It's the eye of evil!" Thorgil bellowed. "Cursed one!"

Kyrin took a small step back, then straightened her shoulders and her chin lifted. She said nothing.

"She hits as hard as you!" Hal shouted back. "And look to what she wears around her neck! The cross. But then, you weren't looking when you had the chance, were you? You were beating a woman in the street. A woman we all know. I worked with Cere in the woods a time or two. He was a good man, and liked his ale of an evening. And his Nell is a good woman. This warrior defended her. Our bout was fair won."

"Witch, I call her!"

Stillness fell over the arena. A lark called on the hill behind Nell. A few in the crowd looked at her. She hugged herself, touched the dagger she'd hidden in her sleeve, and watched Kyrin.

14

Confessions

Senses trained to discern good and evil. ~Hebrews 5:14

Kyrin had turned her back to the sun, to her enemy, and her face was in shadow. She did not move. Lord Jorn's fingers whitened on her shoulder, his face an icy, sunlit mask.

Hal bowed to Lord Jorn, deep and casual. "My thanks for a fair fight, my lord, and best wishes for your lady sister." He gestured with one broad arm toward the inn. "Come one, come all! Join me, my brothers, at the keg, and console my poor, bruised head."

Thorgil shouted, "You're witched, brother!"

Nell dared not speak lest she add weight to the crowd's vote, wavering for or against Kyrin with the rising and falling mutters of the villagers.

Hal withdrew toward the inn, shrugging in good nature. "The end of the warrior's stick argues otherwise," he called over his shoulder. "The blows sting yet. Let's see if the innkeep's good brew will soothe my slow wit." Laughter broke out.

"Na', she's a witch, I tell you!"

Hal's nephew edged against Nell, and she laid her arm around his small shoulders.

"My friends!" Standing at the edge of the arena closest to the inn, Father Ulf's mouth was pinched as if good bread molded on his tongue. He pointed at Kyrin and his voice rose. "There is truth in Thorgil's words. How can a woman, *any* woman, defeat our neighbor Hal, a warrior of great skill, as we all know?" He turned to Kyrin. "Another among us has brought accusation against you. In the name of our Father above, what power do you tap that other men do not?"

Lord Jorn drew himself up in stern ire. "What mean you, Father Ulf?"

"I mean she holds more strength than Hal, a warrior from birth, and it would be good to know where that power hails from, my lord." Ulf bowed his head, not giving an inch, his lips thin in his long face.

Father Ulf did not look at Nell with accusation, but that did not comfort her. The spiritual leader of Bolton dared accuse Kyrin—who held Lord Jorn's favor. He and Thorgil would not wish to hear that jet was said to burn a witch's skin, and that Kyrin's ear was unmarked. For Father Ulf was a dog with a fresh bone. Nell clutched Hal's nephew.

How she wished she were a monk, with the Holy Book in her mind, so she could wield it to help those Father Ulf hounded. She hated his twisting tongue. Cere had known some of the Book, being raised for a time under a brother who loved it. And her Cere never forgot its wonders. If only she had paid more attention as a novice, and learned as he had.

"No woman fights so." Father Ulf threw his words down like a glove.

Lord Jorn muttered something aside to Kyrin. She nodded, impassive. Nell did not see fear in her darkling eyes as she turned and waited quietly, wiping sweat from her chin.

"She is from a far land, but of our faith—" Lord Jorn began.

Brother Rolf pushed between Thorgil and his fat companion, who whispered in the tanner's ear. The burly man shot the monk an annoyed look as he brushed by. Brother Rolf crossed his arms and stood, his back to Thorgil, immovable as a gangly oak, his voice quiet. "I will hear her confession, and then we shall see."

Thorgil opened his mouth, and his companions glared from Brother Rolf to Kyrin.

Lord Jorn protested. "There is no need for a confession, Father Ulf. See here, the bag at her neck bears our Lord's mark. His power is over her, greater than any evil eye." He held up Kyrin's neck pouch, so those closest could see the cross it bore.

Nell balled the shoulder of the boy's tunic in her sweating hand and swallowed hard. The evil eye? Surely witchcraft did not come near Kyrin's heart, one willing to sacrifice her life and limb for another, without thought of gain. One who called her own wandering eye a blessing, and named her one of God's creatures. Though Kyrin *did* ask her to be her handmaiden. What if Kyrin sought to catch her in coils of darkness that seemed of the light? But no, there was naught but kindness and a burden of care on her. Often strangeness, yes, and even anger. But anger that rose hot in defense of others.

"You are right, my Lord Jorn. And wrong." Kyrin's voice spread among them, clear and low. "His power is over me, but it is not his mark that carries the power, but his word. As he says, his writ is sharper than a two-edged sword, dividing even the thoughts and intents of the heart."

Nell raised her hand to cover her astonishment. Here was one who knew the Book. But then, Kyrin did know how to read.

Father Ulf grunted, glancing at Brother Rolf in ire. Most of his audience was dissipating after Hal toward the inn and Hal's keg. Ulf raised his hand, his robed figure straight. "This still bears investigation. Sorcery is a mortal sin—"

Lord Jorn threw up his hands. "Well then, let Brother Rolf take her confession! I trust you have no fear of the good brother?" He asked Kyrin.

She shook her head.

Father Ulf eyed her sharply. "It may be my mind is not clear in this. Do take her confession, Brother Rolf. It is meet for the moment." Displeased, but he was persuaded for the time.

Nell released Hal's nephew, who had been tugging at her to loose him, and the boy raced for the inn after his uncle, all young limbs.

Brother Rolf cleared his throat, frowning at Kyrin, unconscious of Nell's regard. He swung his arm toward the center of the arena. "Come, we'll be free of lingering ears in the ring."

"I'll leave you to it, and to God. But"—Lord Bergrin Jorn's voice frosted—"anything against her, good Brother, bring first to me. Not her confession, if you love me, but facts."

Brother Rolf dipped his light red head in assent and gestured again to Kyrin. "Come."

She shuffled before him to the middle of the ring, weariness at last seeming to weigh her feet. Stiff as a poker, Father Ulf watched, then spun before Lord Jorn's advance and stalked toward the Brewmaster. Nell crept slowly and softly back to her stone.

"In the name of the Father, the Son, and the Holy Spirit, tell me the truth, my sister." Brother Rolf's low voice carried farther than he knew. Nell did not move—none of Kyrin's words would go past her lips.

"What do you wish to know, Brother? My story entire?" Kyrin raised her head with a twist of humor about her mouth. "I suppose you do. Has my uncle told you anything?"

"Naught but that you are a wench after your father's ilk—whom the church has so far refused to condemn." At Kyrin's sigh, Brother Rolf pointed to the cross hanging on his belt. "Tell your story before the Son, so you may be absolved."

Kyrin's gaze did not waver. "He has forgiven me my trespasses, Brother, for I have asked. For by one offering he has perfected forever those who are sanctified. And in another place he says my sins and my lawless deeds he will remember no more. But to answer what concerns you now, I—was a slave in Araby two years.

"My master ordered me to learn the way of the warrior for the entertainment of his guests: his brother merchants and others of the caliph's court. My sister and I had learned unarmed combat in the martial way of the East. We also fought with dagger and staff. I learned the warrior's way quickly out of anger and fear, for my master murdered my mother."

She looked down. "I wanted to avenge her, and my moment came." Kyrin absently rubbed her neck pouch. "But instead, the Master of the stars showed me that anger burns what it touches to ash. And my Lord kept me from wrongful blood." She shrugged. "I served my earthly master's table for a time, then he was false to the caliph, who sent his wazir, who executed my master. The wazir sent me home, and here I am. You would find my sister of more interest, I think, for she has a rare scribe's hand." A smile quirked her mouth, then her voice firmed.

"As for sorcery, though I am a rebel as much as anyone born, the blood of our Lord has cleansed me. But I may freely swear to you, the warrior's way I practice is not witchcraft. Subak uses points of pain to disable an attacker, as I did with Hal. I can show you if you wish." She reached to tap brother Rolf's arm just below his elbow. He cocked his head, watchful but curious.

"A blow or a grab at such a pain point interrupts the flow of the body's humors. A sequence of three such points interrupted will take a man's senses, as you saw."

Brother Rolf's washed-out blue gaze was intense. "You do not deny that your warrior's skill calls on a strange knowledge?"

Kyrin shook her head. "No. It is simply less well known in the West, almost unknown. But it is not evil. My master, Tae Chisun, turned from his people's worship of the spirits of hill and stream. And he thought he must leave his martial skill also, for worship and warfare were often practiced together, and one was thought to feed the other. He was ready to give it up. Then the Master of the stars showed him he must keep his knowledge of warfare for him, the father of lights and giver of every good gift. So long as my master did not look to the spirits, and his knowledge was no form of worship of them, the Master of the stars sanctified his bodily skill unto himself."

Brother Rolf raised an eyebrow. "Master of the stars?"

"In the East the ruler of the stars is the ruler of destiny. Our Lord is Master of all—and so in Tae's mind, Master of the stars." Kyrin tilted her head. "You know better than most, Brother, in our world there are two sources of power, really only one, for the evil one twisted what power he was given. In the end it will be stripped from him. For our Lord took the victory when he cried, 'It is finished!'"

Rolf tapped his chin. "You have more knowledge of such things and the Scripture than many."

"Yes. I study his Book. I listen to it when I may. As Tae says, power from any other besides the Father of Lights is from the evil one, and darkens the heart." Kyrin shrugged. "He gives life and light, makes the hand, head, and eye, the heart and soul. He gives us words and weapons for our hands, for healing." She smiled at him. "Weapons worthy of the war within and without."

Brother Rolf let out a long breath, a crease between his brows. "Father Ulf demands I examine your things."

"So, this was arranged," Kyrin said softly, "from the beginning."

Flushing, Rolf said shortly, "Send Nell for your pack."

Nell began to rise and caught herself. She waited until Kyrin called her. Then she fetched Kyrin's pack from inside the inn. She held out the bag to Kyrin, who had settled cross-legged on the ground across from Rolf.

Brother Rolf's arm stopped her. "Set the things out between us."

Nell looked at Kyrin. She nodded, and Nell laid the leather pack down carefully, untied it, and pulled out what first came to hand.

A folded green cloak, old but thick. Then a short stick of dark wood. Rolf took the smooth, heavy weapon and weighed it in his hand, tapping it against his palm. His eyes stayed on Kyrin, who nodded, without fear, and patiently waited for Nell to continue. Out came black trousers and a tunic, with an embroidered falcon on the breast. Brother Rolf shook the garments out, examined them, then rolled them up as they had been and set them aside.

Nell's hand closed on something cold with a sharp point. The head of a falcon emerged in her hand. So well crafted were the dark eyes, the open beak, the raised feathers down the back of the alert bronze head that Nell suppressed a start. She had never expected such a crafted weapon in a traveler's pack, let alone a traveler without enough coin for a horse.

Rolf turned the falcon dagger over in his hands. He unsheathed the blade and stared at the steel that gleamed through the bronze. "Damascus steel."

Kyrin said nothing. Nell eyed the pattern of light and dark rippled down the once-bronzed blade with awe. Blades of Damascus steel figured in legends. Who was Kyrin?

"Someone went to great toil to hide the worth of this blade."

"It came to me so."

"I see." He turned to Nell. "What else is to be found?"

Nell reached down and her fingers curled around something rectangular and heavy.

"Careful with the book." At Kyrin's words, Brother Rolf shot her a suspicious look and lifted the bottom of the pack for Nell. Nell's fingers tingled.

A book bound in leather, the cover embossed with the tree and the forbidden fruit, tables of stone, the winged man, the lion, the bull, and the eagle of the apostles. A copy of the Vulgate. She had been a novice, she knew its worth. Gold leaf, crimson, and blue and green-dyed leather shone bright.

Brother Rolf drew in his breath. He dusted his hands on his robe, took the Book, and smoothed the cover with faltering fingers. He opened it and held the first page to the light. Nell noted that his fingers against the paper held old ink stains. His voice came husky. "This is wondrous, lady, though I am not sure what I thought might come from such a bag as yours. A fighter, a woman and, it may be, a heretic. Though I do not hold fighting against you." He glanced aside at Kyrin, almost a glare. "I am a fighting monk myself, for all that I love books. I would learn more of this way of fighting, though I am soon to travel for a time. When I return I would cross staves with you." He leaned toward her, a hunting hound with prey in sight. "Where did you get such a treasure as this Book, lady?"

"My Subak master made the cover, and my sister Alaina Ilen scribed the letters while we were slaves in the house of Ali Ben Aidon. My sister wrote it for you."

"What? How could she know me?" His eyes narrowed, fierce, and he straightened.

"No, no, not for *you,* Brother Rolf, for our people, in our tongue." Kyrin gestured toward the village and the Brewmaster. "For those of us, like Nell, and others."

Nell's heart leapt, and she bit her tongue. Kyrin had promised to teach her to read. Her chance to learn had not passed with Cere or the end of her time as a novice.

Rolf's hands tensed on the Book in his lap, though his tone was level. "Do you seek to bribe me, to tempt Father Ulf?"

"No, Brother. I ask only that you let all read it, as often as they will in Bolton church. And that you encourage our people to take comfort in it." Kyrin paused, then said almost to herself, "True comfort is much needed, with my land as it is."

"Your land?"

Kyrin smiled but said nothing.

Brother Rolf sighed. "I will put the Book in a safe place in a church that especially needs it. First in mine, then I will carry it to another. It is too precious for one Abbey to hoard. You may come and read whenever you will. But glory to God!" Rolf smiled suddenly. "You are right, we need his comfort in our times, and every time. I will pray for you."

"My thanks, Brother. I need no absolution but his, but I thank you for your blessing and your prayers for my safety."

Brother Rolf said sharply, "Some of your words are heresy. Never think I do not watch you. "

"I do not fault you for that." Kyrin's smile seemed to push back the shadows creeping across the ring. "All of us should watch for deception. The father of falsehood hunts us all."

"Yes." Brother Rolf gathered the Book in his arms and stood. "Well, my earthly body calls for food and ale. I will tell Father Ulf you are no danger at the moment. But see you do not seek trouble. Father Ulf is sometimes—zealous, shall we say."

"As you will." Kyrin stood and brushed her trousers.

"One other thing. Whence came that black ring in your ear?"

"Ali forced it on me, to mark what he thought my evil eye. But Jesu kept me." Her hand rested on her neck pouch, and her face was sober. "My uncle dislikes me, I think, Brother. He loved me once. I know he loved my mother, Willa. Mayhap I crack the egg of tradition he sits on."

"Ah." Rolf shifted. "I know he deals with a great sorrow. It is why he seeks the peace and contemplation of the anchorite. And the king—but I may not speak of that. Would you open your pouch, lady? I would see it and what it holds also, if you will."

Kyrin frowned. Nell watched Rolf's mouth tighten. He missed nothing, for all that he was younger than Father Ulf. He did not miss Kyrin's hesitance nor the pale, rayed scar when she lifted her pouch over her head after a moment.

Nell kept her unease from her face. Brother Rolf seemed a good man, and his Lord would lead him aright. She would trust in that. Father Ulf—he was the one to watch—and he was Kyrin's uncle. Uncle or not, *he* would burn Kyrin's things as heathen—except the Book, which he would proclaim restored to the proper hands of the church.

Kyrin opened her pouch and slowly drew out a necklace of worn wood beads, a bright bit of irridescent shell in the middle. Brother Rolf reached for it. Kyrin drew it back then fastened it around her neck with a sheepish shrug. "It is only something my father made, but it is precious to me." She lowered her hands and handed him the pouch. "Now you may see them both properly." The shell in the midst of the necklace was carved in the shape of a fish, the early sign of the people of the Book. Streaked with purple and blue, green and rose it shimmered between the wood beads at her throat, over the scar.

"That blow near killed you." Kyrin said nothing. Thoughtful, Rolf bent his gaze to the embroidered cross on the pouch he caressed in his hand. At last he crossed himself and looked up. "I will not demand your second name, since you have not given it to Lord Jorn, though if Ulf is your uncle, I can guess. As far as I can see in God's light you are no sorceress, though you have secrets enough. Now they are mine." His face was young and stern at once, confident in command.

Kyrin bowed her head.

Nell crossed herself and returned Kyrin's things to her pack, biting her lip. Would her words help Kyrin or damn her? The night they met, Kyrin had muttered of in her sleep of a tiger, of falcons watching, and witnesses. And something about the touch of death.

Brother Rolf nodded, his face fell into grave lines, and he shook out his robe and strode past Nell. The moment was lost. But fever dreams bore little likeness to truth, that she knew very well from Cere's last ramblings.

Nell tugged her pale green cloak across her knees with uneasy fingers. Then she smiled. Lord Jorn's gift to her was soft wool. He had been kind beyond need. She wished Kyrin did not always look on him with suspicion.

As she thought of him, Lord Jorn stepped out of the inn. Near the door, with a thunderous frown, Father Ulf listened closely to Brother Rolf. Lord Jorn escorted Kyrin toward the Brewmaster, and Nell trailed behind, skirting Father Ulf, who put out his hand to stop Kyrin.

His fingers shook. "Wait—you say your sister is a scribe, who copied the Vulgate?" His eyes were avid with desire.

"Yes, Father, she did. Not my sister by blood, but by hearth and salt. She wrote it over the years." Kyrin shut her mouth.

"I see." Father Ulf pondered. "Such skill should not be lost, though given to a woman."

"If she comes, and circumstances allow, we will speak with you."

Father Ulf nodded and abruptly turned away.

In spite of Lord Jorn's short, "Well done," Kyrin did not smile. Her eyes glinted amber in the candlelight as she looked over her shoulder after her uncle.

Nell followed her gaze to the dark-robed Benedictines as they walked away, heads earnestly together, arguing. Brother Rolf had forgotten his stomach. He was missing God's gifts. Nell sniffed the steamy scent of seared hart in garlic, and carrot and onion stew.

The men and women who ate and drank at the long tables down two sides of the main room ignored Nell. Their cautious gazes followed Kyrin as she worked her way to a table. They feared anything they did not know, and fearing, they were cruel. Kyrin wished to belong, as she did; but her skin was too dark, her glance too direct, her stride too certain. A woman she was, and yet not such as any they had ever known.

Nell gripped her cloak tighter about her. A few of the Brewmaster's patrons were indifferent, oblivious to all but the bread, meat, and ale before them. Nell sat close to Lord Jorn, and Kyrin ate swiftly, finishing before Nell, who hurried her last bites of stew and bread.

With a grateful glance at her, Kyrin took their leave of Lord Jorn, who let them go with a good will. "I will follow with the shire reeve," he said. "Take Pellam with you. I would not have any accost you on the road."

Kyrin nodded, and Nell followed her to the stable where they found Pellam. "Pel, you are to follow us, by the kindness of your lord."

Pellam stared.

Kyrin reddened. "Ah, I beg pardon, sir. I but thought of you as Pel in my mind. You are rather like a goodly hawk-master I used to know. Forgive me."

The grizzled armsman grinned. "It rests easy on the tongue, Pel does. Call me so if you wish."

It was kindness after the cruelty of the day. Kyrin looked away and swallowed. Seeing the shine of tears in her eyes, Nell touched her arm. And Pel nodded and tacked up, and the bay was soon loaded with Kyrin's pack. They left the stable and turned toward Jornhold.

Nell's breath rustled in and out, their horses plodded down the track, and Kyrin rubbed her head where Hal's staff had hit. She swayed back and settled in the saddle with a long breath of relief. Burned dark by a fiercer sun than Britannia's, she moved like the cats in the wood that Cere had hunted, yet her touch was not ungentle. Her voice flowed soft to the ear, foreign, and yet it seemed Nell had known her forever.

Nell bowed her head, but a smile tugged at her mouth. Kyrin knew much of the Book, but little of a needle, if the work of her neck pouch was any sample. Little of a needle, but much of other things.

Things that would protect Nell against men like Thorgil, even if she learned a tenth of the knowledge Kyrin held. Nell kicked her tired feet out of the stirrups, contented. Here was a companion who did not wish her ill, who treated her as a sister. Father Ulf was foiled for the moment. Witch? Kyrin followed the Christ closer than some churchmen.

A robin sang beside the track, and a wren warbled back. Shadows fingered the green grass and first daffodils. Kyrin twisted her dark hair around her hand, smiled at Nell, and turned back to the road ahead.

Brother Rolf guessed her blood and her house from things he had heard from her uncle. And he did not condemn her. To be such a lady's companion was a dream beyond wildest thought. Did Kyrin yearn for a friend also?

15

Rangdo

Thou hast caused men to ride. ~Psalm 66:12

Nell found Kyrin outside in the sunrise beyond the end of their building, where she sat sewing a rent in her green tunic between bites of bread, cheese, and cold beef. Nell ate the portion Pel had left her, while men emerging from the barracks splashed the last sleep from their eyes in a great bowl of water in the yard, hooting with the chill. One called, "Was it a warrior or a lady you served, Pel?"

"Never a lady like our Myrna," another broke in.

Pel said sternly, "Not like our Lady Myrna, 'tis true, but a lady of honor nonetheless. She's both, I think—lady and warrior."

Bees buzzed over the wall that stretched left of the great hall door, the stones curved around the garden there. The new sun warmed Nell's back. A red and black butterfly fluttered among the yellow flowers that pushed through weeds in a planter balanced on top of the wall. Kyrin looked at Nell with a teasing smile.

"Do you feel up to a practice bout with Hal?" Setting aside her green mending she leaned forward, her dark hair and eyes lively against black tunic and trousers, the stick from her pack in her belt, a part of her.

"What?" Nell swallowed hastily. "He'll break me in two!"

"Hmm." Kyrin looked down at her fingers, brown against black. A grin pulled at the corner of her mouth. "Oh, yes. You are right. Hal is far too large for you to begin training with; but you can still watch and learn. You and I will practice together."

"I will—learn, I mean." Nell gulped.

"Good. With a staff in your hand, soon you will beat two such as he."

§

Hall was surprised when Lord Jorn's gate guard admitted him without demur when he gave his name as Hal Loring. Celine followed him through the wood and iron gate wide enough for two horses. Behind them, the gate and the stronghold's wall rose abruptly from the steep hill-shoulder. Nothing but short grass grew between Hal and the rampart. He cast an appreciative eye over the hall as they crossed the yard.

Jornhold had been built on an open right angle, the double-story wings joined at the center. The stretch of courtyard between the north and south wings made a quarter of a pasty pie, divided again by another low wall into eighths, one of which was a garden. Hal grunted.

Archers in the farthest wing could decimate anyone attempting to reach the iron-hinged, thick door of the north wing, and the same in reverse, supposing by some miracle an enemy made it across the bare expanse of the killing ground, over the wall, and across the yard. Before the porch and along the path to the step lay a bed of flowers, sere with winter dress. The farthest walled court held a bench for visitors, while the closer garden was bare rock and weeds.

Hal shook his head. Poor Myrna. He could not help being glad for her sake that Kyrin had beaten him, though he would never hear the end of Jorn's champion—until he learned Lady Kyrin's skill, defeated her, and stilled Thorgil's tongue. Hal grinned. Her skills would earn him coin with those who could hire him.

If only his foster daughter was more willing. Celine had wanted to learn how to use a staff since she came to his Breanna for help two years agone, but she emphatically *hadn't* desired to learn from Jorn's champion. Her feet behind him were dragging, and here was a better teacher. "Celine! Follow on, girl; follow on. She's a warrior, but she does'na bite, and you'll learn a thing or two."

He caught her hand and pulled her around the edge of the curving garden, and Celine lifted her chin and strode forward without him, her legs stretching her sturdy ankle-length tunic to its limit. She had brought trousers as well, for training in. Hal repressed a snort. He did not understand women, and sometimes he felt overwhelmed by his adopted eldest. Celine ought to be thankful she did not have to lie abed as Myrna did, for weakness.

Hooves thudded out of sight at the end of the hall's second wing, and he sighed and lengthened his stride. The wide ground before the barracks swirled with dust, where some of Lord Jorn's men engaged in mounted drill. Many hire-swords watched, and some watched him and Celine. All of them might soon come to battle, and they knew it.

Hal spat in the dirt. Old Lord Jorn was blessed not to see the rise of wolves such as the likes of Ludwin Mornoth and Nidfael Keffer.

Hal eyed scattered beeches and large oaks beyond the south end of Lord Jorn's sturdy hall and barracks. First leaves shaded the outbuildings, too far from the wall to catch a fire-arrow, and not near enough to threaten the hall if a hearth-fire started a blaze. He nodded approval. This morn he would learn new ways to defeat an enemy, and so would Celine. A woman with such knowledge could survive trouble, as Jorn's champion amply proved. But where was Lord Bergin Jorn?

The path back to the hall porch had been paved in Lord Bergrin's father's time; now a stone or two was missing. Pellam was the man to see in the lord's absence. My Lord Jorn has departed for my lady's medicine, in Lincoln." Pellam strode toward them, arm extended in greeting.

They clasped forearms, and Hal nodded to the grizzled armsman. "That is a hard three days ride."

"Ah, but my lord will make it quick." Keen eyes twinkling, the old armsman bowed to Celine and pointed to a building they had almost passed. "There is the one you seek." Kyrin and her companion, whom she had rescued from Thorgil, rested beside the door, watching them.

Hal's mouth tightened. He'd hoped Kyrin's purse was at least a little thicker for the bruises he'd received on Lord Jorn's account, enough that she need not beg a roof of him. But that was a thought unworthy of his lord. Hal rubbed his sore, shorn head.

Celine was good with the shears. This morn he would not give Jorn's champion the advantage of a handhold on his close crop. His blood rose with his grin, and he dipped his head. "Good morn, lady." Now to learn her foreign tricks.

Kyrin stood, and her companion dipped a curtsey. Celine stumbled beside Hal and found her feet with a glare. Kyrin stared at her, stiffening slightly. "Nell, will you fetch my pack?" Kyrin glanced again at Celine, as guarded as she.

Hal shrugged. Practice would sweat out Celine's bitter humor. Or, if he thought aright, Kyrin would knock it out. He would learn her secrets if he had to watch her a thousand days.

"Sir Hal." Kyrin's solemn bow belied the glint of laughter in her eyes. "Pel says we may use the garden. The dirt is softer there—for my sake."

Ha. The ground he had seen looked more like a bed of small rocks. Jorn's champion jested with him. His mouth twitched. He'd put but few blows on her during their match, for she seemed to know what he'd do before he did. Now she proved herself a wielder of words as well.

When Nell returned with Kyrin's pack, she kept on Kyrin's far side, watching Celine as they walked. Celine said nothing but busily looked about, eyeing Jorn's champion sidelong. Hal stifled a grin.

All in black trousers and tunic, a falcon sigil on her breast, with dark hair and eyes that could bore a hole through a man, not to mention the short ironwood stick she swung as she strode before them, Kyrin was rather fearsome. The more so when Hal remembered her speed and force. Jorn's champion could have killed him. He sobered. She might be just what Celine needed.

Celine was as his daughter. With hair near the same shade as his, she could be taken so. And she needed a strong woman's hand. She had so much of his Breanna's spirit, but less controlled. If she could learn to keep a softer tongue than she had with him this morn, it would serve her well in finding a man to care for her when he was gone.

In the middle of the garden, Kyrin stopped. Nell took a seat against the wall, Kyrin's pack in her lap, and Celine stood like a rock, her arms crossed.

Kyrin faced her, her expression still, careful, her lilting voice formal. She stared into Celine's eyes with strange force. "Is this another who would learn the discipline of Subak?" It might be she recognized a spirit like her own.

"My daughter, Celine," said Hal. He set his jaw. "She *wishes* to learn."

Celine lifted her chin, confident, her eyes hot. "Fear not, I will."

Hal wished again for Breanna's warm, kind hand in his. She would have broken the strange uncertainty that stood between them all with a laugh, an eager question, a smile.

Celine's face was stony. She ought to smile more, but she was not often so angry. In her green tunic she was shapely and graceful enough, and she lit with an aura of kindliness hard to resist when she smiled, bright as her copper hair. He found it so.

§

Kyrin looked at them a long, silent moment. Celine recognized her immediately, for all she'd changed. Would she speak? "Nell, stand there, with Celine. Hal, over here in front of me." When her new students were in their line, she bowed formally, and they awkwardly returned the gesture when she indicated they should do so. "You will discover things stranger than this. You have made yourselves my rangdo, my students. I own your flesh, your sweat, and your blood, for the time. If you have a need, speak to me of it. Know that the way of the warrior is won with pain."

Celine looked sidelong at Nell, who showed no sign of unease. Good. They were warned, and Celine said nothing, yet. "Stand so—" Kyrin showed them how to align themselves, knees bent, standing easy with the right leg drawn back, and blew out her breath. Tae had never hinted how much of his voice it took to teach.

Celine's appearance with Hal had startled her. Though Celine seemed to understand she wished to conceal her house. Though from Celine's challenging words, she was as headstrong and apt to find trouble as ever. There was a dangerous undercurrent smoldering in her eyes. Kyrin nodded soberly to herself. Rather what Tae once thought of her. She would speak to Celine of *why* when she could. Relations among the strongholds were too uncertain, under the rule of a failing king—and Bergrin *had* threatened her—what if he knew she was Cieri's stronghold daughter? She did not wish to tempt him with the coin a hostage would bring.

Quietly, Nell worked on her stance opposite Celine, whose words as they worked together were barbed. But Nell was a strong one, insults from Celine or no. Or maybe she thought to kick Celine wickedly hard, for her constant scowl. Kyrin suppressed her smile. Nell . . . Nell guessed more of each of them than she ever said. Kyrin was sure of it. But Nell did not know their first targets would be straw, bound around wood, until their stomachs strengthened enough to withstand each other's kicks.

Pel brought the mannikins Kyrin had requested, stacked them against the wall, inclined his head and left.

Kyrin pursed her lips. She did not have leather and cane armor for two. During the match with Hal she'd left it off to make the superiority of Subak clear. Now Hal's blows would only make her tougher, and she would need that in the days to come. Picking up one of the mannikins, she set it up before Hal.

"Here." Kyrin tapped the back of Hal's front knee with her stick, urging him to bend it slightly. "Now, when you kick, drive your back knee straight forward toward your opponent. Then turn your body, so, and kick your foot out." She demonstrated. Her roundkick thudded into the wood and straw "enemy" and knocked it flying sideways, spinning. "This blow can fell a man or disable him, if you strike the upper leg or take out the knee."

Nell learned the roundkick quickly, and she and Celine shared the next straw man. Hal made slower progress, but absorbed Kyrin's instruction as intently as her kicks to his stomach, carefully tempered to make him sore enough to gain by them but not drive his breath from him completely. She gave to his ponderous return kicks as a sapling to a falling oak, giving to the force and springing back into place, to deal out whip-quick return strikes.

§

Next morning, near the hall's central fireplace, Kyrin sat with Lord Bergrin, Hal, Nell, and Celine around a long table. A kettle of porridge just off the coals sat on the wood, raisin and cinnamon scents steaming from it. Kyrin's mouth watered, then dried. She would face Myrna this morn.

The medicine had worked well, and Bergrin would not hear of Kyrin leaving until Lady Myrna greeted her. To do otherwise would raise suspicion. So Kyrin wore her Persian trousers and tunic and her kaffiyeh, wound into a turban to conceal her hair. Charcoal circled her eyes, a crude sort of kohl. She was sure she looked a veritable a son of the desert.

When Nell had turned over in her blanket and caught Kyrin applying the last of the coal before the hearth, she'd stared, then smiled slightly. She'd dressed, humming to herself. Finished, she said, "Come, Kyrin, let us go inside. Lord Jorn has been courteous enough since he sheathed the sword he drew against you. His sister cannot be so bad. And the porridge is very good."

She'd said true, it was. Kyrin stared at the pot. Her stomach was in knots. The high, thin east window poured warm sunshine across the worn oak table and bathed their heads. Lord Bergrin and Hal's hair blazed white and red, while Nell's straight, dark sheen found a sparking partner in Celine's rebellious fall of copper curls. Kyrin felt her turban, assuring her honey braid had not come loose. Her fish necklace lay in the depths of her pouch. She had not worn the falcon, and felt naked, without defense.

There was a soft step in the doorway leading to the far wing. Bergrin raised his head, delight suffusing his thin face. "Ahh, Myrna, come, come!" He slid back his chair and escorted her to her seat, then sat on her left beside Hal.

Myrna did not sit at once. "You are well come to our table." Her voice was low and clear. Her cornflower eyes and quiet welcome made Kyrin aware all over again of how delicate Myrna always had been in speech and movement. Fifteen summers she would be. Her flowing blue kirtle and a cream mantle around her shoulders deepened her eyes, while her fine hair reached her waist, lifting as if alive around her hips, rejoicing in the sunlight.

Myrna glanced down then glided around the table, her feet tapping the grey flags. "I thank you for my medicine." She gripped Kyrin's hands, and started.

"Oh! Your hands are like Bergrin's, you must let me get you some of my oil, it softens them wonderfully—" Myrna put her hand over her mouth, her face burning as only one with a fair skin can. "My pardon, please, I did not mean ill; it's God's grace that your hands are rough—to raise weapons against my enemies." Her eyes pleaded for understanding as she stepped back.

Kyrin had not known what to expect, but she had not looked for a storm of confusion and memory. Kyrin frowned. Hal was no enemy, and Myrna named them more than one. Her bones were thin as a bird's. Kyrin folded her hands in her lap and made herself smile. If it was a ploy of Bergrin's, to spring his sister on her, how to foil him? "No harm taken, Lady Myrna, I am pleased for you. Your brother has been *most* hospitable."

"Has he? Yes, I've heard of his welcome for the warriors and mercenaries who pass by our hold." Her tone was dry and amused, and Bergrin gave his sister a rather embarrassed grin.

Kyrin smiled freely back at her. "I truly did little."

Myrna had grown. Before, she would have dared say nothing that might be construed as questioning another, let alone her brother. Myrna was her friend, those seasons agone when she was taken; even Celine had not left her apurpose. Was it best to reveal her name? Surely Hal would temper any ill-thought reaction of Lord Bergrin's. Myrna would not give her away . . . as sure as Seliam.

Myrna's grey eyes considered Kyrin. "I saw you all"—she nodded toward Hal and Celine—"and the one beside you, learning defense and attack in the garden."

"You mean Nell?" Kyrin challenged. She would not give up one friend for another.

Myrna hesitated then nodded. "Yes, I mean Nell. You say you have done little—may I join you in my garden tomorrow?" She seemed hardly to breathe after her last rush of words.

What possessed her to do such a thing? Myrna, gentle, sickly Myrna, wanted to learn Subak. The blood of a hare once brought down by Samson's dive had sickened her. The silence lengthened, and Kyrin swallowed. "You've been so ill . . ."

Myrna twisted her hands, her breath quickening, and she did not take her eyes off Kyrin.

"What if I wish her to learn?" Bergrin tilted his pale head.

Kyrin's lips thinned and she looked at him sharply, then at Myrna. So here was another reason he did not yet give her leave to go. Danger stalked here, running in the drumming of Bergrin's fingers on the table, in the tightness of Myrna's face, her tears near the surface. Tears of need. The helplessness of the prey before the hunter.

She knew that need, and it was greater than her own at present. The danger here was certain, she could feel it, and if she was of greater use to them free . . . Kyrin drew a deep breath. "You may learn with me, Lady Myrna. But—there is something you must know. All of you must know." It was surprisingly hard to raise her gaze to Bergrin's while her face burned. "Of your favor, tell no one. It could bring danger, to you and to me." Silence was thick around the table. Bergrin nodded.

Kyrin gripped the solid edge. She was again trusting her life to Another. "I'm returning home to Cierheld, from slavery in Araby."

Bergrin jerked back in his chair if he'd been slapped, and red rose in his pale face as he stared at her. Myrna's eyes widened, and she raised her hand to her breast. Bergrin muttered, "But that must mean—"

Hal looked from him to Kyrin, thoughts swift behind his eyes. "It means she is Kyrin Cieri, lost daughter of Cierheld. But her voice, her dress . . ." He stared at her.

"I have changed much, and I was freed to finish a task. Do not think ill of yourselves."

Straightening with a frown, Bergrin opened his mouth then shut it. He did not ask why she yet wished to conceal her stronghold name. He could probably guess.

Kyrin looked away from Myrna's wondering astonishment. "I'm going to my father. Then I must find one from Araby named Hamal, enslaved in a place called Cedsel. If I don't return with news or with Hamal by the first autumn moon, Shipmaster Ragad will send men after me. One of them is a man of the wolf-ships from the land of the north. I would not injure him. I also have two—companions—hunted in the sands by the wazir to the caliph, until I finish my task. I may not stay with you long." Kyrin forced her eyes from the pot of hot oats, far less threatening than the awed faces around her.

Bergrin crossed his arms. "The she-wolf gains a pup and soon will find her pack." He smiled, satisfied.

"My father—"

Myrna cried, her eyes shining, "I'll help you find Hamal! And you can teach me Subak on the way to Cierheld. The name Jornhold will bring you gossip, on your road!"

"It might be so." Or the name Jornhold might shut every mouth. Here were unknown currents of power.

Myrna whirled on her brother. "Bergrin, if I go, I'll be safe from Lord Ludwin, and you—you need not fear for me. That is, if Lord Dain agrees I may stay at Cierheld." She looked at Kyrin eagerly. "Ludwin—" A frown marred her brow, and she steadied herself with a hand on the table, her face paling.

Kyrin laid her hand swiftly over Myrna's. "By my oath of bread and salt, Cierheld is pleased to protect you." She was the first daughter of Cierheld and as such could extend the oath. Father would understand the need.

The blood came back to Myrna's face, and she said to Bergrin, "When Ludwin learns I'm gone, he'll look for another match, and he'll leave us alone, brother."

Kyrin said softly, "I've heard things of this Lord Mornoth and Lord Keffer before. What does Ludwin Mornoth want with you, Myrna?"

"It is well thought, this journey to Cierheld," Bergrin broke in. "It might suffice. If Lady Cieri truly wishes it."

Kyrin smoothed the sleeve of her tunic. Bergrin either did not yet wish to call Mornoth his enemy, or he shielded Myrna. A deft turn of the fox, heading off the hound. And he called her Lady Cieri. How had he thought of her when he held her at the end of his blade? But he had been ashamed of that, or seemed to be.

Hal leaned forward. "I have heard Lord Cieri and his men are good in a fight. It is clear where your fighting spirit comes from." He shook his head with a low whistle. "Lady Kyrin, of Cierheld. And your mother's blood comes from the hills . . ."

Kyrin said soberly, "Father and—and my mother were building Cierheld's walls and broadening our fields. Then Ali Ben Aidon's raiders killed her and Lord Fenwer, my godfather, and

I—I was taken." She pressed her lips together; she could not speak of it, not with Celine's hot gaze on her.

"Oh, Kyrin," Myrna whispered. Bergrin looked away, and Nell wiped tears from her cheeks without shame. Hal's neck reddened, his brown eyes stormy.

Then Bergrin's pale brows drew together in decision. "We must get you to Cierheld. Lord Cieri has enemies, and Lord Ludwin Mornoth is among them."

§

They set out in a misty dawn. Kyrin waited on her bay in the yard for the others, going over her gear a seventh time. Bergrin had loaned her the spirited horse—Keltie, to her mind. Keltie's ears pricked and she whickered and stamped, eager for the road.

Hal would come with them as armsman—to see that his Celine was a proper companion to Myrna, so he said. Celine had glared daggers at her foster father's back, but Kyrin was glad for his company. The road wound through dangerous places enough without her having to fight Celine's ill will. Celine had hardly said a word to her since that morn at table, where her scornful gaze and curled lip spoke loud enough.

Kyrin drew Keltie's reins through her hand. Hal knew nothing of Celine hunting and flying falcons in the woods with her before her capture. And then they were parted. Celine thought her at fault. But she had tried to escape, she had. Celine had once looked up to her.

"What are you doing on the lady's horse, boy? I walked the bay a'ready."

She swallowed, dropped her hood and turned.

"My pardon—Lady Kyrin." Hal nudged his white horse up beside Keltie. Kyrin had bound her womanly form, as she had on the ship, and wore her mended green tunic with a brown linen surcoat over top. "That smudge on your chin is something no lady would wear." He looked her over closely. "A serving boy's clothes, and ragged enough. You are not a warrior, are you, Kern?"

Kyrin felt odd, hearing his invented name for her, but it was similar enough to her real one that she did not startle at it. She smiled. "I'm glad I stood the test of your regard."

"Oh, the tunic would fool me—and Bergrin, I dare say. Though you are a trifle small—for a boy or a man." Hal's grin was sly.

"It is well enough." Kyrin ignored his amusement and lifted her hood again to warm her ears against the raw chill. Lord Bergrin's spare sword hung along her saddle, rolled in her blanket, her eating dagger was stuck through her belt. Her stick lay along her thigh, under her cloak. She'd slipped the falcon dagger from sight inside the belt of her trousers, but her recurve bow and quiver openly rubbed Keltie's shoulder. Hopefully, sighted at any goodly distance, it would be dismissed as a bow for small game.

Bows weren't considered serious weapons of war by her people—unless Father had changed their mind with his great war bow. Her weapon was a boy's, her sword carefully hidden. Kyrin steadied the pole in her right hand. Lord Jorn's house sigil dangled damply at the top.

The spear shaft was well used, the steel head concealed by a decorative tip of wood. Jornhold's pennant stirred in the rising foggy breeze. The sigil of a rearing horse snorting upon a dark green field, breaking an enemy spear between its forelegs, riffled out.

Yes, she was Kern the serving boy, until she opened her mouth. As she did now. "Most weapons tend to tangle with women's robes, except for the dagger or bow, one of which is child's play to weild, while the other keeps the enemy at a distance."

Myrna rode gracefully up on the other side of Hal. She pretended not to hear Kyrin. Tapping her sidesaddle on her dappled gray, a light short-sword was buckled under her cloak.

Kyrin frowned. Myrna had better learn to use that.

Hal fingered his sword and the spear in his hand then tapped the plain helm on his head. "We're well equipped," he grunted.

Celine spurred up beside them and tossed her hair back with a laugh. "*Of course* weapons mix ill with a woman's kirtle. That is why I wear them not, though none mistake *me,* whichever I don."

Her mouth thinning, Kyrin glanced at her. There was a slight contradiction in that. And Celine rode astride. Yet she held more of Esther's thought than once she had. Did she forbid herself the hunt with falcon or hound? Kyrin made her face a mask. She suddenly yearned for Cicero's warm tongue, his loyal almond gaze.

Celine mistook her. She did not disdain women's tunics, only wearing them with weapons, a foolish endeavor when an overlong skirt would trip one at the most inopportune moment. Girding a shorter tunic at the hips for the fields was a different matter than a lady's tunic, which flowed to the ground. And such girding would not work for horseback, not unless she ripped the skirt and bound it about her legs. Which was the same as trousers. But long tunic or kirtle, a well-fitted robe made her feel a lady. As beautiful as she would ever be. What would Celine have said if she wore her mail?

But she startled her companions enough with her sometimes quick movements. She did not wish to see Myrna and Nell draw back with uncertainty in their eyes.

And surely she was going to find her father, not to a battle. In Cierheld she would gladly leave behind threat of spilling blood to train her rangdo, to fly falcons in her woods and shoot the bow beside her father, at nothing more than straw. To bathe in Cierheld's waters, where there would be cress at the edges, bluebells on the banks and—

"Well," Nell chimed in from behind, "Our road does not get shorter, and I for one will relish a cushion this night."

"You *would.*" Celine turned in her saddle with a look of scorn.

Nell smiled, serene as a queen in a brown lady's tunic with a green mantle that brought out the brilliance of her mismatched eyes. "Yes, of course. Why ever not?"

Kyrin stared past Keltie's ears, covering a sudden twitch of her mouth with her hand. Their words were not for her to come between. Kyrin's heart beat faster.

Celine had not asked after her seasons in Araby, or spoken of Samson. In a hawk's years, he had to be old, if he yet lived. He had loved the oak outside her window, and the stream. It would not be long, and she would be there.

Lord Bergrin emerged a moment later from the stables, Pel in his wake with a pack-pony. He gave the the pack-pony's lead into Kyrin's hand and cleared his throat. "Fare well. Guard my sister as you would your own." He shot a glance at Hal, who bowed silently.

Kyrin bowed also. "You have my oath, my lord, and I thank you. We'll send word as soon as we may."

Lord Bergrin Jorn bowed over her hand and Kyrin swallowed back her sudden laugh. A lord's son, bowing to her, in a serving boy's dress. But Bergrin was not all bad, not as insufferable as Keffer, or even Celine. That did not mean she would handfast any such as he.

Bergrin drew back, and Kyrin nudged Keltie forward. At the gate, Pel raised his hand in salute, and his old gaze followed them out.

Nell and Celine gradually grew quiet as the mist thickened along their road. Jornhold soon disappeared. Smelling of green woods, the wet gathered in pale beads on their cloaks, weapons, and the horses' manes. For miles nothing disturbed the silence but a horsey snort, the sigh of cloth, the creak of leather or thud of hooves. The mist was a part of their belonging to the road, winding among quiet, dark-limbed trees. Hazel and ash stands and thickening gorse, a cavalcade of those heir to the blood of the hills of olden time; riding with a message, or off to a war or a feast.

Kyrin's fingers numbed on the pennant spear shaft, and she warmed her hand under her arm, switching the shaft and her reins to her other hand. Vague hillsides emerged and disappeared through the grey.

A shaft of sunlight broke the mist, catching a sheen of water over fresh horse prints that marred the muddy road.

Hal jogged his mount forward. A robin sent a joyful note ringing from a flat verge of grass between the road and wooded hillsides around them.

Hal leaned to inspect the prints. "Left less than a bell ago, I'd say." His breath plumed white, and he straightened, his red brows bushy below his helm. "They're moving ahead of us. Could be a messenger."

"So it could." A raven croaked, and his unseen fellow answered. Kyrin's skin crawled, and she lifted her head with a silent plea to the lord of all. It could be anyone. But as Tae said, better safe and alive than sorry and dead. "Let's get off the road."

She turned Keltie toward the trees, and the others followed. The tall trunks and dripping bracken gave away nothing. The woods were empty and wet and cold. She was a fool.

Yet Kyrin's unease grew. Keltie walked on, hooves thudding dull as bone on the wet earth.

Ahead, the road cut between high banks. Kyrin fell back, watchful. Myrna shrugged and sighed, but Celine's lips curled, and she spurred to the fore.

In the midst of them, Hal's gaze moved ceaselessly. Nell watched Kyrin. A stick snapped on the steep left slope. Kyrin looked up swiftly.

On the height, bare trunks stretched between dark fir boughs. A litter of fallen branches lay beneath, old and pale. At the edge of the mist near the crest stood a man in leather. He drew his longbow, leveled the arrow among the bright leaves of young trees struggling among the trunks.

The razor head winked, a prick of light.

16

Attacked

Eyes like doves beside streams of water. ~Song of Solomon 6:12

Aimed at Nell—and the others. Kyrin kicked Keltie, forceful with fear, and Keltie jumped forward as Kyrin screamed, "Left! Bowman!" The man took a step, and was gone into the grey wreaths.

Kyrin dropped Jorn's pennant in the dirt and fought to untie her bow as Keltie thundered past Hal toward Nell and Myrna. Hal was alert, spear ready. He heeled his horse into a gallop, back onto the road.

The opposite hillside and the road seemed deserted but for Celine, galloping through low bracken, her horse swinging around Kyrin to join Hal.

Kyrin watched the trees, leaning low to close with Nell and Myrna, bent over their horses' necks, their hands white on the reins, faces tense. Then her bow was free, and she nocked an arrow. Where was the bowman? He had not looked as if he bore his weapon for deer, aiming at them. At the rear, Hal's shield was up.

Then three riders crashed down through the bracken toward him. Kyrin sat back in the saddle, and Nell's face turned toward her. "Go!" Kyrin yelled, and pointed up the road. She desperately hoped they had drawn them all to this spot and there were not more men ahead.

The horsemen pulled up before Hal, two swordsmen and a spearman. Hal had his hands full, and Celine had no weapon, but she could not help them, for the bowman could strike from a distance. She was their only guard against him. Kyrin swung Keltie after Myrna and Nell, arrow ready. Could she break through the ambush? She looked ahead.

Men with spears rose from the grass, two on each side of the road, flanking Nell and Myrna. Kyrin kicked Keltie forward, raising her bow. But they were too close to Myrna. They did not throw their spears. Kyrin had time to think it odd. Then a heavy blow out of nowhere twisted her out of the saddle.

She tucked her chin instinctively. The ground came up and slammed her shoulder and off hip with vicious force. She came out of her roll and rocked to her feet, half-stunned, her bow gone.

With a shout, a man ran toward her, spear lifting. Kyrin stumbled for the trees and tripped in grass that wrapped her boots. The first tree trunk rose before her. She saw a spear shaft swing up. Pain drew a curtain of darkness around her.

§

Kyrin swam to her senses in flickering firelight. Her forehead throbbed as if it might separate from the rest of her, joined somehow by the pain in her shoulder. Damp leaves tickled her neck. Crushed bracken spiced the air. She heard nothing, and curled her fingers. Her hands were tied in front of her. It was night.

A rough fist closed in the front of her tunic. Kyrin gasped for breath and tensed, fighting not to alarm the owner of the fist. Her ankles were tied too.

"The boy's waken' up, let's have some fun."

"As you please, Curnoth. You've made us wait this long. Said it's nicer, they get to see what's coming," growled a deep voice, full of rough amusement.

"Haven't you ever seen a rabbit squeal, John? He ought to sing well, young as he is."

A small fire glowed like a forsaken ember on Kyrin's left. The huge shadow of Curnoth curled over her.

John spat. "Let's do it, or are you going to talk all night? The ale warms."

Curnoth's grip tightened and he pulled her up. Kyrin's stomach turned over and helpless numbness washed through her as Curnoth's other hand closed heavy on her shoulder. *Wait.*

He pushed and pulled; her tunic ripped. His knuckles brushed her throat, and the old scar.

Kyrin came out of her limpness with a lunge, kicking for Curnoth's shins then slamming her bound hands for his throat. Her feet connected. Curnoth dropped her and fell back with a roar.

Kyrin hit the ground, arching like a landed fish so she took the brunt of the fall rocking on her middle and forearms, and saved her head and chin. Pulling her legs under her, she hopped on toes and bound hands through shadows in frantic haste for what she hoped was a large verge of bracken beyond the reach of the firelight.

Curnoth roared, "Light the torches, fools!" The men moved toward the fire and bumped and cursed. One of them, smarter than the rest, yelled, "Quiet!"

Silence spread under the trees, and Kyrin stopped in the dark. To close, torches flared into flame. She turned her head, and in the moment that most of them were blind, she burst forward.

They caught her in a few strides. Their fingers dug into her arms and legs. Kyrin took a few hard kicks, the last of which left her breathless and groaning. Five of them heaved her between them and carried her back to Curnoth.

"The rabbit didn't get far, and it's lost its voice."

"Hah! Unless he's mute, John, Curnoth'll find it for 'em soon enough." The men laughed. One growled as he leaned over Kyrin, and she flinched at the click of his teeth a hairs-breadth from her nose. He chuckled and cuffed her. They threw her down and she hit the ground mercilessly.

Kyrin stared up at Curnoth, trying to stop the tears rolling down her cheeks.

"Not a spineless rabbit, eh? What should we do with a rabbit that thinks it's a fox, John?" Curnoth turned to the grinning men crowding around them under the flaming brands.

"See if it's got any jewels!" A whip-thin man cried.

"What? On this?" Curnoth shook Kyrin until her teeth rattled. "You crazy, John? This is a serving boy." He turned in mock concern to Kyrin. "You wouldn't have any gold, would you, boy? You caused us plenteous trouble."

Kyrin hoped that meant Hal and the others had gotten away. Horses nickered near the fire, not her companions' mounts. Curnoth slapped her viciously. Kyrin's cheek burned. She looked back at him. "N-no, I don't."

"We'll see, boy, if I have to pare you to the bones." Curnoth slipped the eating dagger from Kyrin's belt.

John and another man stretched her out on the leaf mold, pulling her bound hands above her head, her ankles anchored between the other's knees.

There were more men around her, and the trunks of tall, thin trees. The end of her stick dug into her side. They'd not taken it. But the falcon blade was gone.

Curnoth knelt. "Any money bags here, eh?" he drawled. The dagger slid tickling along Kyrin's stomach. He slowly cut her shirt and tunic straight up the front, grinning as he watched her. Kyrin stared at the sky, her stomach cold. *Lord! Lord!*

Curnoth's men looked on, whispering. "A brave youngling."

"Aye."

"We'll have more fun with 'em."

In a sudden pause, they stared at Kyrin's bronze stomach and the pale whip scars laced around her sides. One whistled. John muttered, "A slave—Bergrin doesn't keep slaves." "But there's—"

Not heeding their chatter, Curnoth leaned forward. He ran his dagger point from Kyrin's ear around her chin, gentle as a lover, then gripped her leather neck pouch and snapped it free. Her shirt parted the last few inches to reveal the cloth wrapping her chest.

"A woman!" Curnoth grunted and sat back. The men holding her leaned in. Kyrin snapped her hands and feet toward each other with all her strength.

Heads cracked together. Kyrin threw herself over Curnoth's body. Ignoring cries of pain, she rolled, gaining speed. Sticks and rocks scraped, she didn't notice. Someone dropped on her back. Kyrin twisted and bit, moving every part of her that would. Blows thudded, and her sight dimmed.

She didn't hear the men's horses mill in panic and scatter into the dark, their riders scrambing after them. She did not feel strong hands grab her under the arms and pull her deserted body into the shrubbery, then through a long stretch of bracken. The warmth of a running horse and the panting figure that held her, looking over his shoulder to make sure they weren't pursued, did not wake her either.

Kyrin opened her eyes to the light of stars. She lay on her back on a blanket, wool by the smell, in an open place. Firelight flickered in the corner of her vision. *Curnoth.*

Chill raised her skin. She curled convulsively and her hand closed around a small dagger. She didn't think, just moved—rolling away from the fire. Blackness and pain crashed over her in a wave.

When she woke again, there was no dagger in her hand. Her palm burned with a line of fire. She turned her head carefully. Her neck-pouch, the falcon blade, and Tae's stick were gone. But her arms and legs were free.

Someone crouched, black against the light, tending the blaze. The snapping heat was closer this time. Her mouth was dry as chaff.

Kyrin reached for her throat. The cool touch of the fish was petal soft. Her necklace had been taken out of her pouch and put on her. The trees above were alders, instead of the firs beside the road. Where was she? They seemed alone with the fire.

Kyrin tried to sit. She could not stop her low sound of pain. The crouching figure whirled and then rose slowly, a jug swinging loosely from his hand. It was a man.

Nothing on him jingled as he moved; he seemed to wear no mail, hold no weapon. His slender silhouette lacked Curnoth's breadth. A careful arms length from her, he stopped and extended the jug without a word. Kyrin couldn't see his face for the crackling fire behind him.

She held her breath, reaching for the jug. Her shoulder protested when he let it go, and she dropped it with a gasp. He picked the jug matter-of-factly from the grass and helped her raise the lip of fired-earth to her mouth.

Kyrin drank thirstily. Pure water and something else—tangy mint. When the tears began to trickle silently down her face he eased her to the blanket again. His tunic smelled of fire smoke and horse, and somehow the wild-sweet of oat straw. The fire gleamed in his hair. He said softly, "You're miles from where you were." He considered every word, as if he thought she might bolt again. "We're outside their reach now, I think. We're well hidden here. I'm Talik."

"Did you see—others in their hands?" Her voice came hoarse, rising at the end.

"No. I chanced upon the swine that had you in the dark. I didn't see or hear any others. You had companions?"

"Yes. A red-haired armsman, Hal Loring, and Lord Jorn's sister, Myrna Jorn. My companion, Nell, and Celine, Hal's daughter." Kyrin swallowed a lump in her throat.

Talik sighed. At last he said, "It's usual in these parts to hold hostages for ransom. You'd better get some sleep if you can."

Kyrin tried to find rest beyond her throbbing body, but dark thoughts kept her eyes open, though she could do nothing for Nell and the others. At last she slipped into dream.

A harsh orange paw with piercing claws smothered her mouth. Kyrin opened her eyes with a cry, hands knotted in her blanket. There was a man's arm in front of her. He was close, full of threat. She struck the upper muscle with the edge of her hand, found a grip, jerked his arm straight, and twisted. Pulling herself up, she thrust her attacker down with a blow behind his elbow. Her elbow continued toward the back of his neck. Her arm lock forced his face into the dirt.

She was on her knees beside Talik. "Aaagh! Easy, easy!" His breath blew dust. Panting as if she had run an Eagle mile, she noted the back of his brown hand, locked in hers, was smeared with ointment so pungent her eyes watered.

Kyrin released him. "I—I'm sorry."

Talik curled his arm to his chest and straightened, still on his knees. He stared at her, as at a mouse become a wolf. Without his arm to hold to, Kyrin swayed and pain knifed her ankle and shoulder. With a quiet hiss through her teeth she gave to it and sank sideways to the blanket. Her stomach rose in her throat; she thought it wise to stay down.

Talik rubbed his wrist, his mouth pursed in a frown, his eyes narrowed. She had not meant to hurt him. *Just breathe.* Kyrin lay still.

His grey-blue gaze was steady, his tan face surrounded by tousled hair the color of straw. He must be out much in the winter. The good scent came from him, of sweet wild oats from the lower fields. Hence the hair. She almost smiled.

His strong mouth tightened, and Kyrin's face burned. He must think her ill-mannered or ungrateful. She dropped her eyes. At least her tunic was presentable, held tightly closed in her unhurt fingers. She glanced at his lean hand glistening with ointment then risked his face again.

He was looking away from her at the dawn-lit trees. Straight and streaked with darker glints, his hair reached his shoulders. A leather surcoat over a green, long sleeved tunic fit him well. Good colors for woods-travel.

He turned back to her grimly. Kyrin wished her face didn't sting with scratches. How to tell him she'd reacted to the threat of his nearness, not to him? Now that she was over her fear, she realized his hand had felt—right, in her grip. Strong, gentle, alive.

She bit her lip. Of course alive. His blood beat strong in his body, did it not? She felt unaccountably silly and irritated. Kyrin lifted her head and her vision swam. She grimaced and glared at the sky. She did not need this, or him.

Talik smiled, a careful smile that did not bait her. "This may help." He lifted a small earthen pot of ointment from the ground. Kyrin sniffed at it, doubtful of the contents. It was the same as that on his hand.

"Hawk likes it, licks it off." He motioned to his sleek brown mare cropping the grass nearby. His lips twitched. He was trying not to laugh, and Kyrin turned her head away. Everything hurt. It reminded her of the beating from Seliam, when he and his companions caught her in Ali's garden. But that traitor was far away, now. And he had been sorry.

She gathered her dignity with a breath and turned back. Talik spread the ointment on her head where the spear had struck. So, she might trust too easily, but he'd had her at his mercy in the beginning. Still did, hurt as she was, if he truly wished her harm. He'd given her necklace back. The ointment took away the pain considerably, though her ankle clamored for attention, and another, closer need.

"Can you sit?" He took her unhurt hand.

With his help, Kyrin was able to keep herself upright and ignore his warm hands. *Quit being a fool.* She moved her arms and legs carefully, while Talik watched.

"Did they break anything?"

"I think not." The ankle, her shoulder, and her head might take a little time to heal nonetheless.

Talik let out his breath. "Good. I bound up your ankle. I'm sorry I couldn't get you out sooner. Tying a bloody squirrel skin to a horse's head is uncertain work."

"I thank you. Most wouldn't have tried, especially against so many."

Talik laughed, short and sharp. "It proved an easy thing, after I got their horses running. Lord Mornoth's men ran after them, and I just dragged you into the bushes, to Hawk there, and rode."

"Well, you have my thanks." So they were Mornoth's men.

He stared into the fire. "I was pleased to do what I could." There was a pause while the fire snapped. "What do I call you?"

Kyrin looked at him a long moment; the name Kern would not hold water with him. "I am Kyrin. My companions and I were on our way to Cierheld. If Lord Mornoth has them, I must find them."

"You would go after them? You are not well enough to ride; you would simply fall into their hands."

Kyrin's mouth worked. "I *won't* leave them to the men who had me." She struggled to rise, and made it up with Talik's arm under hers. "They had a white horse-head sigil on their tunics." Her legs decided to hold, despite her head.

"That would be Nidfael Keffer's sigil. He has dealings with Lord Ludwin Mornoth." Talik's voice deepened. "A dangerous lord, and a wolf to his own people. Keffer admires him."

"A pox on them," Kyrin said bitterly. But after the water Talik gave her, one close need would be denied no longer. "I need a bush."

Talik let her go. Moments later she wavered out from behind some thick gorse, tears falling fast. Talik jumped for her, too late. She sank in a heap.

"I can't walk—" Kyrin turned her head and wiped her face. She must be strong—why didn't the Master of the stars make her strong? Nell and the others needed her.

"Kyrin." Talik touched her shoulder, turning her. "I'll help as I can. But you need to heal. Then we can do something. Until then, leave your companions in God's hands. They are only safe there."

Kyrin blinked. He did not have the tonsure of Brother Rolf, or ink on his fingers, though his long body had the leanness of a scribe, or a runner. Yet he said truth. "I thank you again, sir."

"I'm Talik"—he grinned—"no 'sir.'"

"As you say."

His grey eyes, changeable as the sea, stirred with deeper flecks. "So, you know our Lord?"

"If you mean the Lord of the Holy Book, yes I do. Or rather, he knows me."

"That is well." Talik watched her.

She returned his smile, short and uncertain. How had that inane "He knows me" slipped out? She had better watch her tongue, or she'd be telling him about her father and Cierheld, Hamal, and the falcon dagger and its Damascus steel. Lost though it was.

Talik settled her comfortably and left to scout the road on Hawk. Sext bell came and went with the high sun, though the bell of no church reached here. Kyrin dozed under the whispering alders. Bees buzzed in the grass. When she woke again the shadows were longer.

"You're awake." Talik said, Hawk's reins in his hand, his pack loaded behind the saddle. "Are you well enough to move? I'd rest easy with more trees between us and Lord Keffer's stronghold." His face was closed.

"Lord Keffer's stronghold is near? Why don't we ride for Lord Jorn's? He'll help. And I must tell him of Myrna."

A shadow passed over Talik's face. "I know a good camp a little north of here; you won't get far with that leg. It's dangerous to leave you long enough to get a message to Jornhold." His mouth was set. He sounded as if he knew Bergrin.

He would not go, and he was right about her leg, though he was not telling her all.

Talik did not wish to travel on the road, and Kyrin dripped sweat by the time they covered two Eagle miles, clutching Hawk's pommel with a white-handed grip. Her swollen ankle stabbed her with Hawk's every step.

They stopped in a cup of meadow in the wood, the trees a mixture of hazel, oak, and alder. A wall of blackberry thorns guarded the edges of the clearing. The grass was scattered with bluebells, their sweetness rising in the evening. "Oh!" Tears of more than pain came to Kyrin's eyes.

Her mother had loved bluebells, had woven her a crown of them on her name-day, when she became Cierheld's first daughter. Kyrin found herself shaking. She was overwrought, that was what was wrong with her, and she'd best sleep plenty and eat more. The tears and weakness would pass. Only—she snuck a glance ahead—she'd keep them from Talik if she could.

At her exclamation he'd grunted, staring ahead. But he was watching her now. Kyrin paused. His eyes were shadowed; he'd taken every watch during the night.

She got down from Hawk and clung to the saddle, reluctant to put weight on her foot. "Do you have any sleeping or fever herbs? Hops, mayhap?"

"No. But there are willows by the water, and there might be chamomile about."

"That would be well." The herbs had similar properties.

Talik went to look for them, and Kyrin shook out their blankets on the long grass, hobbled around to start a small fire, and sat down to rummage in Talik's pack. She had lost hers, and her neck pouch from Araby. Talik said he had not seen them. The necklace had caught on his boot when he found her, and he'd snatched it up.

The falcon blade her mother left her, with her bow and Bergrin's sword, all were gone. Her tears ran freely again. She had only Tae's stick. *But,* she said to herself fiercely, *my father is near. And my Father above.*

Talik returned from his search to a fire and a boiling soup of dried meat and a lone potato. He dropped his load of branches beside the small circle of flames. Laying a mound of crisp watercress on top of the wood, he reached in his belt pouch and brought out peels of willow bark and the soft green-yellow of feathery chamomile. "I found them." He shook damp soil from the chamomile roots and laid the bunch in her hand. Kyrin sniffed deep of the light flowery smell. "My thanks."

Munching a little of the cress, she dropped the rest of the spicy herb in the soup. "Might you teach me what you know of herbs? It has been long since—I have been in Britannia." Though she'd not forgotten her mother's lessons, there was always more to learn.

"As you will, when we may." Talik's hands were wet, his hair slicked against his head, bristling again as it dried. He smiled wearily and sniffed at the thin stew with a hungry look.

Kyrin chewed on a bit of chamomile. It was strong. She swallowed and pointed with her chin at Talik's pack. "Who are the sealed messages for? You carry no weapons." There had been nothing, nothing but the blade at his side.

Talik paused the briefest moment, then sat, stretched out his legs, and leaned against his pack. "They are not yours or mine to open." He made a fist and studied it. "I used to be a squire. I've been a juggler, sometimes an acrobat—now I'm a pilgrim on my way to the high hills. Some call them the moors. I left home young. Now I'm going back to see my parents." His ears were red, though it could have been the wavering firelight.

"Are you good with a blade?" Kyrin asked, curious. He had not answered her question.

"A sword fits my hand well and I take pleasure in the challenge of mock combat, if that's what you mean. I do not enjoy killing." His eyes challenged her across the flames, steely.

Did he think she enjoyed blood? Kyrin did not let her gaze drop; she was neither weak nor a murderer.

Gazing at her steadily, Talik played with a stick, shredding the bark with his fingers. "You have knowledge of weapons? But I should not wonder at that. You kept me back easily enough when you thought I might harm you." He glanced at her trousers. Hawk raised her head, her chewing loud.

Kyrin cleared her throat. "I have been taught to keep myself from harm, and to wield a blade, yes . . ." He already didn't think her womanly, by his glance at her garb. She might as well tell him the whole. She looked down then forced her chin up. "I wouldn't have you think I wish to be thought equal to a man. I'm not. Not in strength. Though I am in weaponry and in knowledge. I mean, I wish to live if I am attacked, and keep"—her voice caught—"keep those I love from death, if I can. Subak is a beautiful thing, and strong and good, though I do not always love what I have had to do with it." She stumbled to a halt.

"Subak. So that is the name of your skill. It has a foreign sound. Are you a mercenary from the East?"

"No!" She frowned. "Though my Subak master may have been. He—he was my husband, in name only." She cleared her throat again. "Our Araby master wished us to break God's law and man's. But Tae Chisun is most honorable, a warrior beyond any I have known. His wife Huen waits for him in the Land of the Morning Calm. It was not for lack of teaching or skill that I fell to Curnoth." Her pride in Tae rang in her voice, mingled with pain.

Talik nodded absently and stared into the dark beyond the coals, rolling the naked stick in his hands. He opened his mouth then closed it.

Because she had fallen, Nell, Myrna, and Hal were gone, everyone. As Talik so pointedly had not said, she had failed. A breath caught in Kyrin's throat with unshed tears. "All weapons fail under too great a number of enemies." She hoped Celine had the wit to keep her head down.

Startled, Talik looked at her. "I did not mean you ought not to have fallen."

"We were ambushed, and I was hit in the head and . . ." Kyrin shrugged, miserable.

"A dizzy head does rather keep one down." Talik laughed gently. Kyrin almost smiled. It had been too long since she'd heard anyone laugh. He dropped his grey gaze to his toes. His mouth flattened, twitched, then turned grim. He didn't say what made him sad, amused, and angry at once. She liked the way the skin around his eyes creased with his laugh.

After they ate, Kyrin kept watch through the dark until the healing softness of the willow crept over her in a wave of drowsiness. She woke Talik and nestled into her blanket. Talik would watch after her until the dawn, but she had given him a small respite. In the morn she would think of a way to find Nell and the others.

17

Countermeasure

From the fortress even to the river. ~Micah 7:12

Talik knew he must watch the mile-distant road like a hawk. While Kyrin soaked her ankle in a nearby spring, chill with the last breath of winter, he gathered news from a man he had long trusted. The woodcutter had relatives in Lord Keffer's hold, who had been cheated of wages by their lord.

At Talik's inquiry of unusual doings he said sourly, "Oh, aye, that one caught a prize near here just yester." The woodcutter stared at him, chewing the edges of his mustache, axe over his shoulder. "I've never seen you this close. You're the western lords' messenger aren't ye?"

At Talik's nod, the woodcutter shook his head. "Well then, I know yer' voice if nothin' else, and you should know what passed in these parts. Keffer's na *my* lord." He glared through the pale hair hanging in his face, daring Talik to say nay.

Talik nodded; he could not but agree.

"Well, as of yester-morn, Lord Keffer lets none in or out of his stronghold without clear business or urgent errand. It's said he left a serving boy what was caught to his men's mercies. He took the rest to his stronghold and put 'em under guard by the north gate. One was a lord's daughter, an would na' serve him as he willed. Lord Keffer put her out too, tied to a stake." He nodded wisely and leaned closer to Talik's ear. "They also say she took ill words and filth as meek as my own wife, though I'd never treat 'er so, and ate off the ground as humble as Keffer's dogs. My aunt even said she bought herself and her companions water from the guards with kisses." He scowled thunderously, his mustache bristling. "They've na' been further hurt. Na' that that's na' enough. I'd give my arm to strike a blow for me own." He hefted the axe in his hand.

Talik clapped him on the back. "I thank you for your news. This will not sweeten men's hearts toward Lord Mornoth or Nidfael Keffer. But stay, man, is it not Lord Cieri who keeps mercenaries in his stronghold? I may not retrace my road, but I may have found one of his strays. Give Lord Cieri this"—he pressed a scrap of linen wrapped about a thin bundle into the woodcutter's hand—"as proof of my word. I will pay you well. Lord Cieri may find me here in two days." He gestured at the crossroads.

The woodcutter's hands closed on the bundle. "Oh aye, I will deliver it." He turned away, a big man, with the look of a north-man, but then stopped short. "Lord Keffer says this to any who would take his prize from him—'They will all hang on the wall for the crows—except she who will wed Lord Ludwin Mornoth, stripped of even the tunic from her back, if I receive no dowry in three days.'" He grunted. "Lord Bergrin Jorn will na' be able to meet that, na' in three days."

"I fear he will not. But that's for the lords to worry their heads over, not for the likes of us." Talik saw him off, and soberly wished he'd been to Lord Keffer's hold more often. Nidfael Keffer's messenger to Lord Jorn had gone astray; or had Nidfael even sent one, knowing Lord Jorn's impoverished pockets?

He repeated the woodcutter's news to Kyrin.

§

"Myrna!" cried Kyrin. "He speaks of Myrna—and says he'll kill the others?" Kyrin glared at him so her tears would not fall. "It's usual to keep hostages, is it? And it is at least a hard day's ride to Lord Jorn's for help, and another back, and the same to that rat's stronghold!

Talik turned from her to rub Hawk's sweating neck. "Yes, so it is," he muttered. "But Lord Keffer's a different breed. I'd hoped—but we could do nothing else. You needed the rest."

"I know," Kyrin said softly, her face warming. "I need at least a day more to plan—then to ride for help would make four."

"Yes, we will do what we can. And that is more than you may think."

He was going to help her. Kyrin swallowed. If Tae were here he would already be mapping out the hold, watching the hold's sentries, planning three different ways in and out. Alaina would be gathering needful herbs and readying her staff.

But Tae and Alaina were across the ocean, and she was alone. Alone but for the Master of the stars, who had felt far away since that brief moment by the fire, when she spoke of him to Talik.

Kyrin bowed her head, gripping Tae's stick instead of the comfort of the falcon blade. Cicero did not wait at her heels, his sharp almond eyes eager. There was only this stranger, who had left off his training and did not like killing. He seemed concerned enough for Myrna and respectful of Lord Jorn's interests.

Kyrin glanced at Talik, who knelt, a twig in his hand, frowning at a patch of dirt he'd cleared.

If only she knew that he regarded her father the same. Before Ali took her, many of the lords had despised Lord Dain for his assertion that the peace could not last; there was no unifying force among them, though Lord Dain supported the king as holding the last of what will for peace remained.

Talik sketched out Lord Keffer's stronghold in the dirt, frowning in thought.

Kyrin bent over the rough map; it was a rare man who knew such things. He had not told her all of who he was, not even his surname. As she had not told him. She bit her lip.

Talik laid a large jagged rock on the ground at the edge of his sketch. "This is a steep ridge behind the stronghold. It backs the fortress with a sheer cliff-face." He laid his dagger before the rock, and on either side a line of sticks with two upright on either end. "Two gate-towers rise on the eight-foot thick wall in front of Keffold, here and here. The wall curves like a half-moon to join the ridge." He dug the point of his drawing stick into the ground beside the rock. "The cliff cradles the hall and outbuildings. Each gate-tower houses twenty men, for it is no secret Lord Mornoth favors Nidfael, foot-licker as he is, and lends him men."

"Do you know the bells of their watches?"

"Yes. Two men in the tower above each gate. They change at every bell, standing watch on rotation. The double-leafed gate allows horses to walk through side by side, when Keffer and his ladies go in and out, and wagons deliver food from the farms. The southwestern slopes of his fields yield richly. But he is no lord to his people." Talik's jaw tightened. He stared stormily at Kyrin. "That gate that should serve contented families opens grudgingly for hungry landholders, and traveling merchants who mutter behind their hands of heavy taxes enforced by Mornoth's men." He wrenched his dagger from the earth and rose. "It should not be so!"

Kyrin stepped back. He felt for Keffold's people. "Talik, is—is Lord Nidfael your lord?"

"Hah! How can you think so? I would sooner rot."

As Hal and Nell and Celine would rot in three days, on the wall. Kyrin frowned, curling her hair about her fingers, listening to Talik's low voice as he went on to tell her that Lord Keffer could call forty men from his landholders, besides his hired three score, and who knew how many of Mornoth's.

A hank of Talik's hair flipped back and forth in the wind sighing through the alders. Shadows danced around him in the stiffening breeze as cool evening peered through the high, tangled blackberries. Kyrin reached to rub her itching ankle; the swelling was down. She would soak it as she could while she plotted.

Over supper she told Talik her plan.

He said, "It's risky to leave ropes on the wall."

"We will not need to." Kyrin smiled and leaned forward to draw a pattern beside the fire. Talik leaned over, listening to her description.

Next morn, he left before Kyrin woke and returned near dark with a roll of soft leather, a cloth bundle that clanked, and a sway-backed mare. He would have preferred a mule, but the nag was the only beast for sale, for love or coin he said.

Talik's smile drifted through Kyrin's mind as she carefully ground the fruit of his labor razor sharp with his whetstone. During Subak training Tae had once laid a forged iron frame, long and black, in her hand. It had arched claws extending from it. "Some of the warrior clans west and north of my land have astonishing skills of spying unseen in their enemies' midst. Skills unknown until my master learned, at great risk, how they got inside fortresses thought impregnable." Tae had raised the claw in his hand to clink against the one she held. "They make these for their hands and feet, and wind cloth or leather about them. They are not unlike the webbed shoes for snow walking in your land, except for the claws like a bear's paw. They call them 'claws,' not unnaturally." He grinned. "With them, any warrior can climb wood, or walls of worked stone."

Kyrin hummed to herself as she handed Talik another thong, and wove one through one of her own oblong frames. The first thong on the claw tied about the wrist or ankle, the second slipped over the hand or secured a toe of a boot, while other thongs woven as a web over the frame limited the noise of movement. There. The two for her feet were done, now for her hands.

Talik fingered the finished claws, their tips fine and flexible. "The leather will be stronger and a little quieter than cloth, I think."

"Unless it gets wet—then it may slip. I'll roughen the layers."

"We'll pray there's no rain. Noise is the bigger thing, since I have not your training. I would certainly give us away, on stone or wood." He grinned. Turning the claw over in his long-fingered brown hands, he said thoughtfully, "It has a chance of working."

"They will work." Kyrin tested hers on her feet. She could walk without pain this even. The claws left prints in the earth as of a strange beast behind her, piercing leaf and loam.

"*All* plans are risky," Talik said soberly.

§

On the northern side of Lord Keffer's valley, Kyrin peered from an alder copse on a low hill. After a over a day and a half of skulking travel, she faced Keffold. Three hundred yards away Lord Keffer's wall glistened in the evening. A light shower had left drops of blazing light on every leaf and tipped the blades of grass between her and the wall with fragile diamonds. Inside, her friends were hungry, in pain, and afraid. Behind her, open meadow dwindled into forest glades, then woods farther on. Captivity and glory lurking in the same moment touched her with sadness. "It is not natural." But now she must wait.

Her lip between her teeth, a strand of hair wound tight in her fist, Kyrin watched an ancient horse and cart roll up to the north gate-tower.

The cart halted. She knew mud clung to the wheels and splattered the driver, hunched under a cloak. Likely his feet were as cold and wet as hers.

Men poured out of the gate. They surrounded the cart. Kyrin stiffened.

Gestures swept unhindered across the meadow, though sound had met its match in distance. One man put his hand on his sword hilt. Kyrin reached up and gripped Hawk's thick mane, staring at the man until her eyes watered, but the man made no further movement of threat.

The cart moved on, at a snail's pace. Just before it passed from sight, a piece of wood fell from the back. The cart jounced within and Kyrin slumped. He was inside.

Long hours she waited, listening to the evening, into the dark. A nightingale called sweetly, a fox barked, and once a moth startled her, fluttering in her face. At last a slight rustle. Then the "whip" of branches after a body's passage stilled the nearby crickets. Kyrin waited, heart pounding.

"Kyrin!" came the whisper.

With relief and thankfulness, she slipped forward to take the bundle Talik held out. Moving a little distance away, Kyrin got out of her wet, clinging tunic and trousers and into the dry, dark messengers garb that Talik had taken. He'd left four of Lord Keffer's other messengers unmolested. She'd watched them leave by the gate and split up, each to ride a different direction.

Kyrin slid into the mail shirt last, tongue between her teeth, and searched for the greaves' buckle with her fingers, glad she'd worn such recently. She slipped her feet into high shoes, damp in spite of being sheltered under her blanket, and belted her cloak close.

"You done?" Talik's voice was low, his form unseen among the alders.

"Yes." Kyrin stepped forward cautiously, with the irrational feeling Keffer's men on the wall could hear every cracking twig.

They slept till near dawn. When they rose, frost touched leaf and grass. Lauds bell had rung. They must be out of the stronghold before Prime rang in full light.

In the dark, Kyrin followed Talik across the meadow and a wide, dry moat, careful of her ankle and shoulder, though only soreness was left. At the wall midway between the gates, they donned the claws of metal and leather and climbed. Few would expect to see them daring the stronghold in so vulnerable a way. Trembling with tension, Kyrin found that her claws scratched across the mortared stone and caught cracks easily. They would never work on sheer stone. Her grip felt uncertain. At last they reached the top.

She and Talik slipped rapidly across the walkway as a guard's steps echoed beyond sight of a corner. They slid over the edge of the inside wall and hung silently by their arms, hoping the guard missed the iron tips of their claws clinging to the stone in the dark at his feet.

The guard passed, humming quietly. They crawled to the ground. Wet all over again with sweat, Kyrin's tunic clung to her. She worked her shoulder, relieved it had held up, took off the claws and put on her shoes she'd carried tied around her neck.

They trotted Northeast in the shadows from one building to the next, toward the north gate. There four guards stood duty around Lord Keffer's prisoners, seventy-five paces from the gate and the tower that extended above. The square tower over the gate had windows for eyes. For strength, wide buttresses straddled the wall on either side.

Torches flanked the north gate in wrought sconces, while another flickered near the guards in the yard, near burnt out. Forty paces from Kyrin and Talik, the light moved across bodies curled together on the frosted ground under a tattered blanket, with two more in another heap a length away. Ropes led from them to four tall posts, above the captives' reach. The guards leaned quiet against the posts.

Talik touched Kyrin's arm and turned into the shadows. She forced herself to breathe deep and wait. The clouds above smelled of rain.

One guard of the four looked toward the first green-orange streak on the horizon, waiting for the watch change. The others warmed their hands under their arms, and one stamped cold feet with a curse at the mercs who took warm posts in the towers.

Near a small shed to Kyrin's right, a pebble skittered. She tensed. On the far side of the posts and their captives, the guard near the gate jerked his helmeted head up, his breath pluming. After a suspicious moment, peering hard into the shadows, he rubbed his clean-shaven face and yawned.

"Well, Piter," the nearest guard in front of Kyrin drawled, "See anything?"

Piter growled under his breath.

"I thought you could *see* things in the dark!" His companion slapped his leg, laughing. "The mercs can!"

There came a thump and a muffled thud inside the shed. The guards swung around.

"What could that be, Toby?" said Piter triumphantly. "You think that's just a rat?" He smiled, hefting his spear, and stalked inside the woodshed. He reappeared on a run, cursing a dark, four-legged shape. It darted out between his feet with a high yelp. Piter's brothers laughed. The nearest guard called, "Not a rat, it's a dog after a rat!"

Piter slapped his neck. "Curse these hell-spawned biters!" He spun on the amused guard. "Enough, Toby! What mercenary filth put you up to it, eh?"

"I didn't do nothin'. Put me up to what? No merc told me nothin'." Toby glared at him.

Piter paused then glanced from building to building. He lowered his voice. "Toby, search every crack of that shed. You two"—he lifted another torch from a rack on the post above the nearest captives—"spread out. Watch the gate approach and the road to the south." He lit the torch.

Toby grumbled his way toward the shed. "Oh, give it up, Piter, there's nothin' in—" Toby's spear twitched from his grasp and rose over his head, sliding out of the torchlight up the thatch roof. He yelped. Piter and the other guards rushed to his side.

In the waning torchlight two eyes from under a dark hood peered down at the fuming men from the ridge top, then disappeared. A low laugh drifted back. "Us mercernaries got your post, lazywit?"

A long slither, a thump, and swift steps echoed toward the wood houses and Nidfael's hall, nestled nearer the cliff, at the rear of the stronghold, to the east.

Piter looked at Toby, the sleeping prisoners, up at the lightless watch-post in the tower and then at the two nearest guard stations along the wall. Their humiliation had not yet been noticed. "Filthy merc! We'll get 'em. If our lord hadna' hired 'em—Toby, tell the next watch to look sharp when they get here, lazy scum." Piter stalked toward the shed. Spitting mad, he left Toby on duty with his spear, recovered from the back side of the shed, and sent the others forward with a silent motion of his arm.

A laugh out of the darkness taunted them. The three sped after their tormenter.

The last ring-mail coat disappeared from the yard and the torch dwindled out. None of the guards had worn the look or speech of armsmen who cared more for their lord's life than their own. Mayhap her father simply trained peculiar armsmen.

Kyrin stepped out of the the building's pitch black shadow. Clad in messenger's mail sporting Lord Keffer's white horse-head sigil, she strode to the prisoner's posts. Her heart in her throat, as she drew near she nodded to Toby. She stared into his eyes with the cool curiosity of the warrior. He looked away first. Ignoring all else, she took up Piter's post as if being armed with her stick and Talik's dagger were nothing less than usual.

Toby eyed her sidelong, doubtless hoping she'd seen and heard nothing of their discomfiture.

"Everything quiet? The others leave before your watch change?" she prodded after a long moment. No sound of struggle or cry of triumph came from the houses near the cliffs. Talik had doubtless gone to ground.

"Nah. After troublesome rats."

"Hah!" Kyrin sniffed and lazily kicked the nearest prisoner. Hal, by the vague shape of his larger body. "The rest of *my* watch will be along, and yours better be back." Hal rolled over and glared up at her, his hands tied before him. "Cur!" she growled, stepping between him and Toby. "I'm not paid good coin to watch worthless scum! If this lot could guard a statue, I'd be scouting for the messengers, where I belong. But it won't be more than another dawn, an then our lord will settle your soul."

With the smallest movement, she dropped a dagger. Hal rolled over it as he turned his back to her without a word. Kyrin kicked him again. With a longsuffering glare at Toby, who glared back, she stalked toward a squat building windward of the privy. "I'll be a moment." She stepped inside and stumbled loudly, with a curse. Silent, she turned and peered through a crack of the door.

Near his spitting brand, Toby had his back to her, already leaning against his post. Sweat prickled down Kyrin's back. By now Talik would have eluded his pursuers, and Prime was coming, clouds or no.

Hal was too slow. Kyrin bumbled about a bit then could wait no longer. She strode out. The privy door thumped closed. Then a strong arm nestled about her neck lovingly.

"Where to?" Whispered a breath, hot against the back of her ear. In the middle of her leap of fear, Kyrin slumped and turned her head to glare at Hal. His wide chest shook silently. He was hugely amused. If he were another, she'd have been dead.

But Toby hadn't moved an inch, still with his back to them, though he was strangely straight at his post. Sensing her thought, Hal nodded and slid his cold finger across Kyrin's throat. She swallowed.

Hal had gotten free; that was the important thing at the moment. Now Nell crowded behind him with Celine and Myrna. Their quick breaths steamed the air. All that was left on the ground were her friends' blankets, the dark bundles on the ground slightly flatter.

Kyrin turned and reached for their loosened neck ropes, her dagger in hand. Hal caught her sleeve and shook his head. He gathered their noose ends and handed the handful to Kyrin, then turned his back pointedly. He was right. Kyrin readied her dagger against his spine, and marched the prisoners down the dark lane between the privy and the buildings. No yell rose from the wall.

Prime would ring any moment, and her friends walked before her, stiff and cold, limbs cramped. Where was Talik? They'd be out soon, or it would be too late. The sky was grey.

Kyrin urged them around the corner of a cookhouse—and face-to-face with a boy dipping a bucket of water from a spring. She nudged Hal straight past him had a bad moment when Nell hesited, but she turned toward the tower.

The boy stared, his startled face pale in the dawnlight. After an eternity came the gurgling splash of his released bucket as he returned to his work. Beside the barracks, Kyrin glanced back.

The boy carried his dripping load the other way, without a glance over his shoulder. Keffer's sigil was not interfered with in his stronghold. Kyrin sighed in relief.

They stopped out of sight behind the barracks. While Hal stripped Myrna, Celine, and Nell of their ropes, Kyrin took her half-hidden climbing claws out of a grass-clump, dismayed. She needed more training. She'd not hidden them near well enough for the light of morn, and Talik was not back. Everything felt wrong. A sprinkle of rain fell.

At the bottom of the inner side of the stronghold wall, Kyrin put Talik's claws on Hal, fastened her own and then demonstrated their use. Raindrops pelted her head. Looking up, rain falling in her face, Kyrin saw no guard, though that meant nothing. The wall's height and width concealed anyone at the low battlement looking out. Celine, Nell, and Myrna waited below.

Kyrin counted in her mind as the guard passed overhead, out of sight but still humming. To sing about one's work was God's gift. He retraced his path as her last count to a score predicted. At Kyrin's motion, Hal started up the wall in the streaming rain. She felt almost sorry for the guard as she followed, licking water from her lips.

Edging her head above the walk at last count, she saw the battlements were empty clear to the tower. Kyrin pulled herself onto the walk and ran, slipping on the wet stone, to the battlement she and Talik had chosen for their descent. Her ankle twinged. No time to stop.

She motioned Hal in front of her and slid sideways through the crenel slit after him. Hal descended while she waited, a dark shadow splayed just below the edge of the stone, for the guard to pass again. When he was gone and she was on her feet, Hal threw up Talik's claws and a rope. Panting and hot despite the rain, Kryin returned across the wall for Nell and the others.

Agile and quiet, their bare feet quicker on the damp stone than Kyrin's slippery, leather-clad claws, Nell and Celine came up the rope, sure as frogs up the stone inside a well. A wind was kicking up. The sky glowed under forge-steel clouds.

A last time Kyrin went down and put the spare claws on Myrna, last and lightest. Near the top, Kyrin took a moment to scan the quiet stronghold over her shoulder. Still in shadow, she saw no sign of Talik, and nothing from the men who had followed him. It was as if they had all disappeared.

She frowned. Two horses waited outside in the alders for six riders. Because of her ankle they had planned for her to go to ground and Talik to run beside one of the horses. They had found only one other beast besides Hawk for their need. Talik said he was good at running. But he was still inside.

The guard should be near the end of his route, soon to return. Kyrin urged Myrna up, slithered atop the wall, and helped her over.

A shout rang inside the stronghold. Not yet on the ground, Myrna fell the rest of the way with a squeak. Head below the walkway, body braced, Kyrin listened for Talik. Nothing, no steps of the guard either. Desperately, Kyrin lifted herself, straining for sight.

A horn-call rang out. Torches blossomed near the shed, clearly lighting the posts where Lord Keffer's prisoners had been.

An arrow whipped past her head. With a low wordless cry, Hal leaped up and yanked her back and down into Nell and Celine's arms in a somersault. Kyrin rolled out of her friends' grip, grabbed the longbow Hal shoved into her hands, and shot the guard who stared down at them. His surprised mouth open to shout, he stumbled back. The claw swinging from her wrist destroyed her aim and threw the arrow high in his shoulder. She hoped he would live to sing again.

Feet thundered. Echoed commands passed like fire along the wall top. Hal furiously dug Talik's weapons away from the base of the outer wall and thrust them into the hands of the others. Kyrin's companions took the daggers, wide-eyed, and Hal belted on Talik's short sword. Kyrin threw a blanket to each.

"Lackwits!" A cracked shout pierced the air. "Is a mercenary too quick for you?" It must be Talik, that laugh of joy in the dawnlight. Triumph lurked in his voice.

Kyrin ran for the stones as a roar of outrage crested the rampart. Her claw found a crack and held. Hal pulled her to earth. She sprawled, crying low and fierce, "Talik's in there!"

Hal picked her up, took Talik's claws from her, stripped hers, and snapped, "Run!"

Kyrin ran. She dragged her arm across her eyes and forced her feet on. Safe in the alder copse on the far side of the meadow, she looked back, hands on her knees, gasping.

Lord Keffer's men crowded the wall. Four of them raised bows, the rest brandished spears or swords. *Had* that yell been Talik? Was it his ruse or another's?

Nell and Celine raced across the meadow through the drizzle. Hal followed, half-dragging Myrna, who struggled to keep her feet. Arrows thudded into the ground around them. Then they were out of range and plunging toward her. They sped into the shelter of the alders.

Celine shook as she gulped for air, Nell had tears on her face, her hands steady about Kyrin's blanket—no, Talik's. Kyrin bit her lip hard. She could not think of him. He would tell her to go.

She had told him to run without her, if he must; she had not thought to leave him.

"Get on the horses!" There was nothing to do but follow the plan as best she could. Kyrin shoved Myrna up on Hawk, and Nell behind her, then threw up Talik's bag. Hal swung Celine on the sway-backed mare behind him.

Kyrin slapped Hawk's rump and lunged for her stirrup. They headed for a nearby stream that joined the river.

Prime bell and a horn at the north gate sounded together. Lord Keffer moved fast, as they had thought he would.

Kyrin strove to run faster. They broke from the trees into a glade. Tall grass whipped Kyrin's greaves.

Talik now struggled for his life or lay beyond caring. Chest aching, Kyrin gazed at the dip on the far side of the meadow, which meant the stream. She could send the horses on and lose any dogs that followed—and look for Talik. The farm chosen for her to go to ground in lay upstream.

If they reached the water before Keffer's men saw them they could lose the scent. Kyrin clenched her hands and sped through the grass. Her ankle ached. Flame licked her legs. Her ears thrummed with her blood-beat.

Tae would call it foolish.

She didn't hear nearer hooves approaching until Myrna screamed, "Kyrin!" and pulled out her dagger.

18

Surprises

If your heart is wise . . . ~Proverbs 23:15

A dark horse thundered up on Kyrin's left, near two hands of riders behind him. Kyrin's heart sank. That mailed figure was not Talik. For her, escape was over.

For her companions—she raised her stick to strike the lead horse's knee, then scrambled to keep her feet as Nell reined Hawk violently aside.

"Kyrin!" The lead rider's hoarse shout brought her gaze up from the horse's heaving belly and flashing legs to his outstretched arm. Her falcon dagger flashed in his gloved hand, held by the sheathed blade. She might do more for Hal and the others if she was close. Close enough to unseat him or take him hostage if she must. Kyrin reached out and grabbed the strong mailed arm.

It was not unlike taking Tae's hand as he raced along the top of the garden wall in Araby, ready to swing her up, training her for just such a move. *Leap with the lift*—the man swung her onto his horse, belly down, never slowing. Kyrin landed with a thump and reached back along her side for the pommel. His hand was heavy on her back. There was no possibility of talk.

She breathed when she could, turning her head, watchful. The nearest men held no drawn weapons. Those on the outer fringe did. None seemed to bear Lord Nidfael Keffer's sigil. All she could see of the man holding her was flashes of black tunic and boots.

Larger oaks and ash trees closed in around them. After an Eagle half mile the horses slowed to a trot. The man released her and slid back to allow Kyrin to swing a leg across the saddle and ride astride, then pulled her close against him.

Kyrin gripped the horse with trembling legs and steadied her arms, regaining her breath. None seemed to be pursuing them. The arm around her middle was steady, though the man's breath was fast. The horse's mane streamed over her hands, and Nell and Hal's eyes were on her.

Warily, she watched their abrupt companions, silent but for that one shout. Wherever they were going, at least it was away from Lord Keffer. What did this lord want, and where had he gotten her mother's weapon? He had called her name.

The man raised his arm, and ten riders galloped up in a wide V, surrounding them. Each had a black ribbon tied about the right arm. Close on either side rode an armsman in autumn-brown, with a sigil on his breast. A sun on blue and a moon on black, divided by a red-shafted arrow. The pennon on the man's long spear at the rear flew the same sigil. It was none Kyrin knew. Shafts of sunlight lanced the clouds, and hazels and shrubs thickened among the trees.

Hal spurred toward them. "My Lord—"

Who was he? The man behind her was tugging off his helm.

As she turned, Kyrin's heart shook with a great leap. Then her arms were as far around the dark haired man's neck as she could get them, sitting in front of him as she was, and his arms were around her, Hal forgotten.

After long moments the horse turned abruptly east at his rider's urging. They moved toward the river, and Kyrin had to find her seat again or slide from the saddle as they rode down the bank. Her back heaved with sobs against the mailed chest of her rescuer. After long moments walking down the watercourse, they moved southwest into the hills at a walk and let the horses blow.

Kyrin was smiling so wide her face hurt. She was surprized to realize that her and Talik's last camp lay ahead on the side of a hill. When they reached the high spot, Nell and Myrna gingerly slid from Hawk. Celine collapsed when her feet touched the earth, but rose on her father's arm. She tossed her head with a glare when she noticed Kyrin. Never mind Celine.

Their rescuer waited—for her. Kyrin slid down the dark horse's shoulder, gripping his mane to keep her suddenly weak knees straight. She turned, breath held.

He dismounted easily, helmet dangling from the strap on his saddle. The years had gilded her father with a quiet sternness, until he smiled. Then crow's feet hemmed his eyes in his tanned face, lending him a kindly look. Silver flecked his brown hair at the temples, adding to his air of authority.

Slowly he laid sinewy hands on her shoulders, as if hesitant to touch her for fear she would vanish. She was as tall as he, though he was far wider of shoulder.

Kyrin shivered and gripped his arms. His tannin-brown eyes drank her in then lifted to her face in wonder. "My daughter, you are truly—my Kyrin! You've grown; you're so quick and strong. My daughter—" Tears filled his eyes. He pulled her closer.

"You're here!" Her voice shook. *He* saw no black eye of evil. She buried her face in his shoulder. And he hugged the breath from her.

One of her father's armsmen, dark-skinned and whipcord strong, walked over to them with an apologetic clearing of his throat. Nith. It had to be he, armsmaster to Cierheld. But why was he here instead of in Cierheld's training yard—unless her father had emptied Cierheld for her sake? But there were not enough men for that. Lord Dain Cieri let her go, though he kept an arm about her shoulders. Kyrin wiped her face. Nith glanced aside in respect, then back at them.

"My lord"—Nith bowed, including her in the gesture—"Lord Bergrin Jorn's man, Hal, tells us that one of them was left behind. He ran as bait, so our lady"—he indicated Kyrin—"and the others could get out."

Kyrin touched her father's hand, felt his strong, rough fingers close around hers. "Please, Father, Talik took me from Lord Keffer's men. I wouldn't leave a dog to Nidfael's mercies. We must get Talik out!"

Dain's gaze was warm and steady. "We'll do what we can, daughter." He turned away, clearing his throat, and beckoned to another of his men. "Berd!"

Berd bowed to Kyrin as he approached. Kyrin inclined her head. He had been a boy when she last saw him, now he was a man. No longer gangly but strong and wide of shoulder, though still fair-skinned and dark-haired. His level glance took her in, not pausing on her earring.

"I give you greeting, my lady. It is good to see you."

Realizing she was staring, Kyrin reddened. "And you."

Dain said, "Berd is second armsman now, and Nith"—he nodded to him, and Nith inclined his head gravely—"is our first armsman as well as first armsmaster."

Kyrin drew herself up and bowed formally in the way of the East, one warrior to another. And then flushed again, deeper, as they stared at her. Nith cocked his head, a gleam in his eyes, while Berd said,"Well met, lady. I—", and Kyrin could not quite meet her father's gaze.

Hal strode up, grinning. "My lord, one more bell and we would have been skewered to Lord Keffer's wall. Your presence was most welcome, and I give you thanks. Though I think you have found something of even more worth." He turned to Kyrin. "Aye now, so you're home. I'm glad, my lady." His eyes twinkled as he looked at the others. "You've seen nothin' yet. She beat me in the Brewmaster's own ring with a warrior-way of her own. Like nothing I've ever seen. Subak, 'tis called. She's teaching me. Wait till you see."

Kyrin swallowed hard.

Putting an arm around her shoulders, Daid said, "Let's get our man out and our women home, first."

"Aye."

Around a fire speedily kindled by Berd, they wolfed down meat and bread and last season's wrinkled apples, brought out from the men's packs. Kyrin sat between her father and Nell.

"Talik blends in with other ways of speech and thinking easily," Kyrin said soberly, remembering Keffer's guards and Talik's taunts in the dark. "He may yet be hiding inside."

Her father's glance was piercing. Kyrin frowned. If she only knew Talik's surname. Her father might think him a wastrel, chance met by her.

"I'll send a man to mingle; then we'll know." Dain glanced aside. "Berd."

"Sir." Berd rose, and Dain beckoned him close and spoke to him in a low voice. Berd moved swiftly to a group of five watchful riders under an ancient oak and picked out a tall youth whose bony hands stuck far beyond his sleeves. His scarecrow form moved well as he stood; and better than that, Kyrin thought, he looked like every man's apprentice.

"Father, shouldn't he wait till after dark to go over the wall?"

Her father smiled. “No. Lord Keffer won’t expect a sortie while the sun is high.”

That was well thought. “What do you know of him?” she asked curiously.

“He is a dishonorable man.” The short words held volumes. He said nothing further.

The fire crackled and leaped, comforting despite the sun, filling the silence and Kyrin’s vision with snapping orange. The color of fire, and orange and black fur.

Her father held another bit of bread out to her. “Speaking of going over the wall—”

“My Lord Dain?” Hal interrupted.

“Yes?”

“These might help your man.” Hal held out a pair of the iron claws.

Dain took them, fingering the tips and testing the strength of the thongs. He measured the frame of one against his broad hand. “Where did you get these?”

Hal grinned. “Lady Kyrin used them to get me across the wall. We climbed like squirrels.”

Kyrin remembered her foolishness at the wall and her face heated. Hal said nothing more, and Kyrin let out her breath. Nith leaned forward from his place across the fire, interest in his face.

Dain looked at Hal, then at her, then at the claws in his hands and carefully set them aside. Nell fingered them where they lay, picked them up, turning them over.

Kyrin said hastily, “We made them how my Subak teacher taught me, Father, in Araby. I have so much to tell you of Tae. An honorable warrior, he was a second father to me. He protected me from the sailors and raiders and my master—”

Dain's face had gone still. He rose, and stepping to the far side of the fire, he stared into the trees, his back rigid. "And I'll hear it gladly—at another moment." Those about the fire were silent.

He turned and smiled awkwardly at Kyrin, slipping the falcon dagger from his belt. "You'd best keep this. Later we will speak. Rest now. I'm leaving Berd to watch over you, and going with the men. We should be back sometime after dark. Pray for our safekeeping, and for Talik."

"I will, Father, but I'm going with you!" Kyrin rose.

Dain picked up the claws he'd strung together and tossed them across the fire. Kyrin reached to the side and caught them effortlessly, picking a harmless end of the spinning bundle out of the air.

Nith smiled. Lord Dain grimaced. "Rest here. You're more tired than you know, Kyrin. We'll speak of Lords Mornoth and Keffer and these things when I return."

Kyrin stared at him, mouth open to argue. Talik was her friend, and she could shoot and—and her father asked it. "It is well. Go in God's blessing," she said at last. And Nith's smile widened, a glint of approval in his eyes.

Dain moved close to grip her shoulders, and touched the leaping fish at her throat lightly. "My Kyrin, I'm so glad you still know him." His voice gruff with emotion, he laid the falcon in her lap, pulled up his hood, and his smile retreated into stern shadow as he turned away.

A pall crept over Kyrin. The lord of Cierheld was the same, and yet her father was different. He might guess some of what she wished to tell him. What would he say when he learned she could kill a man with a seeming touch, and that she was learning the sword? Though Jachin would never finish her training. She would have to find one to teach her in Cierheld, though it would be a different discipline than Jachin's. Kyrin sighed.

Her father strode toward his horse, his short cloak of dappled green and brown, black side turned in, concealing his mail tunic. His sword was sheathed, his heavy bow in his hand. He mounted and rode away, his men behind him in single file. Kyrin swallowed hard when they disappeared among the trees. She felt as if he might not return. But that was in the hands of the Master of the stars.

Hal looked away from Kyrin's shaky attempt to smile. In sympathy, Nell offered Kyrin her apple. Kyrin held it, looking at the four Cierheld men left under the oak, now her men. For she was Cierheld's first daughter.

They carried short spears and swords, dappled by the sun through the leaves. In addition, Berd bore a bow where he stood sentry. Very unlike her father's great weapon, it was one of the short recurve bows used in the East for fighting on horseback. Where her father had found such a bow for the pattern? Evidently he hadn't discovered the glue to bind the horn and sinew backing to the wood, for Berd's was bare. If she could show them how hers was made, but it had been stolen, along with the sword Bergrin gave her.

Thank the Master of the stars Lord Keffer hadn't gotten her mother's falcon dagger. But somehow it had come to her father's hands. If someone served him within Lord Keffer's ranks . . . but none knew her as Cieri's daughter, or that the falcon dagger was her mother's, or even of Cierheld. None had known except Uncle Ulf and Talik. Talik. She had only asked him about her pack and neck pouch. If he'd found the dagger and sent it to Cierheld without speaking to her—how dare he?

Her sore shoulder and ribs ached, and by the way Myrna moved, Kyrin thought her companions must feel the same. One did not climb walls every day.

She asked Berd for the makings and brewed a large pot of tea, pushing back thoughts of her father and Talik. There would be later moments to speak of the falcon blade and of trust.

Berd helped her brew the tea, stirring the pot with an ash stick, absorbed in the task. "Lady," he said, soberly looking into the depths of the pot, "We're glad you're back. Lord Cieri thought you dead with your lady mother, though he hoped still, at times." He raised his gaze, avoiding her slit tunic front, which she'd stitched together with thin strips of leather. He must think it an unfit garment for his first daughter to wear. "We pulled the pyre apart afore it burned much, and we found her. Your father mourned you for seasons. It was a hard time." He turned his attention back to the tea. "Lord Cieri strengthened the stronghold. Now he has forty men inside Cierheld's wall at all times. He teaches every man and boy who calls him lord, the blade, the spear, or the bow. And wherever brigands go, Lord Cieri comes, asking only food, drink, and half the spoil of those we catch." Berd's dark eyes gleamed. "You know—" he stopped suddenly. "Pardon, my tongue runs away."

"No! I hear you gladly, please, go on."

"You—do you remember? Old Cernalt taught you to make jesses for the hawks. Only he was not so old then. You called him 'Hawkman.' Your lady mother loved the birds, too."

She thought Berd had been going to say something else. She remembered a night when he kept her from Esther's cunning designs, when her father first gave her Samson. Had Berd been the one to pick Samson up, the lost one, the outcast from the nest? He seemed good at finding those who needed him. But if she remembered further the tiger would certainly come to her tonight.

Her key! Kyrin straightened. The key of Cierheld, the stronghold key every first daughter carried, it too was gone with her pack.

Berd eyed her uncertainly. "You're not offended that I talk of—before?"

Kyrin pulled herself back to the moment. "How can I be offended, Berd? It's been a long day, is all." She sighed. "It is only I feel I am yet at sea, caught in a storm I cannot see through."

Berd watched her, his head on one side, and said nothing.

Kyrin smiled crookedly. "How is Cernalt's Thelmae?"

Berd grinned. "Spirited as ever! Cernalt, his boys, and the garden are in good hands."

Kyrin laughed; then another thought touched her. "Does he still train falcons? I had a peregrine once, Truthseeker, a gift given in the East. But she was taken from me."

Berd nodded wisely. "Cernalt yet trains them well, my lady. And we'll soon have another for you."

Kyrin nodded, weary, and stared at the pot in silence. As if sensing her wish, Berd tended the tea in quiet.

Myrna sat by the fire with Celine as midday wore toward evening and Compline, or last light. Kyrin took Talik's horn cup from his pack and filled it with the strong tea for Myrna. Myrna took it with grateful thanks and sipped. Kyrin was glad to see she seemed strong enough, after her ordeal. When Myrna finished, she took the horn to Berd, who refilled it then passed it to Nell and Celine. Finished, Celine moved to the fireside and dropped the horn in Kyrin's lap without a word.

Kyrin chewed her lip, holding the cup for Berd to fill, then blew on her tea till it cooled. She gulped it down. And found Celine's eyes on her, a slight mocking smile on her lips, so like

Esther's. It was sand in a wound. What cause did Celine have to spurn her?

When dark fell, they lay in their blankets on piles of heather far enough from the fire to avoid sparks. Two men watched, and the rest played dice on the far side of camp with Hal. An early moon cast netted shadows under the trees. Kyrin listened to her companions' restless movements.

Nell rolled over on her stomach. "Kyrin, what happened on the road? I saw you running for the trees, and then that man hit you. I feared for you—"

Celine said shortly, "Could any harm come to *her*, first daughter that she is? But she fell like the rest of us. Despite her foreign Subak."

Myrna curled closer, an alarmed rustle of her heather bed.

Nell said fiercely, "Celine, how could you! Kyrin took us from Keffer at the risk of her own skin! You—you—"

"No, it's all right. I did fall." *Though I got up again—with help.* Kyrin gave them the bare facts of her terrifying time with Lord Keffer and Mornoth's men, and told them of Curnoth. "Talik, he took me from them. He was kind, even before he knew my name." Let Celine chew on that. *Though he suspected I was more than I said.*

Nell smiled at Kyrin knowingly. "Whoo! That Talik is both bold *and* very kind."

"I'd like to meet him in the morn"—Celine laughed low—"to thank him properly. If you will, first daughter." She glanced at Kyrin, the anger back in her eyes.

"It is well," Kyrin said quietly, wishing Celine might never see him, and then she wondered if any of them would.

Myrna said nothing, staring into the fire. If she knew Kyrin's tangled hopes and laughed at her foolishness . . . There was much of Esther in Celine. Kyrin clenched her fist. She would not let it rub off on her. She would not doubt Myrna.

The others were silent. Celine propped herself up on her elbow, a kind of triumph curving her mouth. "Why do we not pray for protection for Talik and Lord Cieri?"

"That is well thought." Kyrin sat up, holding out her hands to Myrna and Nell. Hesitating, at last Celine took theirs, and Kyrin raised her face to the sky.

When they had finished, Kyrin looked thoughtfully at Nell. "What happened to *you,* Nell, in the hold? Did Lord Keffer or any other speak with you? I would know more of this Mornoth."

Celine snorted. "Speak to *her?* None of us but *the Lady Myrna* were worth his words!"

Myrna said nothing and looked away, her lips tightening.

Nell shot a sideways look at Celine and said in a low voice, "They were rough, and we were *all* cold and hungry and dirty. Myrna wouldn't let me take her place with the men who came for water-toll kisses."

Kyrin shuddered. "My thanks, Myrna," she said softly.

Celine's voice bit. "What, you think Nell one of your precious Cierheldans, and you her first daughter, that you would protect her? You take that place, when you come from chains, yes"—Celine shrugged as if it were a small thing—"but also rich gardens, hummingbird tongues, and endless learning? Of what use is sacrifice for a handmaiden? Here, you could have anything—"

Kyrin found herself on her knees, leaning into Celine's intent face, every muscle taut. "I would *die* for her! And for any other Cierheldan! The least peasant has a heart and soul, and dreams as we do. You should know, being one yourself! And she is not my handmaiden, but my companion. It is true, sacrifice is a first daughter's place, but you do not know of what you speak. It is not so easy, nor so hard. Not when you love someone," she whispered. *If you love them enough.* Kyrin breathed hard. She sat back and looked away, while Celine stared.

Silence reigned about the fire, even the men pausing in their game. Berd did not turn his head, and said nothing, though surely he heard. Kyrin wished she had not drunk so much tea. It felt like to come up with memory of torchlight and her mother's fall. She shuddered. Blades and blood.

If she failed again in time of need, she was no first daughter. Though it was a gift given that none could take—unless there was question of fitness. She could not be unfit, she would make it so. To keep those close to her from harm. "I need a bush." She smoothed her tunic with shaking hands.

"Kyrin," Myrna whispered, catching her hand as she stepped past her, "there would have been no stopping them, once the guards found out who Nell was, with no husband or father to hold them to account. Celine had Hal."

Nell smiled at them, her face lit by the rising moon.

Kyrin squeezed Myrna's hand.

"Humph!" Celine scowled and turned her back to feign sleep. Soon the others also slept, but for those on watch.

Kyrin's eyes remained open. She'd lain so, on sand and stone instead of heather, so many nights beside Alaina. Alaina, who always had a warm heart. *Master of all, keep her and Tae. Let them know I think of them, running to escape the wazir's reach in the sands. Keep Hamal, and help me get him to the wazir soon.* She yawned. The fire had sunk to a few bright, winking eyes, like those of a tiger. But two strong Cierheldans faced the darkness a hundred strides from camp, where they were not blinded by the light. She was safe.

Kyrin opened her eyes to the lazy rustling of oak leaves above her head. The warmth of the early sun and the murmur of men's low voices was comfortable. Talik! She sat up.

A few feet from her, he slept in his cloak, a green blanket wound about him. His pale face was drawn but peaceful, and there seemed no hurt on him. So he'd not been caught, then. She rubbed her face. Where was her father?

There was a light step behind her and Kyrin spun to her knees. Dain greeted her with a wide grin. Red morning highlights shone in his hair. Loving laughter twinkled in his eyes. Kyrin's face heated, and her father grinned again.

"It's not what you think—where did you find him?" *Father* felt odd to her tongue this morn. "He truly *did* take me from Keffer's men." Her words stumbled.

"Talik found us outside the hold." Dain stroked his chin. "Lord Keffer's men never saw him after the alarm horn. He hid in a loft, still wearing Keffer's tunic. At dusk he joined Lord Keffer's men on the wall, moving steadily. He has a quick wit and tongue. After dark, he jumped for a spot of soft ground and crawled on his belly to the wood, where we took him for one of Lord Keffer's men and almost spitted him."

Kyrin thought of that long, slow journey over the open meadow and meeting a spear at the end of it. "My thanks, Father," she whispered. He'd saved her, and all of them from whatever purpose Lord Mornoth had.

"I am glad," her father said simply. "Come, let us walk a bit, if you are well enough." He did not seem to notice her ill-mended tunic or trousers, rather the worse for wear. They walked among the oaks, and Kyrin found herself telling him everything, and learned many things in return.

His hands clasped behind his back, Dain said at last, "Talik Wyman sent me your mother's blade, you know."

"I thought he might." Kyrin's voice tightened. So, Talik's surname was Wyman, fighter, in the old tongue.

"He was right to do so. With things as they stand between certain lords and the king, it is wise to know who one deals with. He had to be sure of what he thought."

"I heard the king was ill."

"Yes." Dain glanced at her. "The double sigil I wear endears me little, in the hearts of many." He sighed. "After your mother fell, I swore to find justice for her and for your godfather. I did find it, some would say, defending our shore against a wolfship out of the mist. The king declared me guardian of Fenwrd hold and formally Lord Fenwer's second heir. When Fenwer's sickly nephew, his true heir, died, the king gave Fenwrd stronghold to me."

"Is that why you changed Cierheld's sigil from the willow and eagle?"

Dain's voice was soft. "Our Willa is gone ahead of us, yes. I had no more heart for the willow. Then the king ordered me to be an arrow in his kingdom, to guard the sun of justice and the moon of peace by day and night. He thought the double sigil fitting, since I rule two strongholds." He looked up through the tree limbs. "In truth, I am hard pressed between many; Cierheld and Fenwrd, the king and my brother lords. I stand between those who seek peace and those who seek their own gain." He straightened his shoulders. "But I am glad you have come, though I regret you step into such a broil. I thought I would never see you again, yet God has given you back to me. I thank him with all my heart."

Kyrin wiped away her tears and hugged him a long time.

When they returned to camp, the company ate, put out the fire, and set out for Lord Jorn's stronghold. As Dain told Kyrin briskly, he wanted to take council with Bergrin Jorn. "And Lord Keffer won't expect us to take *this* road to Cierheld." He grinned.

Riding quick and bold, they reached Jornhold by evening. The snug homes on the road leading from the village were empty. Lord Jorn had heard something, then, and might have drawn his people inside the hold. Kyrin nudged her horse on.

When they came in sight of Jornhold, the watchman blew his horn at the gate, and men thronged the high walk, spears bristling. The wail of a child drifted down the slope to Kyrin. She drew a sharp breath. Crouched behind a scaffold at the nearest crenel, a bowman aimed at them. A bowman, here?

Kyrin nudged Talik's ankle with her stirrup. He inclined his head but said nothing. So, he didn't think a lone archer, likely a hunter with a weak bow, of much moment. Kyrin's arms prickled and she forced her eyes away. She knew what a bow *could* do, if Lord Dain's method of defense had spread.

Talik might be used to having arrows aimed at him. She was not.

19

Challenges

When my anxious thoughts multiply . . . ~Psalm 94:19

Nith unfurled Cierheld's banner at Dain's command. A cautious messenger descended the hill. He started when he recognized Myrna, and eyed the carefully worked sigils on the men's tunics in doubt. Lord Dain greeted him amiably. Looking relieved, the messenger gave them welcome.

At Myrna's side, he led the way up the slope and across the defensive ditch, newly deepened in the dark earth, the horses' hooves booming on a new, thin wood span leading to the gate.

Kyrin passed through the tall, heavy portal with her father. Lord Bergrin Jorn strode to meet them, and Myrna dismounted and ran to him. Their blond heads rested together a moment, and Myrna murmured something in Bergrin's ear. Then the lord of Jornhold turned to Kyrin and Dain Cieri.

"Lord Cieri, what has happened, that you ride with so many men? I see no hurt among you . . ." He pointedly noted the armsmen behind Nell and Talik.

"No, my lord, no harm has come to us. Not for lack of trying, as Lady Myrna, I'm sure, has told you. But I've not heard the whole story, myself. There's been haste, but we will learn all tonight. Our first daughter has returned, of which I've heard somewhat." Dain looked from Kyrin to Lord Bergrin, his eyes afire, his smile thin. "Lord Keffer is a threat to all who wish to keep the peace. May we speak of ending his influence?"

Kyrin cleared her throat. "Father, Lord Jorn"—she bowed to Bergrin—"other lords may know of Myrna, and Lord Keffer's demand of her. My Lord Bergrin, Talik stopped a messenger on his way here to demand a dower for Myrna. But there were four messengers sent. We don't know where the others went, or with what word."

"Does he plot against you, my lord?" Dain looked closely at Lord Bergrin.

"Let us see what we may do." Bergrin compressed his lips, a glint of challenge in his eyes. He bowed. "Be welcome to my hall, come, take some wine and bread."

"With a good will."

Kyrin trailed the others to the hall. A strong current of cool air rose from the west, a growing storm front swirling her hair, sweetened with mint from the garden in the evening. She stared idly at thick spears of sunlight that shot through the towering thunderclouds of the advancing storm. The beams bathed all around her with glory, revealing gloom beyond their touch, below the wind-brushed hill and the fields. She bit a hangnail wearily, and wondered what the morn would hold.

Myrna showed Kyrin, Nell, and Celine to a prepared chamber. Dimming light fell across the room from a tall, west-facing window. Myrna gestured Kyrin to a comfortable bed on the far side of the room, and she sat with a sigh. A bed off the floor, with a mattress. She stroked the linen coverlet.

Myrna was rolling out a pallet for Nell, while Celine had the other bed, near the door. Rich tapestries on either side of it caught Kyrin's eye.

In the first, woodland animals rested in a field of bright flowers around a waterfall. The second had a wide, pitch-black border. Inside, a white tiger reared, strong shouldered, heavy paws reaching after a quail, its orange-red eyes mad with desire. Kyrin took a short step back before she could stop herself. It was such a little bird. But it was not a falcon—and she was not a quail.

"Kyrin." Nell grasped her elbow, with a little frown. "My lady."

"I am well." Kyrin didn't look at the tapestry again, though the tiger's gaze followed her. Shivery unease dug claws in her back.

She snuck a glance at the tiger. She'd remove the tapestry as soon as possible. It looked made in Araby, though none who honored Allah would make an animal or human likeness. Lord Bergrin's father must have traded for it. It had nothing to do with her.

Myrna was an able hostess and kept no comfort from her rescuers, offering Kyrin a hot bath as soon as water could be heated. "If you wish it," she added quickly.

Kyrin hid her smile as she slid her stick under her pillow. Myrna would laugh, at least giggle, mannerly as she was, if she knew Kyrin bathed two times every seven-day now, summer and winter. Kyrin grinned. "I've become a little less than a complete barbarian."

After the others bathed, she joined them, Lord Bergrin, her father, Nith, and Berd for supper at the great table. The rest of Cierheld's men propped their weapons against the wall behind their seats on the long benches of tables farther down the hall.

The first wood table held a feast. Kyrin eyed the expanse. A monstrous kettle of stew held the center. Loaves of bread and rounds of cheese were piled around it. Apple pies from last season's dried apples, no less sweet for that, steamed at either end. Bowls and cups of fine-turned wood with Lord Bergrin's sigil carved on the side graced the settings. A flower in a fluted wood vase bowed its blue head in shy, delicate beauty to peer at the guests.

Kyrin would swear the vase, too, came from Araby. Someone in Jornhold traded with the world. She would never have thought it of Bergrin. She buried thought of the tiger, striking up conversation with Lord Jorn's steward about Araby's trade goods, to much lordly amusement, which she ignored. Kyrin guided the steward into news of local trade, and was especially interested in what he said of a slave trader who worked southeast of Jornhold.

"There are few slavers here. The nearest, he sells his ill goods north and south of here, for he wouldn't survive in these lands," the steward said, with a pointed glance at Lord Dain.

Kyrin looked up. Her father touched his chin with a finger, eyeing her. "Tell us how this slaver bears on your tale."

Kyrin pursued her account, beginning with Ragad's ship. When she came to her first meeting with Hal, Hal broke in jovially. "Ye're sure to leave the interesting bits out, my lady." And he cleared his throat. Men at the lower tables leaned forward.

Hal grinned. "I meant merely to teach her a thing or two, of my generous arm and the quality of our staves in Britannia. Instead, a lady of the highest steel bested my hide. Taught me, she did, that width of frame and a different knowledge can mightily deceive a warrior's eye." He went on, to tell her part in his warrior's education lavishly.

Kyrin's face heated, and Celine reddened.

Kyrin hastily took up her story with Thorgil's charge of witchery, her confession to Brother Rolf, and Lord Jorn's defense, while Celine chewed her lip, glaring.

Kyrin's suspicion grew. Celine had *no* right, no cause.

Before she blew out the candle beside her bed, while Nell threw out the wash water, she walked over and decidedly removed the tiger tapestry from the wall. Celine watched, tight-lipped.

Suspicion became certainty. Kyrin dropped the hanging on the table between them. "Well?"

"Well, what?" Celine's eyes narrowed with caution and a kind of excitement.

Kyrin shook her head. The fester had to come out. Her heart beat faster. "Why did you accuse me to Father Ulf at your father's match?"

"I didn't—"

Battle loomed. "Don't lie to me."

Celine glanced at the doorway, as if hoping Myrna would step in.

"Why?" snapped Kyrin.

Celine flinched but her eyes blazed. "You know it all, don't you, first daughter of Cieri? Ever since my father told my brothers and me how you stood up to Lord Jorn with his sword at your breast, it's been nothing but Lady Cieri this and Lady Cieri that! If I knew Subak as you do, I would use it better. In the stronghold I could've found Lord Keffer in his bed and killed him for what he did. I would have uphold my honor. But no, you didn't, and we almost got caught. Talik was almost killed, and now Lord Keffer's coming. And my father only says, 'Lady Cieri is such a strong one, with so much ahead of her, it's a pity after everything that she's landed in the middle of this.' Well, it's your own spilt flour! Who else should sweep it up?"

"So you don't believe I'm a witch or a heretic?"

"You?" Celine hooted. "You wouldn't know a witch or a heretic if they bit you, though you can beat five men with a twig."

Kyrin blinked. After a moment, she said, "We used to swim together, and fly Samson—"

"And then it ended!" Celine's breath came hard. "Before I came to Hal and Myrna, I stayed with Esther. You were gone, and she taught me well the way of women of standing. She was my sister. But then she—her heart is closed." Celine turned her back, picking at her coverlet, her voice muffled. "So I don't care. I helped Breanna and Hal and sought to learn the staff with my brothers, until you came back. You, you draw everyone after you. Just leave me to find my own way. After I learn Subak, I will go."

"What have I done to offend you, Celine? If it seems good to you, we'll walk in the wood tomorrow, and you can tie my hands and pound away. We'll say it was practice." It would be, of a sort. Kyrin stifled a wry laugh and sobered. "I would have you for my friend."

With a swift look for the amusement Kyrin hid, Celine said, resentful and a little regretful, "Why? That's silly."

Maybe truth would dull Celine's anger. "The only thing I need fight is *that.*" Kyrin pointed at the rolled tapestry, utterly serious. "Not Esther, or my friend."

"You are not my friend. You left." Celine rose and unrolled the tapestry, staring down at it. She frowned. "This can't be. With everything you are, you fear this beast?"

Kyrin's eyes went to the raving tiger in Celine's hands, to her pursed mouth and puzzled brow. "Believe me, that moment at Keffer's wall, when Hal pulled me down, I lacked wit. And the tiger—if you hear me dreaming in the night, don't wake me. I might take your head off." Celine didn't know the half of what she was. Her unarmed skill was nothing to her ability with the staff and the bow. Not to mention the death touch. The sword she had just begun, the weapon took a lifetime to master. Kyrin sighed. "More, I fear what may come. The beast comes with destruction, *is* destruction I think, in a way."

"Esther said you would be changed. But even she did not guess so much." Celine's rage had dampened to confused questioning.

Kyrin lifted her chin. "I didn't think Esther would even guess. But anyone who has been chained, as I have, *would* change. Either for good or for ill. They couldn't help it. Celine, I couldn't come back. I wanted to, but I couldn't leave Tae and Alaina behind to die for my escape. My master's temper was not kind.

"But enough of that. I would we could swim together again. The bluebells are out. It has been so long. There is little water in the sands."

Celine did not answer, still frowning.

Kyrin let out a silent breath. "Well, mayhap another time. Good night to you, Celine." She went to her bedplace and pulled her tunic over her head. She raised the coverlet and slipped her legs under. Nell slipped in, doused the candle, and crept across the room to her own bed. Kyrin wondered if she'd been waiting outside the door.

Later, she turned on her side by a warding fire. Flame shadows leapt across the sand, and she gripped a sheathed blade. Her nemesis threw back his head with a savage snarl, ears pinned to his skull. Kyrin yanked frantically on the sword, drawing the beast closer. The blade did not budge.

Above, a falcon cried. She circled, screaming. Then she dived, crying down the wind.

Kyrin's heart dove with her. "No!"

Her queen of the air was an attacking blur to defend her, wings swept back, beak open, talons extended.

The tiger lunged, reaching up with a massive paw. He swept the falcon from the air. Her defiant cry broke off in an explosion of feathers.

Kyrin stepped from the light. She could not leave the falcon to his mercies. But it was too late. Tears wet her face as she whirled the sheathed sword in a humming arc.

Ignoring her edgeless weapon, the tiger kept malevolent eyes on her, hunched over the bundle of grey-blue feathers with a throaty growl, cracking bones in his thick jaws.

The falcon! She should not have come. Not for me.

Amber and gold flame danced in the watching jet eyes of the tiger's collar. They seemed to gaze at the stars, at a sky of distant lights and a cold silver moon. Where was their Master and hers, who governed all? *But love is loyal, always. And I know he wills only the greatest good.*

Kyrin edged back to the fire and sank to her knees, wiping at her face. Glinting in the moonlight, the watchers about the tiger's neck gazed at her, at peace. And another eye winked into existence among them.

Kyrin stared in wonder. No falcon was caged and wingless among them. They were part of the cloud of witnesses from ages past. Her mother was one witness, and the falcon dagger one of a different kind. Kyrin's skin burned with cold. Would they witness aught but a fallen first daughter? She must get up, must learn to draw the sword in her hand against the beast, must fight it.

Next morn, a messenger from Lord Keffer brought a missive to Lord Bergrin. By his anxious look as he bowed before his great chair, the messenger wished he could disappear. Jorn wrote a terse reply.

He agreed to peace if one Lord Ludwin Mornoth withdrew all claim on his sister, Lady Myrna Jorn, of Jornhold. Keffer's messenger beamed, vastly relieved, when Bergrin sent him to the kitchen for a hearty meal and then to the stable with orders for a fresh horse.

Missives went to and from Cierheld over the following sevenday. The tiger pursued Kyrin through the dark bells near every night. Often the falcon fell, by claw, tooth, drowning, or in flame.

Kyrin began sitting in the garden alone, sometimes with Nell, once wandering it with Myrna and Celine. She could not speak of her dreams to Nell, though she wished she could walk with her father again. He would drive the beast back with his wisdom. But he was closeted with Lord Bergrin and his men or practicing at arms. They had not invited her to their drills, and Kyrin thought it best not to approach them without invitation.

Nesting, chirping birds, the flowers, trees, and garden herbs, even her quick pupils failed to pierce the fearful darkness that shut Kyrin inside her circling thoughts. She practiced the way of the warrior till her limbs were leaden with weariness. All her skill of heart, hand, and blade availed nothing.

Curled on a bench in a nook in a corner of the garden-wall near a rosebush, Kyrin sniffed back tears. The steward's gossip had led to nothing about Hamal. She was failing Tae and Alaina, trapped in the sands, hunted by the wazir and the caliph. Lord Keffer and Lord Mornoth were aware of Jornhold's defiance. And she herself drew their enmity against Bergrin and Cierheld.

If they did not yet know who took their prizes from under Lord Keffer's nose, they soon would. Her father was stretched thin between Cierheld and Fenwrd strongholds. Her godfather's hold had burned so fiercely the foundation stones of Fenwrd cracked, forcing them to begin rebuilding elsewhere within the wall.

There was Celine. Kyrin wiped away a tear. And one would think Uncle Ulf, since she was cleared of witchery, would hasten to seek out Cieri's daughter, his niece, however busy he might be. He also believed her unfit.

Her father had shaken his head with a sigh when she asked after her uncle. "Father Ulf comes to Cierheld seldom and does not stay long. He is no longer Cierheld's priest. I fear he blames me for Willa." Then Dain smiled. "But Cierheld's key is yet guarded. The raiders did not take it, and it will come to you. I found it on Willa. And you, you had laid her straight, Kyrin. That gave me hope. For we found you nowhere, but your mother lay in peace in that place. I know your Uncle Ulf would thank you for it, if he were here." Dain hugged her. "It was well done. Though when we reach Cierheld, there are changes." He had frowned, pain in his thinking look, and she did not ask.

Kyrin lifted her bare feet to her chill rock bench and curled cold arms around her knees, her throat aching. The scent of new roses was heavy, but the warmth of the sun felt thin. Because she failed, her mother had lain still and silent under the cloak she'd wrapped around her. She could smell the very stone.

"Kyrin?" Far too close, Talik looked down at her in concern, his sinewy shoulders and steady gaze alive with strength. "What ails you?"

She shrank back, buried in a place where every living thing she loved was dead or lost. Turning her head away, she blurted, "Nothing, I'm fine—"

"Don't say that." Talik's grey eyes were narrow. "You haven't been well for days."

Kyrin clenched her jaw. It did no good; tears gathered and fell.

The stone bench shifted as Talik sat on the end and stared at the pink-streaked, red blooms of the rosebush. Then he turned and gripped her shoulders abruptly.

Kyrin flinched, and he released her. She couldn't look at him.

He lowered his head till his eyes found hers. "What is it? What grieves you so?"

"The tiger." She gulped. "It hunts me. I thought it was gone."

Talik frowned.

She searched his eyes for understanding. "I—there's a tapestry—in my chamber. There was one like it on Ali's ship. The beast has followed me in my dreams since my mother died. I haven't even told my father that, or that the sword that took her did this." Miserably, Kyrin slid the fish aside from the scar on her neck. "I was afraid of blades, and the tiger came. But I broke the fear that gripped me in ice, the fear that grew when any blade came near. And I thought the beast was conquered too, when I freed the falcon in Araby. Our chains shattered."

"What do you mean?" Talik's voice was gentle.

"I gave it up—vengeance—and fear." She kicked one restless foot back and forth under the bench. "Vengeance was empty, dead ash. Mother did not want that, nor the Master of the stars, nor I, in the end. I fought my hate, and the falcon and I flew free of our chains. I did not dream of the tiger any more." She lifted her head with a small smile. "But the tiger has returned, nearer since the wazir sent me home." Scorn like a hot wind erupted and burned through her restraint. "I have come back, but still I fear. So the tiger comes." Her voice hardened. "To wield a blade with my body is not the same as wielding it well in spirit."

"Besides this tiger, do you blame yourself for your mother?" Talik asked softly.

"At times." Kyrin bit her lip. "Though I know it was not my doing. Father is sad when he thinks of her."

"And so glad to have you."

She shrugged a shoulder. "I am not the first daughter they think me." She touched the ring in her ear.

"No." Talik grinned. "But they love you nonetheless." Then his smile faded and he shifted. "His word can be a blade for defense. What do you fear?"

"I—" Kyrin looked down. "Many things. As well as the task to find Hamal for the wazir, for Alaina and Tae, as first daughter, I must protect Cierheld and my family. Now Lords Mornoth and Keffer threaten us all. Did I not once say I was stronger than they dreamed?" Her mouth twisted. "My father and the others, they expect something more, and so I fail again."

"All know you are not a coward, for you fought Lord Keffer's men, and in Keffold again. It is wisdom to avoid raising your blade until you see your target." Talik shook his head. His smile was wry. "You know, courage isn't a question of strength or failure or gaining what we seek, but trusting the one who made us. Then we can go forward, whether we fall or rise."

Kyrin looked at him and wished she had a sweetmeat to give him for saying "we." Then her smile pulled to one side. "Go forward? We do little but deal with messengers, who give us naught. No news of Hamal or Lord Keffer or Mornoth. And justice—what law or judge in this land can help Myrna and Bergrin, since the king cannot? What but the strength of our arms and the favor of heaven? The church will not, Father Ulf sent Brother Rolf to tell us it is none of their affair."

Talik crossed his arms. "You are wrong, I think. No news means our enemies stir little. And Brother Rolf looked none too happy to bear such a message. Father Ulf is but one of many deans to many priors and their abbots. But should you not forgive yourself first?"

"For what?"

"For not being what they want, even what *you* want." He shrugged. "It often helps, speaking truth. My washbasin overhears many things, of a morn, when I speak to God. I will help you tell this truth, if you like."

Her smile trembled. So was the blade raised against the tiger. By truth. By her hand and Talik's, together. As he looked at her, did his gaze warm? *Don't be a fool.* "My thanks."

"Well then." Talik leaned back and looked above the garden wall, addressing another. "We ask you, Father, give our daughter of Cierheld your cleansing and your courage, and I also. Uphold our hearts and holds and land by your truth. Keep us abiding within. We give you all thanks."

He said it so simply, and stopped. Uncle Ulf would frown. Kyrin added softly, "May it be so."

He looked at her with a smile of deep solemnity and joy. Kyrin said low, "You saved me from Nidfael's men, Talik. I will never forget that." She paused briefly then hurried on. "I don't trust Lord Keffer where I can see him, much less where I cannot. Lord Mornoth has more men than my father and Lord Jorn together, and wielders of power like Mornoth never stop. They are like the tiger. I've brought their regard to Cierheld and my father. Such destructive, ravening hunger. And my thoughts are the same; they circle me like beasts."

Talik nodded. "Yes, of a certain they can be beasts. At times black, fiery, and hungry. But they cannot stand against the Master of the stars's word. It is a blade of truth. Bind and destroy every false thought as it comes; you are the shire reeve of your thoughts. As for Lord Mornoth, he has had his eye on your father for some years. Lord Dain is ever in his way."

Kyrin stared. Talik sounded as if he fought the same war in his mind. As if he knew somewhat of the intrigues between the lords.

Talik shrugged and spread his hands. "Thoughts dart in and out like birds. Or vultures, depending on their nature. God demands right acting. So long as you don't follow your fears, you do well." He looked at her intently, a little anxious, and rubbed strong fingers on his knee, disturbing an insect that rested there; it spiraled up, buzzing gently amidst glinting, diaphanous wings. "It may be I speak too much." There was a silence, and Talik bowed his head, a slight crease between his brows.

"You speak right. I've been a fool. I forgot to ignore my heart when it was false." Kyrin swallowed back more tears.

"You know, you *are* silly." Talik grinned, taking the sting from the words. "If you don't hit yourself over the head for one thing, it's another. Let not regret poison this morn. He has the past, and the future. This day, live true."

"Yes, I can see that." Kyrin gripped her hands in her lap. If only her heart agreed. It seemed she must wait and think aright, until her heart aligned with truth.

Talik touched her hand. "As for us and Lord Mornoth, we have been made able to fight evil where we find it, by inner and outer battles. This you have done. It was not chance I passed by Mornoth and Keffer's men that night, to get you out of their clutches. The Master of all has given you knowledge and skill for a reason, probably many." He grasped her hands.

"Yes." She knew it well—there were so many ways to fall short as first daughter. Kyrin moved to pull away.

"No, wait, please."

His hands were so large, guarding hers.

"You *are* Cieri's daughter, always Lady of Cierheld. None can take that from you. Only you may give it up. I do not think you will. Do not forget that." He released her and sat back.

But if she were unfit—but as Talik said, courage wasn't a question of failure or gaining what she sought, but trusting. "Thank you, Lord Talik."

Talik laughed. "Why do you call me 'lord'? As far as you know I'm common born."

"I—well," she stammered. He acted like one.

"No matter." His voice light, he reached to finger a rose on the bush beside him. "What kind of rose is this, Lady?"

Myrna had called it Heartsblood of Love. Kyrin's face heated. She opened her mouth, and Talik looked over his shoulder at her then began to redden. He cleared his throat and stood, even as she did. "I brought you something—"

"I'd best go in soon. I told Myrna—" Smoothing her tunic, Kyrin glanced at her bare feet. How Esther would giggle, that a man came upon her in the garden with her toes bare. She looked up.

Talik held her pack and a blade in his hands. She stared at them, mouth open.

His lips twitched, and she snorted at him, and then they were laughing until Kyrin held her stomach. "Where—where did you find them?" she gasped at last, holding close the pack and the sword.

"I bought them with a little coin off Nidfael's man, Curnoth, after letting him know who he attacked. I whispered the names of your father's armsmen in his ear, and he was eager for these stolen goods to find their rightful owner. I'm afraid Keltie is gone for good." He sighed regretfully.

Kyrin shot him a sideways glance, smiling as she opened the pack. Her fingers closed on her Araby tunic. And Talik had gotten Bergrin's blade besides. Now she could return it with honor. "I thank you again." She bowed briefly then held the black cloak to her face, remembering Tae's sly humor, Alaina's grin, Cicero's happy bark as he circled her, waiting for a run. The hard shape of her stronghold key pressed against her cheek. Kyrin smiled.Tears of relief could come later. She had a friend.

Talik plucked a half-furled rose and held it out. "For a lady and a first daughter, returned to take her hold by storm."

Uncertain, sweet chaos. She took the rose, careful of the thorns.

His eyes were full of merriment. Beneath lurked steely purpose.

Kyrin's middle turned to water. What things did he purpose?

20

A home for the lonely. ~Psalm 68:6

Birdsong was in her ears. Kyrin sighed under her soft blanket. Talik had gone to his parents and his work, though the warmth of his smile remained. From the posts of the bed, gamin faces in the polished grain peered at her cheerfully. The cured hide springs creaked slightly, while the mattress of straw and feathers delighted her. She had tired of sleeping on the ground. Celine and Nell's beds were empty.

Kyrin slid out of bed and felt like skipping to the basin of heated water that Jornhold's servants had gotten used to supplying her every morn. Energy rose as she washed her face, and trailing the rough linen towel, she followed her eager feet to the nearest window. The wood shutters were thrown back and morning air crept in, fresh with dew, twining about her ankles. This day, she was on her way to Cierheld.

Over their morn meal of fruit, porridge, and eggs, Dain turned to Kyrin and said in a low voice, "There is something I must tell you. I have a wife. Her name is Elinor, and I have a half-son of nine years. Meric is a good boy."

Kyrin swallowed the suddenly large bite of apple in her mouth.

He ran his hands through his cropped hair. "I am sorry. I could think of no way to tell it easier."

Kyrin stared at the table then forced words around her thick tongue. "Does Meric—like hawks?" Surely he did.

Dain let out a long breath. "No. Meric studies books more than anything else. He's even delved into the text of a general that my grandfather had. *De Re Militari,* on the Eagles' military training. But Elinor, she loves to watch me shoot. And Meric shoots at times." He laughed a little. "Her tongue is sharp, though her heart is gold." He settled back. "Well, you will meet them soon enough. You will be interested to see the wall, and we've added entire fields to the plow. Your inheritance is full, my daughter." Hope and pride shone in his face as he kissed her cheek. Kyrin smiled, enjoying the warmth of his arm, while the rest of her felt rather numb.

Lord Bergrin saw Myrna off again, though he'd said she could stay with him if she wished. But Myrna was determined to learn the ways of Subak. She mounted, packed on her horse between Nell, Celine, and Kyrin's mounts, for they would travel inside a ring of Lord Dain's men. Berd crowded at Kyrin's back, and Hal rode in proud attendance. The band camped two nights on the road and neared Cierheld the third afternoon.

They entered the woods and wended along a wide dale. Kyrin's blood quickened. The hills that surrounded her valley were tall, and beautiful with trees. Just before the low pass leading into Cierheld's valley, a helmed man in chain mail stepped from a copse of elm, twenty men with ready bows at his back.

He looked straight at Dain and cried loudly, "Aster!"

Dain did not blink an eye. "Kyrin's peace!" he roared. The guardsmen stepped back into the trees, and Dain slowed his horse to rest his hand on the leader's shoulder. "Well done, Cid."

Dain glanced at Kyrin as his horse moved on. "I've ordered the men to challenge all who pass, regardless of who they appear to be. My command has been followed well." He grinned and combed an oak leaf from his hair.

Kyrin looked from the staring guardsmen to the elms overshadowing them. In a candlemark they left the woods and rode out onto the higher floor of the valley. The fields about Cierheld were indeed larger.

Men and women readied the dark soil for planting, their weapons beside them. Even the ploughman had a sword at his hip. Kyrin looked sharply over her shoulder at Berd. He nodded. Cierheld was on alert.

More of the trees had been cleared. Every man, woman, or child made some gesture of respect as Dain passed, and some bowed to Kyrin. Her hands grew clammy on the reins. These were her people.

A worker's steady eye caught her's, and he bowed solemnly. Kyrin dipped her head in return. Her father had always received steadfast love and loyalty, but that his people showed it so openly declared something more, an allegiance. Her father rode straight in the saddle, garbed in mail and leather and black linen. He bore the sigil of two strongholds over his breast. And what did she bring him?

Kyrin's eyes misted. In the morn, at his side, she would practice at his shooting butts, the first daughter of Cieri.

A lush, low-cut meadow extended farther than a bowshot from the walls. Sparse grass grew on the mound above the ditch. They had not been attacked recently, or that rampart above the moat would have been churned to mud.

Lord Dain had warded Cierheld well with her godfather's stone. The stronghold wall was thick enough for two to walk abreast, and a moat and the broad earth mound surrounded that. The great wood gate with metal hinges had a smaller door. It opened for them, for one person to enter at a time. Dain waved Kyrin ahead, grinning.

She dismounted and passed through, leading her mount, sniffing at the stone and moss, the homey smell of horse and hound, the mouthwatering scent of porridge and plum cake. The narrow entryway had high walls and no roof. Armsmen peered down at her until another door, with a loud scrape of three bars drawn on the opposite side, opened to admit her. Kyrin stepped through. And paused.

To her left were the mews, stables, and smithy, with the chicken shed and kennels behind. The kitchen faced her on the right, with the cellar beneath. Beyond the kitchen, the well was out of sight behind it, but she glimpsed archery butts further down the lane. The great hall itself was little changed to her eye, though the grounds had grown between it and the kitchen. It remained twenty-five giant strides long, or seventy feet, as she jerked into motion and strode toward the stables. Wide steps rose to the same thick oak door she remembered.

Kyrin gave her horse's lead into a man's hand, Berd and the others having followed her toward the stables. Lord Dain halted at her elbow, and Hal and the others gathered behind. With a deep breath, Kyrin slowly stepped around the hall steps and looked past the corner of the hall.

The live oak she'd climbed so long ago, now towered above her window, and the barracks stretched farther than they had, with a new woodshed at the end. A hawk called overhead, short and harsh. Kyrin stopped dead.

A dark shape bobbed on a branch high in the oak. Kyrin held her breath, leaning forward. A hawk sidled along the branch, regal head streaked brown and white.

"Father, one of the goshawks is loose!" She pointed.

"Ahh." Dain squinted up at the bird, then turned to her. "Don't you remember? He was cast out of the nest."

The goshawk cocked his head to examine her with a red-gold eye. "Samson! He still lives."

"Yes. He comes to the oak now and then. None of us can touch him."

On a sudden impulse, Kyrin raised her arm, wrapped it in the tail of her cloak, and whistled. Samson looked down at her and screamed. Kyrin chirked back, her heart in her throat. He lifted his wings and floated from his perch. Then the wind of his hover fanned her face, throwing back her hood. He had grown into the largest tercel she'd ever seen. Kyrin chirruped again softly even as her heart beat fast.

Samson folded his wings and dropped to her arm. She steeled herself as he thumped to rest, his talons pricking through the cloak. She stroked his soft head and down his back as he eyed her close.

A cheer burst from the crowd of men, women, and children who had moved forward, unnoticed as she coaxed Samson down. Samson flapped furiously, and Kyrin bent, her face hot, to talk soft nonsense to Samson as she covered his eyes to quiet him.

"Well, I'll be!" Dain put his hand on her shoulder, and a joyous laugh sprang from his throat. Not to alarm the goshawk, he stepped away and spread his arms and spun slowly, gesturing toward Kyrin. "My daughter has come home! Our first daughter has indeed returned!"

A second thunderous cheer roared between the walls, joined by Hal, Nell, and Myrna. Celine grimaced.

Kyrin fiercely willed her knees steady, and bowed to the ring of strange, excited faces. Cierheld men and women smiled and called greetings, but she saw none she remembered.

Samson clacked his beak aloud, and Dain pointed Kyrin toward the mews. "We must get him to a perch and a meal."

"Yes." Kyrin walked as smoothly as she could, not to jar him.

Cernalt's short, thick frame filled the mews door, his scarred face bearing a wide smile. "Well, the lost ones have come home." He bowed his head and held out his arm to usher them inside, then turned to retrieve a hawk's hood from his supply against one wall. Kyrin stayed close, her cloak shielding Samson's eyes.

"Well now, there ye are." Cernalt walked the hawk onto an empty ash perch.

Kyrin remembered something else, and glanced down. Under Samson's perch and the littered floor, the tunnel out of Cierheld began, to emerge within the mill outside the gate. Not many enemies who gained the walls would look for an escape route in the mews. It was known only to her family, and the eldest armsman—Cernalt. But this was no time to think of enemies.

Cernalt pulled the end of Kyrin's cloak from Samson's eyes. With a small sound in his throat, the hawk looked at the perch between his talons then with a flap and a sudden hop, he found her arm again, driving her wrist down beneath his weight. Kyrin rocked back a half step and stroked him with a shaking hand.

So he felt it, too. This night, her hawk would have no tether but his oak at her window. Unless her old room was another's. No, not her room, her chamber. And only if Cernalt was not angered by a bird that refused his keeper.

"So that's the way the wind lies, is it? Unusual, a hawk that takes to a human." The grizzled armsman nodded, and his washed-out blue eyes flashed over Kyrin from head to foot, quick and sharp. His gaze lingered on her necklace, as if he could see the scar beneath, and Kyrin flushed, fingering it.

Cernalt eyed her, grunted, then gave her the formal gesture of respect. He pressed his fist to his heart, touched his forehead and flicked out his fingers, pledging her his heart, head and hand.

Kyrin shivered. This was the inheritance she had returned to. Cierheld and all its people, many of whom she no longer knew. But Cernalt did not think more of her than she was.

"Old friend," she said low, and stepped toward him. He hugged as much of her as he could reach, with Samson on her arm, then coughed and, with a bow and an apologetic nod to Dain. "My lord."

Dain simply grinned.

Kyrin covered Samson's eyes with the hood Cernalt handed her. Cernalt had the high, thin windows that ran lengthwise under the eaves unshuttered for light and air. There were five other hawks, but the corner where Esther's gyr once rested was empty, and the remaining perches seemed lonely. Kyrin cocked her head, wondering at their emptiness, though Cernalt cared for them well.

Dain sighed. "Once I had the desire and the days to devote to hunting. Now I hunt more two-legged than four-legged prey." He grimaced. "At least you can eat the four-legged; the first is generally worthless. But with you and Samson we'll have some grand hunts. Meric will have to leave his parchments for a moment, to help gather us hare and duck." Dain's eyes twinkled. "But now, my lady and the hall waits to welcome their first daughter."

The hall awaited. And her mother was not there. Kyrin followed him across the yard, and up the wide steps, wishing she could stay with Berd and the others to unload the horses and gear. The oak of Cierheld's great door held the strength she remembered, perhaps smoother and darker with weathering.

A young woman opened the door, and her gaze went to Samson. She hesitated a bare instant then stepped aside, clutching her tunic with work-worn hands. She was tall and strong, and her wide grey eyes were clear beneath wheat-brown hair braided gracefully about her head. It was streaked with gold from the sun. She smiled at them. "You are well come, my lord, and—our first daughter."

Her voice was soft, her smile faultless. Kyrin's skin prickled. Elinor could not be more than a hand of years older than she. She kept close watch on her frozen feet for Samson's sake.

§

The pain of Elinor's thought wiped away her smile. *Will she have any of Penni's gracefulness?* She forced her smile back in place, but her first daughter's careful bow and even more careful, "My thanks, my Lady Elinor," struck her with cool wariness. Elinor blinked. Did she expect unkindness?

The first daughter of Cierheld strode past her. Clad in a black tunic, she carried on her arm the untamable hawk that haunted the oak and Elinor's beloved chickens. Her full trousers were gathered at the ankle, and beside the dagger in her belt rested a short, dark stick. She caressed the gleaming head of the dagger without thought.

It was also a falcon. The same sent to Dain, that took him from her side. Elinor swallowed. This—Kyrin—touched it as if it comforted her, as if she knew well how to use it. *For Dain's sake I wish her to love me, if not as a mother, as a sister. But how can Dain allow that hawk in the hall?* But she had been a slave.

Dain's daughter swallowed and dropped her gaze, and Elinor flushed. A lady should never give less than full welcome. She motioned her further within. "Come to the table," she murmured. "Cook will have the lamb ready in a shake."

"My Elinor." Dain squeezed her shoulders, and Elinor smiled at him, but her gaze followed Kyrin. She walked before them as Elinor had asked, her eyes intense in her rather thin face, a gaze that gave away nothing, roaming about the hall. She fingered her stick, and paused, eyeing the weapons rack beneath the stair.

Elinor frowned. Her new first daughter seemed apt to turn to weapons, far more than a lady should. Of course, she had no one to defend her but herself in those burning foreign lands. Elinor pursed her mouth. Here there were armsmen, despite what Dain said of a weapon in the hand. Kyrin would learn so, though she was Dain's daughter. She must give her time. Elinor nodded.

§

Kyrin made her way toward the high table. Though civil enough, she thought Elinor did not merit Margye's calling her "sun hair."

A weapons rack hung on the back wall, where her instincts sent her gaze under the shadowed stairs after a quick glance around the near-empty tables. The rack held ash spears and clubs for the most part. Talik had said her father trained everyone. He spoke true. Either Cierheld was on a war footing or her father had reason to be cautious. Blades *were* dangerous for the untrained.

Though Cook would be lethal with her chopping knife, with daily training on vegetables. Was she the same kind, crusty woman who'd helped her mother weave Kyrin's last name-day crown of bluebells? Kyrin swallowed. She'd worn two crowns that day, one of knotwork bronze as first daughter, the other of bluebells for her name-day. Crowns and conflict seemed to go together.

She laid a hand on Samson's soft feathers. Considering Elinor's sigh when she first opened the door, she might be on a war footing herself.

A lump blocked Kyrin's throat. Instead of wiping her eyes she looked up. The rafters were thick and familiar, as was the twice man-length fireplace on her left, at the end of the hall nearest the door. The stone floor spreading beneath three tables set end-to-end on her right was clean, and the sparse hangings she and her mother had embroidered and woven had been extensively added to.

A tousle-headed youngster rose with a rustle of cloth on wood from the long bench opposite her father's seat and Elinor's at the high table. He moved quickly forward and stopped in front of her. Wide grey eyes stared up at her from under long lashes and shoulder length, white corn-silk hair. He was slight, yet sturdy enough. His face was thoughtful.

Meric looked from her strange tunic to her weapons. "You are my sister, Kyrin. I'm glad they didn't kill you too." He stared at Samson curiously.

"Meric!" his mother gasped.

Kyrin's smile widened. His words might be taken amiss, since her return sealed her inheritance that might have been his. But he meant his words. This brother of hers did not call false "well come" when he did not know her. Though he looked ready enough to smile. "Yes, I am glad too." Meric's deserted book rested on the corner of the far table. "Did I interrupt your reading? Father says you enjoy *De Re Militari.*"

"You know it?" His quick look saw that she did not mock, and his face lit. Catching his mother's frown, he said, "But it is time for supper. Mother has ordered a feast." Reddening under their eyes he bowed to Kyrin jerkily, then ran to wrap his arms around Dain's waist.

"Oh ho!" Dain hugged him and laid his hands on his shoulders. "Meric, what companies have you routed this day among your pens and ink? Fear not, between you and Kyrin, we'll soon have these petty squabblers running with their tails between their legs, with all honor to the king, or my name is not Dain Cieri." He cleared his throat. "Kyrin, you'll want to see your chamber. It is the same. Elinor has prepared the chamber near the stair for the Lady of Jornhold." He gestured toward the door of the small guest chamber beyond the fireplace. Myrna curtsied to him and led Celine toward it.

"Yes, Father. Nell will be with me—" But Nell was already at Kyrin's shoulder, and followed them up the stairs, while Samson kept his balance, talons clenching Kyrin's arm, flicking his tail.

At the top of the stair it was seven strides past the room her father and Elinor shared, to a second chamber on the right at the end, near the rooftree. The chamber on the opposite side was doubtless Meric's.

Kyrin drew a breath and stepped into her old room. The window, smaller than she remembered, opened east, nuzzled by the great limbs of Samson's oak. A small table with two unlit oil lamps and a spun pottery basin full of wildflowers stood below it, in the last light of the window. Her rough-hewn bed stood on the other side, the stolid head posts close to the chimney for warmth. The knots and running gold grain were bumpy under her fingers. It felt familiar, and yet not. One lady of Cierheld was gone, and another had taken her mother's place. Kyrin bit her lip.

Elinor did no ill, that she comforted her father. And Meric was kind for a boy of his summers. She'd have to see he became no spoiled lord's son.

"Well." Nell beamed. "This is beautiful."

The floor had been swept, and the embroidered linen coverlet on the bed invited Kyrin. If she could only lie down. But no, it would not be kind to her family or the rest of Cierheld. And her stomach growled at the smell of roasted potatoes and lamb. The kitchen was busy.

"Be welcome here," she said to Nell. "Put your things wherever you like." Kyrin indicated the space beyond the bed with her chin.

Nell glanced at her in doubt, shrugged, set Kyrin's bags by her bed, and then her own against the wall. She smoothed her skirt uncertainly. "I'll get water for washing."

"My thanks." Kyrin touched the soft cup of a bluebell as Nell slipped out the door. She smiled at the gingery smell and leaned across the table to set Samson on the window sill. At least she had Nell.

Removing the hawk's hood, she stroked his back. He eyed her with his bright orange gaze, cocking his head. Then he flipped about, hopped from the window to a branch, and moved deeper into the gloom of the oak, a sleepy noise in his throat. Kyrin chirruped good night and watched him until he disappeared.

She sat on the bed, hands resting on her belt near her weapons. Forcing herself to relax, she pulled out her dagger and stick to test their familiar edges. She need not fear, Elinor would be quick to say, this was Cierheld after all. Kyrin slid the falcon dagger under her pillow and the stick back in her belt.

Nell pushed open the door, carrying a basin of steaming water and a burning pitch sliver. "Here you are, my lady." She set the basin on the table and lit the lamps, then doused the sliver. The smoke of the pine smelled better than Ali's best frankincense.

"Back so soon?" Kyrin teased. "The well must have been at the bottom of the stair."

"No, lady, a girl handed it to me, nice and hot, but I will get more in the morn—"

Kyrin grimaced. Nell was also uncertain of her place. "You think your worth lies in how much you slave for me, after I served Ali, and know what it is to be bound to another's will?"

"Should you not—might you not—need a handmaiden now that you are a lady and in your own place? All serve you here." Nell looked at Kyrin steadily. Her hands gripped her tunic.

"No. You are my friend, Nell, far above a handmaiden. I only agreed to it because you termed it so. To my mind you have always been my companion. You only serve me as handmaiden when you wish, if you wish."

Nell's lips firmed. "I do. That was our bargain."

"Very well." Kyrin inclined her head and moved to the basin. Word of her strange washing habit had preceded her, it seemed. Nell meant to take her duties seriously, and she could not fault her for it. She combed out her hair and brushed dust from her black tunic.

No first daughter would wear such. She had wanted all to know who she was, but she ought to have worn the tunic and trousers she'd bought in the port this day, for all they were not so fine. It was not her purpose to shame Elinor, no matter Elinor's first distaste. Her Araby garb would look very odd at table. But it was too late. Both tunics were dirty, and the black was the best of the two.

Kyrin took off her boots and opened her pack to find her soft, leather winter inserts. The wood floor warmed her bare toes, heated by the fire in the fireplace below and the chimney near the end of her chamber. She could have dry feet at least. As she tugged on the last leather sock, a soft tap sounded on her door.

"Come in."

Elinor looked around the corner of the door, glanced at Nell, unpacking her things, then back at Kyrin. "I—I asked Dain—I mean your father—if you had a tunic for this night. Please, take no offense," she continued hastily. "Your father said he didn't know, but I have something you might favor." Eagerness peeped around the edges of her nervous smile.

"Yes, I would like that. I have none. Thank you. My mother," Kyrin added, with an awkward, shy smile. Already turning away, Elinor stumbled.

Kyrin frowned. "Did—do you want me to call you Elinor?"

"No, no, not at all," Elinor whispered, without looking back, and fled.

Kyrin bit her lip and frowned at Nell. She had thought calling Elinor "Mother" would please her, though Elinor could never fill her mother's place. It was just a word, applied to Elinor.

Her recovered key meant far more. The moment was not ripe to show it to her father or Elinor. She had carried it so long, and it held so much memory . . . and promise.

21

Hamal

Like the cold of snow in the time of harvest is a faithful messenger.
~Proverbs 25:13

Elinor and Dain occupied their chairs at the head of the long table. Kyrin was seated at her father's right elbow on the closest end of the bench. On the opposite side of the board, Nell, Myrna, and Celine lined up on Elinor's left hand. Kyrin wished Celine would smile, rather than avoid her gaze. At least Cernalt, across from her, kept conversation lively and smiled often. Nith joined Cid, the sentry who challenged them at the pass that afternoon, and his men down and round the far end of the table. Hal sat on Kyrin's right, and Meric peered at her around Hal's bulky frame. Berd stood near the wall behind her father's chair, fully armed.

It was a festive gathering. The green-and-brown mottled tunics of the men were grass and earth to the women's bright dress. Such would blend well in the woods. Elinor's kirtle of robin's egg blue brushed the floor. Kyrin stroked her embroidered collar. The one Elinor loaned her was near the same shade. The griffin, bird, or dragon, she was not sure which, strode around the sleeve cuffs and hem, interwoven with knot work of green and gold. It was beautiful, worthy of a first daughter and of the blood of the hills. Her mother would have clapped her hands in delight and asked her to twirl, that she might see the full effect. Elinor's needlework rivaled old Aunt Medaen's. But where was Aunt Medaen?

Kyrin leaned forward. "Father, Aunt Medaen, is she—"

"By the blessed saints! Pardon, daughter, it's just that I forgot. My sister has gone to stay with Lady Ynglida Govannon."

Talking with Cernalt and Hal, Nith turned his head. Celine, who had been laughing at something Myrna said, closed her mouth. Silence fell.

Elinor sighed. "It's a long, old story, not fit for airing the night of your welcome. It would be better if we speak of it later."

"Ah, yes, quite right." Dain nodded.

"As you will." Kyrin smiled and looked at her wooden spoon of potatoes. She hoped nothing was amiss. The rest of the hold soon jested over their food at the other two tables, and her smile widened. It was good to hear clean laughter again.

Ali's table had been privy to schemes, oily flattery, or brittle silence. Cierheld's board would never resemble his, as she was first daughter. Elinor stared at her plate when conversation lagged, her eyes tired. It was the only thing that marred the delicately roasted lamb and mouthwatering, spiced potatoes, for Kyrin had not tasted potatoes since her capture. Dain held Elinor's hand gently in his. He caught Kyrin's eye, and his grin bloomed, eyes twinkling.

It was an old sorrow then, nothing to do with her. Kyrin ate another bite of potato and grinned at Meric behind Hal's broad back. Her new brother's *De Re Militari* interested her. Tae would approve. And Tae would skin her if she didn't learn more of it. He studied all the different systems of military combat, tactics, and strategy that he could get his hands on.

In bed, after Kyrin snuffed the lamp, Nell began to snore. Kyrin rolled over. Her window was open to the night and the rustling song of the oak. She wondered where Talik was. Did he sleep safe or somewhere in the open on a dangerous scout? Her father and Bergrin Jorn had pledged each other to keep an eye on Lord Mornoth. Talik might be part of that, within his duties as messenger.

Would her father stay in Cierheld, since her return, or would he be all the more vigilant against thieves and marauders? If he went out, she must find a way to go with him. She might even see Talik again. As for the wazir—Hamal slept nearby under these very stars, and would soon be found. Then Alaina and Tae would be safe. Kyrin nestled into the black tunic she'd rolled into a pillow. It smelled faintly of desert smoke, camels,and rosewater.

In the morn she went down to breakfast, in black again. Her father was gone. She should have been with him, shooting at the butts or doing whatever he thought fit, but he and Hal had gone out with Nith before dawn. Elinor knew nothing more. Kyrin swallowed her disappointment and said little over her porridge.

Myrna and Celine joined them. As soon as Meric finished his last bite, Elinor cleared the table and sent him to his studies. Kyrin rose. She could go with Nell to her room, to Myrna's chamber, or outside. Elinor tentatively invited them to join her at her embroidery.

"My thanks, my lady, but no." Kyrin suppressed a shiver. She had plans involving her rangdo, a horse, and Samson, not displaying her inept hand at a needle. Why had her father left her alone this first morn?

Elinor nodded and turned sharply from the table.

Myrna said in her soft voice, as if she'd meant to say it all along, "My lady, I would be pleased this eve if you would show me the stitches and colors for that tapestry of the hunt," and pointed at a hanging on the wall of a helmed warrior in a forest, with a hawk on his arm. "Since I am not truly robed at the moment for sitting before a hoop"—Myrna glanced at her trousers—"I must practice with the others. But it would please me well to sit with you."

Elinor smiled. "Lady Myrna, it pleases me well also." She turned toward the stair gracefully, her handmaid behind her.

Meric looked after his mother, tucking his lower lip behind his teeth. Kyrin wished she had not forgotten to call Elinor "Mother." Meric caught Kyrin's eyes on him and his *De Re Militari* rustled as he quickly found his place.

Kyrin asked Nell, Celine, and Myrna to meet her and Hal on the bit of flat ground behind the mews. She had no wish to display her skill before the men in the barracks, though the ground was wider there. She gathered her pack, went out the small end door of the hall and peeped within the kitchen, where Cook gave her a pasty.

As Kyrin ate quickly, Samson flew to perch on the mews' ridgepole. Celine and the others ran around the chicken shed and the kennels and then did warming exercises. Kyrin showed them a round-kick drill she'd done every sun with Alaina. It started on a slow tempo, ending with them kicking each other as fast as they could. There was little strength in their blows. Kyrin frowned as she watched. Her rangdo were blessed without knowing it. Next time they'd run the entire yard, from the west side well, around the shooting butts and the woodshed, past the armsmen's quarters and barracks, then between the hall and the smithy, stables, and mews, back to Cierheld's gate.

She'd get Berd to find her some old, straw archery butts for the morrow. She must also find a leather-worker to make bodyshielding for her rangdo—but she had no cane. Would simple layers of leather work? Talik might know. Rangdo must learn to give and receive full-power strikes, and never to depend on metal armor.

She looked up. The feathers on Samson's head crested in the light wind, one orange eye peering at her then the other. Once or twice he shrieked softly and cleaned his beak on the ridgepole under his talons. Cernalt sat mending the hawks' leather hoods in a patch of sunshine before the mews, absorbed in his work.

Kyrin drew a deep breath. This morn her rangdo struck naught but air. She showed Hal the snapping front kick: crippling to the instep, the knees, the inside of the legs and the groin, not to mention the stomach. Celine's attempts at punches, Myrna's open-hand blows, and their front, back, and sidekicks improved a little. Kyrin went through the kicks beside them and left her place often to correct position and speed. When Myrna began to gasp for air, set her mouth stubbornly, and kicked on, Kyrin sent them all for a drink from the well beyond the kitchens.

Then it was back to mock hand strikes to the throat, neck, eyes, temples, and back of the head. Once they had solid targets, they would work the same areas hard, followed by the staff and then the short stick. Working with climbing claws and other weapons would come later. She must establish her own practice pattern before she began to teach blades to her rangdo. Kyrin wiped her brow.

She needed that body-shielding. It taught one how to take a strike and redirect the force. Then a hard blow was not debilitating, and one could learn to fade away from it with the proper exhalation, and the *kiyop*, the short sharp yell that tightened every core muscle of the body for defense or attack. Striking at full strength without injury brought learning to both attacker and defender.

The barracks were astir. Berd's voice echoed down the lane between kitchen and hall. "Right side—hold! Left side—close up. Shields up, spears forward! Your enemy will not stop unless you stop them!"

Kyrin cocked her head. Men thumped and clattered and yelled in the unseen give and take of blows. It sounded as if Berd filled the place of second armsman well.

Terce neared, and her rangdos' last strengthening stances. Legs braced wide, knees bent, toes straight ahead, in moments the horse stance had their legs shivering like leaves in an autumn wind. Kyrin grinned. It was good the ground was yet packed and damp, without the choking dust and heat of summer, or of Araby. "Enough!" She had talked continuously, done the drills with them, and still had strength and breath to correct them. Kyrin's mouth quirked in a pleased smile. Her breath and walk were yet long and even.

Myrna panted, "How—did you *ever*—get so tough?"

"I ran out of breath, until I hardened. There are more drills."

There was a collective cry of despair.

Kyrin caught back a laugh. "Don't fear. You will learn more every time you practice, I give you my oath. Even if you do not think so, your limbs will learn and strengthen." Kyrin touched Myrna's shoulder. "Your hand strikes are strong." Myrna smiled and stared down at her fingers. "And Celine, your kicks need directed aright, but they are fast and hard." Celine scowled. Kyrin lifted her chin. "Soon you will take a man from his horse. Mayhap that will tame your ill humor."

Celine opened her mouth and closed it, and Kyrin turned to Nell. "Nell, you learn quickly." Nell grinned. Kyrin frowned at them all. "Remember, work on what I told you during our practice. I am going to do my own training. I will be back in a bell or so. Good day!"

Ignoring their open mouths, she picked up the bundle of food she'd gathered from the kitchen when she talked with Cook, who'd cried on her shoulder, overcome at her return. With the bundle was a hawking glove from Cernalt.

Kyrin pulled it on and whistled. Samson flew to her arm, and she slipped the hood over his head and walked toward the stables. Celine led the others toward the well, feet shuffling with weariness. Celine wiped sweat from her face as she went, red hair sticking to her temples. Kyrin felt Cernalt's eyes on her back. Had her father not taken her with him because he felt her a bone of contention? Or weak? Worse yet , had Elinor convinced him to leave her at Cierheld this morn? She must go. In the woods could she drive off the thoughts that plagued her.

§

"It's orders, my lady." The sentry at the gate stared somewhere over Kyrin's left shoulder, where her horse whuffled in her ear.

"Whose orders, sir?" Mayhap he did not yet know his first daughter's face. "Are they meant for the first daughter of Cierheld?"

Berd's voice came from behind her. "Yes. Lord Dain's orders keep us all. No one is to go out alone."

Kyrin spun. Her horse backed a step, flinging his head up with a snort. "Ever?" Her voice swung higher. Never to have the wind, water, and wings in her ears, without the voices of men?

"For the time. And Twr is not to speak beyond what his watching demands. He must have eyes for the sentries further out, who forward messages from beyond the wall." Berd's dark gaze assessed her as Twr turned hurriedly to his post.

Kyrin reddened. She ought to have known not to speak overlong with a warder. It was rare she could get a guard at any gate to listen to her long, even when she was a slave at Ali's. Why did she feel enslaved again—it was a reasonable order, given the nature of things at the moment. She nodded and turned away, her whole body heavy.

"I will go with you where you wish, as long as you do not seek Lord Keffer's gates." There was a small curve to Berd's wide mouth.

He meant to make her laugh. But it *would* be better to go to the woods with him than not. She needed her own practice and the quiet outside the hold. She would also learn if she could trust his tongue not to wag. Keeping Subak's secrets would be hard for an armsman who depended on learning of warfare. But she was his first daughter. Mayhap he would.

"My thanks." Kyrin led the way through the small door Twr opened in the gate, Berd following. Berd might even teach her a bit of the sword he wore so well. Or speak to her of Lady Ynglida and old Medaen, since her father seemed none too anxious to meet her questions.

Kyrin sighed. That was unworthy. The lord of Cierheld did nothing without good reason, and a good reason there must be for him to leave Cierheld without her the very morn after their return. She might also discover the answer to that.

At the midday bell Kyrin returned, well satisfied, her hair damp. Berd had let her swim in the stream alone, and she had not been long, for the water was cold. Nith strode alongside them as they came in the gate. "Lady Kyrin, I trust you enjoyed Cierheld's woods?"

"Yes, indeed." Kyrin grinned. "Where is my father?"

Cernalt took their horses' bridles at the stable entrance. "Within, at the midday meal." He and Nith exchanged glances.

"My thanks." Kyrin dismounted and hurried toward the hall while Nith walked with his second toward the barracks, speaking low and swift. Kyrin smiled. Berd had been most helpful in dispelling her fears. Her father indeed had cause to go out early.

Over the next seven-day she trained herself and her rangdo hard. There was need of it if even half of what Berd told her was true. Then the messenger her father had sent for news of Cedsel and Hamal returned.

Kyrin ran up the steps and into the hall, past Elinor's frown. She waited until the messenger had delivered his word to her father, bowed, and backed respectfully away, before she strode to the side of Dain's great chair.

"It seems we have found a bargain, Kyrin." Lord Dain's smile was grim. "Lord Nidfael Keffer will meet me in two days in the valley of Buckden Pike—with one of his slaves that he bought from Cedsel, who matches Hamal's description. I will pay a sum, and he is ours." Dain sighed, and sent her a sharp look under his brows. "I will buy him even if he is not the one you seek."

"It is well. I hope he is Hamal," Kyrin said somberly. "The one you sent could not find out?"

"He could not get close enough." Dain's smile slid sideways. "Lord Keffer suspected prying eyes, and rightly so. Will you come? You know the hardness of slavery, and the ways of his land."

"I do. I will gladly come."

"Hah! I suspect it would be hard to keep you back."

Kyrin's mouth twitched, and her father shook his head, smiling. "It is good to have you with me, Kyrin."

§

Kyrin waited on Cauldron's black back in a meadow below Buckden Pike. Her father had gifted her the stallion. Clad in her pale Araby robes, flowing around Cauldron's dark sides, she was a sight the Cierheld men behind and before had never seen. The leather circlet Elinor had insisted on making to replace the worn band of her kaffiyeh fit perfectly. Across her forehead three falcon's talons hung from the braided leather, while the cloth tapped her cheeks. The wind rustled the tall grass about her ankles and twisted Cauldron's mane around her hands. His ears twitched forward, and he arched his neck.

Ten riders emerged through the boughs of an opposite stand of evergreens, three slightly ahead of the rest. The middle rider glowed in a brown tunic so rich it neared purple. On Lord Nidfael Keffer's right his armsman carried a standard. On his left was a slight figure mounted before a thick-bodied armsman. Stiff and straight, Hamal sat as far from his captor as possible, and looked neither right nor left, his arms tied at wrist and elbow, his ankles bound with a length of rope passed beneath the horse's belly. Dark of skin, with gazelle eyes, he looked almost—beautiful. His face was full of poison, the coppery taste of hate Kyrin knew well.

Hooves thudded on the grassy ground behind, and Lord Dain and the tensquad spread around Kyrin. Lord Keffer stopped.

He raised his hand. "Let your first daughter retrieve her prize, so there is no possibility of mistaken unpleasantness." His voice was rich, yet it lacked something.

Without turning his head, Dain said to Kyrin, "He has always barked about Mornoth's feet. Our men have scouted well. This time and place do not favor him, not unless his wits have left. He knows we will start nothing if you are in his reach, and that we will kill him if *he* does. Go with care. We will watch."

"If he forces our hand, he will find more than he can chew." Kyrin urged Cauldron forward. As she neared Keffer and his men she suddenly wished she had a blade in hand.

Hamal's hair had been haggled short, probably with a knife. Patches of it had been jerked out by the roots. Bruises darkened his cheek and temple. His face was strained and pale, his lips cracked from lack of water as he licked them. A linen rag the poorest of the poor would have scorned hung about his thin body. He caught pitifully at it to keep his frame covered. Wrath and tears rose in Kyrin's throat, then his gaze rose and caught her's. His lip trembled and stiffened, and he lifted his head higher, if that were possible.

Nidfael laughed. "I said send your first daughter, not some wandering servant from a far land—"

"I am Kyrin Cieri, of Cierheld!" Kyrin cried, and closed the last distance between them. She halted Cauldron beside Hamal and dismounted, staring coldly at Lord Keffer's armsman as the man gaped at her. She turned and held out a heavy leather bag toward Nidfael. He watched her, lip curling. Kyrin took a step and dropped the bag into his palm, ready to strike him first if need be. "Your price."

At his lord's nod, the armsman slid down and loosed the captive's feet, pulling him free to stand on the grass. Hamal blinked, stepped toward Kyrin, and his legs buckled. Only Kyrin's quick grip under his arms saved him from rolling under Cauldron.

"So you buy this sack of dung, do you?" Lord Nidfael Keffer's lips were wide, his curious blue eyes just too far apart to add charm to a face most would call handsome in a soft way. "I would think you would wish no reminder of Araby, first daughter. Or do you want him for your idle hours, and pain?" He smiled, with a toss of his head. "Your uncle has spoken of you. Though you seem to have a talent for climbing walls, better you should take a strong lord to rule beside you."

"If you have met him, then surely you know there are many kinds of strength, my lord," Kyrin said between her teeth, ignoring his reference to her raid on his hold. "Kindness is one, and true dealing another." She boosted Hamal up and helped him slide one leg over Cauldron's great back. "As for the slave, he is near beaten senseless." She glared at the armsman and twitched free his mount's reins then slid onto its back.

Nidfael sputtered "First daughter, the beast was not in our bargain!"

"No, but the coin is yours, double what you asked. And know this. The wazir of Araby's vengeance will be swift if you follow, or touch Hamal again. I was sent for him."

Nidfael gaped as she turned the armsman's beast, urging Cauldron and his burden toward her people. His voice rose. "Think not you can turn your back on me! One day you will face me and fall, first daughter! Your father cannot always guard your tail." He cursed and shouted after them, "Cierheld is a kennel of heretics and treacherous dogs!"

Kyrin did not look back. Hamal stayed at her side. She watched her father's men, counting on their watchful faces and hands poised on weapons to reveal any treachery behind. They reached the tensquad and, leaning toward Hamal, Kyrin cut the cords that bound his wrists and elbows. She muttered in his ear in Arabic, "You have eaten of my bread and salt." And pressed the falcon dagger into his dirt-stained hands. Sagging over Cauldron's neck, he clutched the weapon as if it were life and death.

"You affront my honor!" Lord Nidfael Keffer yelled.

"What of the damaged goods?" Dain shouted back.

Nidfael scowled and gestured his men toward the trees.

"I would not have him say Cierheld took aught of his." Kyrin got down, turned the horse's head, and slapped its rump. The beast trotted across the meadow after its master, and Dain nodded. The men were silent, Berd's face giving nothing.

"Forget not my words, first daughter!" Lord Keffer cried, gesturing for the armsman to catch his horse.

As they disappeared, Kyrin said softly, "I will not forget."

Nith brought up another horse for Hamal. Before she mounted Cauldron again, Kyrin took off her kaffiyeh, set it on Hamal's head, and gently pressed the band down to hold it over the matted hair. But that face that turned to avoid her gaze was too fine-drawn.

Not a him. With a catch of her breath, Kyrin whipped off her cloak and wrapped it around the girl. Who she was did not matter now.

Berd brough her a horse. Tears ran from the girl's eyes as she smoothed the kaffiyeh, drawing it about her face, pulling the cloak around her shoulders. The men's silence became grim.

"Move out!" Dain growled. The order whipped the band into motion. The girl jerked in fear, and her horse sidestepped. Kyrin pretended not to notice as they trotted away from Buckden Pike to join the twenty more Cierheldens concealed a bowshot back.

When they reached camp, midway to Cierheld, Kyrin whisked her charge into her tent and shouted for the hot water kept on the fire on her order. She pulled the kettles inside one by one and emptied them into Elinor's largest pot, meant for the cookfire, resting in the middle of the tent. When she had added enough cold water, Kyrin gently gestured the girl from behind the curtained alcove of her bed-place and showed her the bath. The girl shot her a dark glance and bent over her knees, shivering beneath her rags. Kyrin shrugged and changed into her own tunic and trousers. With a smile, she left her thawb from Araby and her precious scrap of soap beside the tub.

Warming herself over the fire in the middle of camp, Kyrin smiled. Something about the girl reminded her of Nell.

Nell had grown more Elinor's companion than her own, since so many stronghold duties took her out of the hall to deal with animals, crops, and the defenses. Nell's strengths were with Elinor's herbs and her needle, though her growth in the way of the warrior was swift—despite Nell's tendency to hold her breath and clutch at things, mayhap with a little scream, when something frightened her. They had been cleaning the guestroom when a rat rolled out of an old cover and leapt to scurry up her arm. Kyrin's smile wavered. Regardless, she had refused Nell's coming. Her companion would not be a part of this dangerous errand of the wazir's. And now her questions multiplied. Returning some time later to the tent with two bowls of savory stew and a hunk of bread, Kyrin ducked under the tent flap.

All had been straightened, the bath water dumped, the pot sat beside the door, and the girl waited gracefully upon a cushion, her hair rolled damp against her neck. She never took her eyes from Kyrin, fingering the soft cushion beside her. Kyrin knelt and set the steaming dishes between them, with the half-loaf in the midst. The girl bowed until her forehead touched the ground.

"I heard of a price?" she whispered, and dared a proud, broken glance at Kyrin.

"No, not mine! My father will be repaid once we get to the ship. I was sent by the wazir, Sirius Abdasir, with coin for Hamal. Lord Nidfael may have deceived us, but it is well spent, and we will yet find—"

"How can this be, that you have come for me?"

Suddenly wary, Kyrin stopped. "What is your name?"

"Hala."

Kyrin sat back. The name was too close. "I see. Hala, I was sent to find you, or Hamal, for my freedom." No need to mention Tae and Alaina's freedom.

Hala let out a long sigh. "Hamal was my cousin, a traveler. I searched but I did not find him. Then—but my father has found me. It is well he has the caliph's favor." She shook her sleeve, and the hilt of Kyrin's dagger gleamed in her palm. The falcon's eyes glittered as if with secrets. The bronze was no harder than Hala's face. She held up the dagger, eyes blazing. "This dagger—you took it—but you also took me." She stared at the falcon. A shuddering breath shook her, and another. "Where—how did this blade come to you?"

Kyrin's heart twisted. What Hala had suffered. "I found it on my mother when—after my master's men killed her." She took the falcon and held it to the light, turning it slowly. "They near killed me," she whispered. "That gaze draws the eye and the heart, does it not? Cries to you to fly up after it. Even your father asked to see it, after a fight, once. He gave it back to me. So brave and beautiful."

"Then it cannot be what I thought. It may not buy me his favor."

"The falcon blade has seen many things." *I fear how far it sees, sometimes.* "But why would it buy you favor?"

Hala looked down wearily. "I am no longer my father's pure daughter."

Kyrin swallowed. "I sorrow for your loss." She paused. "But you are yet your father's daughter." She touched Hala's knee. "Their filth is not yours."

Hala gave a ragged sob. "How, how may I face him—"

"Do you love him?"

"More than the light of my eyes," she whispered.

"Then bring him that love."

Hala smiled wanly. "Wise words, from a slave."

Kyrin looked away. "What wisdom I have was won at cost. It is not yet fully mine, or at least, I am growing into it. But," her voice lightened, "the most excellent Sirius Abdasir was angry, you know, that the caliph forbade him to come find you."

Hala brightened. Kyrin spoke long of her last visit with the wazir and offered the bread to Hala. Hala broke off a chunk absently, as Kyrin spoke of her escape from her father. Then, realizing the obligation of the bread, Hala looked at Kyrin sharply.

Kyrin grinned and took a big bite. Hala smiled and dug into the stew. They talked late into the night of many things, and left the tent in the morning, companions.

Lord Dain was pleased to ride hard the five days it took to get to the coast and Shipmaster Ragad.

Kyrin stood on the dock. She looked after the wazir's vessel, dwindling into the grey and blue streaked meeting of river and sky, then glanced down at the falcon dagger and the thawb and kaffiyeh she had loaned Hala, secure in the crook of her arm.

She had escorted her onto the ship after a tearful good-bye, with a letter for Tae and Alaina, whom Hala promised to find quietly after her father's warrant against them was settled. Kyrin smiled. She could trust Hala to champion Alaina and Tae and the end of her task. Though wounded in spirit, Hala was strong.

The last tip of the sail disappeared down the estuary, carrying Hyl with it, the wolfship warrior on the lookout for sandbars. Kyrin turned, and her father nodded and handed her Cauldron's reins, then nudged his own mount toward the end of the echoing wood planks.

Kyrin snuck a glance back at the wharf. It caught her by surprise, the wish for a moment that she went with the ship. She sighed. She never quite belonged in the ladies' embroidery circle or the conversations of cooking and children. These days she received many sidelong looks. Elinor did not quite trust her. When the men's talk turned to the hunt, the drill ground, warfare, or local gossip of doings outside Cierheld, then she listened, yet did not fully join in. When she stopped beside a fire, talk died to silence. Was it the dark ring in her ear? It would get better. She was home, and she was first daughter.

22

Change

Thou hast refined us as silver is refined. ~Psalm 66:10

The company returned to Cierheld, and spring wound by without incident. Talik arrived during a thunderous morning storm long after Cierheld's fields were planted, in the first week of the warm season. Elinor went to the door at his knock and let him in on a gust of misty wet. Talik shook his wet head and rubbed his hair with the scrap of linen Kyrin handed him. Small rivulets flowed from the green cloak he laid over the hearth near the fire. By his smile at them all, he was glad to hear the rain drumming on the roof instead of his head.

"Well come, well come. Sit you down." Dain pointed to the nearest bench.

"You are most gracious." Talik obeyed with a grin. Then he sobered. "I bring news. The king is dead."

"Ah." Dain stared unseeing at the guest room beyond the flames, stroking his chin.

Kyrin said nothing. It was not unexpected. Nith came in, followed by Berd, and sat behind Dain.

Talik nodded acknowledgement to them and went on, "The regent has taken his seat. He bids all lords to keep on as they have been."

Elinor snorted and Lord Dain laughed, a quick, short bark. "Whisper that in some ears and you would lose your head."

"Aye." Talik grinned. "But your head is wiser than to contemplate such a thing."

Kyrin smiled with the general steely amusement. She wished the tunic Elinor had not yet taken up for her did not sag in the middle. She brushed at it, and tucked it flat as she could as she found a place to sit, in the warm corner of the hearth beside Meric, who solemnly hung on Talik's every word as he and Dain spoke of Uncle Ulf. He had finished his pilgrimage and was soon to be walled in by his brother monks at Bolton church as an anchorite, as he wished.

Kyrin twisted a bit of hair thoughtfully about her fingers. Was Bolton not the church Brother Rolf served? And Nell had been a novice in a house of nuns there, before she married Cere. It was curious that many lives she knew met there. And her uncle in the midst of it. And if Alaina's copy of the Vulgate were yet in Bolton, she could scribe some of the Book for her own use. Her recall of some verses were not clear. Then she could also talk to her uncle, find out why he avoided them so.

Talik glanced at Kyrin almost apologetically as he said, "He is a strange man, especially for a priest."

"How so?" Nith's gaze speared Talik.

"Usually relatives serve an anchorite and his needs, but he has declined to have anyone from this house. Instead, Lady Esther goes to Bolton often, though Halwende stronghold is another day's ride on top of the two from here."

Nith looked at Berd, and both turned to Dain. Kyrin's gaze narrowed, and in her mind the tiger raised his head.

Uncle Ulf was yet priest to Easby church in Richmond. Why had he not applied to be an anchorite there? Mayhap he did not scorn them as much as he said. Kyrin's mouth firmed. If

Esther meant to drive ill will further between Uncle Ulf and Kyrin's family, she would find a determined defender in their first daughter.

Lord Dain grimaced and raised his hand. "I know, I know what you would say. It may be Lady Ynglida of Halwende was part of Lord Edsel's downfall, but she has not stirred from Halwende since my sister Medaen went to help her in place of my Elinor." Smiling, he gathered Elinor in his arm and pulled her to his side. He looked at Kyrin. "And Esther is not Lady Ynglida. Since her public disappointment with Lord Mornoth, Halwende's first daughter has devoted herself to those more needy than she. That is all to the good—"

Kyrin swallowed. So Lord Mornoth had refused to handfast Esther, whose lands were not so poor. Had he tried for Myrna to give him a foothold, or simply a bone to pick with the northern Northumbrian lords?

Elinor frowned playfully. "Fie, my lord. Esther but wishes to sit beside a strong lord, as any woman of sense does." She glanced at Kyrin. "Safety is not to be scorned—"

"Not at all, my lady." Dain's voice was dry. "If Esther wishes to serve my brother-in-law, I wish her joy and Father Ulf less bitterness. Never forget, he is our blood. Besides, whatever his wisdom, his influence as an anchorite in Bolton will be small."

Talik shook his head. "I wish it were so, but Bolton is growing rich, and much trade and gossip flows through it, so Lord Bergrin says, and he should know. There is talk of the king to come. Will he will listen to the lords of the northlands? There is gossip of the Northumbrian lords good and ill, and also of the two-legged wolves who have been marauding about."

"You mean robbers?" Meric said, and glanced at Kyrin intently, as if to be sure she noted it. Elinor's lips thinned, and she looked away. Kyrin inclined her head to Meric. *He* held no ill will. Would it ever be the right moment to show Elinor her key, to openly claim it, and wear it on her belt? But she seldom wore a tunic befitting a girdle these days. Elinor likely thought it just as well.

Lord Dain said, "Yes, robbers, Meric. The brigands are thickening despite our vigilance." He threw up his arms. "But enough, come, it is time for supper. We would be honored if you would stay within our walls this even', Talik."

"I had hoped you would ask." Talik grinned, rose and ruffled Meric's hair. With a bow for Kyrin, he walked toward the high table after Nith. Berd followed, while Meric smiled after Talik, and Kyrin's knees dipped in a return curtsey. Then her face flamed. It was the first time an instinctive curtsey had ever caught her unaware. Berd looked back at her, dark eyes steady in his fair face. Looking between the three of them, Elinor shook her head. Kyrin's smile disappeared.

After supper Talik sat with them around the fire again. Berd positioned himself near Kyrin, watchful, quiet, his wide shoulders blocking some of the firelight. The rain slackened. The fire spat. Talk turned to weapons, and the men bent over maps at the near table.

Kyrin could keep her mind on nothing, her thoughts always sliding back to Talik. Nell and Celine worked on their stitching. Elinor was in the kitchen, instructing Cook on the morrow's meals, and Myrna was near asleep. Talik's face was quiet, as he listened to her father. There was strength and beauty in that face.

The next morn, Talik accompanied Kyrin to the fields where she went to watch over the workers, carrying Cierheld's horn of alarm. She'd slung her bow and quiver over her back, for there would be time to practice after her watch. Her father outshot her at the long butts, while she was slightly faster and as accurate at the closer butts.

Meric tagged after them, swiping at plants along the track with a stick. Talik swung around to catch him and lift him up on his shoulders. Meric whooped.

Kyrin frowned at her brother; she'd seen Berd lean down to whisper in his ear and give him a little shove after them as they left. She did not need a minder in Cierheld's fields with all her people about. Had Elinor set him and Berd to watch her? She frowned.

The beaten clay path was slippery. In the fields near the center of the valley, the last misty clouds parted and the sun shone down; steam rose from the dark earth, warm and sweet. Talik looked over a field of calf-high grain to the taller corn, then at the workers, hoes rising and falling, their weapons girded close. He grinned, and bounced Meric, who squealed.

"I thought your father did not work on the seventh of a seven-day?" Talik eyed Kyrin.

"Not often, no." She smiled, then sobered. *"You* were the one who told us more of the lowland field-robberies. It worries him. Lord Landyl's stronghold, Fresen's Fresenheld, and Gadral of Aysgarth, have banded together to protect their food and wealth. Other holds, it seems, have been destroyed for the same. Not that Father's coffers aren't bare. But we must guard the crops, and get them in as early as may be."

"Yes, it seems my news precedes me of late."

Kyrin glanced at his closed face, pursed her mouth, and stared at a grass clump. "Even their crops still in the ground were ruined. The brigands faded away like the wolves they are. Of course, Father has not gone out since—"

"I know nothing certain. But all holds should be wary, especially with the king gone."

Kyrin jerked about to stare at him. Was there trouble with the new regent?

"I have spoken to your father. Mornoth's men are training daily, strengthened by mercenaries from the lowlands. Lord Mornoth claims they are to defend him in case the lowlanders get too hungry, and against the brigands. Lord Jorn and I have reason to believe he is up to something." Talik's eyes were intent.

Kyrin straightened, her mouth flattening. "It is well Father decided not to sell the ransom weapons from the wazir. As he says, we may need them. My thanks, we will watch well, sir." *Against the tiger, too.* She would not forget the blade of truth.

"Call me Talik," he protested, laughing, "It has not been that long since I saw you last!"

"Talik," Kyrin murmured, flushing.

"Ha!" Meric pointed at her and laughed in glee. Kyrin's cheeks burned brighter, and she glared at him. He should stick to *De Re Militari.* Meric giggled. Talik smiled a knowing smile.

"Upstart brother! And you—" Kyrin kicked the dirt clods near her feet at Talik. Talik dodged, and Kyrin picked up more clods. Talik retrieved one and handed it to Meric, and the clod war moved rapidly down the cart track, her laughing prey weaving to finally dodge into the trees at her watch point. She followed, her heart lighter.

Talik left the next morn with messages from Myrna and Lord Dain for Jornhold. Hal returned with him, for Lord Jorn had made him an offer he could not refuse. Hal had learned enough Subak to pass on more than a hand of good defenses to his lord's men, as Bergrin's new first armsman. Kyrin was content. He was a good man.

She walked beside her father in the woods behind Cierheld, a breeze stirring the grass, her bow over her shoulder. Afternoon sunlight slanted through the trees. The oaks hung heavy with sweet scented leaves and acorn nubs. The blackberry briers between the trunks were thick with fruit. Her father carried his great bow and long, dark-shafted arrows at the ready in case of game. A stick cracked under her foot.

"What are you thinking of, daughter?"

Kyrin sighed. "Elinor, why is she so—well, she seems angry at me, at times afraid, and then also to love me. Last morn after my bell on watch I came back with Meric and Talik. She gave me a tunic and apron that she and Nell had made me. Blue linen, with a most becoming border. With the same embroidery on the green apron. Such work takes many bells. And I like it well. But, she is also smothering Meric. When he went out with Talik and me—it was the first he's been outside the walls since I've come."

Her father's face remained calm, waiting. Kyrin waved at the woodland. "Elinor refused to let me take Meric anywhere without at least two armsmen. Meric, the wise little man, he turned red when she said that. But he seems to know something I don't that makes him obey her."

"Ah." Dain stared at a bright bough swaying overhead. "Well, daughter, part of this is my mistake." He nodded at the tops of Cierheld's wall towers peeking over the trees.

"Elinor told me before she married me that she wished no interference with her child. I agreed. It was not a wise decision. Your stepmother asked it because two years ago her daughter, Penni, begged her leave to ride a real horse instead of a pony. Elinor gave in, and the horse ran Penni under a tree. It killed her. That is why Elinor lets Meric go nowhere alone. And you," Dain put his arm around Kyrin's shoulders, "she sees you as another daughter—but she fears your fighting skill. The way you follow the courage of the falcon, your willingness to risk yourself. She fears you may lead Meric to the same." He sighed. "But know there is this also. When I told her about your mother and your time in Araby, she cried."

So, fear made her angry. *It is good I hold my key, and not Elinor. It still smells of Qadira's scented oils. I wonder why father never gave Elinor Mother's key. She is the lady of Cierheld.* Kyrin said, "Her anger is not that I came back and pushed Meric out of his place as first son?"

"No." Dain looked at her, startled. "I assure you, nothing is further from her mind, or mine."

Kyrin sighed. That was well, at least. "Father—"

"Yes?"

Her face heated. A bee buzzed about its work on a blackberry bloom, crawled over a green berry and a red. "Berd watches me. Does he, well, do you think he cares for me?" She scowled.

"Hmm. I think not. Not like that."

Then how *did* he see her? Kyrin stepped over a prickly blackberry vine. Men and family and raiders. She wanted to snort. But Elinor said it was unladylike. Among all her uncertainty, one thing was certain. She looked up. "Father, I—I love you. There were so many times—on the ship, in the desert, in Ali's house, when I could not say that. Now I can." She moved close to lean her head against him.

"I love you, too. I always will." He squeezed her shoulders. Together they skirted a meadow. A hare hopped around the trunk of an ash, two hundred paces off if it was a yard.

"Look!" Kyrin shrugged her bow into her hand and reached for an arrow.

"Here. I think your draw is strong enough now." Dain held out a black arrow from his quiver. Kyrin took it, and he reached for another. They drew together, loosed as one, and the hare fell.

Walking up, Dain said, "Right good shooting!" and lifted the hare by its back legs, one shaft through the neck and the other through its middle. Either shaft would have gained it for the pot. They grinned at each other.

Nith strode toward them over the grassy rise. Dain lifted the hare. "Your first daughter aims well!"

Nith grinned at Kyrin. "So I saw. Near two hundred paces. Well done, my lady."

"My thanks." Kyrin nodded. Nith paused, waiting, and Kyrin looked from him to her father. "Shall I take the rabbit to Cook?"

Dain pulled the shafts out and handed the hare to her, with the black arrow she'd shot. "Keep it. May it serve you well."

Kyrin smiled and bowed to Nith. He nodded as she turned toward the hold. She smiled at the summer sky, the butterflies fluttering about the flower-strewn grass despite the creeping clouds. Samson screamed overhead. Kyrin looked up to a blur of wings, and he plummeted onto her arm. Laughing, she stroked his back. "Greedy-guts, you." The tiger was far away.

§

The grain ripened as long days baked the earth with heat. Kyrin was busy from dawn to dusk. It was hard to find time to practice with her rangdo, but she persevered and was proud of their progress. Berd continued to go to the forest with her. By now he knew more of her skill than any other in Britannia. Often he'd helped her by playing the part of attacker, and he watched closely. And she learned more of his sword work.

Kyrin helped with the harvest, for Dain ordered everything gathered as early as possible, and Elinor and Cook and their helpers in the kitchen preserved every berry and fruit that she, Celine, Myrna, and every other woman and girl could lay hands on. Every family in the stronghold and surrounding steads bent their backs to their labor.

For rumor brought evil news. The lowland brigand remained active, the northland lords watchful and suspicious of their landholders, freemen, peasants, and their brother lords. Lord Dain sent spies and patrols out in vain; no one professed to know anything.

It was said the brigand leader did not accept new men, though his ranks seemed undiminished, and Dain said he had lost a few. His men dissolved before pursuit like mist, only to regroup and strike elsewhere.

Talik came often, whenever messages or errands brought him by Cierheld, and he worked at whatever the family did that day. One hot evening they ate supper outside the wall by the mill pond, where everyone dabbled their toes in the water.

"Hold!" The sentry's cry came from the wall near the gate.

Talik spun, sitting by Kyrin, and his wet foot hit her as he shot to his feet, near knocking her into the water. On the bank above them, Berd drew his sword. Every head around the pond turned to stare toward the wall, where the sentry cried again, "I said hold!" All heard the swish of the arrow and the cry of pain.

What happened the next morn was something Kyrin never forgot. As the sun peeped over the rim of the world, the lord of Cierheld drew his men up before the barracks in ranks. Nith strode back and forth before them.

"Are we not brothers? Do we not uphold our oath?"

"Yes!" roared more than two hundred throats. One hundred were Nith's, the others were tradesmen and freemen of Cierheld.

One man said nothing, the mercenary who'd tried to sneak out of the smithy with a new-forged sword. Stamped as it was with Cierheld's arrow between stylized sun and moon, it would have been hard to sell. He was a fool.

Cid, on the wall, had put an arrow through his arm. Now the mercenary stood bound to a post before the oak, glaring at them. He was well-muscled, with a crooked nose between hot brown eyes.

"He has betrayed that oath!"

"Yes!" the angry roar answered Nith.

"Can he repay the four times coin our lord justly requires?"

"No!"

Nith said quietly, "Then what is our lord to do?" Silence fell.

"Take it out of his hide!" someone yelled.

Dain stepped forward. Behind him, Kyrin stood with her hands on Meric's shoulders, with Elinor beside her. Fully armed, Berd kept her father's back. Still, the tension in the air had Kyrin watching for anything out of the ordinary.

Her father's voice was deep. "I say he has not the coin. What does he have? That is something to think on. And I know one who thinks much, who is wise and says little. Let us ask our first daughter. For she will guide you in future. Let her begin now." Dain beckoned to Kyrin.

Her eyes widened. Elinor sighed as Kyrin moved past her. So the thief had naught to repay, naught but his body. Kyrin stopped beside the lord of Cierheld, her legs shaky. In the crowd someone cried, "Aye, he can pay with his head! Then he'll take none other's goods. It's a lean 'nough year as 'tis!"

Kyrin waited. They quieted, and she lifted her chin. "Let him pay with his sweat. That may teach him something of what he took from you." She dared not glance at her father. Her people would weigh her judgment.

Near the front of the crowd, a burly smith said, "That sounds fair, lass, that he work. But what to do with him after?"

The thief spat at him. The spittle plopped in the dust short of the smith.

"If he shows no repentance, turn him out."

The smith looked at the bound man soberly and raised his arm, turning to the rest of Cierheld. "So let it be!"

Staring straight before them, the mercenaries yelled as one, "So let it be!" Dain echoed them, with Elinor and Meric.

Cid led the man away to a cell between the armsmen's quarters and the barracks. So the thief labored through the rest of harvest. He spoke little but curses, shouting at all who came When Kyrin was about, his brown glare followed her. She made herself ignore his hate and stare past his crooked nose. A first daughter could not be weak. And then Nith turned him out.

One night not long after, Dain said, "Elinor, you will have to do without me a few days." He grinned. "Even you, Meric. Lord Teth"—he glanced at Kyrin—"needs help with his wheat."

Kyrin tensed. Teth should keep his own counsel and not take her father, who had enough to do between Cierheld and Fenwrd hold. Dain's steward at Fenwrd brought problems enough to his attention, let alone the messages that flew back and forth between them and their allies in Reeth, Middleham, and elsewhere.

Nevertheless, early in the morn Dain swung into the saddle before the hall steps, two squads of men around him. Meric handed up a small sack Elinor had filled with bread, cheese, meat, and apples. Dain gripped Meric's shoulder with a fond shake and leaned from his saddle to give Elinor a last kiss.

Kyrin followed him through the gate, past the mill, and through the fields. When they reached the end of the plowed ground, the men stopped at Dain's signal. Riding on a little, out of earshot, Dain turned to Kyrin. His mount stamped.

"Double the guard posts while I am gone. I left instructions with Nith. He and the men will follow your word."

Kyrin swallowed hard at his serious face. She could not lose him again. "Will you not take Berd with you?"

"He is needed here. What would you do without your Subak drills in the woods? And Cid is with me. He is a good man." Dain smiled wryly. "I know you are not hare-brained, daughter, but I gave Nith room to use his judgment and give advice, should you ask it. He's been with me on many marches. Worry not, he trusts you already. I will see you in a seven-day!" He clapped his heels to his horse.

Kyrin's bare feet curled against the morning-cold ground as the others clattered after him. She made her way back to the hall, cutting around a field of grain stubble. Knowing no danger, content, the cows ate the gold wealth at their leisure.

If she could only be a cow or a child again, just for a little while. She paused, remembering Talik in Lord Bergrin's garden. It was so easy to forget the Master of the stars's undying power, the faithful hands of him who held everything in being. Mayhap she could pass to Elinor the wisdom Talik showed her.

A day later a messenger came with news that Lord Cieri had arrived at Lord Teth's. Kyrin went to find Nith.

The armsmen's quarters were simple. A room divided by a curtain into two, each containing a desk, a chair, and a second curtained alcove for a bedchamber. Leaning over his desk, Nith straightened as she came in.

"Yes, first daughter, what is it?" His short beard accented his hard mouth. He was altogether lean and dangerous, his eyes hard.

Kyrin bowed. "My father has arrived at Lord Teth's."

"Ah. That is good." Nith's face relaxed into a smile.

"Yes. I—" Nith waited without expression. "I wondered, might we post men between us and Teth's to take faster word between us if there is need?"

Nith nodded. "I think that would be wise." Kyrin smiled, and he grinned. "What, girl, you think I would not take a good thought from you?"

She bowed again, deeper. "My thanks, armsmaster." She had thought exactly that. How had he known it?

Cernalt stepped around the curtain at her shoulder, clearing his throat. "That's the first lesson a good armsman learns—take every good idea from anywhere, at any time."

Kyrin inclined her head and soon took her leave, wondering what she would do, facing men in straight battle. Single fights with Seliam and Curnoth did not count. One day, as first daughter and Lady of Cierheld, she must lead Cierheld's men. They expected it.

The heart of the falcon would never break, not while it breathed. But her heart was weak. Nith and old Cernalt's war-hardened hearts were hers, and she must keep all of them strong. If she broke—the thought brought back the cold fear of the blade.

Cierheld went on. Elinor kept supper at the high table gay with wry, humorous conversation whenever it threatened to turn foreboding about the coming winter. She was an able first Lady, though never wielding a weapon.

Everyone knew the brigands in the lowlands had stolen Malton stronghold's goods then destroyed the rest. Three strongholds banded together a short while after the attack, to hunt the despoilers. They did not find them. The peasants who escaped hoarded and fought over what was left. Already some had fled to the mountains, watched by the local lords, jealous of their own food supplies. A few peasants with needful trades found shelter and work. The others lived and begged as they could.

Kyrin threw herself into Subak and Berd's instruction in the sword. He took her one morn to the smith's small armory and helped her pick a blade of a right weight and length for her strength. The simple war of body and blade against an attacker pushed the deeper war against the tiger to the back of her mind

23

The hand of aliens . . . whose right hand is . . . falsehood. ~*Psalm 144:11*

Kyrin dreamed, walking a dim, grey desert. A thunder of pursuing horses she could not see clattered up to the dark, boiling sky and echoed back, reverberating through her head as she began to run. The tiger raced ahead of her in long bounds, chasing the falcon, its wingtips brushing the ground. Someone called to her.

"Kyrin!"

Kyrin sat up with a jerk, her cover half on the floor. Hooves thudded around the oak below her window, before the barracks. Men called to each other amid the sound of rattling arms.

Nith pounded on her door. "Kyrin! Wake! Teth's hold burns!"

Kyrin croaked, "I'm coming!" and rolled out of bed, rushing for the black tunic and trousers she'd put in her clothes chest, thumping blindly in the dark. Nell sat up in a rustle of her blanket. "Nell, Teth's hold is afire! Elinor will need you."

A white shadow in her undershift, Nell stood quickly and grabbed Kyrin's arm. "Where do *you* go?"

"To my father." That was her place. Kyrin's heart thundered.

Nell lit a candle. The light flickered over her flat mouth, and her brows drew together, but she picked up Kyrin's tunic, laying her cloak over her other arm. Kyrin donned her trousers, breathing deep to steady her fingers on the drawstring fastenings, hastily taking her tunic and cloak from Nell.

Nell hugged her. "Be safe. I will pray."

Kyrin hugged her back. "Take care for yourself. God is with us all."

Down the hall, Nith called to Elinor as Kyrin fastened her sword belt. She loosened the long blade in its sheath, settled the falcon dagger on the opposite side, and picked up Tae's stick. The wood felt good to her hot hand, almost as if Tae were beside her. With a deep breath, she opened the door.

Nith carried a torch. Shadows wove around him. "A message came, first daughter." They moved swiftly down the stair together, Celine peeking at them over Myrna's shoulder from the guest chamber on the lower floor as the rest of the hold woke. "Lord Teth is under attack, his hold is being overrun. During the first confusion someone threw a peasant on a horse and told him to come here. He met our man on the road, and came with him, then our man was shot down. The peasant made it."

Outside, stars and a westering moon lit the sky. Up on the wall, Kyrin stopped at a crenel. A cold breeze blew around her as she gazed north at a flickering red speck. Someone had attacked Teth's.

"They must have fired the whole stronghold!" she whispered. Her mind spun in horror. Her father must be alive. "How many men do we have, besides the patrols out?"

"A hundred fifty, lady." Nith waited, his face canny and strong under the dancing light of his torch. "I've already called three squads to the wall."

"If it seems well to you, bring fifty men to me, mounted, then arm the others and put them on the wall, but keep the second fifty in reserve." She paused. "Less any scouts you need to send out. Tell Berd we will send him back a message from Teth's. What hour is it?"

"Mid of night, shortly before Matins. But Berd will go with you. I must stay here."

Did Nith ward against an attack on Cierheld? It was no time for questions, but for trust. "As you will. My thanks, Armsmaster Nith."

He gripped her shoulders. "There was no one on the road beside the archer that took our man when the peasant came through. That may change, first daughter. Watch well. Send out scouts. Listen to Berd. Have the people brought inside with their families, if any walls stand and—you will know what else to do when you see it. It is enough."

"Yes, Armsmaster." Kyrin bowed her head, glad of his presence, his warmth and will. Did every person feel so alone in the face of uncertain battle?

"Now go, and show them your mettle with wisdom." Nith gave her the formal salute of respect and called orders as he turned from the wall.

Below was swift flurry. Torches sputtered into existence, men called to one another. Cierhelden warriors, hold-born and mercenary alike, crossed the yard, arming even as they ran to stand along the wall. Archers stopped at arrow slits, swordsmen and spear men settled between crenels. In the yard, women filled water containers from the well against fire-arrows, following the lord of Cierheld's practiced order of defense. Would these walls ever see Lord Dain again? Kyrin's throat closed up as her foot touched the earth of the yard.

Berd had the men ready before the barracks, and while she told him their road, a man led up Cauldron, provisioned and saddled, her bow and quiver waiting for her. Bless Nell. Cauldron nuzzled Kyrin's neck. She gripped his mane, put her foot in the stirrup, and swung astride.

At the gate the sentry, his hair glowing red under the torch he held, trailed his hand along Cauldron's neck, muttering, "His blessings," as Kyrin entered the cold darkness. Once outside, the walls behind her twinkled with light.

Berd rode at her side. He flung out a silent hand and four men peeled off, one on either side, the others behind and before. The rest of the company strung out, two by two.

They did not follow the main road but went by small ways through field and wood. Over moor and into wood again, they made all the speed they could in the dark. Shadows under the trees slowed them to a walk. Through field and meadow they trotted. It was nearing Lauds, just before Prime, when they slowed again.

The edge of the fields around Teth's stronghold appeared as they picked their way through the trees, blackened stubble and sparking patches amid last wreaths of smoke. They drew nearer. The burned fields, silent buildings, and wooden walls were vague looming shadows. Did the attackers wait for them, were they gone, or were all dead inside?

Scouts circled the hold while Kyrin waited with Berd, sword ready. It was yet too dark for bow work. Red winks of light glowed between rents in the stronghold palings, a dog howled mournfully, and Cauldron shifted beneath her, his teeth grinding on his bit.

The scouts returned empty-handed; they had seen nothing human, heard nothing. Berd left some of the horses before an empty stone granary outside the wall, under guard, freeing a tensquad of spearmen and swordsmen for groundwork. Scouts posted in the fringe of the woods would give warning if the attackers returned that way. Unless they waited within.

Surrounding the tensquad with riders, Kyrin and Berd led a short rush through a break in the timbers of the wall. They took the first building within, a smithy. It proved empty, though tools, metal, and weapons had been taken, the space ransacked. Bodies were scattered outside, too dark to discern faces.

"It is good we brought extra torches. We must find my father—"

"We will." Berd was grim. "After we know what this place holds. You take these"—he motioned to two mounted tensquads—"we'll leave the men on foot here, to clear out this mess and ready the smithy for any wounded. I'll take a squad around the west side, while you take your two to the east. Though these brigands have a history of strike and run, if either of us finds trouble, we'll cover the other's back. If we both find trouble, fight through till we meet at the south end. We'll find Lord Cieri." Flame bloomed as a Cierhelden mercenary lit a torch beside them. Berd's dark eyes snapped in the light.

"They may have captives, Berd. Or they may attack from without, after luring us further. But if they're gone, can we search out their trail or must we wait for light?"

Berd sighed. "Lady, I would help anyone left alive here and wait for light. Forewarned, with this many men, and walls to fall back on, we are strong. Our torchlight in the woods would give them the advantage. The enemy has the dark, and as far as we know, and would hide or kill any captives long before we caught up, supposing we even found sign. Sign which close fighting here can wipe out."

"You are right," Kyrin said huskily. "We meet on the far side." Torchlight grew as the men lit more brands in the smith's banked fire. She left her bow and quiver with Cauldron at the smithy. Any fighting would be close work until dawn, and there were the dead to search.

Glowing mountains of red coals hissed and settled around foundation-stone rubble and scattered kitchen pans and the great hearth, all that was left of the hall. Smoke and scorch-smell choked her, one of the men coughed, and the ashy mess slid under their feet. Kyrin hastened from the hall to the partially burned barracks, searching feverishly for her father, turning over the bodies while Twr, whom she'd met at the gate the first morn, held a torch for her. No hail or cry came from Berd and the line of torches and men working their way along the other side of the hold.

Everywhere was the reek of burned flesh. Kyrin came upon a family: father, mother, daughter, fallen within three paces of each other. A dagger was clenched in the man's hand, his wife had dropped an iron pan, and a rag doll rested asprawl, flung from the girl's fingers.

Sickness crept over Kyrin. She folded her arms across her stomach. Lord Teth had been caught by surprise. Where would her father and Cid and the men have been? If they were in the hall, her father was ash. Ash: grey, empty, dead. Just as her mother had fallen.

Kyrin crept behind a bit of wall, where Twr found her wiping her mouth. He swallowed hard. Sweat gleamed on his face when he jerked his gaze to her. "It unsettles the stomach."

"It is not something you should ever get used to." Twr nodded, and Kyrin touched his shoulder, her hand shaking as her voice did not. "See them so you can fight with greater strength against the beasts that do such." There was a new straightness to him when he followed her to the base of the east wall.

Kyrin met Berd at last at the south wall, her heart beating against despair when he shook his head. Teth's ruined stronghold sheltered nothing but embers and bodies and blackened stone.

"Do not give up hope. Your lord father is resourceful." Yet Berd's face was bleak in the growing light. A sparrow lit on the wall and chirped, wind ruffling its feathers. It cocked its head, a shiny black eye on them.

There were survivors, found by the scouts, though none of their men. Back at the smithy, Berd questioned them. Two cooks had hidden in the wood and nervously said they knew next to nothing. The last three men shifted their feet, jumping at every movement, hugging the shadows of a stone shed looming behind them, its roof and door gone. At last a tow-haired man stepped forward into the torchlight.

"Your name and trade?" Berd asked, sitting on a stone block at a makeshift plank table before the smithy.

"Ber, I—I'm the cowherd—was," said Ber miserably. "Till they took my cows."

"What do you know about the attackers?"

"I—" Ber twitched and looked around, blinking in the ruddy torchlight. He looked down then abruptly lifted his gaze and squared his shoulders. "My lord, it was a horrible thing—"

A wiry, soot-blackened arm and dagger rose from the shadowed group behind the cowherd. Then another figure leaped from behind the shed wall and thudded into the attacker, yanking his arm back. There was a quick, confused struggle.

Ber's attacker fell with a gurgling grunt, the blackened dagger he'd meant to use buried in his own soot-streaked neck. He carried Lord Pesen's rooster sigil on his breast. The second man reeled after him, with an unintelligable rasping croak. He stumbled and fell face first beside him. The cowherd gaped and backed away as the men of Cierheld surged forward with a growl, raising torches and weapons.

His broken nose and rough brown tunic backlit, the third survivor yanked a spear from a mercenary's hand and ran toward his fallen brothers, raising the weapon. The man on the ground turned his head, brown eyes wide.

"No!" Kyrin screamed, barely hearing Berd's bellowed, "Hold!" In a split moment of fear, she elbowed aside two men in front of her, lunging for the spearman. She kicked out desperately at his descending arm. Her boot struck his wrist.

The man howled. The spear slewed into the dirt near his target as small bones snapped. His cry of pain turned to a snarl. He ripped a dagger from his boot with his other hand, spinning toward her, aiming for her ribs. But Berd was in front of her, deflecting, sweeping her behind him with one arm, the other burying his dagger in the man's chest. Berd released the weapon to draw his sword. The man fell away. That nose—Cierheld's banished thief.

Her own sword drawn, Kyrin covered Berd's back. He was yelling, Cierheldens forming up around them facing outward, swords and spears ready. Kyrin dropped to her knees beside the thief's intended victim, a burned, bloody bundle of flesh and rags. She grasped his shoulders and turned him over. Dain looked up at her, breath coming in harsh puffs. Kyrin smoothed his ash-laden, singed hair from his eyes.

"Ky—Kyrin," he gasped, moving his head a fraction to indicate the dead men around them. "Betrayed us—let them in. All raids—to bring war . . ."

Kyrin nodded. "Shh, shh." Dain's eyes fluttered shut. Her hand flew to his neck. "The healer—where's Crag!" she screamed.

"Here." Panting, Crag burst through the ring of men and knelt on the other side of her father, motioning her back. Swallowing down sobs, Kyrin obeyed. The old man felt Dain's wrist and peered under his eyelids, then began to strip away his charred, tattered tunic. Kyrin's breath choked at the black and red burns that patterned his chest and neck.

Crag took off his cloak and hurriedly wrapped his lord in it, then barked, "You and you! Bring him. Easy now!" Two men gently lifted Dain and carried him toward the smithy, Cierheldens ranked two deep around him. Crag hustled after. Berd ordered the cowherd and the cooks put under guard, and his men formed into a square about the smithy.

Inside, herbs stewed over coals, filling the air with sharp, bitter-sweet steam. Dain moaned as they laid him on a pallet. His eyes opened a little, and he gripped Kyrin's hand. "Berd—" he gasped.

"I'm here, my lord."

"Crag, witness." Dain crooked his fingers. The healer hovered closer. "Berd—is first armsman—for my daughter. Say—you will." His eyes pled with Berd.

Berd glanced at Kyrin quickly then bowed his head. "It is my honor, my lord."

Lord Dain Cieri sighed and his eyes shut.

Kyrin met Berd's silent question and nodded her acceptance. He had saved her life. He touched her shoulder, and their unspoken oath went deeper than words.

Crag ordered everyone out but his apprentice, while he went to work over Dain. Kyrin stood beside the hastily curtained door, tears drying on her cheeks.

Who sought war? Against whom? Who had betrayed them?

Lord Pesen, though a southern lord, was a kindly man. She had talked with him often after her return. Lord Kem Landyl's stronghold, Fresen's, and Gadral's had seemingly been destroyed for their goods. Now Teth's, not known for its wealth. Had her father had word that Teth's hold lay next in the brigand's eye?

Had he gone in search of the robber in his own way, since his spies failed? Her brow furrowed.

The attacks had made lords and peasants suspicious of each other. The common people resented the lords' surmises of uprising. Muttered rumor said the lords must be hiding something or someone of their own behind the attacks. But no lord had brought men against another. Until now.

What had possessed Lord Pesen to destroy Lord Teth? If they *were* Pesen's men. In the fight before the smithy, either her father or Cierheld's thief had killed Pesen's man, who attacked them. But why? Then the thief clearly meant to kill her father. Was he simply erasing witnesses, or was there something deeper at work? Regardless, there would be war.

Berd was now her armsman. It gave her a queer feeling, seeing how willing he had been to die for her. Standing beside her, Berd stared at the growing light. Finally he sighed, lifted his hand, and dropped it. "If Lord Cieri wakes, try to find out more. I'm going to make certain the watch has been doubled."

If he had ordered it doubled, it was so, but waiting came hard. Crag began dressing her father's burns, and after a moment listening to her father's pain, Kyrin followed Berd. She caught up to him on the other side of the hold, directing temporary fortifications of the wall. Berd straightened, giving her a solemn nod and a level look. "You have done well, daughter of your father."

"My thanks. You also."

Berd only nodded. "Has Crag spoken to you of Lord Cieri yet?"

"No." Her eyes came back to him.

"Then there is hope." His chin jutted. "Ber had true news, I deem, since our thief tried to kill him. Ber says that in the attack on Lord Teth's, Lord Pesen's men struck down Teth's warriors and those of Cierheld in the yard. Then the brigands came up behind and killed Pesen's men. They fought as trained mercenaries, killing everyone in the hold. They did not want witnesses."

"To destroy Teth and my father at once," Kyrin said thoughtfully.

"What?"

"Everyone knows my father also keeps mercenaries. They are a potent force, one any attacker must take into account. What if they could be accused?"

"By all that's holy," breathed Berd, "I believe you speak true. If one or two of our fallen could have been brought forward as proof that Cierheld mercenaries fought here, and murdered . . ."

"Our thief tried to steal a new-stamped sword. Did he bring it here for such proof? And now they have more Cierheld proof than they wish, living men, who will testify of them. We must get back to Cierheld's walls."

"Aye. Nith must know." Berd spun away. "I'll send out the riders."

It was Prime. Kyrin paced back and forth in front of the smithy. The dead had been removed and the cowherd was not in sight. Nearby, Berd spoke softly to Twr.

Crag's apprentice beckoned from the smithy door. Kyrin beat her first armsman through the curtain. She stopped beside her father's pallet, and he stared up at her.

Kyrin smiled. Her face felt stiff. Dain raised his hand and she gripped it, leaning close to hear his raspy, halting whisper.

"Not Lord Pesen—think other lord's men, disguised. Gate opened. They cut down Cid and—my men. I hid. Could trust no one, must find out . . . who our thief—" He paused for a labored breath. "Who did this, who is behind. . . He sank back, breathing hoarsely. "Kyrin, you've come back to me. Where, how—" he muttered, his gaze wandering from her face with his wits.

"The bastards!" Berd strode outside, flinging back the curtain.

Kyrin looked back at her father. Her skin crawled. This had been planned, to bring the lords against each other. Which lord plotted to destroy the others and rise above his fellows? Ludwin Mornoth, for one. With the king gone, there could be more. Kyrin stared at her father as his eyes closed. The tiger walked amid the stink of heated metal and the smoke of the smithy. Chasing the falcon. When would it bring her down? It breathed, creeping behind her.

A hand fell on her shoulder, and Kyrin struck it away with a wordless growl as she spun, hands coming up to attack. She froze, and pulled the falcon blade away from Crag's throat. "My pardon, sir."

He swallowed hard. "The fault is mine. I should not have startled you."

"Will he live?" Her voice cracked, her throat dry.

"He is badly burned, lady. I do not know."

"Care for him well, Crag. Call me if he wakes or worsens. Berd will know where I am."

"I will, lady."

Kyrin left the smithy.

One of the messengers returned. He had no trouble on the road.

Cierheld was quiet, but ready. Elinor and Nith awaited their return. Elinor had sent messengers to warn neighboring strongholds of the attack at Teth's, and for them to guard against all men, no matter what their sigil, whether peasant, freeman, or lord. That night everyone slept uneasily, heads on saddles, weapons close at hand. They silently cheered the foggy dawn.

24

Wounds

I have seen the wicked . . . spreading himself like a green bay tree.
~Psalm 37:35

Kyrin studied the old hay cart, thinking of ambushes and the need for speed. Berd examined the altered cart bed.

It rested lighter upon its wheels, rid of cumbersome width and length, fastened to two horses instead of one. Straw had been laid knee deep inside. The waterproofed roof rippled in the dawn wind. Wary men surrounded the first wagon and another behind, as decoys.

"It must be enough," Berd muttered. He raised his arm. The wagons creaked forward, unseen scouts flanking them as they wound into the woods. They arrived at Cierheld without incident, exhausted by constant watchfulness.

Dain was settled with quiet speed in his own bed, and Elinor took Kyrin's place beside him at Crag's order. Kyrin made her way down the stairs and collapsed in her father's chair. She awoke to a tug at her foot in the evening light. Meric looked up at her, his face serious, in the middle of removing her boots.

"I thought you would be more comfortable, sister." He set the boot in his hand on the floor.

"My thanks, Meric." Kyrin smiled. He grinned lopsidedly and brought a stool and lifted her feet. Kyrin looked from the stool to his face, and her eyes teared.

Meric patted her shoulder awkwardly. After taking stew from the kitchen to Cierheld's lord and lady upstairs, he brought her a bowl. She took a couple of bites, then lowered the bowl and turned her head to hide her tears. Meric was too quick for her.

"Kyrin, is—is Father very bad?"

She gulped. "Crag does all he can." And so would Nell. If only Tae were here, with his knowledge of healing. Hers was less than Crag's. She reached for Meric, as if he could keep the thought that rose between them at bay.

"Oh," he said. Then, very quietly, "My thanks, for telling me." He moved to pull away, but Kyrin held him. He struggled a little then leaned against her, shaking. Kyrin hugged him tight.

"Brother," she said in a soft voice, "he's not—not so bad."

"No!" He burst out. "Lie not to me!"

She straightened. "I do not. We do not know what will happen. He may heal quickly."

Meric crumpled, and said on a sob, "Penni—I could not give her farewell—"

Kyrin touched Meric's chin and turned his face to hers. "If—if it comes to that, I will make sure you can see him." Elinor would not stop them. She would see to it.

Meric looked at her with a deep, shuddering breath. At last he wiped his face with his sleeve and wrapped his arms around her neck, laying his head on her shoulder.

§

The youngest child in the stronghold knew there was trouble. No more crops and strongholds were burned, which in itself was troubling, for it cast doubt on the lord of Cierheld, though

Fenwrd was bursting with those who had nowhere else to go, for both holds took all they could. Lord Cieri did not improve.

In constant pain from burns but partially healed, he held close to his bed; sometimes he made it to his chair by the fire for a bell or so. Healers from other strongholds came to him, shook their heads and left. Elinor and Kyrin did not speak of what loomed before them.

Aunt Medaen came from Halwende, with Esther Govannon. They gave their horses to the stableboys, and Kyrin met them on the hall steps at Elinor's side.

Elinor smiled. "You are well come. Please, come in."

Medaen's foot had touched the first step. She looked up at Kyrin and stumbled.

Kyrin sprang down the steps to her side. "Aunt—"

Old Medaen, wrinkled but as comfortably shaped as ever, threw up her hands in the old gesture and burst into tears. "My dear, oh my daughter—" She hugged Kyrin, her arms still strong, if a little more wrinkled. "I could not leave Ynglida before, but she has taken a turn for the better. My brother, how is he?" Her face was anxious.

"It is all right, Aunt. It is good to see you." Kyrin swallowed. "You will bring Father joy."

Medaen touched her cheek, her eyes gentle, then her gaze found the jet earring, and Kyrin stiffened. Aunt Medaen's smile trembled, but she said nothing. Kyrin hugged her again and stepped back.

Esther waited beside Aunt Medaen, her eyes downcast, resplendent in a red tunic over a blue undertunic, trimmed in gold. Neither would lend itself to nursing an ill man or helping about the hold. But Esther's face was sober.

Kyrin reached out. If she wanted peace . . . "Esther, be welcome."

Esther raised her head, as if she did not see Kyrin's hand. "Kyrin Cieri." Her small smile held an unholy gladness, her blue eyes the distant curiosity of a sated hunter, lazily watching fresh prey. She eyed Kyrin's ears, one pierced and free of a ring, the other bearing the sigil of jet, of shame and slavery. Kyrin's neck heated. She'd think it evil, or at least an opportunity to treat her as if it were. With the respect due a guest, Kyrin stepped back without a word and let Esther precede her up the stair. Battle was joined.

Elinor went upstairs to sup with Dain and Aunt Medaen. With the lord and lady of Cierheld absent, only Berd attended the high table as armsman, and stood at Kyrin's back. She spoke as little as she could.

Esther sought to draw her out. She stared at Kyrin over the rim of her cup. "But did you never find any of them well to look upon? I hear the riders of the desert are dark with mystery, bright with jewels, and absolutely heavy with silks."

"There was one. But you would not have called him rich, though he was a prince." Faisal was far richer in spirit and heart than Esther.

"Ah." Esther's brows arched. She glanced at Celine and the others, drawing them in, and leaned forward. "Where is he now?"

"In the Araby sands, with my sister and my second father."

"You have much to tell us, I see."

Kyrin said nothing. Alaina's letter, arrived after her father's wounding, had indeed had much to tell.

My dear sister, we are well. Faisal shelters us in his tents. How are your father and your stronghold? Have you news of Hamal? The wazir presses close through Umar's Hand, though all in the desert mislead him.

I miss the Umar who threw my staff to me. He has changed. No one here dares give Tae away. They would die at their brothers' hands—or Tae's. At least such is his reputation. At the caliph's word, the Kathirib will attack to bring the Twilket and Aneza to the caliph's mind over a tax on goods brought through the sands.

I miss our sparring; I practice still. Here I sleep alone, without you at my back. I would I could be at yours. A scop is not needed here, nor a scribe, nor my staff.

Tae says not to be anxious, the Master of the Stars has all in hand. I know that, but I cannot feel it. The only thing to do is what he has laid before me.

Faisal has enemies among the sheyk's men. Their leader, one Hafiz, would be sheyk when Gershem is gone. And Gershem will not choose between them as yet. It threatens the Twilkets from within—and so the peace of the Oasis of Oaths. Faisal sees this; he is not dim.

Hafiz seeks to humble him before their warriors. I wish I could stand for him—the prince does not deserve their hard words. He shields us from the Kathirib, though he is angry at times and struck by dark moods.

I wish I knew how to protect with a touch, as you do, but Tae thinks it best not. When will our father see I am ready? When will I not need to be protected? Am I so different?

I must be strong. You know me, sister. You have my love. I am writing our Chronicle from the time that Ali Ben Aidon took us. If the Master of the Stars allows, you will read it.

Send Hamal swiftly. Umar hunts us. We have heard no mention of you in any news of the desert or of Baghdad. You are in our hearts.

The Master of the Stars keep you in his hand. Your sister by blood, by hearth and by salt. I must end, but you will be glad to know Cicero will have pups soon by Sahar, Faisal's hound. You could hunt every morn here, in the hills.

Your sister, Alaina Ilen.

Alaina clearly esteemed Faisal and walked between many dangers. Kyrin bit her lip.

"How could this prince not favor you, our first daughter?" Esther's voice was sand in her teeth, grating against thoughts of war and Tae and Alaina.

Kyrin shook her thoughts away. "Your pardon. He may have been the prince you say, but not to me. I was a slave." And not of his heart, not then. *I am glad for you, Alaina, my sister. And for you, my brother.* Kyrin smiled a little. She could read between the lines. Her mouth tightened. She would not expose Alaina to Esther's laughter; a low-born peasant who loved a desert prince.

Celine leaned in. "Why such a secret smile, sister? Esther speaks truly. A prince of any land is a worthy prize." She tossed her head with a little pout. "But *you* were the one there, in the caliph's court. Is there naught you can share, even of their ladies' tunics, if the men were so ill to look on? They say their robes truly are silk, come by the Road from the East. Do the women veil their faces to their eyes and fear to look on foreign men? And what happened, that they disfavored you? Though you were a stranger, it must be said." She clasped her hands. "But their embroidery is fine as a queen's! Especially their beautiful tapestries, coming even from Baghdad. Lord Bergrin has one; it was in our room in Jornhold. You remember, the one of the tiger." She smiled sweetly at Kyrin.

"But then, you would know more of the trade of silk and thread than its uses. You brought back no prize but the gift of war. I say true, you are very good at that. I have been glad to learn at your feet." She tossed her head and shot a glance at Esther. "It has been too long since I learned. Now I can ward myself well." The challenge in her voice could not hide her longing for Esther's notice and her triumph over Kyrin.

Kyrin clamped her jaw on a surge of anger. Celine thought she handed Esther trophies: that Cierheld's first daughter disdained men, held secrets of trade and love, and trusted them not. Celine did not remember that Esther killed her own prey and disliked the help of others in doing it. Baiting Esther was more dangerous still. The rest of Celine's words deserved no answer.

Very level and quiet, Kyrin said, "I was never in court; that was Alaina, and only for a season. We had naught to do with the caliph's trade. The wazir's errand here was not about that." She frowned. *She* had naught to do with his trade. Alaina was now forced to war over it. "Yes, the women conceal their faces." Kyrin smiled grimly. "And it is quite true that silk and thread do not lend themselves to my hands—"

Myrna broke in earnestly, "But as Celine said, there are other things that do. Your Araby tunic and the trousers, the black ones with the falcon—could you give the pattern to Nell? Might we make some like them for ourselves, with our house colors on the breast, and another pair for you? The men have their house sigils, to wear with pride. Is not the art of Subak and our first daughter worthy of Cierheld's sigil?" She looked around at them. "The tunics will be beautiful! If Elinor would cut the cloth, Nell and I and Celine could wield needle and thread and make them." She looked at Kyrin with such shining hope, Kyrin felt a sting in her eyes. She nodded. If Elinor did not think well of their plan she would find a way to buy the cloth.

Myrna smiled, and it was as if the sun broke over land new washed by rain.

Esther sniffed. "Truly, Myrna, you take joy in the smallest things—"

"Yes, isn't it wonderful?" Myrna said, undimmed.

Esther rolled her eyes and turned to Celine with a rather venomous smile. "Celine, knowledge has an end. Your learning at Halwende is done. I see nothing more I may teach you. You, of all those of your birth, should know that."

Celine opened her mouth, turned very red, and stood.

Rage knotted in Kyrin's throat. Celine had burned her last bridge, and worse, Esther watched it fall with glee.

Nell rose, with a glare at Esther. "Celine, I would ask your nimble help with the tunic pattern." She turned toward the stairs.

"Ah, so you also work with the ill-marked? It seems to be catching." Esther looked Nell up and down. "It must be something about your eyes, that people think you witchy. Things of earth and things of heaven never do meet."

In one person, they did meet perfectly. Once. Once in history. And Nell was not witchy. Kyrin opened her mouth, "She is—"

At the same moment Celine gritted, "*Her* heart is unmarked by ill will. Is it not a gleam of heaven?"

Esther stood, eyes flashing, hands clenched, and rounded on Kyrin. "A gleam of heaven, is she? What of you? Why did they give *you* such an earring? The eye of evil, is it not? Do you share Nell's sorcery?"

Kyrin lifted her chin. "We share the letters I teach her from the Book, where we learn of our Lord."

"Ah, so she *is* your handmaid. What darker books do you study while others sleep, first daughter? Does she follow you out to read earth and sky in basins of water in the night?"

Hands clenched, mouth tight, Kyrin took one step, and from the stair Elinor called softly, "Come, come, my lord sleeps at last. Lower your voices, if it please you."

Her head high, a small smile on her lips, Esther rose, regal, and walked to the guest chamber. She shut the door. Meric said not a word but watched them with wide eyes from where he studied.

"Celine, we am glad to learn beside you." At Kyrin's words, Celine shrugged and turned away. Kyrin sighed. She wanted to call her friend.

§

Kyrin woke screaming in the paws of the tiger. Striking and kicking, her palm hit wood. Her fingers closed on the stick and she pulled it close, against the resistence of a live body on the other end.

"Kyrin, wake!" Nell hissed.

Kyrin started. "Oh Nell!" Her father, Elinor, Esther, Celine—all tumbled inside, mixed with flame and fur, sadness and the call of the falcon. The tiger would kill them all. Kyrin put her head in her hands.

Nell dropped the staff on the bed and her arms went around Kyrin. "Shh, shh, my sister, it's all right, all will come right." Kyrin sobbed, safe in her kind arms.

The next evening Kyrin went to her father's chamber. Mayhap she could lay one thing to rest before she sought her bed again. Dain heard the door and turned his head, biting back a pained grunt. Kyrin walked around to the front of his chair. She glanced from the oozing bandages about his neck and the stain on the front of his tunic to his face.

With a bitter quirk on his lips, he spread his hands. "Ah. As you see, I am helpless, and not even old."

"Father—" Piercing claws squeezed Kyrin's heart. She must ask, and she could not. It would beggar Cierheld, and their people.

"It's all right, daughter." Dain's face flushed. "I should not say such." His hands closed on the blanket over his legs.

"I'll get Mother."

"By all means, fetch my Willow lady."

Transfixed, Kyrin jerked to a stop and stared. With a soft smile, Dain laid his head against the blanket-cushioned back of his chair. Kyrin crept out. *Please my Lord, my friend, Master of the stars, our Father! Do not take him from us!*

Dain's bout of fever passed. Next day, the chamber seemed unchanged to Kyrin's eyes, her father's great chair in the same spot. He cleared his throat and turned questioning eyes on her. This time she must ask.

"Father, can we not send for the healer from Londian? I have heard he knows how to heal all ailments of the skin."

"Sit, daughter."

Kyrin sat gingerly across from him and leaned forward, rubbing her fingers over the wood arms. Her knuckles whitened.

"Such a man would cost much," Dain said softly. "I will not give Cierheld or Fenwrd for my life, when winter hunger lurks outside our doors."

"But, Father—" Kyrin's heart swelled even as her throat tightened. There was nothing more to say. Honor was his. "I love you, my father." She stood and kissed him, and turned away. She could not stay her tears, though she held her breath to keep them from falling.

"Kyrin—" He caught her arm and led her back in front of him.

"I must not tire you." Kyrin lowered her head and blinked at the fire.

"You do not," Dain said, his stern mouth melting with his old, small smile. "Nor do your tears, daughter. You make me stronger. You will rule well," he continued softly.

Early the next misty morn, Kyrin called Berd. He found her saddling Cauldron in front of the stables. Kyrin said flatly, "This morn I must go alone. Ride a wide circuit about me if you must." She yanked the cinch strap, and Cauldron snorted, turning his head to nibble at her hair.

With a long look, Berd said only, "As you will, lady," and busied himself about the stable door.

Kyrin pushed Cauldron's anxious nose away, her heart hot. Berd could wonder all he liked why she wore a flowing woman's tunic this morn. Green linen apron over sky blue tunic. Earth and heaven did not meet, hah! Kyrin sniffed, her hands swift about Cauldron's bridle.

Aunt Medaen's fashioned chemise under the blue tunic was soft and warm. She wondered what Esther would say of Talik if he came this morn. But he might not come. And it was as good an hour as any to test the tunic's limitations when she used a blade. Esther would have no edge on *her,* ever. Whatever she finally wheedled Celine to show her of Subak.

Kyrin felt Berd's eyes on her back as Twr let her out the gate. Her first armsman led out his mount as she turned for the grey-wreathed woods.

At the edge of the high meadow where she and her father had hunted there was a dark shape in the dew-beaded grass. Kyrin stopped, then nudged Cauldron closer. Mist curled above outspread wings, wisping away in the dawn. Kyrin dropped from the saddle.

"Samson?" Carefully, she reached down. He did not stir at her touch. He was stiff, his feathers wet with dew. He'd been there the night. There was no wound on his dark-barred breast, his orange eyes closed, talons clenched. Kyrin lifted him under his widespread wings. He would ride with her one last time.

Uncaring of her tunic skirts, she held him on the saddle before her and kicked Cauldron. They tore across the meadow at a furious gallop, heading for the trees. Kyrin rode until she had no more tears.

Then she turned back along the stream. She would not break her word to Berd, unspoken though it was. He thought her to be within his protection, and so she would be.

She buried Samson upstream above her pool, on the bank where the bluebells grew thick in the spring, under a clump of bracken. When she was done, Kyrin looked at her dirty hands, thick with earth and the smell of leaves, and her dulled falcon blade. The sun had grown warm while she dug, and Aunt Medaen's thick-spun chemise was hot along her back.

Kyrin stripped off her blue tunic and apron and waded into the water. It was less chill in summer. Medaen's white undertunic tugged cool around her legs in the current. Kyrin almost smiled. Aunt would raise her hands and exclaim, and mayhap rap her on the head, for swimming in it. But what was a garment, if not to wear? She would treasure the chemise always.

A mossy rock turned underfoot and something pricked Kyrin's ankle with quick pain.

A long shape glinted in the water under ripple and shadow. Kyrin tucked her hair behind her ear and reached down. It was a blade. She gripped and lifted it, and scrubbed the blade clean with a handful of sand. Wiping it dry on her chemise, she held it up in wonder.

The sharp length of the weapon reminded her of Hyl and his wolfship. And his ravens gathering about death and darkness, as the shadows did about the blade's watery bed. She shivered.

Samson was gone, her father like to follow. And men gathered against Cierheld like a swirling cloud. Samson kept his heart to the end.

She stared at the sword's bright edge. Somehow the gathering dark did not seem so black. *Fierce cry in the sky, wild and high . . .*

"Kyrin, what are you doing?"

Kyrin spun, and fell with a splash. Spluttering, blade in her hand, she rose. Esther stood, looking down the bank. Talik was beside her, her arm in his.

He loosed her and leaped lightly down the bank, a falconry glove on his arm. "We were looking for Samson. Cernalt said he should have been back last even. But you found a sword—in the stream?"

"Yes. Catch." Kyrin tossed it to him, and Talik caught it expertly in his gloved hand. He stared at it, then looked up and flushed, belatedly turning his back.

Kyrin said, "Esther, would you—?"

"Of course, first daughter." Esther took Kyrin's tunic from near Samson's grave and picked her way down the bank. She graciously spread the garment between her hands to ward Kyrin as she walked from the water, staring at her over the top. Esther's grimace at the wet chemise flattened as she saw Kyrin's scars. Kyrin was not sure she wished to read her expression as she glanced away and swallowed.

Kyrin dressed hurriedly. Taking the tunic from Esther, she pulled the soft blue over her head and hugged it around her, then handed over the wet chemise.

Talik hefted the sword, eyeing it. "This is a fine blade, meant for an offering to the spirits, or sent after a warrior on his last journey."

Esther crossed herself.

Talik turned to Kyrin and held out the blade. "Now it is yours. It may be a Damascus blade or better." His fingers lingered on it.

They walked up the slope toward Cauldron, Esther having captured Talik's arm again. Talik paused at the fresh mound of dirt, his brow furrowing. "Did you find the sword here and take it to the water to clean it?"

"No, Samson lies there."

Esther said nothing, only her lips flattening. Kyrin looked from her to Talik, who stared at her and then crouched to run his hand over the dirt. "I sorrow for you. But that sword is worth—" He stood, head cocked, watching Kyrin.

Esther shrugged. "Quite. A blade like that is worth fifty falcons."

Kyrin tied her apron strings with more force than necessary, eyes burning. "The sword will not leave us. Samson has."

"True enough." Talik sighed. "He was more than just a good hunter to you." He touched her shoulder.

Kyrin's heart warmed. "Will you help me find some flowers for him? I know it is late in the season, but—"

Talik opened his mouth. Esther glared at Kyrin. "What a broil over a bird! It is good he left this morn—"

"This morn? You saw him this morn? Where?" Kyrin stepped closer.

Esther glanced aside. "I—"

Then Kyrin knew. She choked out, "*Why*?"

"He's filthy. They all are, and he near made my horse throw me before the gate, swooping down over my head like that. One of my men declared him a danger; I agreed."

"He was *mine*." Kyrin shook with a great sob as her anger rose. "You—you . . . Leave me." Her grip whitened on the sword.

Esther backed away. Talik stared at her grimly. "You'd best go back to the hold."

"You would leave me to go alone?" Esther's voice grew shrill.

"No. Talik will go with you. I will take my lady." Berd nudged his horse from behind the trees and bracken and stopped beside Kyrin.

Kyrin stepped to his stirrup. "Berd, my thanks. Talik—"

Talik eyed Berd with a dark frown. Kyrin said hastily, "Berd is my first armsman now." She handed the sword up to him.

Talik glanced sharply at her and away. "As you will." He strode aside, gesturing Esther ahead of him. Kyrin mounted Cauldron and Berd closed in beside her, handing back the blade.

On the ride back, Kyrin was quiet. She looked over her shoulder once. Talik walked beside Esther, his arms swinging free. Kyrin twisted at her hair uneasily, a knot in her throat. She had not meant to hurt Talik, only to get away from Esther before she hit her.

Kyrin unsaddled Cauldron in the stable, Berd working quietly beside her. She said softly, "Berd, think you the blade would buy Father a healer from Londian?"

Berd pursed his mouth. "It is fine steel. You could ask Cernalt or Nith."

"Cernalt knows of swords?"

Berd grinned. "He has done more than tend the falcons, you know."

That was true. Once her father's armsman, always an armsman. Kyrin nodded, thinking. If she did nothing, Cierheld might fall with its lord. Meric, Nell, Myrna, Elinor, Nith, and even Berd, who took the blade from her to examine it again. Even angry Celine, and Twr, with his near worshipful awe; they were hers, to be defended. *Master of the stars, let us not fall.* She was first daughter. She could not let them fall.

At supper Samson was mourned. As Twr said, raising his horn of mead with the others in a toast, "Samson brought in the tenderest duck this side of the Ouse!"

Kyrin told no one who had brought Samson down. Esther was quiet, glaring at her. It was not hard to avoid speaking with the first daughter of Halwende, for the blade Kyrin had found was closely studied by every male at the high table. The retelling of its finding abounded about the hall, and the men eyed her with admiration.

Cernalt pronounced, "It's a good blade, that."

"Aye." Talik took the blade from him and hefted it again.

From the next table, Twr looked at it longingly. "It's a blade I'd buy myself, had I the coin."

"That's if the Lady of Cierheld didn't want it—your pardon, Lady Elinor, I meant the first daughter of Cierheld." Talik bowed smoothly to Elinor, leaving his question in front of Kyrin.

"No, I don't want it. I mean to give it for a healer, for my lord father." Laughter and talk at the tables fell quiet.

"A healer might take coin better."

Kyrin looked at Talik in surprise. "We have none." Her neck heated. "Though I might sell the blade for coin in York or Londian," she added, thoughtful.

She left the weapon in Talik's hands and went to her bed, lighter in heart, though wrung by the day. Curling under her blanket, Kyrin stared at the rustling oak. Samson was gone.

Fierce cry in the sky, wild and high, echo my heart's cry . . . She would write him an ode. *Break the bars of wrong, cross over the wall.* Her hand closed on her stronghold key. Falcon's Ode . . . it was fitting to honor him. And she would wear the key, be it only under her tunic.

25

Strife

For such a time as this. ~Esther 4:14

Kyrin woke. Light streamed through the oak, patterning the floor. She slipped out of the room as Nell slept, her face peaceful. Kyrin crept down the passage. She would not wake her father.

The door of his chamber opened, and Esther slipped out, a small smile on her face. She lifted her head and jumped, her hand on her breast. "Goodness, how you do creep about. The painted people of the hills have nothing on you."

Kyrin looked from her to the door. Below, Elinor called, "Esther, did you bring Dain the clean bandage?"

"Yes, my lady." Esther smiled at Kyrin, turned and swept down the stair. Kyrin followed, wished Elinor a good morn, and sat down to her porridge with a will at the far end of the table from Esther. Then she blinked.

Elinor must have bid Talik remove the blade last night from the table, for it was not there. Meric joined them. Myrna and Celine emerged from the guest chamber, Celine rubbing her eyes. Talik came in from the yard with a grin, Berd behind him. Meric piped, "Where's the sword?"

Talik's eyes flew to the table, then to Elinor and Kyrin. "I left it here last even—"

"I was first down, and I saw it not." Elinor's brow scrunched, and she finished poking up the fire vigorously. "Mayhap arms-master Nith—?" She turned in hope.

"I'm sorry, my lady." Nith shook his head. "I know not. Let me ask the guard without."

The guards had seen nothing.

"How dare they?" Talik's face was thunderous. "I am sorry, lady. We will find it." Berd nodded dark agreement.

The porridge kettle deserted, all of them searched the hall, careful to leave Dain undisturbed. Esther helped and only raised a superior brow when Nell tumbled down the stair long after her mistress. Despite a growing headache, Kyrin searched again. Under the table and benches, in the guest room, on the weapons rack, the stair and beneath, even inside the chimney.

Nith and Berd drew the men up for morning inspection and went through the barracks. Medaen lifted every pot in the kitchen, and the mews, smithy, kennel, and chicken house were thoroughly searched. Kyrin went to look in the well, where someone might have hung a blade over the lip of stone by a thread, and behind the hall, Nell lifted the garden's cabbage leaves. She straightened and shrugged in answer to Kyrin's silent question.

After circling her oak, staring up into the branches, Kyrin slumped on the bottom step of the hall. Berd was leading a squad along the walls, searching every inch of the yard, dirt or stone. Cierheld's great gate was closed. Who hated Cierheld or its lord so much he wished Dain to die? Or was the blade simply too great a temptation?

Nell sat beside Kyrin with a sigh. Above them, Esther said, "I must needs return to my mother, since Medaen says she will stay with Lord Cieri until the sword is found, or her brother improves."

Kyrin swallowed the knot in her throat and wiped at her eyes. If Esther had Samson removed . . . She had always been good at manipulation. Kyrin strode up the steps and planted herself before Esther. "Did you do it? Where is it?"

Esther threw out her hands in disgust. "What would *I* want with a sword? And where would I hide it, under my kirtle?" When Kyrin only stared at her grimly, feeling Cierheld's key sliding beneath her own tunic, Esther huffed, "Oh, very well!" She pulled up the edge of her skirt. Kneeling to check, Nell glanced at Kyrin and shook her head.

"Satisfied?" Esther glared at them. "You'd do better to search this wench or Celine; they might have some use for it. Or yourself."

Kyrin did not even glance at Nell. Celine stared at Esther from behind Elinor's shoulder, her face white. She shook her head mutely. Behind her anger, Kyrin wondered if Celine had taken it. Mayhap merely to prove herself Kyrin's equal with a blade, and then she'd been afraid to tell them? She could not wish Dain ill. "Celine—"

"I did not; how dare you think it! I am not without honor." Celine turned on her heel, and in a moment the guest chamber door thumped loudly.

"Well." Esther lifted her chin. "I will leave you to it, and take my leave of Lord Cieri. Halwende has need of me."

Her bags had been loaded on her horse. Esther descended the stair a last time with a bolt of Elinor's cloth under her arm. Kyrin eyed it. It was long enough to conceal a blade. Esther folded the black linen, and Kyrin's hope died. A prim smile edged Esther's mouth.

Standing among Cook and her kitchen help, Talik watched the first daughter of Halwende depart, arms crossed. None seemed sorry to see her go.

§

Berd found Talik in the stable, readying his horse. "Leaving so soon?"

"Yes. I've done enough here," Talik said. He'd been worse than useless, losing the sword.

"Talik Wyman," Berd mused. He took out his dagger to pare a nail. "Did you take it?" He shot a hard look at him under his brows.

Talik snorted. "Your suspicion is misplaced. I would not harm Kyrin or Cierheld."

"You're a lord's son. You may wish to tell her. She has no love of lord's sons, even those Mornoth has disinherited."

"How know you of that?" Talik's hand tightened on Hawk's brush.

"It is my duty, my oath, to know of all men near my lady. And women."

"So Esther draws your narrowed eye also?"

"Aye."

"They searched her."

"Not when she left."

She had been upstairs, in Dain's chamber, with moments enough to move a blade from a bolt of cloth to her skirts. But Dain would have seen her. And as Lady Govannon said, what would she do with it? It was far more likely one of the men sworn to serve Kyrin had taken it. Talik straightened suddenly and faced Berd, his eyes glittering with grey storm. He took a step closer. "Do you seek to drive me away? Do you serve Kyrin also in this? I've seen the way you look at us."

Berd slid his dagger back in his sheath, his nostrils flaring. "I will protect my lady of Cierheld even against herself, so—"

"She does not need this now," Talik gritted. "Her father and Samson and the missing sword are more than enough."

Berd glared at him. "Keep from Lady Govannon if you care for the heart of Cierheld's daughter."

"What mean you?" Talik balled his fists.

"Walk not arm in arm with Esther if you seek Kyrin. She feels herself enough of a wren beside a peacock without your lordly help."

The loss of the sword, the land, choked Talik. And Kyrin. He swung. His fist connected with Berd's jaw. Berd grunted, slid away from his second fist, and landed a blow to his ear. Talik's head rang. They stood toe to toe until they'd absorbed enough punishment to dull their inner pain, then they swung apart again, panting.

"Do we have to do this?" Talik snarled.

"Idiot! Did you have to break my nose? I was only saying—"

Talik drew back his fist, and Berd hastily put out his palm—"Wait, I only meant, ward her well."

"So?" Talik eyed him suspiciously.

"So ward her with your life, man! As a hawk, she needs gentle handling. Though in some ways she hits harder than you." He smiled. "Still, a dagger in the back will end the strongest life. Ward her. With all the skill of a lord's son." Berd touched his nose gingerly.

"I mean to."

"So what are we fighting about?"

"Nothin'."

They glared at each other.

"Good. I can't have my men killing each other. Not when Lord Mornoth lurks." Cernalt swung easily out of the shadows of Cauldron's stall and crossed his arms, his old eyes sharp.

"Sir." Talik bent his head, and to his surprise, Berd did also, wiping blood from his nose.

Cernalt held out a parchment. "First armsmaster Nith has a message for Jornhold, to be delivered without delay."

"Yes, sir." Talik took it, tucked it in his tunic, and turned toward Hawk. Berd was settling her saddle.

Talik gave him a crooked grin. "Still wish to be rid of me, eh?"

"Nah. Kyrin will be waiting for you when you return." Berd held out his hand, and Talik grasped his forearm.

"Pardon my hasty blow." His neck felt hot. "So you fear for her—does this fear have a name?"

"I know little enough. And my tongue could have been more skilled just now. Keep your ears and eyes open." Berd turned toward the hall, and Talik watched him a moment, and turned Hawk's nose for Jornhold.

§

The lord of Cierheld grew no better. Over the following desperate hand of days, Nith informed Kyrin that Lord Bergrin Jorn had no coin to borrow. She offered to teach the warrior's way at the Brewmaster and tried to sell Cauldron in Bolton, to no avail.

Leading Cauldron out of town toward her meeting place with Celine, Kyrin eyed the stone church beside the abbey and the river. She paused, uncertain.

Celine had disappeared within Bolton with six of Berd's ten-squad. When she'd asked Kyrin if she could go, Kyrin had been able to think of no reason to refuse. And so Celine had come to barter for cloth for Myrna and Elinor, while Berd and the other four men attended Kyrin. Brother Rolf might have news of any in need of a horse or of her skills. They could as easily hail Celine from the church as from the trees beside the road. And Uncle Ulf was not yet an anchorite, walled within.

While the others dismounted around Kyrin in the churchyard, she tied Cauldron to a nearby tree and nodded to Berd, who turned to watch the road.

Kyrin stepped inside the nave. It was quiet, without voice or movement. A large book lay open on the altar at the end of the aisle. Was it Alaina's Vulgate? Her leather shoes whispered along the aisle. Bending over the altar, she sniffed the familiar smell of leather and paper, not scraped parchment, and reached out to caress Alaina's familiar hand. Her skill had wrought such a thing of lasting worth . . .

"I wondered when you would come."

Kyrin yanked her hand back, and Brother Rolf shook his head with a smile, rising from his knees in a corner. "None has a better right."

Kyrin nodded and turned to the Apostle John. *Abide in me. I am the vine, you are the branches. Abide in my love.* She was trying, though the falcon was hard pursued. Kyrin bowed her head.

"What troubles you?"

Kyrin told Brother Rolf of Cierheld's plight. He shook his reddish head. "Ah, with the burned wheat and barley, so many destroyed holds and homeless families, everyone clings to what coin they have to fend off starvation.

"Bolton is pressed beyond our means. The infirmary is full, all of us living on turnip soup, and it is not even winter, though the nights grow chill." He rubbed his arms. "Still, our Lord's arm is not shortened." He smiled then sobered. "I would tell you to ask the king's household, whom Lord Cieri has served well, but alas, the regent is not of our late king's mettle or resources, not even for my brothers' flock of Bolton. But"—he held up a hand—"if your sister should come soon, your uncle admires her scribing. You might prevail upon him to pay well for her service." He looked at her patiently, his lanky arms strong, hands clasped in his dark robes. He cleared his throat. "I once spoke of matching staves with you. I regret, my coin has already gone to hungry mouths. As soon as I may—" he sighed and shrugged.

Not soon enough for Dain. Still, Kyrin thanked Brother Rolf.

He grinned. "It may ease your mind to know Thorgil speaks no more of witchery. And I have heard naught to bring me to your hold. In fact, Father Ulf employs him as a bearer of messages and burdens. Thorgil seems willing enough." He watched her, ice blue eyes gleaming beneath hair of pale flame. "God go with you on your road." There was a fire in him. A banked fire, but a fire all the same.

There was no game along the road from Bolton to Cierheld. Many had gone before them. The first real snow hit the ground as they made their way homeward, covering the land with a mantle of white a hand deep. Sensing Kyrin and the men's mood, Celine was quiet.

The whisper of the tack of thirteen riders seemed at times interspersed with the padding tread of a tiger. They reached Cierheld and Kyrin wearily pulled herself up the steps. Soon she sat before the fire in the hall, with her father. Nith and another had carried his chair downstairs. Kyrin ignored her damp cloak and the growl in her stomach.

Abide in me. The falcon lived in the Master of the stars's peace. If only she could do so. Idly, she twisted and pulled at the head of the falcon dagger to lessen the tingles in her warming hands. The proud head loosened. Kyrin tightened it again.

She smiled at Dain, bittersweet, and he smiled back, reddish stubble about his chin. It was good to sit beside him, with his warm smell of cinnamon and the oak logs in the fire. It did not matter if they talked much or little. He was there.

If only she could get the coin for Londian's healer. The falcon was cool under her fingers. Why did the Master of the stars not help her father? Was he to die so soon after she found him? Would the tiger bring them down? Her teeth clenched and her hands tightened. With a *crack,* the dagger's head turned and slid. The blade twisted to cut the edge of her palm.

Her mouth open in a hiss of surprise, Kyrin stared at the Damascus blade and the falcon head in her lap. The bronze was jagged where the join had broken. A pile of dust spilled out of the hollow within, onto her tunic. She poked at it. The mound loosed a slight musty odor.

"Kyrin, are you hurt?" Her father sat up straight.

"A small cut." A thin line of blood ran near her little finger. "I'm well." There were hard lumps in the dust.

"You'd best get that bound up." Dain tried to shift in his chair and peer into her lap. "What is it?"

"I don't know." She picked the hard bits out of the oily dust, rubbed, and opened her hand. There lay a round white stone. No, a small pearl. Excitement tightened her stomach. She'd seen the like at Ali's. Another white pearl, a black, a rough red ruby, and two blue stones of differing shades, streaked with grime.

"Well, look at that," Dain whispered. He picked one up. "This is a sapphire. I wonder how they came to be inside the head of your falcon blade, and for how long."

She knew. The Master of the stars put them there long ago, through a human hand. For such a time as this. "Father?"

"They cannot be used for me, my daughter." There was tender, sad firmness in his voice.

"Why not?" Kyrin's voice rose. The heat of the tiger's rage bloomed inside.

"I received a message."

"May it burn!" The missive could only be from Talik or another on the behalf of the northern lords. Talik, who left her without a word of Samson or the sword or her father, though

Berd said he carried a message for Nith. Talik might have given her a moment to speak with him before he went.

Dain grew stern. "Things are very bad in the strongholds. Listen, daughter, and think."

Kyrin gripped the jewels in her fist. This could not be the Master of the stars's design!

Elinor called greeting to someone at the door, and Dain laid his hand on Kyrin's arm. She turned her head, tapping her foot since she could not reach her hair. Dain's lips twitched. Kyrin's mouth flattened. There was nothing amusing about his stubbornness.

A cloak swirled as a man turned to shut the door, revealing a bit of wet, straw-colored hair gleaming in the firelight. Talik dropped his hood. His grey gaze flickered over them.

Dain grinned when Talik eyed his drawn face sharply. "Welcome, stranger." Her father shot a mischievous glance at Kyrin. "Come, warm yourself."

Talik bowed and sat on the edge of the hearth. Kyrin shifted back to give him room, her skin tingling.

"Good evening, Lady Elinor, Kyrin, and good even' to you, my lord," Talik said solemnly.

Kyrin gave him a brief nod, the heat of anger and something else swirling in her. There was a receding greenish bruise around Talik's eye.

"Your first daughter will stay for the word I bring?" He glanced at Dain.

Kyrin gripped the pieces of the falcon dagger in her lap, her face heating to equal her heart. Talik wished to speak to her father without her? What was he about? Surely he had more wit than to mention the sword—unless he'd found it. But then he would have spoken to her first. Mayhap she could make him see the wisdom of convincing Dain it would be best for all if the lord of Cierheld was on his feet, that it was good to spend one jewel for a Londian healer. She clenched her hands in hope.

"Yes, Kyrin must hear this. She is first daughter."

"Very well." Talik's face was hard. He stood restlessly and gazed past Dain, toward the end of the hall. "They die, in the lowlands around the Humber. Lord Mornoth brings war earlier than we thought."

Kyrin glanced at her father, startled. War was far more than a brigand who burned holds or conflict between a few lords. If her father's surmise was right . . . "So, Lord Mornoth sent the robber to Lord Teth's?"

"Yes, Lord Jorn's man found out, with the help of Nith's eyes and ears in York." Talik turned. "We do not yet know the lackey's name, only that he gives fealty to Mornoth. I'm of a mind to help your father and Lords Gadral, Fresen, and Landyl, with our other Northumbrian allies, drive him and his band of brigands to ground. The regent is not strong, but he is all we have. Without him we fall into chaos, and we know who will ride at the head of *that* wild hunt." He rubbed his chin and sighed. "The strongholds aligned against Ludwin Mornoth are few enough. The regent does nothing; he cannot, not without appearing to refuse the will of his council. Mornoth has done his work well." He shook his head.

"The children of York look at me with such hope. When I turn away it eats at my heart. Lord Ludwin Mornoth begins his full bid for power in the south, but he will extend his reach to us. A hold near Bishop's Dale is soon to fall. Each hold he overcomes gives him more strength to oust the regent." Talik's gaze bored into Kyrin. "Even if by some miracle we take Mornoth's stronghold near the mouth of the Humber, we will need more than the food he stole. We don't have enough to last the winter. And to fight in the snow—" He sank down by the hearth.

Kyrin looked at the floor. The firelight flickered. Talik was right, and her father. Their very land and people were in danger. The heart of a falcon never faltered once the needed course was seen.

"I—I found something." The hall was silent but for the hissing pop of the fire. Kyrin cleared her throat. "What I have found will get us men and supplies."

Talik raised his head, sorrow fighting hope in his grey eyes. She poured the jewels in his hand but for one hard blue spark trapped between her fingers.

Talik rolled the rest in his palm, tipping them toward the firelight. "Half these would pay for more men, and the others will gain us food, both for us and the needy souls from the burned strongholds."

Those at Fenwrd, and Bolton. Kyrin nodded.

He looked up. "But what of Londian?"

"You will not use them for me." Dain's voice was firm. "I will heal, or not, as God wills."

Kyrin said nothing. Was it not sin to disregard means given?

That night, his fever rising, the lord of Cierheld went to his chamber. Berd and Talik carried him up. Kyrin made him as comfortable as she could, and then Elinor waved them out, pressing a cool cloth to her lord's brow. Kyrin and Talik descended the stair after Berd.

Dismissing Berd with a nod, Kyrin stopped at her father's empty chair. "Talik—"

"My lady?" He turned beside the hearth.

She laid her hands on the carved willow crest of Dain's chair, her knuckles whitening. "I am first daughter, it is true; it is also true I am a woman and untried." Her arrow that once brought down a Twilket raider to save a child did not count—that was no battle. Neither was the time she fought Seliam. She drew a deep breath. "When the moment comes, our allies must not falter. Between Nith and Berd and I, you will give us a leader Cierheld can follow."

Talik flushed. "I have not the gift of command!"

"Berd says it would be well for me to speak for Cierheld. And for you to lead our northern lords, Talik Wyman, son of the old rebellion, once Lord of Alkborough." Her voice was steel.

Talik shook his head and muttered, "That lord was my father's father. Now my father and my mother live in Gordale Scar, below the falls, in the wood. He is lord of nothing."

"And you?"

"I go where the road and the message take me."

As they would take him again. Kyrin could not look at him. "And do you wish to be a lord's son?" It was almost a whisper.

"Berd should not have loosed his tongue—"

"I asked him."

Talik ran his hands through his hair. "Why do you believe our Northumbrian lords will not follow you?"

Kyrin glared at him. He avoided her question neatly. "You know why!"

"You yet doubt your place as first daughter, or your fitness?"

"My place is with my father—"

"You would say so, when Cierheld needs you?" He stepped closer, his eyes narrowing. "You love your father, I know, but your gift in warfare—"

"The question is not of gifts! It will look ill if Nith or Berd take the field with our men, without my father. I cannot take his place. As Lord Alkborough's son, you can lead Cierheld. You must!" She would take back her words about lords' sons.

Talik turned white and stepped closer. "Why do *you* stay behind? You are not one to be caged, except for a purpose. It is not in your nature." He shook his head. "Look to yourself! Give what you promised!"

Kyrin flushed, openmouthed. He had seen the blue jewel she kept when she dropped the others in his hand. "I keep my oaths!"

"But not the spirit of this oath, this gift of your father's?" He was unyielding. He swallowed, and closed his eyes.

Better it was anger; his sadness would break her, with her own. "The spirit of things, is it?" She said bitterly. "What of you and Esther, and that sword?" Had he taken it?

"I do not deny I wanted it, but never did I seek Esther." He eyed Kyrin warily. "She wishes my regard, I think."

No, he hadn't. Kyrin sighed and leaned on the back of her father's chair, seeing in the light of the fire the raised poker in Esther's grip long ago, her mother's crippled hand curled around the chair arm, her father seated in it, asleep. And then the chair was empty. "Talik, please—" Her father had need of the blue jewel. The rest of them were enough for food and men. Peasants were used to making do. *She* was used to it.

"He does not wish it," Talik said, sober. Then softly, "Stay the course, Kyrin. Lord Mornoth and the brigand who serves him will be brought to justice." His eyes glittered with tears.

He reached for her hands, or the dagger. She cared not. The falcon mocked her pain. Fumbling, clumsy with despair, Kyrin drew the blade, dropped the blue spark inside, twisted the head, and threw it at his chest. "Take it! With your place at the head of Cierheld!"

Talik caught the dagger and stared at her, his mouth firming in an angry line. "Do not forget *your* place, first daughter. I will not forget mine. To protect and serve." He bowed stiffly and strode out the door of the hall.

From the coals of the hearth, the tiger turned and looked at her.

26

Secrets

Thou hast refined us as silver is refined. ~Psalm 66:10

Talik stood by Hawk across the yard, readying to ride with Nith to Lord Landyl's of Reeth in the north, for a gathering of their allies, men, and arms. Talik would lead eighty men.

Kyrin's mouth twisted, dry as dust. If she had but one jewel, all would be well. She swallowed hard. That was not true. More was at stake than the life of the lord of Cierheld, though he was her father, and dearer than life. The north desperately needed every mouthful of food and every man the jewels could buy. Though she was torn in two.

Talik was to lead Cierheld in battle, and she—she was to ride to bargain her father's life away. To meet Father Ulf, who had been chosen to carry Cierheld's gift for Bolton Abbey and payment for the men and supplies, for during his travels her uncle had gathered connections with many lords and their holds, north and south.

Talik pulled Hawk's head around, with a last glance at her. His face was as bleak as the clouds. His mouth worked then he turned away. Kyrin could find no words for him. The morning was as cold as the distance between her and the Master of the stars.

After the sound of Hawk's hooves died, Kyrin trotted out the gate of Cierheld with Twr and a tensquad fully armed with spear, sword, and shield. Berd reined in beside her.

North, the way Talik had gone, the trees were a dark wall beyond the mill and the meadow. If only she had told him she was sorry.

Kyrin turned Cauldron's head toward Bolton and the south. Prime bell passed over the line of silent, alert riders behind her. Then it snowed in fits.

The second day out Kyrin called to Berd. The armsman legged his horse beside her through blowing white. The drifts were deep as the horses' knees and growing. If they could only travel in the trees where the snow was thinner, but the undergrowth was too thick.

"Yes, lady?"

"Berd, we must not stop for the midday rest or we will not meet Uncle Ulf by Nones."

He looked at the sky, sniffed the wind, and said, "Yes, my lady."

The men followed her order without comment. Did they think ill of her for bringing them to this pass? She could not tell from their shoulders, hunched against the cold, or the quick, darting glances that looked from her to possible danger on their flanks. Warmth wafted from the horses' backs and steam from their nostrils. Fog chuffed from the men's mouths. The air stung Kyrin's nose where she walked behind Cauldron, who grunted as he broke trail at the head of the column in his turn. The cold whiteness around them seemed without end. The silence and thick falling flakes swallowed the clank of horses' bits and the *shush* of their steps.

On the south side of Bolton, Berd, who had forged ahead in the dimming light, gave a low hail. Father Ulf and the men around him were dark, white-dusted shapes on the meadow spreading white and wide along the river. Kyrin grimaced.

She would have been pleased if her uncle had agreed to meet in Cierheld. But he feared another attack along the road, so he said. She shrugged slightly. He was a cautious man, keeping to lands he knew in time of trouble. She would see him as she had wished, and face that anger again. Did she have the courage to ask him why? He could hardly call her witch now.

She shoved through the snow toward them, after Berd and Twr and another, who broke trail. An armsman and two monks, neither of them with Brother Rolf's tall gangly frame, eyed her curiously.

Then Uncle Ulf turned and stared at her, his long face as still and concealing as the snow. He turned to one of his brothers. "Assist her," he ordered.

The small round monk sighed and nodded, walking forward past Berd and the others. Uncle Ulf settled his hands in his sleeves.

Kyrin's lips tightened. For a soon-to-be anchorite, sought for his wisdom gained from solitary contemplation, he involved himself much in traveling and business. Such as dealing with the coin between the church and local strongholds. But it was true the affairs of Cierheld would affect Jornhold, and thence Bolton, whose walls were soon to swallow him.

Her key heavy about her neck, Kyrin bowed and briefly told Uncle Ulf what they knew of Lord Mornoth and his dealings with the brigand.

He eyed her, raising an austere brow. "It seems my thanks are due you. This scourge must be stopped. To sniff out evil at its source is a hard task for any man. Though"—he shrugged—"we know the king was ill fit to lead such a hunt." He bent his sharp gaze on her, his mouth thinning. "But I will speak no ill of the dead." He seemed impatient to finish his errand.

Kyrin quickly removed the falcon dagger's head, took the hand-span wood chest Berd held for her, and dumped the jewels inside. She closed the lid.

The morn after the falcon dagger gave up its treasure, her father's brown eyes had been steady. He pointed toward the dark beams overhead, struggling to rise further in his chair, and said gently, "We have him, and that is everything. This life and pain is passing; the world to come is eternal. Rule justly and with love. Rule yourself well in both; and bring your people to knowledge."

Bowed over the chest, gripping it hard, Kyrin sighed, snowflakes blowing across the wood, chilling her fingers, swirling into her eyes. Father Ulf's face tightened when she paused. Kyrin wiped her eyes, unseeing. But Berd's gaze narrowed, and he watched Father Ulf's every move, his hand near his sword. Kyrin shoved the container into the awed monk's hands.

She moved forward as the monk hurried to his horse, and stopped at her uncle's knee. "Uncle, we would welcome you at Cierheld. My father is ill, as you have surely heard, and I—" She looked down. "I find I would not lose any of my blood, especially to ill will."

"*Ill will?*" Father Ulf leaned over. "What know *you* of ill will? Speak to me again when you have lived without your lord of Cierheld as I have endured the days without my Willa." He stared at the hills behind her. "God's pure work in flesh: tainted, twisted, driven to wallow in uncleanness, driven by her love of a man. To *heresy*." His gaze dropped to her and his jaw jutted. Kyrin backed a step. "There will come a day when your heresy will be recognized—"

His brother monk legged his horse up beside them. "Father, we must go."

"Then go!" Kyrin cried into the rising wind. "Take Cierheld's gift and payment and go!"

Uncle Ulf smiled, a thin gash in his face. Berd, standing at her shoulder, took a step forward. But Father Ulf turned his beast.

Tracing the shape of her key beneath her tunic, Kyrin slogged back to Cauldron. It was good Brother Rolf had not witnessed their meeting. It seemed Uncle Ulf had so little regard for those who bore the name of Cieri that he spared no thought for their pain. Cauldron threshed through the snow and bore her, her heart and feet numb, to the end of the forlorn column. Kyrin stared at Cierheld's horn in her hands. It was done.

She raised the horn and blew a loud blast to bring in the scouts, her dark cloak snapping in the frigid wind, coated thinly with ice, and led her men into the shelter of the trees.

That night she huddled in her cloak by a fire swiftly kindled by her first armsman. He knelt to crouch beside her. The wind drifted cold fingers of snow down their necks. Kyrin both longed for and dreaded her bed. She had no wish to watch the falcon's life flow away again under the tiger's paws. Since the night she discovered the jewels, she had not been able to lift the sword against him. It was little comfort she had chosen rightly in the end. She had said she was *stronger than they dreamed.* Well. She licked her lips and stared into the flames. "Talik will have reached Landyl's by now, will he not?"

"Yes." Berd rose. "You'd best get some rest if you wish to rise early on the morrow, lady."

Kyrin nodded dully, went to her fur robe and cried herself to sleep.

She woke with a sense of peace. The tiger had not come, and it could not in the grey light of dawn. Muscle by muscle, she relaxed, comfortable in her furs. The low voices of men and the crackle of flames growing in the fire-pit warmed her spirit. Pine smoke tickled her nose. The warmth of her furs did not reach her cold cheeks. But the quicker they moved on, the better. She rose and soon dug into a bowl of porridge Berd handed her. They broke camp and rode on.

Kyrin scanned a long white ridge clothed with scattered pine on her right. It descended into lower ridges, thick with trees, some bare of leaves, that came down to meet the road. They were yet two nights from Cierheld, slowed by the snow and their late meeting with her uncle.

Cauldron snorted. Then he reared with a scream of challenge. Kyrin drew her sword and he dropped back to earth, pawing the ground. Mounts squealed and blew as Berd's command rang in her ears. Her men formed up around her, steel drawn, spears bristling.

A man wearing a mountain cat's skin, staring through the empty eye holes, the furry edges concealing his head and shoulders, gazed at them from the edge of the trees. A score of men on horses that showed hunger in hip and rib rode out around him, taut and bristling with anger. There were a few swords among them, but most held ash spears. The cat-man twitched a stick with a white cloth tied to its end ceaselessly against his leg, a spear in his other hand.

So. Unless he planned treachery, he meant to speak. He did not take his attention from her, and the silence stretched. The rest of the skin and the tail of the cat trailed over his back and a soft-tanned tunic and leggings. The pines whispered overhead.

Kyrin's skin prickled. Her squad would not fare well against these hungry outlaws, twice their number. She shrugged, nudged Cauldron, and her men parted to let her through. Berd followed, his drawn sword across his saddle. A horse-length from the cat-man, Kyrin stopped.

The ill-dried cat skin stank. The man's blue eyes snapped behind the cat's snarling face. There was something familiar about the straight way he held his head. He dropped the stick in the snow.

"Sir, what need you?" Kyrin asked quietly.

"I am Brother Rolf, no betrayer of a lord!" Rolf ripped the hide from him and threw it clear. Berd swung his horse around in front of Kyrin. Rolf cried, "This day I am a hunter, and proud to be! You. False raiser of our children's hopes in Bolton! What say you before I take what was promised?" His horse stamped in its place. He ignored Berd.

"What do you say?" Kyrin's stomach turned over. "The jewels for the south people, Brother Rolf, they've been given." She forced herself not to look away from his drawn face, set with inner pain.

"Have they?" Rolf leaned forward. "My warrior days are not so far behind me. The law of the land falters. Our Lord calls all men to do justice and ward the defenseless. This morn we found my brothers curled in speechless agony, slain by poison, and Father Ulf gone. How could you? Where are you keeping him? Or did you drop him when you finished with him, for the snow to cover? By our Lord, I will whip your treacherous back for this!"

Berd kicked his horse. Before the last word was out, he knocked the spear from Rolf's hand with the flat of his sword, and set the edge to his throat. He growled at Rolf's men, "Be still. I would not murder a man of the church."

Kyrin flung out her arm. "Stop! Brother Rolf, I gave the jewels to my uncle early last even. Our meeting lacked fair words on his part, it is true. But there was no treachery. Might the brigand under Lord Mornoth have struck again?"

"Hah!" Rolf's face was pale, but he sat straighter. "You would know more of that than I. Has not this robber ceased his attacks since the lord of Cierheld took to his bed? Or would you deny that knowledge also?"

"Have a care for your tongue, man," Berd gritted. "Our lord took his death wound protecting you. He has only ever served his king—"

Kyrin held up her hand, and Berd shut his mouth and lowered his blade. Kyrin swung down from Cauldron, turning her back to Rolf, hiding her stricken face. Her father *was* failing. Berd only said what they all knew. But she did not believe Brother Rolf was a backstabber. And she trusted Berd if her belief failed. She drew a deep breath, clutching Cauldron's saddle.

Her questioners must see the fearless face of innocence, so the real traitor might be found the swifter. She turned, her face set. "Brother Rolf, my uncle may have been taken. Or, he may have left the trail where the new snow hid his tracks—or those of his attackers."

Uncertainty clouded Rolf's face. "Give me proof of what you say."

Kyrin lifted her chin. "I have none. None but my men's word, and the question of what we do on the road without Cierheld's walls, if we did *not* fulfill our word."

"Then some of us will die here." Brother Rolf smiled, his eyes hard. Berd tensed. "Better now than of hunger."

Brother Rolf would fall, and his men, poised to strike, would then fall on Berd like wolves. "Wait! I will give better than proof!" Kyrin cried. "Take me and"—Berd caught her eye fiercely, but she paused on the youngest in her company. "And Jost, as prisoners for Cieri's word. Take us with you and hunt down Father Ulf."

Berd turned. "No! My lady, you cannot. *I* will stay."

Rolf glared at him.

"Berd, I will endanger no one else for my uncle. Besides, I doubt not Brother Rolf will find him quickly, mayhap exchanging his ill-gotten gain for coin, for the brigands have never yet dealt in poison." Kyrin's voice was bitter. Jost legged his horse toward her and Berd.

"Do you have so little faith in a Father of our abbey?" Brother Rolf protested.

Kyrin looked at him sadly. "Do you have so much? My uncle is different than the man I knew. Bitterness devours him."

Rolf shut his mouth in a flat line and said nothing.

"I could never speak before your father again if I let you go," Berd protested. "I am your first armsman—"

"And it is not your decision." Kyrin's neck heated as Berd stiffened. Why did he oppose her in front of the others?

Rolf said stiffly, "I will take this Jost, and him"—he indicated Berd with a tilt of his chin—"and count it enough, Lady Cieri. It is not right that a stronghold first daughter ride with us. Your armsmen will not be harmed, for I hold *you* accountable. I pray that my judgement was right about you, that you do no witchery here, and I will find you at Cierheld, your word redeemed." He spun his horse on its haunches, without a glance at Berd. Berd's stare should have burned holes in his back.

"One thing, Brother Rolf." He turned, and Kyrin continued, "I will wait for you here two days." And she would send a messenger to Cierheld, while they watched the road. "Also, be wary of any men of Lord Mornoth and Nidfael Keffer's. Mornoth supplies the brigand." It *was* possible Uncle Ulf had not betrayed them. She would pray so. "They may have my uncle. It is probable they have much of your lowland goods."

Rolf's men looked at each other. One muttered hotly, "I knew it!"

"We'll get 'em!" another cried. "Whoever they be." He looked darkly at Kyrin.

"Peace!" Brother Rolf raised his hand. "We will ride to look into it. Lester, as you love me, ride with the lady. I will not leave her with her guard under strength." A huge man with black curly hair dismounted and walked his horse toward Kyrin. She watched, her cheeks hot, but did not refuse Rolf's man. Brother Rolf might mean what he said, and also wish a witness to her word.

"Fare you well," Rolf said, and nodded curtly to Berd.

"My lady." Her armsman saluted, sheathed his sword, and fell in at Rolf's side.

The band disappeared into the lower wood, breaking through the crusting snow. Berd and Jost did not look back. Jost held his head high, proud he served her and Cierheld. Kyrin hoped they did not have reason to curse the stupidity of Cierheld's first daughter. She sighed and picked up Cauldron's reins. "Twr."

His mount was between her and Lester in a moment. Kyrin nodded, glad for his company. Even less than a squad as they were, she'd take her Cierheldens over twice that number of any other lord's men. Twr rode beside her, silent. He seemed to understand she wanted Lester near so she could keep an eye on him.

The man was quiet. He kept a smile on his face, but he noticed everyone and everything. Kyrin's smile quirked. She was oddly unafraid. Lester was most unthreatening, despite his giant frame and watchfulness. He might even be one of Rolf's Brothers from the abbey, though the heavy blade at his side was worn. Kyrin shrugged. Mayhap he was a brother from Rolf's past.

§

Brother Rolf found sign of his quarry at the edge of a large meadow off the road, where the daughter of Cierheld had stopped her squad to dig snow away from the grass to provide the horses feed. Father Ulf's horse, among others, *had* left the trail.

Rolf could not tell if more than his brother monks' beasts had passed that way. Rolf gave low orders, and the men of Bolton slipped through the trees and bracken in a wide net on either side of Father Ulf's tracks. They were near enough Pately Bridge and Keffold. On foot, Rolf warily followed the marks in the snow with one of Bolton's watchmen and Berd at his heels.

Brother Rolf ached for his monk's habit. Though rough, it did not chill him with cooling sweat as the tanned skins did. His books and the abbey were softening him.

"Brother," the watchman offered, "Cierheld *has* always been true." Rolf grunted. He wished Berd did not grin so prettily at the watchman.

The road to Pately Bridge, having crossed the main road to Bolton elsewhere, passed through the trees ahead. The noise of their feet on the snow crust was too loud for Brother Rolf's taste. He stopped, and Berd a moment before him, he noticed with a sigh. The watchman took another crackling step and winced. It comforted Rolf, and he shook his head at himself.

Next moment, it was driven from his mind.

Somewhere on the road that appeared thorugh the trees, a voice he knew said indignantly, "If they see me they'll kill me!"

A lower voice growled, "I tell you *again*, no one will know you in that tunic! Find out when and where any southlanders will ride to Kem Landyl's hold to join Cierheld. There should not be many, since you have their promised coin. Remember, it is half your payment."

"And not near enough. God's house requires—"

"Prate not to me of your house!"

Slowly, his heart cold, Brother Rolf crept forward and peeped between the leaves of a low-growing oak, Berd on his heels.

A thatcher in homespun with bits of straw in his clothes sat his horse. He tipped back a wide hat, and caught it as it began to fall. Father Ulf jammed it on his head again and grinned unpleasantly, straightening to his full, ascetic height. "Lord Cieri and these cursed northlanders will have an unexpected greeting at your hands." He blew on his reddened fingers. "That nest of rebellion has been fat for far too long, my lord—"

Brother Rolf turned his attention to Lord Mornoth, a lord out of a tale, his wide shoulders clad in black, his white stallion restive. A conical, unmarked helmet on his head winked sliver and blood in the afternoon sunlight, his hawkish face and yellow beard adding strong lines beneath. Groups of armed men squatted on the snowy ground beyond their lord. Their fires extended beside the road, wending beyond Brother Rolf's sight. Evening drew shadows across blue-white snow in the grace of feathery evergreens and the bare bones of other trees touching the sky.

Rolf slid back behind the trunk of the tree, collapsing at its base, lowering his head in his hands. He would gather the men of Bolton, and they would catch Father Ulf when they could. Rolf brushed at his eyes. Father Ulf had once wanted only peace. He had turned from that path.

Or had he sought peace on his terms from the beginning—with his God, his family, and his life? Brother Rolf wanted to ride, his spear high, and dash evil to the ground. He also longed for Bolton Abbey, and even more, the great book on the altar. His mouth tightened. From this moment, he would hide more of it in his heart. But now—he met Berd's eyes and nodded. Now was the moment to capture a traitor, to find a true lady, and give her what he knew. He would not leave the daughter of Cierheld in doubt of him.

§

Kyrin stared after Brother Rolf as he departed for Bolton with his men, his head low, with the jewels resting in a bag over his heart. Talik must be warned.

"First daughter! Pah!" Father Ulf spat at her from the line of Cierheldens behind her, struggling against Berd and Twr, who bound his hands. Berd swung him around so she was out of reach of all but his voice. "First in deceit, who uses a woman's flesh as it ought never to be used! It is not for a woman to ride so; not for a first daughter to take the lead, nor to take the place of men." Ulf glared at her.

Kyrin turned her gaze on him, bleakly sensing the rise of the tiger. "It was forced upon me."

Uncle Ulf shot her a sly look. "Can you deny that you take joy in the way of the sword? That you revel in your devilish Subak? That you are pleased with men's tunics, which free your stride, and that you take pleasure in the love of these who follow you?" He flung out his arm at the men, who shot him grim or disdainful looks. Jost stared at him, red and rigid with anger. Kyrin swallowed, forcing her words into cold formality. "I am the same, whether I wear a woman's tunic or that which is suitable for Subak."

"*Are* you like these?" Ulf gestured with his chin at those around him. "With that sign of black evil in your ear? Search your deceitful heart, and see if it speaks a different tale." Ulf grinned. "I will hear your confession."

Berd jerked him toward the back of the line. "Keep your ill will behind your teeth. She has had all the confession she needs. And our Lord has accepted her."

Uncle Ulf glared at Berd but fell silent. He did not long remain so. Berd had him gagged when Ulf insisted on reciting every ill the late king, Lord Dain, and every other had ever done him, adding more to the litany of Kyrin's wrongdoing.

Kyrin frowned. Was there a seed of truth in his words? Was her weak heart unfit? She missed Samson flying above them, Nell's gentle voice and strong common sense, even the falcon in her dreams. She rested her hand on the falcon dagger's empty bronze head. *Mother, how I wish you were here.*

In a sevenday of hard riding through Coverdale and across a plain to the next dale, Kem Landyl's Reeth came in sight. Kyrin smiled, thinking of a fire instead of blowing ice, and hot soup and cider. And she could take off her mail, of which a stray ring was wearing a hole in her shoulder.

But Talik, with Cierheld's force and Lord Landyl's, had gone on. The steward shook his head at Kyrin's news. "My lords all saw fit to go on to Cattraeth. Their scouts have chased the brigands that far."

Kyrin squinted up. The sun was near Terce. They could yet make a full day's ride if they kept on. She turned back toward Cauldron, legs and shoulder aching. She rubbed her shoulder absently. Did her father still oversee Cierheld from his chair? Surely he had remembered to remind Cernalt, first in command in Nith and Berd's absence, of the tunnel in case the hold had need of a back door? But Cernalt knew it well, as her mother's old armsman and keeper of the mews. Kyrin frowned. He often seemed more than the hawkmaster, with his solid frame and sharp glance, the way the newer Cierheldens watched him, and Berd and even Nith deferred to him. She pulled herself back into the saddle with a grunt. When one once held the place of first armsman, one never quite retired.

The cold grew, and at times Kyrin dozed in the saddle. Through the day they went. At Cattraeth, at dawn, Twr's hand on her arm alerted her, and she raised her head.

Talik and their men had camped on a grassy meadow among the companies of the northern lords. Kyrin blinked at Twr, and he bowed his head, indicating she was to ride ahead.

She was so cold she couldn't seem to catch her breath. It was an effort to lift her arms to guide Cauldron among the scattered rude shelters that covered the trampled meadow, around men who lay sleeping wherever they found room. She winced; her mail had dug a hole in her flesh. Her neck creaked.

An older man looked up from sharpening his sword, and a young messenger gaped in amazement at Lady Cieri, garbed for war in mail, with a sword at her side. The rumors that Lord Cieri's daughter was no stranger to weaponry and fighting were true. He shouted to another, and ran to alert—someone—she supposed. Other men were awake, stirring steaming porridge and toasting bread on sticks over the fires. They stared at her as she led her stern tensquad toward the larger tents in the middle of the meadow, Jost smiling in irrepressible spirits on her left.

Father Ulf, his feet fastened under his horse's belly, his hands tied under its neck, struggled to rail at their watchers then kept red-faced silence as they wound through the ranks of eyes. The nearer men bowed to Kyrin.

She saw them through a haze, and hoped they pardoned her slight nod. None of her squad had slept much since Brother Rolf departed, leaving behind her fully satisfied first armsman and her men, Brother Rolf's deep apology to her and Cierheld's name accepted. Kyrin's mouth was numb, but she smiled wryly inside. Brother Rolf had promised to join Cierheld's forces after seeing the recovered jewels safe on their way.

Cauldron's feet crackled over skeins of ice, frozen thaw-melt, and shuffled through deeper snow. Surely it was not much farther? Ah, there.

Cauldron halted before a wide tent of dark cloth, under the Cieri sigil, flapping in the bitter wind. The moon and sun, with the red arrow between. The sigil wavered before her. She was so cold and weary and her shoulder hurt . . . Would they welcome her, Nith and Talik, after her hard words back in Cierheld? Cauldron would not mind if she stayed on his back a moment. But a shadow moved within the tent.

Her legs buckled when her feet touched the ground, and she clutched at her saddle. Strong hands caught her from behind.

27

War

He trains my hands for battle, so that my arms can bend a bow of bronze. ~Psalm 18:34

"Are you well?" Talik kept her from the ground, gripping her shoulders.

"Cold. Lord Mornoth comes from the south . . . Southeast road." Kyrin's jaw spasmed and clenched. She managed to open her mouth again, but nothing came out. Her key had slid inside her mail, a freezing brand against her skin despite her thick wool cloak and an extra fur Berd had found among the men. *Samson—your fierce cry—would my heart were as strong to do no wrong. But evil's hand is long, seeking heart and song, with forgotten shadow throng.*

Talik shook her, his brows drawn together. A beam of sunlight topped the eastern hill. Kyrin felt its warmth on her stiff cheek. Talik shouted orders as he helped her stagger inside.

"My lady!" Nell rushed to take her hands and draw her toward a chair. Kyrin stumbled and Talik's hands gently stopped her fall. She shivered in the chair they set her in, glancing out through the flap at men about their errands then at Nell. Nell, here—how?

Nell knelt, taking off her snowy boots. "I couldn't let you ride to all your battles alone, now could I?" She said softly. "And I am your companion. Elinor and I agree on that." Her smile was satisfied. "Berd has other duties here; he cannot be by your side always—and in a camp such as this it is not proper. Here, let's get you out of that wet cloak."

Kyrin leaned forward and shifted to dislodge the hilt of her sword that dug into her side. The mail pained her shoulder as Nell whisked off the cloak. Kyrin fumbled with her sword belt. It was far from the girdle Elinor said should grace every first daughter.

But she could not be angry with Elinor, as Nell *tsked* and shoved Kyrin's hands away to give her room to release the belt. Kyrin had not known she could hardly move her fingers. "Nell—thank you."

"Of course, my lady." Nell turned her back to tug a brazier nearer. Kyrin rested her sword against the chair but left the falcon dagger in her lap. Weariness of heart crashed down on her. The falcon's eyes were dull and opaque, its farseeing gaze blind in the dimness of the tent. Why had help come for Cierheld but failed her father? *I will counsel you with my eye upon you.*

Her mail removed, Kyrin clutched a dry, warm fur Nell laid about her shoulders. In the tent door, Talik called something to Nith, who strode past, leading Berd and her men toward food and rest. Kyrin's nose was thawing in the heat, letting in the smells of fur and horse, fire smoke and an undefinable scent of men. Cierhelden guards had unbound Father Ulf. He moved shakily between them, more supported by his captors than restrained, as they followed the rest. How would she tell Nell of Uncle Ulf, or did she guess his treachery, seeing him brought into camp bound?

Talik dropped the tent flap, and spoke softly with Nell. The sword hilt removed from her ribs, Kyrin relaxed into the warmth of fur and her eyes closed. She jerked as something hot and heavy touched her hand.

"Easy," whispered Talik, and held out the mug of tea again. She sipped then drained it to the dregs, cradling the heat of the mug. The hot roil in her stomach warmed her.

"What is this you say about Lord Mornoth?"

"He—he's almost here, a day's march—if he hasn't pushed his men." The tea's heat crept deeper. She shivered convulsively. Nell went to the chest in the corner for another fur.

"I see." Talik strode to the door and called a messenger, then gave Kyrin more of the fragrant mint tea, his frown deeper, as he pulled a chair before hers.

She must speak the words in her throat, heavy as stones. "Talik, I sorrow for my words before I left. I should have—"

"The fault was also mine." He shook his head soberly. "Though our words were true, their spirit was bitter. Now we may begin again." He smiled a little and pulled the fur higher around her shoulders. Tears welled up. The warmth of the tent stung her cold fingers fiercely. Nell busied herself on the far side of the tent. Weary beyond caring, Kyrin let Talik grip her hands and leaned her forehead against his shoulder. She whispered, "Have you heard anything of my father?"

"No." He patted her knee and whispered, "But at this moment, no news is good news." Kyrin gulped back a silent sob, then another.

Nith strode inside without ceremony and they broke apart. The tall armsman's battle-dark eyes warmed; then his smile fled.

"I sent scouts to confirm Lord Mornoth's whereabouts; they are still coming as Lady Cieri said, up the southeast road."

"Thank you, first armsman." Talik rose. "We should gather the men for council."

Nith nodded then glanced at Kyrin, and a grin spread over his face. Talik went outside. In a moment he returned with one of Kyrin's saddlebags and handed it to Nell with a word. She tugged out Kyrin's black falcon-embroidered garments and laid them in her lap."Change your tunic, you've got a council."

Talik left, paying no heed to Kyrin's questioning glance. If plans had changed and they wanted her in council—she could hardly think over the shouted commands outside.

After a moment she dressed slowly with Nell's comfortable assistance, as close to the brazier as she could get. She left her key outside her tunic. If she was to play a part . . . Nell smiled at her, a small, proud smile. Her sword restored to its place, Kyrin ducked out of the tent.

The companies had drawn up in ranks. An open lane between respectful lords opened before her. Middle-aged, blond Kem, dark, tall Lord Lanner Fresen, and brawny young Cor Gadral, his red hair reminding her of Hal, watched her. More men than she'd hoped had gathered against Lord Ludwin Mornoth. She smiled and bowed to each, for the tea had thawed her enough.

They bowed in return. "Lady Cieri."

Farther down the line, Berd and the other lords' first armsmen waited, watchful before their squads. Kyrin returned their courtesy with full honor, a first daughter to equals. It was only a part she played. She could do that. Soon Mornoth would be destroyed, and she could return to see how her father fared.

The line of armsmen ended with Nith, Cierheld's men drawn up in ranks behind him, and Kyrin hesitated, unsure where to go.

Nith inclined his head slightly and she walked up a low, south-facing hillock where Talik waited. He put out his hand and helped her up on the rock beside him, turning her to face their assembled allies. A slight frown tightened Kyrin's brow.

This was no council. She raised her chin, questioning him with a look. The stillness was absolute, and her breath quickened.

The new sun gilded every face in the sea of men, one side in golden glory, the other stark shadow.

Limned in the dawn-light beside her, Talik bowed and tucked something in her palm. Proud and clear, his gaze steady, he said, "Lady of Cieri," Then raised her hand in his above their heads. The blue and black ribbons of Cierheld streamed from their joined hands. A cheer roared from the foaming sea of souls at their feet. Kyrin's toes were yet numb, but her heart warmed, remembering the oath of first daughter she'd given. *To keep faith—to seek their meat and protection and honor as my own—and as Tae taught me, Subak for my land, for my people, my family, and my Lord.* Kyrin's mouth went dry. She tightened her fist and straightened. The squads quieted.

"My thanks." Her unwieldy tongue was impossibly clear. Kyrin looked at Cierheld's allies and then Cierheld's men, ninety of them hers. "We fight for our land, our oath-brothers, and our king!" She shook her hand within Talik's, the ribbons rustling. "Together we will stop Lord Ludwin Mornoth and the brigand at his right hand!"

Someone shouted, "The king is dead and his regent is worthless!"

His eyes locked before him, Berd cried, "We fight for the king who will come, in justice and right!"

Kem Landyl stepped from the line of lords, eyeing Kyrin keenly. "You have need of an armsman to speak for you, first daughter?"

Kyrin cocked her head, breathless in the sudden silence. Talik's hand tightened around hers, his mouth pressed into a white line. He glared at Lord Kem.

Kem's words pressed hard, though his voice was mild. If he wished to know where she stood and tested her . . . in the end it mattered little. Something else mattered far more. "I have need of every man who speaks truth, whether he suits *my* need or not." She stared at him, gaze level.

"Well said." Lord Kem saluted and turned to his place with a satisfied grin. The Cierhelden tensquads, joined by the others, took up a chant that shook the earth, "Cieri! Cieri! Cieri!"

Kyrin put her fist over her heart, touched her forehead, and ended her salute with an outward flick of fingers, meeting their eyes. Berd bowed. It was all that need be said. She had no more words.

Kyrin turned away, down the back of the hillock, pulling away from Talik, who would have kept her close. He shrugged and followed, directing her toward Cierheld's tent. Berd came to escort her through the smiling crowd.

"Lady Cieri! Lady Cieri!" The call followed her amid a storm of salutes. Her mother last bore the approval in that name. Lady Cieri. Kyrin nodded to Nith as she passed him. Mayhap they *would* have followed her. Esther would always take what she could—as Celine would also counsel. To use the men's regard and twist them to her ends. And then none of them would live in her heart.

Kyrin bit her lip. It might be too late for Esther, but she would not give Celine over to such a heart of stone. She would not. She rubbed at a rising ache in her head, wincing at her shoulder. Celine *was* her rangdo, even if she was not a Cierhelden, and she was also a sister, if a quarrelsome one. Kyrin's step faltered, and she shook her head.

Did Nith mean to ask her to ride before the men of Cierheld? Leading in the field . . . This moment, here, as first daughter, she was someone the men fought for, not an untried leader. If they were *not* uncertain of her leading in battle, they should be. They did not know that she would bend as the need arose to the wisdom of the other lords. Tae had never trained her to lead men where they would die. The thought brought a coldness to her belly, and the rotten, hot breath of the tiger on the wind.

An answering defiance rose in her. *Fierce cry in the sky, wild and high.* Kyrin breathed out. *Be true as the faithful snows. Truer yet as the board is set. Give not in to enemies; break their net.* She smiled. *Samson, your Ode grows, though not in order. But as Aunt Medaen would say, when did I ever follow order? Though I follow it more now than I did.* Sobering, repeating the new lines under her breath, Kyrin rubbed her shoulder and sat down in the tent to wait for Talik and Nith.

Men bearing buckets of boiling water entered. Nell directed them behind a curtain that closed off the rear of the tent. The steam rising from their work bore the scent of mint, pulling at Kyrin, but she could not think of the glad prospect of a bath. Not yet. If Nith sensed her misgivings would he dismiss them as uncertainty, or worse, think her a coward? And what was Talik about, leading the men to honor her—was he seeking to resign his post?

Talik and Nith entered, smiling. Kyrin drew a deep breath as she rose. They waited.

Best to know and get it over quickly. She lifted her head, the straight look of one warrior to another. "Armsmaster, I will not command our people. I know little of battle besides hand-to-hand fighting, and I am not enough of a warrior to lead them. I—" her voice came softer, "I know of killing, but nothing of companies and squads and strategy."

Nith nodded, sober. "You've but proven your wisdom, my lady. As you say, a battle is no place to learn these things. You will first listen and watch from a secure position. As your father wishes, this is the beginning of your training. Later, if you agree, you will earn your place in the squad file." Kyrin breathed out in relief. His tone lightened. "The men know what training you have received as a slave, and that you are willing to stand good for your word. It is said you risked your own skin with a certain warrior monk." He shot her a hard look. "Though it was not your skin to risk. Remember you are our first daughter. We do not have another." He glanced at Talik.

"As with Lord Wyman, it heartens all the men to see you here. My faith, lady! It is not so long since the queens of the old blood ruled these hills and led our people to victory."

"I see." Kyrin smiled a small smile.They did not mean her to lead, and they did not object to the blood of the hills as Esther did. "It is well, then, first armsman." Though she would listen to what the men said of her when the armsmen were out of earshot. Nith bowed his way out.

Talik tilted his head. "You spoke well, on the hill."

Kyrin shrugged, and dared touch Talik's sleeve in Nell's presence. "My thanks. I left when I had no more words."

"No matter." He whistled tunelessly to himself, watching her. The last man went quietly out with his empty bucket. She wanted a bed to fall into and brief, restful silence. He took her hand and bowed over it. "Take your ease and rest, lady. I will see you in the morn." He ducked out, and Kyrin breathed another sniff of perfumed steam. Shoving back sleep a little longer, she found her way behind the curtain and slid into heavenly liquid heat, sprinkled with dried lavender and mint. Her shoulder stung.

§

A blare of horns whipped all dreams from Kyrin. She opened her eyes, and her hand closed on the falcon dagger beside her. The tent had disappeared. Instead, above her nose was pulled an oxhide, smelling of smoke, and a tree trunk rose not far behind her head. A horse whinnied.

She slid from under her bed-skin, the ox-hair beaded with frost, and shifted the falcon dagger. Nell was thoughtful to lay the blade she'd forgotten in her chair where her waking hand would find it. Her shoulder reminded her she was thankful not to wear mail this morn. She would don it soon enough.

Men pulled up tent pegs, calling to each other. The other tents scattered among the trees fell in orderly rhythm. There was no sound of combat. The lords were moving their men into position. She had slept late, but needed it. Kyrin frowned slightly; she hoped Nith thought so.

A young messenger noticed her, trotted over, put a courteous fist to his chest in salute, and held out her sword and a bow. Kyrin's mouth twitched as she took it, remembering her father's arrow and a rabbit. She trusted Nith had gotten a bow that fit her draw, and meant her to test it. She sheathed her dagger and, her belt fastened at last by cold fingers, the sheathed sword tapped her leg as she strode into the bushes.

When she came out, the messenger pointed into the trees. Sunshine streamed around the broad boles, turning the ground mist into white glory. "First armsman Berd waits for you, lady." Yestermorn's snow had vanished. Kyrin thanked the messenger and moved toward Berd and Talik who were tacking up six horses, one of them with—she stopped short—her saddle. Kyrin hurried. Mayhap there was need of mail?

"Lord Mornoth and Lord Keffer have split their forces," Talik said tightly, staring at the horse's flank as he lifted the saddle to its back. "As we thought, they never were on the road together." He jerked a leather strap into place. "They have a devilish plan. So says your uncle. Lord Nidfael Keffer is on his way to attack Cierheld." Talik looked up, his face full of fury.

Kyrin swallowed hard. "Do they know—"

"He has been reminded there is a hidden way into every stronghold. Yet you can reach Cierheld before him, lady, light as you are. Twr will go with you, and Berd." Talik indicated Twr nearby, who saluted. Kyrin nodded to him.

She was light, if she wore no mail. Berd was not. Berd's dark gaze pinned her. She turned to eye the rump of her first armsman's stallion, rippling with muscle. The beast looked strong enough to bear a giant at speed. And well so. Her first armsman would not be parted from her for any need but her life. Kyrin's mouth twitched. Berd's shoulders relaxed when she inclined her head. Had he expected her to balk? She did rely on him, whether or not they were likely to meet an enemy on their road. Berd said nothing but bent to straighten a stirrup. Kyrin smiled a little and ignored Talik's glare.

The big mare he readied for her was not Cauldron, but all her gear was on the saddle, even the stick she'd left on Cauldron last even'. With her shoulder, if it came to shooting . . . there were not many archers among the other lords' men. Only Mornoth's. Kyrin swallowed on a suddenly dry throat and coughed. Twr offered her a waterskin.

She took a swig so icy her eyes teared. Lord Jorn's men had last reported Lord Keffer in Pately Bridge. So, he moved against Cierheld? Her stomach tightened. Nidfael Keffer would not find them unready. He must not.

Talik shoved a spear into her saddle thongs. "Nith says we must defeat Lord Mornoth here. Then we may ride for Cierheld or the other strongholds, as need demands. You must hurry. Cierheld can hold out much longer than Nidfael thinks—if you guard the tunnel and none slip inside to unbar the gate." Not looking at her, Talik hung a quiver of arrows on her mare's off side. He cupped his hands. Kyrin lifted her foot, and he threw her into the saddle. "None but Nith and I know where you go."

His hand brushed hers as he withdrew. He looked up, his grey eyes deep. "Here is something for you." He reached inside his tunic and pulled out a hooded hawk. Against injury, her body, wings, and talons were wrapped tight. "I found her last even' in a tree, its naked branches red with sunset, flapping in a late falconer's net. Let her not fall to Samson's fate—at the hand of treachery."

Kyrin carefully took the peregrine from Talik's warm fingers and slipped the bird inside her tunic. *Take up your being, queen of meaning. Falcon deadly swift, farseeing; my heart, ever kenning.* If she could but understand her own heart so well. "I will not let her fall so," she said softly.

Quickly, Talik pressed a biscuit and a bit of meat into her hand. "Lord Mornoth's forces grew during the night. He has twice our number, and Lord Keffer about two hundred. The reports are sure. Where the warriors came from, we do not know; Nith believes them mercenaries from Mercia. Lord Bergrin Jorn arrived early this morning, and will send fifty men to your aid. They follow as they can." Talik nodded and slapped the stallion's rump. "I will see you again," he said low, and glanced at Berd. Twr waited on his mount behind.

Kyrin's legs tightened against the horse's brown sides as she sprang forward. Talik's stern face worked as he whirled away from her, his back tense. "Don't despair!" she cried across the distance widening between them. "Fight! An he wills it, I *will* see you again!" The mare lifted over a log and its front hooves slammed down on the other side, jolting Kyrin's teeth. *Abide.* The falcon made a harsh noise and nestled against her heart. The woods thickened beyond the edge of the near empty clearing. Kyrin could almost see Tae, hear his low voice, "Fight well."

So many things could happen to those she left behind. Kyrin sent an earnest plea upward with her glance then turned her attention to threading through the trees. Berd and Twr nudged their mounts up on either side, remounts in tow.

Sometime later, branch-scratched, they emerged from the forest and trotted across half open meadow. The ground was bare in many places, steaming in the sunlight. They switched mounts and followed a dim, half-frozen cart track through a chain of small meadows and thin forest. At midday they found dried meat, bread, and onions in their saddlebags. Kyrin and Berd ate as they rode. The bread was dry and going stale. Tae said trail rations always did. Then Berd watched, while Twr ate hungrily, without the noise of chewing to hide sound of approaching danger.

A bell passed. The grey and blue shadows of the trees lengthened. The track they'd chosen disappeared among low, rolling groundswells, thick with trees and bracken. Kyrin lay low along her horse's neck to avoid a branch, wishing she rode Cauldron with his night-wise ways instead of the mare. They trotted up a rise and then down, through a line of willows. Their horses' hooves thudded unexpectedly upon a road. Kyrin was across before she knew it.

Armored men in six long files rode away from them, fifty feet on the right. A long-dead oak towered before the troop, naked of bark in the evening, marking the Wensleydale road toward Cierheld. Heads turned and mouths opened in alarm. Her horse danced when she pulled on the reins. They carried no sigil she could see.

Kyrin kicked the mare back across the road, Berd and Twr beside her. They had to get to the nearer pass; old unused, and rough as it was. They could not outrun this force all the way to Cierheld by the roundabout valley road.

A shout rose. Kyrin glanced back. Mounted men swung from formation and raced to cut them off. The setting sun washed their helmets, chain-mail, and tunics in hazy gold.

Berd and Twr made it into the trees a length ahead of her, glancing over their shoulders. Kyrin urged her horse under the leafless branches. The trunks separated them.

Shouts and the thud of hooves echoed between the trees. One of the shadows resolved into a man who swung his horse before Kyrin. His mount surged against the mare. He struck Kyrin's leg with his boot to unbalance her, raising a short spear. Kyrin leaned back, sword half-drawn.

The spear struck her side, glancing off her leather belt. She let go of her sword to grab the spear shaft as it withdrew. She yanked. The man slid sideways, releasing his spear as he struggled to keep his seat. Kyrin whipped the shaft back at him, a scythe on a wicked back-sweep, and toppled him.

More pursuers flickered in and out of existence under the trees. An arrow struck her horse's rump and glanced aside. The mare's stride lengthened.

A thicket parted, and she saw Twr galloping toward her across a small clearing. Two spearmen closed in on him from either side.

Then Berd was beside her, his mount's hooves pounding beside hers. Kyrin swerved away. "Go!" Berd shouted. Sword out, he charged Twr's attackers.

She did not bother to answer, but pulled her mount up to string her bow. She was ten times a fool for not stringing it before they started, and she should have worn her mail, regardless of weight.

A blow across Kyrin's back flipped her off her horse. She gasped for air, struggling toward her feet. Her hands empty, numbness spread across her back. There was a muffled squawk, and a sharp beak pricked her stomach. Kyrin gasped. *The falcon.*

A mounted archer circled her, grinning. Her bow was broken, one shattered limb sticking up from the ground. The spearmen were down, and Berd's saddle was also empty, though he was on his feet. Twr rode toward him, his arm outstretched to pull Berd up behind him.

A second archer came out of the trees, his arrow leveled at Kyrin. The rider circling her saw him, cursed, and also drew on her. Berd leapt for the archer near the trees.

Kyrin jumped. She strove desperately for height with all the power of her legs gained kicking straw men off Ali's garden wall. She was aware of Berd crashing into the second archer's horse as she came up and lashed out. Her axekick smashed her attacker's bow-arm across his body—then her other boot took him in the throat. An arrow whipped past her ear with a wicked, thick-voiced whisper.

As the archer fell off the other side, Kyrin reached for his saddle and thudded across it, belly down. She pulled herself astride, gasping. She was the only one left ahorse.

To one side, Berd pulled the second archer's horse around to mount it. He staggered as an arrow slammed into his back. Twr's bow was up, his mouth tight, shoulders aligned to his shot—squarely at her. There was no moment to fling herself off or turn the horse. She turned her head as she ducked.

Behind her, another bowman released. He twisted as Twr's shaft seemed to sprout in his eye, and fell.

Kyrin straightened. Twr's saddle was empty. The archer had changed his aim and Twr was down, with an arrow in his throat. She needed a weapon.

Berd made a high sound, an animal scream of wordless protest. The back of his neck white as chalk, he gripped the horse's mane to keep his feet, body sagging. Nearby shouts propelled Kyrin from the saddle.

She whirled Berd around, lifted his foot to her stirrup, and shoved with all her strength. "Pull, Berd!" He grabbed at the beast's mane and gained the saddle then dropped bonelessly across its neck. The horse sidestepped with a nervous whicker.

Kyrin stepped on top of Berd's foot, lunging for a seat behind him. When her foot slammed into its off side, the horse burst into a gallop, but she was moving with it, and faster. Pinning Berd with one arm, Kyrin grabbed a handful of mane, lowered her head and rode, chest heaving. She had lost Twr; she would not lose Berd.

They descended into a gully and the horse jumped a fallen tree. Kyrin dodged branches that rushed for her like living arms. They tore at Berd. Her legs were tight about the horse's hot, sweating sides, her tears lashed dry by flying mane. Beyond the ravine, the black horse climbed a low hill, grunting with strain.

Kyrin touched Berd's neck. It was cold and clammy, and his blood-beat was as fast as her breath. Their pursuers were too close to stop. The arrow in Berd's back had struck his shoulder blade and slid around the side, out through the flesh under his right arm. Blood trickled from the wound. Somewhere in their wild flight the shaft had broken. The head and a bit of shaft remained. She must stop the bleeding, though their pursuers were too close to take out the arrowhead.

Kyrin tore away a strip of her black tunic and packed it around the arrow as best she could despite the jolting of the horse. If Berd began to bleed in earnest he needed crushed yarrow and someone who could tend to more than fighting enemies off his back. She pressed the cloth hard. Cierheld was not the closest but it was safer. Berd needed a bed. She checked his blood-beat often.

At last there was no sound of pursuit. She pulled the horse down to a lope. Was it possible thier pursuers had lost their trail, perhaps when they hit the ravine?

The falcon moved against her chest, settling as dusk crept down around them. Kyrin found herself shaking. She wished she could stroke the falcon. Instead she switched her grip on Berd and whispered, "Good bird, you'll grow up strong as Samson." Tears streamed down her face, unheeded. "You'll fly high and far. As brave as Nell, as loyal as Berd, as true as Twr, who saved his first daughter." *His first daughter, who killed him.* Kyrin shied away from the thought. Where had Lord Keffer gotten so many archers? Only the Welsh across the mountains used bows for much more than hunting. Such archers could harry them now.

The horse stumbled. Kyrin slowed him to a walk. There came a faint hoofbeat behind. Kyrin urged the beast to a trot again, drawing her sword. Did their pursuers guess where she went, who she was? They *must* reach Cierheld before Nidfael's men, if those on the road had been his. The pass was close.

Kyrin poured water from a skin over Berd's lips, trying to wake him. He remained pale and unmoving, breathing heavily. The sound reminded her of the chuffs of the tiger. But it was nothing more than Berd's breath and the wind in the cold trees.

Falcon, with your amber eye lead me to the rock that is higher than I, there in your eyrie, never to die. Kyrin drank from the skin as they moved cautiously into a dale, hugging every tree and rock. They came to another road, blessedly empty, and moved higher into the hills. They gained the pass into Cieri's valley as night fell.

Kyrin's back was a bar of fire from straining to hold pressure on Berd's wound and keep him on the horse. She was so weary she was half lying on him. The saddle brushed the walls of the rocky defile, scraping her aching legs and knees. The wind plucked at her scratched face.

It was no good to kindle a warning fire upon the great outcrop of rock nearby. Few in Cierheld would ever see it against the full, rising moon. Not until the fire became a blaze. And there was no time.

She hoped the man on Cierheld gate was alert. Somewhere down the long defile behind, a hoof struck stone.

28

Siege

Distress . . . ~Deuteronomy 28:53

Kyrin tensed. There was no cry behind her. Whoever it was had not seen her yet—or they had and meant to kill by stealth. *Let it not be another archer!*

Kyrin edged the black horse from the trail. Skirting the rocks, she rode down into the trees. Nothing else moved in the forest border or meadowland below the pass. She blessed the Master of the stars for the moonlight over the rocky ground. An Eagle mile would see them home.

At last the track wound before them, gleaming with water and mud, up to Cierheld's gate. Kyrin looked over her shoulder. Nothing. The man on the gate would bring a torch if she called or knocked, lighting them up clear enough for the worst archer in the world. If they yet followed. Her neck prickled.

It was a perfect night for the tiger. Ought she to try to get Berd in through the tunnel? The mill was a silent dark shape on her right. Did not Tae say the most dangerous moment was when one thought one was safe? She would take the less obvious way.

At the back door of the mill she tied the horse and eased Berd's limp weight to the ground. She bound his arm to his body and tugged him inside. She felt no fresh, hot blood on her hands, though the coppery scent was thick. Under a high window that sent a shaft of moonlight across the pale wood floor, Kyrin lifted a darkened plank, revealing blackness below. A cloud of grain-dust billowed around her, and she muffled a sneeze. Grimly, she wedged Berd through the opening, then crept back outside. Stripping the horse, she tied it and carried the saddle and bags inside to hide them behind some flour barrels.

Kyrin's nose ran and her eyes itched fiercely. After a drink to ease her throat, she took the last of her enemy's skin of water and poured it over her face. The water eased the swelling a little. She tore another strip from her tunic, wet it, and bound it over her nose. The damp cloth would keep out the worst of the dust.

She reached for the falcon, a warm bundle against her stomach, for the tunnel would involve much bending. A low, muffled voice on the other side of the wall froze her where she stood.

". . . they suspect nothing. I will look at the way and report back. Go." One pair of feet strode away, and all was silent. Kyrin eased toward Berd and the tunnel. She slipped between the boards and had the dark plank almost in place when the mill door creaked open.

Kyrin eased the wood down over her head, holding her breath. *This* enemy had come for the hidden way into Cierheld, not for her and Berd. Unless he stumbled over them. Surely he would not bring a torch, for fear a gleam near his goal would give him away. That light would give her and Berd away as well.

The man crossed the floor, his steps quiet. His dusty tracks would disguise hers, not to mention those made during the miller's work. She must move now, while his steps covered the noise of her own. Praying Berd would not wake, Kyrin seized him under the arms and dragged him down the pitch-black tunnel. The falcon struggled a little against her tunic.

The dirt floor was damp. After twenty yards Kyrin stopped, lungs heaving. Within forty more, the world had closed in to her heart that beat in time with the falcon's, the rasping strain of her and Berd's breath, and the growing certainty that death stalked them. The fear, pain, and weariness on top of the grain-dust had stirred her lungs to full fire. Only air would quench her need now.

Their enemy must be in the tunnel. How far had she come along the twice arrowshot passage that ran under the moat, the wall, and up inside the mews? Her arms and legs burned.

Berd groaned. Kyrin let him down and touched his cheek. He twitched, and lifted a hand to grip hers, wariness in that strength.

"Shhh," she breathed. She could not risk more.

"This hole's black as Mornoth's pit!" A distorted voice growled down the tunnel.

With new urgency, Berd's fingers fumbled up her arm. What must it be like, waking to dark and pain, not knowing who loomed near? Kyrin held still, and he found her key, dangling from her neck where she bent over him. His hand dropped away and he let out his breath.

Straining for any sound from the man behind them, Kyrin urged Berd up again, her shoulder under his. Berd pushed to his feet, as tense as she. Nothing broke the silence.

Was the man behind them deaf as well as blind? All he need do was slip up on them with a dagger. Lungs heaving, Kyrin dropped her left hand to the falcon blade, bursts of light floating before her eyes. She did not have the breath to use it.

Berd's hand closed on hers and plucked the blade away, and he pushed her on. He would not thank her for being stubborn. Her breath rasped. Kyrin ducked her head and struggled forward, a roaring growing in her ears.

The floor of the tunnel rose. All she could hear was her whistling breath, the catches in Berd's when the pain took him. She was thankful he stayed close. Her fingers met earth.

Kyrin reached for the wood panel she knew must be above her head. Berd shifted at her back to face down the tunnel. There was a muffled cry, metal struck metal, a thump, and Berd grunted and fell. He lay heavy against her leg.

Desperate, Kyrin pulled her sword free. Lord Keffer's man must not get past her. The tunnel was too close for a freely wielded long blade, but held reversed along her forearm—she could use hilt or edge. If he could be goaded to run in . . . Swiveling her blade before her with all the air she could gather, she croaked, "Cieri!"

No blow fell. Kyrin dragged in another breath and coughed.

"Kyrin?" The voice was guarded—one she knew.

"Cer—" Kyrin dropped the sword and felt herself following it. A broad arm caught her, and a hand brushed quickly over her face and the fish necklace at her throat.

Cernalt shook her, "Lass, what's wrong with you? You scared me out of twenty years training. Thank our Lord I but gave Berd a sore head. Or is it Twr? But you're not breathen' right, nor him." His accent thickened. "Ye're hurt—we'll get yeh out, just wait a moment. Why'd yeh not come by the gate?" He stepped over Berd, stretched his arm up to the door, and even the smell of his fear sweat was sweet.

She must tell him. Kyrin drifted a bit, dragging in air, while Cernalt rapped the wood overhead in a complicated pattern.

When they lifted her through the floor of the mews, Kyrin raised her head. "I'm—not hurt. Keffer! He's coming. He knows." She coughed heavily. They set her down, and she leaned on a hand. Feathers and clean rushes smelling of mint rustled softly under her fingers.

Aunt Medaen knelt beside her, garbling words in her horrified haste, "Oh, dear daughter!" A sudden urge to laugh exploded through Kyrin. Aunt Medaen's face split in a smile, and for a moment they giggled together. Then in the light of the lantern that Cook held, Cernalt rolled Berd over and hissed at the wound he found. Cook nodded to Kyrin, a large kitchen knife in one capable hand. They sobered.

Cernalt grunted and said, "I sent my man to bring up the squads out on patrol, quietly. Am I right we need to set a guard here and in the mill?" In the lantern's dancing flame, his wrinkled face was a weathered oak come alive, wise eyes looking across the ages at her.

"Yes," Kyrin breathed, and smiled. Old? Cernalt was as frail of mind as a fox. The falcons on their perches muttered, restless. Her falcon stirred, head tilting against her middle. Kyrin closed her eyes and dragged in an easier breath.

Aunt Medaen urged her up, hands gentle. "Come, Kyrin, you need tea for those lungs and your poor eyes! And I daresay a bath and something to eat will not go ill either, and then bed."

Kyrin squeezed her hand. "My thanks, Aunt, but"—she turned her back on the men and reached into her tunic to pull out the falcon, who twisted her head toward Medaen's voice.

"Ahh." Aunt Medaen smiled. "Best we give this one to Cernalt before we go in."

Cernalt rose from Berd's side. He looked from the falcon to Kyrin. "Ye're full of surprises this night."

"There is more. Talik sends word Lord Nidfael has two hundred men—last count. Talik and Nith and our allies face another four hundred with Lord Ludwin Mornoth. I do not believe Lord Keffer or Mornoth know I brought warning. Though we had trouble—on the road." Her throat closed. *Twr.*

"Ah. Hence you did not use the gate."

She nodded. "Lord Jorn sends us fifty men, if they have not met the same trouble. The falcon's name is Truthfinder." Somehow her name seemed important, as Cernalt lifted the bird from her hands. Kyrin got the rest out with an effort. "Twr. He kept me from an arrow, and fell." Cernalt did not look away, acknowledging her pain. He did not hide his own tears. "It was well done," he said steadily.

"And I acknowledge it, and my fault in the matter." Kyrin leaned heavily on Medaen.

Cernalt's gaze sharpened. "*We* will speak of what happened, *then* if there is fault, you may say so."

She bowed her head. "As you wish, armsmaster."

His eyes twinkled. "So you've figured it out at last, have you?" There was no trace of accent in his voice. Cernalt shrugged. "Men speak freely when they hunt with their falcons, and few pay heed to an old hawkmaster beside them. The same goes for the feasting table or the harvest."

Kyrin shook her head. Hidden armsmaster of Cierheld, master of messengers, and what else? Cernalt held depth upon depth; she would think on them after her mind cleared. She hobbled away beside Aunt Medaen.

Meric caught up with them at the hall steps, while Cernalt sent men running to the four winds with orders.

"Kyrin!" Meric squeezed her tight, small arms hard with muscle.

"Meric." She smiled down at him, but a head shorter than she. His helm and mail shirt reflected the light of a torch as it flamed to life. A short sword hung from his belt. She stared at him, bemused. *De Re Militari* had inspired him, it seemed.

Meric stepped back. "The messenger said you caught the traitor who stole the jewels! Lord Mornoth won't be pleased now! He can't buy men with air!" Meric laughed exuberantly.

Lord Mornoth *had* bought archers with something. What other surprises had he bought? "Our position does not look a lark, either, brother." Kyrin paused for breath, and Aunt Medaen told Meric of Lord Keffer and the tunnel. Meric sobered.

"He won't touch father or mother," he said with a frown, his hand on his sword.

"I know." Kyrin nodded at the same time as Aunt Medaen, and they shared a smile. Then Kyrin bit her lip. "How is father?"

"About the same," said Meric.

Kyrin frowned. She mistrusted the tiger, and herself, and her sinking thoughts. Always the thickness in her lungs brought them. But she *must* think. "Arm him and Elinor and dress yourselves in servant's clothes. Will you find Celine and tell her I have need of her—and Cook?"

"But Kyrin, I want to stay with you—"

A wave of breathlessness hit her. "Go!" Kyrin said shortly, and he went, mouth quivering. Kyrin stumbled into the hall with a sigh and submitted to Aunt Medaen and Cook's ministrations.

§

By Vespers, the stars and moon gleamed over Cierheld and its manned, silent walls. Unlit torches and covered clay pots of coals sat by many feet. Kyrin drew a clean, easy breath of chill air and let it out in a cloud.

The terrible itching that had, at the last, made her scratch even her scalp, was soothed by Cook's oat water brew. Berd was well tended in his quarters by Crag's apprentice, who'd stayed to tend Lord Dain and any others who needed healing in the hold, while Crag had departed with Talik and Cierheld's forces to battle.

Kyrin rubbed her face. Celine had loftily declared she would look in on Berd. She'd seemed of the same disdainful, angry mind as when Kyrin left to take Uncle Ulf the jewels.

Things had gone worse with Elinor. Kyrin was feeling a little better, sitting in her father's chair close to the fire, when she heard Elinor protesting the servants' tunics Cook had sent up. Kyrin climbed the stairs and stopped just outside Dain and Elinor's door.

Within, Meric had his back to her. "Mother, truly Kyrin has reason to tell us to disguise and—"

"What reason?" Elinor's voice came tart from where she stood out of sight on the other side of the doorway. In her mind, Kyrin saw her straighten, regal head high, pale hair a coronet, her blue eyes flashing.

Meric looked down, and Kyrin sensed his troubled frown. "I know not, Mother, but—"

"But nothing. Take them back."

"No. I—I can't."

"Meric—" Elinor seemed more stunned than angry.

He lifted his head and his shoulders straightened. "You need weapons, too. Bring Father his sword. Wake him up. Or—or I'll get Cernalt. He agreed." His voice trembled a very little, with tears underneath.

Elinor sniffed. "That girl has filled your head with nonsense. So alone, so ready to fight." She sighed. "Such a strange first daughter. I knew it, I knew she was trouble."

"She's my sister!"

"Your *sister* she is *not!"*

Kyrin could not leave him to face Elinor's wrath alone. She stepped inside the doorway and laid her hand on his shoulder. "Thank you, Meric. If you would go to Cernalt and assist him as he asks, that would be well." Meric smiled at her gratefully and went.

"You!" Elinor exploded in a furious whisper, the red rising in her cheeks. "He is only a boy!"

"Yes. A boy who will have to be a man very soon. He will face what I faced," Kyrin whispered. There, it was out, the specter between them, a dying father and husband. Kyrin found tears running down her face but did not turn away.

Elinor slapped her. Kyrin swallowed, bowed her head, and stepped back. "I did not mean—Meric will have you. I did not have my mother. But no one can replace my father. I—"

"Go. Get out!"

"Elinor—"

Elinor turned away, face in her hands, and said in a weary, choked voice, "Just go."

Kyrin went, and climbed to the wall.

It was time to raise the sword. By her key, her scar, the earring in her ear, and the strength of the falcon blade. By what she was and the gifts they bestowed by the Master of the stars's working, it was time to fight. *My loyalty give I, to lord and land.* She drew that knowledge about her as a shield. The tiger paced after her across moonlight and stone.

Kyrin sighed where she crouched behind the crenels. A pot warmed her toes, and she rubbed her sore shoulder. Of Cierheld's present hundred defenders, there were seven tensquads. She'd dispersed fifteen of the other thirty among the seasoned tensquads and prayed they would pay attention to their teachers, and that their teachers made no mistakes when they covered their flanks. The last fifteen men, if she could call women and youngsters men, knew how to use their chosen weapons just well enough to be a danger in the ranks, and were positioned with more space between them. She wished she had one rangdo beside her. Even Celine. Mayhap especially Celine, with her fiery spirit.

A faint, far *clink* drew Kyrin to alert tension. Quiet blanketed the stronghold. There—a horse's hoof clipped stone again. She leaned forward, her bow and quiver casting slivers of shadow across the stone. An owl called in the mews. Moon-gilded shapes rushed over the ground below. Closer, closer. They were on foot, some with ladders.

Kyrin eased aside the pot lid and thrust an arrow into the nest of coals at her feet. The tip burst into instant, hidden flame. She stood and swung above the crenel, and aimed over the swarm.

There was a yell, and she loosed and ducked. Her brand rose high, flaming bright. It curved down beyond their attackers, a thin crescent trailing into blackness. Red fire exploded, rushing in a great circle around those below.

Men caught in the edge of the fire-ring became pillars of screaming flame, others milled, trapped between the wall and the pitch fire. With a shout, the rest of Cierheld rose up, keeping behind shields and crenels as best they might. Arrows whistled to and fro. Some of the men on fire ran for the moat, only to set the oil there ablaze. Arrows hissed down among them.

After an age, Lord Keffer's first attack slid back through a burned out gap in the pitch fire, near the woods. No enemy had gained the wall.

Cernalt sent a boy to the hall with word that only five Cierheldens had fallen to archers and sling stones. A cheer from Elinor and the women who moved about gathering water against fire arrows and setting up a place to care for the wounded, gave new determination to all on the wall. Truly, they fought for those they loved.

Kyrin wiped her eyes. It was good Celine did not know of Twr. She was thankful for the night—that her face was hidden.

Lord Keffer's men ordered themselves. A second line rode some distance behind the line of foot, charging again.

Under the rising roar of their approach, Cernalt's steady voice beside Kyrin was a comfort. "Stay together, now. Hold—hold fast." Kyrin waited until the attackers' eyes shone wild in the light of pitch fire. "Strike true!" Cernalt cried. Then she drew an arrow from her quiver.

At that moment Cernalt shouted, "Down!"

Kyrin dropped. A spear scraped heavily across her mailed back, driving her flat, without breath. Rolling to the edge of the wall, she lifted her bow. On the nearest ladder a man lifted a spear to cast at Cernalt. She shot. "Tend the wall! Worry not for me! " Before her target crumpled and fell, Kyrin turned to the next threat, the smell of death and flaming oil in her nose. Cries further along the rampart told of other Cierheldens hit. The top rungs of more ladders thumped against the stones.

Cernalt sprang past Kyrin, grabbed a ladder, and strained to shove it off, arms creaking. More men piled onto it. Kyrin dropped her bow at the base of the wall, ducked under Cernalt's outstretched arms, and grabbed a lower rung. They heaved together.

The ladder slid sideways. Crashing down, it took another ladder with it, spilling some attackers into the moat, raising splashing geysers of water and flickering patches of oil into the air. Their short span of the wall was clear.

Panting, Kyrin checked her quiver. Five arrows, and her sword and dagger were still with her.

Yells rang louder on her right. She sprinted toward men bearing the pale blots of Keffer's white horsehead sigil in the gloom. They'd managed to secure a ladder against a thin line of Cierheldens struggling to hold their ground.

Cernalt swept past, charging three men beating down a Cierhelden, screaming "Cieri! Cieri!" He blocked the first man's sword and killed him with a backstroke, and slid past his companion to thrust a third through the throat. Kyrin drew, dodged the strok of the dark haired man Cernalt had bypassed, then her blade took his life.

§

A bell later, she ached from giving and taking blows. How many more times would Nidfael throw his men against the wall?

Cernalt assumed a group of Lord Keffer's men had reached the Cierheld road before Lord Jorn's, since their attackers seemed well ordered and no relief had come. Kyrin thought Nidfael Keffer himself had arrived.

Most of the men Cernalt had sent to secure the tunnel entrance where it emerged in the mill had disappeared beneath a cave-in. Two men returned to tell of it.

The last of the pitch and the lamp oil waited in vessels above the gate where the fighting had been heaviest, leaving parts of the wall, like this one, near undefended. Dawn drew a broadening line in the sky. It was a brief moment of peace.

She lifted her face to the sky. There were a few stars left. But their Master and hers heard every incoherent word and silent inner fear. Kyrin let out her breath in a low fierce laugh, touched by sadness.

Her sword and the falcon were loose in her clammy hands, her body gripped by chill. But the day was past when the ice of fear could halt her. Though the eyes of the falcons set to watch from the very neck of their enemy might witness her fall, they would also see her rise. Samson, a witness in his own way, was among them. *Your keen amber eye on the first and the last, feathers sun-kissed, at sacrifice not aghast, you flew, knowing your cast.*

Bow in hand, Kyrin smiled at the nearest defender, a strong youngster of twelve summers. His dark hair reminded her of Berd. The sigil Myrna had embroidered on the breast of her tunic would rise or fall this day, taking with it the fate of two strongholds. A shout rose from the forest. The boy answered, lifting his spear in defiance. The call gained speed along the wall, but from far fewer throats. Kyrin drew a grim breath.

Lord Keffer's men charged again over the seared ground toward Cierheld, shields above their heads. Two men deep, the line spread beyond Kyrin's sight, surrounding them. A rope and hook seemed to leap from every hand to strike the wall. Many caught and held. Kyrin moved toward the nearest, nocking an arrow. Though she'd replenished her supply as often as she could, she had few left. Not enough for even the three tensquads at the gate. But she would keep back as many as she could from the boy lost in the press behind her.

A clear horn call tore the air. Dark against the mist-swathed oaks, a skein of mounted men galloped toward the hard fighting before the gate. As their spears lowered, Kyrin raised a cheer, "Jorn! Jorn!" Her voice cracked, but Cierheld echoed her. The riders swept on. They thundered over Keffer's men, fierce as a legion. Those remaining of the squads attacking the gate retreated in disorder, calling the rest from the wall, and his few mounted forces protected their withdrawal.

Kyrin leaned on her bow and closed her eyes, listening to Lord Bergrin's riders mill outside the gate, the Cierheldens calling joyful greeting. Her heart sang.

"Lady! Lady Cieri!" The youngster who had stood beside her threaded through the men along the wall.

"Here!" she cried, and he dashed up to her.

"The men—the men at the gate—not Lord Jorn's," he blurted. "Berd—"

Kyrin did not stay to hear the rest.

On the walk above the inner gate, right arm bound to his side, Berd gazed down at Brother Rolf. A strip of white cloth flapped from his spear, and his was horse as restive as the tense tensquad around him. None of them wore a monk's robes. The dark-haired giant on Rolf's right was Lester, in mail and leather armor, as were they all.

Ignoring Rolf a moment, Berd turned to Kyrin. "Must we always meet like this, I standing between you and other men?" His words were stern, but his dark eyes glinted at seeing her whole.

"If the occasion warrants." She met Rolf's battle-tight gaze below, and grinned. Berd nodded, his lips thinning, hiding his amusement. "So I thought. And you'll use any weapon against our enemies. As a monk he has turned his back on war. You know it." It was more a sigh than a grumble.

She answered lightly, "But not on his brothers. We may trust him that far."

Berd shook his head but waved his hand. The inner gate opened, as an archer stepped up beside Berd, bow ready.

"You insult us so?" Brother Rolf pulled his horse's head toward the outer gate.

Berd raised his eyebrows but waved the archer back. "You are well come to Cierheld, Brother Rolf."

Rolf shot him a dour look.

"My pardon, Brother Rolf." Kyrin bowed, fighting her twitching lips. "Your assistance is timely."

Rolf grinned at her. "No offense taken." Then his glare skewered Berd, who shrugged.

Later, resting on the wall while they watched the ground between the wall and the woods, Kyrin soberly met Brother Rolf's eyes. "You saved us many lives. I thank you, though now you are in the same trap."

Brother Rolf looked down. "I thought you a traitor, lady. And worse, in my most shameful moments. And then, we didn't *try* to stop Lord Keffer, to the church's shame. You don't shelter a viper. You crush it." He pounded the stone with his fist absently. "I would have harried him when he retreated into the woods, but my men were too few." He lifted his hands to stare at them, rubbing his fingers and thumb together. "I turned to the quill because of my hot blood—and now, it is different."

"Yes. But Rolf, you've given us a chance. If Jorn yet comes—"

"Ahh, you thought we were Lord Jorn's. To my sorrow, we are but ten men retired from violent service until now. I would redeem our numbers if I could." Brother Rolf tapped the stone thoughtfully, raw-boned, red-haired, and of an age with her, despite his mail. "Do you have much porridge meal?"

"We have plenty, Cernalt says enough for five seven-days. Our meat will give out first, if they siege us."

"I heard you're out of oil but for the pots above the gate. If meal is boiled it sticks well and burns long."

Kyrin sent for Meric.

Meric dashed to the kitchen and gave the order to Cook. Every available pot was to be kept full of boiling porridge. He laughed at the kitchen women's stunned expressions.

"No, the enemy has not come to break fast with us. It's instead of burning oil, at the gate, *and* for breakfast, so be quick!"

Red-faced with relief, Cook threw an apple at him. Meric dodged, and the apple struck the doorframe. He stopped short and reached around the post for the spinning apple. He shared the sweet fruit with Kyrin in the early sunshine as they paced upon the wall.

"Kyrin, can I fight?" Meric begged. "I have my bow! The one Father taught me to shoot! There will be no danger. You deal with the swords, and I'll shoot the ones farther away."

No danger except from other archers. "No, Meric. Stay in the hall. You can take one of the upstairs windows." If Nidfael's men got that far, the wall would have fallen. Meric's face soured. Kyrin swallowed. "I would have you with me, but I would not see you fall." As Twr did. As Penni had. As Meric could not bear to see her face danger without him. Kyrin touched his shoulder. "Twr died, and you're my brother—and your mother. I can't." She had cast *that* in his face. But all her choices were evil.

Meric walked away, head down, savagely scuffing the stones. Kyrin sat and laid her head wearily on her knees. The dead lay beside the woodshed in carefully arranged rows. Men, women, and a few children. Crag's apprentice tended the wounded in the shade of the oak, then moved them inside, where Elinor and her handmaid divided attention between them and Lord Cieri. Cook and her helpers gave out water, food, and Crag's pain-deadening herbs. Men whose hurts were not crippling refused the herbs and returned to the wall.

Nearby, a man who had taken an arrow through his arm stalked back and forth behind the crenels, fingering his axe dourly. Celine darted in and out of the hall, her hair a red flame.

At the Sext bell, Kyrin left the wall and sat with her back against the kennel, eating with Berd and the four men Cernalt had assigned her. She had a spoonful of hot lentil stew to her mouth when the alarm horn blew over the gate. Kyrin dropped her bowl and ran toward her post.

Four tensquads marched along the road from the forest, straight past the mill. Kyrin's heart sank. They carried a form of pike she had never seen. Wicked, hooked, it was long enough to pluck a man from the wall. A line of men before them carried shields to guard the polearm company from Cierhelden arrows.

"You! Find Brother Rolf and get him to the gate!" Kyrin sent the boy off and dashed for the back door of the stables. She slung her short nomad bow over her shoulder. Her foot was in Cauldron's stirrup when a sudden thunder rocked the air and earth. Cauldron reared and tore away. Kyrin stumbled for the door, ears ringing.

29

Love

I have seen a violent . . . man. ~Psalm 37:35

She stared across the yard. The outer gate hung on one hinge. Black, bitter smoke curled around it like mist. Kyrin shook her head; it still rang.

Men with a white horse-head on their tunics poured through the inner gate before it could slam shut. The first squad spread in a swift line before the shattered outer gate. A few of their brothers had made it through the second gate. They must not hold it open.

Kyrin ran forward and her sword rose and fell to good account. Cierheldens were jumping down from the wall and more formed up around Kyrin. The small postern door slammed, shutting most of the enemy from sight. Her men drove the others back. Trapped, Keffer's men leapt forward, pushing. Kyrin's sword was a thick length of wood in her hand. In the circling crush, the bar of the inner gate was paces behind her. She deflected a blade stabbing for her belly with a grunt.

Berd lunged and slashed down another man, his sword awkward in his left hand, his right useless. A man knocked him down and the others surged forward, trampling him.

"No!" But she had no time for anything but the attacking blades. Berd would want her to live. He would want Cierheld to live. Kyrin deflected and thrust, her heel nudging wood.

A belligerent horn blared. There was a thunder of feet on the other side of the gate. Kyrin straightened.

And then it was as if the world ended. A thunderous noise and a slap as of a giant hand hurled her back against the gate and knocked her sprawling on a blast of air and shards of wood. She rolled over in the mud.

The inner gate creaked, buckled, and splintered, in the same bitter stink and cloud of dark smoke. Her vision blurred in and out. She hardly heard Lord Nidfael Keffer's men give a great shout and run forward.

And Nidfael Keffer rode through the gate on a white horse. It paced past Kyrin toward the hall, so close she could have touched his stained stirrup. Kyrin's breath froze in her chest; she couldn't move.

Wherever her blurred gaze fell, Cierheldens were being disarmed. Her men were gone, dead or fled the sorcerous blast. Sorcery, or . . . Tae had said something of a strange black powder holding enormous power when joined by flame in a contained space. The men of the East held keen wit for inventions of death. And now Lord Mornoth used it against them. Where had he come by such knowledge, and did Nith and Talik fight the same power at Cattraeth?

Kyrin staggered and sank to her knees in the thawing mud. She realized she held herself up by her sword, point first in the earth. Around her, a few of Nidfael's men lifted their blades warily. One man tilted a pike toward her, ready.

Before Cierheld hall, Lord Keffer's mailed back was straight. A polearm guard of six bristled around him. Both gates were packed with men bearing the white horse-head. Kyrin looked at her sword, and let it fall. There was no escape. Cierheld was lost.

She sagged to her knees, too sick to cry, and her bow dug into her shoulder, the tip on the ground bending dangerously. She could save that, at least. Muzzily, Kyrin laid her bow on the ground with shaking hands and slid her quiver over her head, lowering it to the earth. A weapon cared for was a later friend. The quiet was torn by the cries of their wounded under the oak, those who could, doing their best to flee. Nidfael's men blocked them.

The horn sounded again. Nidfael called in a voice generous with triumph, "Come, come, you may keep your houses in peace. If you yield, you will be spared."

It smelled of a treacherous messenger. Kyrin swallowed.

"All but for those of house Cieri." His voice sneered. "They have been found treacherous to the king and will be punished." He straightened. "But you—you acted in ignorance." His gold hair shone in the sun, a lesser glory than she remembered Lord Mornoth's to be. Nidfael offered a deceptive peace before the deathblow.

Tae also said, *Never give up.* She was not what she wished, but better she than no one. These were her people.

The edges of her vision frayed about Lord Keffer. Kyrin slid an arrow from her quiver. Steeling herself against a blade or an arrow in the back, she stood slowly, leaning on her bow, one arm limp at her side. She did not feel the shoulder her mail had plagued earlier.

"Do not be foolish, this is the last grace I will give," Nidfael cried. "Surely, you cannot all be fools?" His blue tunic rippled, bright as his disbelieving scorn.

Lord Nidfael's men watched him implore and demand. A few chuckled. The closest was seven paces. Kyrin quietly nocked the black arrow her father had given her. Scent of sweat and blood and bruised grass hung in the air with that of bitter smoke. *Rise over stone, for hope to vie*—she raised her bow. And the arrow flew. *Your shadow nigh.*

A pike rose in the corner of her vision. Kyrin raised her bow over her head. The hooked pike descended, the bow cracked. She was hurled into darkness.

The tiger bounded toward her, ears up. Kyrin turned to run. It jerked to a halt, ears pinned back. About its neck the falcons' eyes blazed in the golden light streaming from behind her. Soundlessly, the collar broke and slid from the tiger's shoulders to the earth. With a yowl, the tiger spun. Then it was gone.

The light remained, and the witnesses. Kyrin turned, as a flower toward the sun. *There* was a place lit by love and life and joy. Her mother—and the Master of the stars. She hastened along the path to meet him, sword in her hand. He barred her way.

Was it the blade? Kyrin dropped it, but he motioned for her to pick it up. In that place, somehow she knew he smiled his approval, but she was not to pass. She could not see his face.

Kyrin wept. Her tears fell on scars marring the strong palm he cupped for them. Flowing down from that hand, her tears were red as blood. She bowed her head, and dared reach out in honor to catch the last drop. For he had given every drop of his life.

She turned back and began to walk. His face, here, was not hers to see, not yet. But the joy she thought she left behind with every step grew inside her to peace. He loved her, with all the strength of his blood, and that of his Father, beyond all time. He walked with her, unseen.

Something tickled Kyrin's neck, something warm and wet. There was a weight across her chest, and thin arms about her quivered. Someone sobbed, shaking her head to fierce pain. Kyrin opened her eyes.

The ceiling beams of her chamber were dark overhead. Cornsilk hair she knew waved before her nose. Her father sat in a chair beside her bed, a hand on Meric's heaving back, his other hand over his eyes, mouth twisted. Kyrin tried to make her tongue work. He looked better, despite the pain in his face.

Dain's hand dropped. He lifted his head wearily, and stared. Startled joy bloomed with his inarticulate cry. Meric sniffed, and then his wet eyes met Kyrin's. With a wordless noise, he tightened his arms around her neck, nestling close. Dain knelt and gathered them both in his arms, crying, unashamed. After a moment, Meric wriggled out and ran from the chamber.

"Mother! Come quick!" A wild yell of delight filled the hall.

Kyrin heard later that Meric whooped his way to the door, ripped down the black linen nailed there, threw it on the ground, and did a victory dance on it.

There was a clatter of steps on the stair, and Elinor rushed in. "Oh, Kyrin!" She cried, and smiled as she looked at Dain. Her arms slid warmly around Kyrin. Kyrin remembered other arms. She laid her head against Elinor's shoulder. Elinor's hand shook on her hair.

Crag and his apprentice came in frantic haste, wide-eyed Myrna in their wake. The healer felt Kyrin's pulse, looked in her eyes, and finally poked about her bandaged head, his fingers firm. He made her raise her arm. It was barely sore.

Crag let out a long breath. "You're better." Grinning, he kissed her forehead as if he could not help himself for joy then growled at his apprentice and left to tend his other patients.

"What—who fought Keffer's men back?" Surely Nidfael had fallen. She thought she remembered that.

Meric's eyes widened. He jumped on the end of her bed. "You didn't see? I heard a great noise and went to my window, and Lord Keffer's men came running in. Then you came out of the stable with the others. But you moved so much I couldn't shoot." Meric shook his head solemnly. "Then Lord Keffer rode in. And most everyone put down their swords. I thought the men would kill you if I shot one of them, so I didn't. You dropped your sword. And I couldn't see you until you raised your bow. Then one of Lord Keffer's men raised his funny spear, so I shot him. Only I was too slow. My arrow got him, but he still hit you.

"He dropped, and you did. I shot the next man, since Lord Keffer was down." Meric shivered. Dain rose from his chair to hold her brother's shoulders, moving as if he had no pain.

Meric looked down. "Lord Keffer's men backed away from you. You looked dead. Blood all over, and you so still. We saw Father's black arrow in Lord Keffer, and Cernalt and everyone turned on his men. We were angry, that you should fall alone. We rose for Cieri." He looked up at her eyes wide and sober. "Then twenty riders galloped in the gate. Only they turned out to be Lord Jorn's, so we won." His smile was shy.

Elinor hugged him. "I am proud of you, my son."

Meric reddened and looked from her to Kyrin. "I have to tell you, sister. I almost went to fight on the wall. And then—you would have died." His throat worked.

"No, brother. God would have sent someone. But I am glad you kept your post." Kyrin smiled and moved gingerly to hug him. He hugged her back, with a grin of pure relief.

"Well." Dain coughed and looked from Elinor's smile to Kyrin. "We are mightily glad to have you back, daughter, but we'll let you take your rest now."

Her sight was blurring again. She lay back. "Berd?"

Dain took her hand. "He's in the same place you are."

Kyrin smiled and drifted away.

When she woke again, Elinor held a cool, wet cloth to her forehead.

Abruptly remembering, Kyrin bolted up, hands fisted in her covers. "Talik! And our men! Did Lord Mornoth fight them with that strange weapon and smoke?"

"Shh, Kyrin, rest. Just rest." Elinor tucked Kyrin's hair from her face. "Nith returned a day ago. Your Lord Talik Wyman is well." She smiled and eased Kyrin back. "Ludwin Mornoth died in clean battle, and the stealer of your jewels, well, the church insisted Nith let your uncle go, on condition he be walled into Bolton Abbey soon." She frowned, then shook herself. "But Nell and Myrna and Celine wait to see you."

Kyrin put a hand to her head. "How many bells have I been here?"

"Since yestermorn."

"Oh." She saw circles of weariness around Elinor's eyes. "I'm well, Mother, or nearly. My thanks for staying with me, but you should rest."

Elinor kissed her. "I thank you, my daughter, but you do not tire me." She hugged her a moment and rose. At the door, she turned. "My pardon. It near fled from my head. Lord Wyman wishes to see you also."

Talik. Kyrin smiled. "Would you ask him to wait a moment and send Nell in?" She looked for her comb and the water basin.

After Nell pinned Kyrin's hair up in a manner she deemed worthy of a first daughter, Kyrin perused her creation in the bronze mirror with a small smile. Nell departed with a lilt in her step.

Then Talik's lithe frame filled the door. His grey eyes were deep as he took Kyrin in. He sat on the stool beside her bed, saying nothing. The memory of their last parting shone in his eyes.

So much had happened. Kyrin swallowed, awkward thanks for Truthfinder in her mouth and a flush on her face. What came out was, "Well, how went the fight against Mornoth?"

"Well enough." Talik paused. "I am to take up training with Nith. I could wish to be an armsmaster such as Cernalt, but for that, I need have started as a stripling."

Kyrin's mouth twitched at his regret. "Cernalt is very good."

"Truly." A thrush twittered, and Talik stared out at the afternoon sunlight flooding the oak.

Kyrin hoped it would become Truthfinder's favored perch. Outside was no clash of swords or screams, but only the cluck of a hen, a dog barking from the kennel, and the sound of Nith, ordering drill before the barracks. The scent of thawing earth wafted around her. And that sweet straw smell she knew. Kyrin sighed, contented. "You're strong enough, my lord, and grow ever stronger in the ways that matter most."

With a quick smile, Talik took her hand. He sobered, and rubbed it gently. "I am glad you think so, Kyrin." His grip tightened. Warm and callused, his fingers slid over a glassy-smooth spot on her palm. He tilted her hand to the light. "What is this?"

In the middle of her palm, a teardrop shape gleamed crimson as the blood pulsed beneath. Kyrin pulled her hand back and rubbed at the mark, the size of her thumb. Painless, it lay even with her skin. Awe and remembrance tingled up her back.

With a sharp look at her, Talik leaned forward. "What happened?"

"Nothing ill. I'm not sure how to say it yet . . ."

"I see a joy in you, so I am glad." A shy grin lurked at the corners of his mouth. "But you've made me curious, lady."

"I will tell you when I can." Kyrin laughed and wiped her tears.

With the Vespers bell, worn out by a stream of well-wishers, Kyrin's eyes drooped. Nell shut the door on any more visitors. Kyrin's head ached. Returning to see if she had need of anything, Talik went for a basin of water to ease her himself, instead of calling Nell. The cool cloth on her brow was of his courtesy. After he had gone, Kyrin stared into the dark oak. Her thoughts refused to cool.

She had been at fault in their last quarrel. Was she worthy of him? If only she might walk through life with him, so strong in spirit when he needed to be, and kind. As an arrow, he aimed well, to follow the Father. The Master of the stars would bind them together if they handfasted. Not that there would never be quarrels. Her selfishness battled all loves. And her pride was so easily wounded, if one knew the points to touch. In some ways, she was far less than Esther thought her. When he knew of Twr, would Talik look at her with disdain? Kyrin's breath caught.

What *had* he shown her of his heart, beyond a certain care for her well-being? She frowned. He had never mentioned he cared for her in that way. But with nothing to do but think, she was becoming a fool. She had better ask the Master of all. And if he did not approve, or Talik did not return her feelings, then the Master of the stars had something better for them both. If only Talik did not despise her, she could be content. She could.

The next morn Crag said simply, "Heads are hard to treat." He would not hear of Kyrin rising but insisted she lie flat, as she was still dizzy. "Better to let them heal clean than suffer from moving about."

The quiet bit hard the second seven-day she was captive in her bed. She'd asked for company. Myrna and Celine sat about her chamber, embroidery needles busy, heads bent over their work. At the foot of her bed, Nell patched the tunic Myrna had made Kyrin, rent by the spear slicing past her back in the fighting on the wall.

Kyrin looked around the room, restless. She had progessed to sitting up, hands yet idle. There was a rap at the door. She looked up, not waiting for Nell to open it. "Come in."

Berd bowed. "Lady Cieri. You have guests."

Kyrin's brow creased. Everyone she could possibly have laid eyes on in Cierheld had been to see her. Berd stepped aside and gestured formally. Two in mud spattered cloaks moved inside. A short, dark-skinned, wiry man and a woman with red-gold hair. Kyrin straightened, eyes wide. "Tae! Alaina!"

In sheer surprise she swung her feet over the side of the bed and stood, wavering forward. Nell sprang around the end of the bed but Tae reached her first and steadied her. Alaina helped him put her back to rights. Breathless and smiling, Kyrin let them, crying for joy.

After the brief flurry, Tae bowed to all those now standing around him. "I am Tae Chisun."His face was grave but his eyes warm, wrinkles deepening.

Nell closed her open mouth. "I—you are well come. I am Nell Trinley. This is Myrna Jorn, and Celine Loring. We—"

"They are my rangdo," Kyrin broke in with a grin, and Alaina's eyes widened.

"I see." Tae glanced at Berd, who stood near the head of her bed, arms crossed.

"Not him—he's my armsman."

Berd inclined his head, and Tae returned the gesture.

Alaina sat on the edge of the bed and looked hard at Kyrin. "You've been through quite some doings, I hear." She leaned in. "You *are* pale. Are you sure you're well?"

"I'm on the mend." Kyrin smiled. "And no, I'm not weary, except of this bed. I've been fussing to be let out." She grinned, wiping at her eyes. "It is so good to see you. More than I can say." She gripped Alaina's hands, wordless. Then turned to Myrna and the others. "This is my sister, by more than blood. When I woke on the slave ship, she helped me. I'll tell you her tale sometime. But Alaina, you and Tae must be tired from the road. Celine, would you mind asking Elinor for some of the aged mead and refreshment for our guests?"

A flush high on her cheeks, Celine moved her stool nearer the bed for Alaina and pulled Kyrin's clothes chest out from the wall as a seat for Tae, with a short bow. Not meeting their eyes long, Celine quickly slipped out for the mead and oatcakes. She returned with the mead in cups, on a platter of bread, cheese, and meat. Berd rescued a jug of cold cider from Celine's other hand. She thanked him and sat quietly at the foot of Kyrin's bed, watching.

They feasted, with happy talk and laughter, until a scratching at the door and a whine brought Kyrin's head around. Her gaze darted between Tae and Alaina. "Cicero?"

Tae shook his head, with a slight smile. Alaina said, "No, his daughter, Gwenich."

Kyrin clutched her covers. "You brought one of the pups? Let her in!" Berd lifted the latch. A dark nose followed by a moon-pale face and pricked ears eased the door open. Gwenich looked straight at Kyrin, her almond saluki eyes considering. Tall, long-legged, a regal sight hound, she eyed them. Celine rose, staring, and whispered, "What a beautiful dog!"

Gwenich suffered her stroke for a moment, then trotted to Kyrin. She put her cool nose on the bed and snuffled under her hand. Tears rising in her eyes, Kyrin ran her fingers down Gwenich's smooth, wiry back. Red hairs dusted her coat, pale as Cicero's, red as sand under moonlight.

"Cicero runs with his Sahar in the sands, catching my prince plenteous gazelle." Alaina smiled. "Faisal remembers you. But Gwenich—we brought her for you. Prince Faisal asked it, and it was in my mind also. We thought her younger bones would better stand the voyage than Cicero's, and it would be easier for her to grow a warmer coat here. I also brought this." Alaina went and dug in a sack she'd laid down near the door, rustling about in its depths.

Gwenich nudged Kyrin's hand again and licked her fingers, crooning a love song deep in her throat. "My thanks," Kyrin whispered. They would catch many rabbits and ducks, running below Truthfinder's wings, as she had with Samson. She'd only wanted to see Cicero's pup, and Gwenich was hers. "It's so much." She rubbed the pup's silky ears.

Alaina moved back and shook her shoulder gently. "No, it's not too much. Not for my sister. You deserve much more than this. You kept us from the wazir and Umar's Hand. But see this." She laid a book in Kyrin's lap, and Kyrin's eyes widened.

She caressed the leather cover and looked up. "Alaina, I *will* get you a good blade for this. Our Chronicle." She hugged it to her. Elinor would treasure the volume. Crag might let her read it. If only the sword she'd found in the stream had not disappeared. If it could be found, it would be fit payment. Berd stirred, as if he knew her thought. Kyrin shot him a look of apology.

Alaina's smile turned impish. "I am sure you will. But I have much to tell you of my prince. The desert is so full of beauty and life once you have eyes to see it. We ran, and we fought, and . . ."

Kyrin listened, rapt, until Crag insisted they all leave. Gwenich stayed.

30

Thou did'st make men ride over our heads;

We went through fire and through water. ~Psalm 66:12

Crag's proscribed third seven-day rest passed. Kyrin was no longer dizzy, and both Truthfinder and Gwenich joined her and Berd on gentle walks in the woods. First daughter and first armsman healed together. They practiced what they could, going through Subak stretches and the steps of the sword without blades. During those days, never did Kyrin neglect to stand beside Dain as the sun lifted over the world, their arrows whisking away to the straw butts, regularly skewered at two hundred paces.

She wished she could practice with Talik, and looked forward to that moment. She had much to learn of the sword before she could cross blades with him. And in unarmed combat, he had much to learn from Cernalt before he could think of facing her and Subak.

Early one morn Kyrin practiced Subak forms with Tae for the first time since the pike had struck her. Her legs shook after one form. She had used to do so many without a halt. But the joy of movement would banish the shakiness of her limbs in time. At the end of the form, she took an uneasy step.

Tae watched her, arms crossed, chin in hand. "Very good. You will test for the black sash in two moons."

Kyrin's grin vanished. Three would be more to her liking. *If* she could get back into fighting form so quickly. And good? She was weak as a rat. Would she remember the Subak drills she'd practiced with her rangdo and Berd? She'd had no one who knew Subak to drill against, to push her to the cutting edge. She had focused on defending against Berd's skill with the sword and spear, and Cernalt's unarmed system of combat, more fists and wrestling throws than open hands and kicking. Alaina would wipe the earth with her. Nevertheless, it *would* be good to work again with her sister. And all Cierheld would be watching.

You've fought warriors for your very life, and you fear the eyes of your people? Kyrin stared at Tae with a faint frown.

Tae smiled. "You will be ready, daughter." At least *he* was certain. Tae clasped his hands behind his back and paced one way and then the other.

Kyrin stared. She'd never seen him so *un*certain.

"I have a son—Ryung Suk. He waits for me with Huen." Tae turned suddenly to look her in the face. "I will go back when you have gained the black sash of mastery."

Kyrin nodded, throat tight. "I am glad." She had known he could not stay, and Alaina had told her she must return also.

Tae gripped her shoulders. "You will always remain my daughter," he whispered.

"Yes—my father." It was one of the last times she could call him that. Kyrin gulped. She would make him proud.

Tae sighed. "You should know the wazir sails for Britannia. Sirius wishes to give you your writ of freedom himself."

Kyrin touched the ring of jet. *Your word must break this one.* Now he counted her word fulfilled. He'd freed Tae and Alaina from the threat of his Hand. Sirius would not sail so far simply to honor a slave. Did the wazir also come for trade? "I will speak with my father of any silver, leather, or goods that may interest him. He will drive a canny bargain—"

"He yet wishes the touch of death."

Kyrin looked at Tae sharply.

"I know not whether he seeks it for his caliph, or himself, or if he sees me as a threat to his land. I have been but once to the caliph's court. Or the excellent wazir may seek only trade." Tae frowned. "He may also wish me at his back while he seeks the caliphate himself. When Alaina and Faisal were wed, he asked me to serve him. I told him my Huen waits for me and put him off. I fear our hunt is not ended."

"Ah. Alaina told me Seliam warned her to beware the asp."

Tae shook his head. "Faisal said there was an oath between the wazir and his brother. Sirius Abdasir may yet search for his nephew, Hamal. Or if there is another traitor, he has not shown his coils since Kaish was killed." Tae looked at her. "But we must beware the sword before us, then the spear that may come for our backs."

Kyrin pursed her mouth. "Hala told me Hamal was a traveler here." She brightened. "Does Hala come with the wazir?"

"She may. But Hala may not know all her father's plans. Sirius Abdasir is not one to leave at your back, unaware."

Kyrin nodded. She must speak with her father of the wazir, and with Elinor, of what to have for the feast. Not pork, of a certain. Hala might be coming, and the wazir might wish to break their journey at Cierheld.

Soon preparations for the foreign guests and the following festivities were in full swing. Elinor, Cook, and every pair of hands they could command cleaned and cooked ceaselessly.

Celine seemed no less angry, but quiet. As a hurt animal retreating to its den, she said little to any. Aunt Medaen had gone back to Lady Ynglida of necessity, for the Lady of Halwende was frail. Esther attended Uncle Ulf, bringing him meals, books, quills, and parchment in his walled-in cell in Bolton Abbey.

Kyrin snorted. Anchorites—if they claimed to wish solitude, why did they choose to be walled into a church? Her father had recently given reluctant leave to the steward for an anchorite to be walled in at Fenwrd the following moon, in a deserted part of the ruined hold above the lonely ocean. The anchorite said he wished to pray for the souls of those fallen. *He* at least seemed sincere. He wished his name and face lost to the world.

Kyrin wondered how many bells Esther spent with Uncle Ulf, and how many with Lord Mornoth's nephew, now free to declare her the most beautiful woman in the Northland. The new regent reaffirmed his ties with Northumbria by gifting Lord Dain Cieri some of the holdings Lord Mornoth's nephew had inherited, for defending the king's interests. Interests soon to be Cieri's own, the regent hoped. Impressed with the allies' effective tactics against Lord Mornoth's forces, he'd also sent some of his men in rotation to train under Nith.

The old regent had retired to the country and was thinking of the church. Which, Brother Rolf said, he was far better fitted for in temperament.

Always about the hall, Elinor was peaceful, her smile warm, her laugh quicker. She often joined Dain and Kyrin at the butts while the robins sang in the early sun, then would leave to help Cook at the breadboard.

When Tae was not training Kyrin and Alaina privately, he followed Nith or Berd or Cernalt about their duties, soaking up new customs and ways of warfare. Meric was in awe of Tae, who admired his *De Re Militari* and questioned him often and at length in the hall after supper, to Meric's great joy. Nith and the rest of the men would crowd around as well, and conversation often turned into a heated debate over a tactic, strategy, or technique, sometimes not settled until Tae or Nith ably demonstrated a point in the yard the next morn, ending with someone getting a mouthful of dust.

A hollow sensation flooded Kyrin whenever she thought of her test for the black sash. She filled her free moments with rigorous practice. Tension heightened as everyone in Cierheld looked from her to her reticent teacher and wondered what marvels they had yet to see.

Nith pitted Berd and Talik against each other in sword work, where they were near equal, and against Cernalt for unarmed combat. "I'd back Cernalt against any in our stronghold, except Tae." Nith eyed Tae sidelong. "And our first daughter."

Tae tipped his head, his round, brown face giving nothing. Cernalt avoided Nith's challenge with a silent, wolfish smile.

The victor was yet to be proven, when time could be taken from the mopping up of brigands for a match. For Margye had sent a missive to Lord Bergrin Jorn that her village had been raided again. Margye had used Kyrin's gift well, and was now an unofficial elder of the village. Kyrin rubbed her falcon dagger. There was one who was not slack. Margye had life in her old bones yet.

Lord Bergrin had carried her letter to Cierheld when he came to see Myrna. Myrna welcomed her lord brother and they walked often about the mill and the fields, two slender figures with ash pale hair. Kyrin smiled wryly. Nell kept company with Myrna more often than Celine these days, for Hal's daughter threw herself into Subak with a vengeance. She seemed not to care who she sparred with, though she fought hardest against Alaina. Kyrin shook her head. Alaina gave more than she got, being far ahead of Celine in the necessary strength and muscle memory. With Kyrin, Celine was cautious, almost restrained.

She never spoke of Esther. Cierheld's first daughter watched her warily, hoping her rangdo would turn from her anger.

She was thankful that Alaina took up Nell's instruction in letters, and that Nell joined in Alaina's study of herbs with Crag. For Kyrin was occupied with hold duties, practicing for her test, and business with the church and the other lords. Kem Landyl, young Cor Gadral, and Lord Fresen were fascinated by the upcoming test of Lord Cieri's first daughter, along with every armsman, freeholder, and peasant among the holds—as far north as Aysgarth and south as Alkborough.

Alkborough. Her father had declared to Talik that he held the regent's gift in trust for him, as his father asked when consulted about the status of his former hold. Lord Dain and Cierheld's armsmen remedied Talik's ignorance of a first son's duties. Talik would be a lord in his own right, amply proven at the battle of Cattraeth. Kyrin thought it fitting. As her father said, what would he do with three strongholds? Both his first daughter and Meric already had an inheritance. Kyrin's smile faded.

There was to be a large crowd for her testing. Brother Rolf declared that not even Father Ulf's displeasure could keep him from Cierheld on the fateful day. "This marks an important turn in Bolton's affairs, indeed, in all Northumbria, and the church should witness it."

Early the morn of her test, Kyrin rode out with Truthfinder, Gwenich, and her bow after rabbits. Berd ranged wide and kept constant watch, though Nith's patrols had scoured every road. The rabbits escaped while Kyrin listened to the wind in the ash leaves, smelled the bluebells and bracken, and laughed at a bright-eyed squirrel tapping its paw, furiously scolding Truthfinder, who whirled peacefully above the trees on a warm updraft. The falcon turned and twisted, the wind riffling her feathers. *From far shadowland I return; to lord, to love, and to you, loyal on my fist and true.* Kyrin watched her for a time, penning the bits of Samson's Ode on a piece of parchment on her knee.

Fierce cry, in the sky, wild and high. Echo my heart's call. Far from dungeons cramped and small, follow arrowing wings across the wall, where lies a stronghold rescued from the fall. . . . Kyrin's quill scratched to rest, then on. *Falcon deadly swift, farseeing; my heart, ever kenning. Loyal to her maker, to her created nature; awe, to behold such stature.* No more words came. The midday bell would see her test begin.

She put her things back in her saddlebags, mounted, and rode Cauldron at a gallop over a meadow sprinkled with spring flowers, through the woods, past the mill, and over the causeway. Just after Terce, by the sun, she pulled Cauldron to a halt before the gate. She flung Truthfinder toward the sky. He lifted from her arm and winged over the wall toward the oak. She dismounted. Gwenich whined, watching the falcon, hoping for a rabbit. "Later, girl, later." Kyrin stroked her furry head.

Meric grinned at Kyrin, his back against the wide-open gate, arms crossed. "Did the hares escape you?"

She shrugged.

"Well then, Sister, join the company inside!" He smiled expansively.

Kyrin scowled. She wished she *had* a rabbit—to throw at him. Her brother knew she was nervous. Still, he awaited her test and the demonstration Tae had arranged with rampant excitement, fostering speculation among the Cierhelden men and boys. Only Hyl's word fit such a brother. She drew herself up and glared, laughing inside. "A snotling, you are." Meric grinned and returned her shrug.

Kyrin paused at the open inner gate, with a clutch at Cauldron's rein. She knew that rapid, liquid tongue, that voice. Despite herself, she tensed and slipped the falcon dagger out of sight in her tunic. The low murmur of Arabic swelled as she strode across the yard before the stables, Gwenich at her heels.

Men in robes of flowing crimson surrounded a turbaned man in white, who stalked toward the hall beside her father, flanked by armsmen and more men in red. The wazir, Sirius Abdasir, lean and keen as ever. Surely Hala was about? Peeping past Cauldron's neck, she did not see her. Cierheldens led their guests' mounts across the yard behind her, the horses' heads small, their steps fiery.

Kyrin's stomach tightened. Her hair was tangled as a bird's nest from her fast ride, and from twisting it while she wrote various knotty verses of Samson's Ode. She allowed Cauldron to clop faster toward the stable, concealing her. If she could avoid notice until she gained her chamber, she could face the wazir as a first daughter should, elegant and dignified, with her key. Or could it be she was not ready to face the man she'd out-foxed?

In his stall, Cauldron nuzzled her with a comforting whicker. Kyrin pitched his hay and brushed him down, listening to the voices near the barracks, memories crowding. She loosed Gwenich into the kennels and scrubbed her dirty hands together, then braced herself and crossed the yard toward the hall.

One of the men in crimson thawbs bowed and left his companions with the wazir's tent before the barracks. He watched her, his kaffiyeh framing his pale face as he met her eyes, hand ceremoniously on the long sword in his sash. "Kyrin Cieri."

Kyrin forced her long stride to slow, her hands not to clench. She breathed slowly through her nose. "Umar." The falcon blade was in her tunic, not to hand. But he knew her debt was paid. He had not threatened *her*, last they parted. He had harried Tae and Alaina hard, but then, he was the wazir's Hand. Somehow, she'd thought he would stay with Ali's household in Oman. Her old master always had reminded her of an eel.

Umar's smile was wide. "I wish to give you my thanks, for myself and Jachin." He paused and cleared his throat. "I have heard that this test has an uncertain outcome. I would not miss the fortunate moment to speak with you."

Kyrin stared at him and fought back a laugh. "No. There is not much danger. It is like, well, like the testing of a bodyguard for his sword. There are idle tongues about."

"Your news lightens my heart." He bowed.

"But for what do you give me thanks?"

"Ah. Hala Abdasir is the light of my eyes." He gave a bare lift of his shoulders. "You extended to her the hand of peace."

"Yes. I was most glad to do so." Kyrin nodded. "But you escort the Honorable wazir, Sirius Abdasir. And Jachin, is he here?" It was not done, to mention Hala again, but she could ask after her old swordmaster.

Umar inclined his head, and his mouth soured. "Jachin oversees the house in Oman." He drew himself straight. "I have the honor to guide the Excellent One to a place little distant, where he has news of something he seeks. Your Lord Cieri graciously invited us to take refreshment, and to stay for this *test*."

Kyrin smiled slightly. She had told her father of the desert guest law and asked him to bind the wazir by it. Thus all were safe. "My thanks for your good wishes. Be welcome in our hall." She bowed to Umar and edged around him. Why had she bid him welcome? Because she meant it, she supposed. Her hair was still a mess.

Umar let her go, staring after her. His mouth flattened. Kyrin found she twisted her hair uneasily, and shook it back in irritation. His smile was yet too wide, as his father's had been.

Berd caught her before she reached the hall steps. "Tae asks for you in Nith's quarters. You are not to see any who might distract you from your trial."

Too late for that. Kyrin pushed her hair over her shoulder. Useless. Alaina would have a brush, and Tae's wish this day was a command. She turned toward Nith's quarters then glanced back. "Berd—"

"Yes?"

"Umar. He was not always a friend. Would you see that he is watched?" Guest-right or no.

"Count it done, my lady."

§

Sext bell had rung in Bolton, though Lord Cieri had done the honors in Cierheld with Uncle Ulf's hand bell he used to call mass with. Now it called another gathering.

Next to the mill, Kyrin faced Alaina in the midst of an open square marked out in a fallow field. From the sidelines a child stared wide-eyed, his hand clasped by his grey-haired grandfather. Armsmen, tradesmen, freemen, and stronghold servants milled about the square, greeting familiar faces. Behind the crowd, five Cierheld squads were drawn up in ranks.

Along one side of the square were set benches from the hall. Talik sat with Meric, the other lords after them. Cor raised his fist in encouragement, but it was Talik's slight nod that Kyrin answered with a smile. On Dain's left sat Elinor, eyes bright, and Meric, still and intent.

The wazir sat apart with his men and Hala. Kyrin smiled. Tae had whisked her away just after she got in the gate, and told her Hala was ill from travel. Even now she was pale. Kyrin bowed to her slightly. After the test, she would ask Nell to attend her with soothing herbs.

Kyrin smiled crookedly and forced her chin up. Myrna had outdone herself. Kyrin tugged straight her tunic of black linen, pleated at the waist, and smoothed it over her blue wool trousers, brilliant as sapphire. The sash Tae had brought her in Nith's quarters was startling white against the colors of Cierheld. She would not disappoint Nell. Nell, who'd fought for the honor of embroidering an exquisite falcon on the breast of her tunic, with a red arrow in its talons. Nell ever had faith in her.

The earth beneath her feet was soft. She would dance with Alaina this morn, in Britannia. Free in her home, in their land. *Subak for Cierheld, Subak for my king. And for Tae; he has waited long for this hour.*

Silence fell in a thick blanket as Tae strode into the roped-off square, clad in black silk, compact and lean as a mountain cat. Her master of the way of the warrior had never walked so sure and strong. Kyrin repressed her smile of pride. It was like practice in Ali's garden again, only better.

Tae bowed before Lord of Cierheld, then to their watchers. His voice called every eye. "You have honored me with your interest in Subak, the warrior's way of my land. I and my rangdo will endeavor to give you a more accurate knowledge of that way."

Tae paused. "Do not lightly attempt anything you see this day; it is dangerous for the untaught. My rangdo learned over years. This day Kyrin Cieri, your first daughter, will be tried for the black sash of mastery." He smiled, and it was the smile of the hunter. "Let us begin!"

He bounded across the grassy ground to the center of the square and drew his sword, thrusting it with a flourish between Kyrin and Alaina.

Alaina, garbed in a white tunic, trousers, and sash, the ends fluttering in the breeze, smiled at Kyrin. It was a sly smile. Kyrin drew all her mind to her opponent.

Tae snapped the blade down in a swift glittering slash.

Sliding her toe under the staff at her feet, Kyrin flipped it up to her waiting hands. Alaina plucked her staff from the ground, rolling to meet Kyrin's overhead blow with a resounding *crack.*

Kyrin circled, with a flurry of quick jabs. Alaina deflected and attacked Kyrin's feet then darted for her middle. Kyrin smacked her staff away, pushing forward. The staves clattered, vibrating furiously. Kyrin's hands tingled as she evaded and diverted and countered.

Alaina struck for her toes, middle, and head, then leaped, spun, and came down. Her staff lashed out like a snake's tongue, and the end glanced from Kyrin's head. Kyrin squinted, eyes tearing. She shook them away.

Her breath came quick. Her staff whistled for Alaina's head, knees, and middle in lightning succession. Alaina blocked and slid away. Kyrin growled wordlessly. Alaina had been training in that desert indeed. In that space of thought, Alaina dropped to a crouch, thrust her stick between Kyrin's ankles, and twisted. Kyrin fell flat on her back with a yell. Alaina stood, then bowed and stepped back with a surprised flicker of a smile. Whistles split the air, with yells of disappointment and acclaim.

Kyrin rose, the heaviness of defeat in her chest. But Alaina would never defeat her in the last of the four tests. It was not yet the fourth. Kyrin's mouth flattened in determination.

Then it was Tae's turn. He gave Kyrin and Alaina each a bright sword with an apple speared on the tip. He faced the crowd and knelt. Meric ducked under the rope with a rippling black blindfold in his hands. He let it unfold and held it up, the silk blotting out the sunlight, and bound Tae's eyes.

As Meric walked back to his seat, Kyrin lifted her blade high. This also was a test. Of trust. A wind whispered past the edge and the blade sang softly. *Keep it still; keep it still. Trust Tae. Trust him to hear. To know, to move correctly.* She must trust herself, if his mistake required she save his limbs. Double edged, it was. *Breathe.*

Tae rose, composed. His head cocked, the tails of the black silk about his eyes tapping the back of his neck. Every soul about them waited with bated breath. Tae faced Kyrin in one swift, smooth reversal of his bare feet.

Then he yelled. The crowd gasped even as he leapt, spinning backward in the air. His whip kick drove his foot up and back, speeding toward Kyrin's blade. The apple exploded. The sword flew from her hand. Still twisting, Tae snapped his other foot out in a tight arc. Alaina's apple disintegrated in a crushed burst of white pulp. Tae landed in a crouch on the grass, silent and still, deadly. All gaped a moment. His brown feet were unmarked by blood. Then they roared. Armsmen, lords, and peasants stamped their blazing approval. Alaina removed the blindfold with the ease of practice, Kyrin bowed beside her and Tae before their audience. Her heart beat hard. Tae Chisun was a master of Subak. But three proofs of *her* mastery were yet to come. Every eye of her imagining was on her. She dared not fail. It was time for the second test. Fists tightening, she bent her knees slightly, ready to move any direction. *Just breathe. They will not know if you make a mistake. Tae will.*

Tae faced her and barked sharp, gutteral command.

Kyrin slid forward and struck low, then pulled her leg back as her fist descended in a hammer strike, to step forward with a fast, sure punch. The sleeves of her tunic snapped with the force flowing through her strikes. She fought within a combat form, a series of attacks too dangerous and deadly to use with a live companion. By the end of eleven forms she was breathing hard and wet through. Sirius watched, intent, fingering his chin.

For the third test, Tae and Alaina each took a long fighting stance on either side of Kyrin, feet wide apart. They held square pieces of smooth pinewood. Tae braced his over his head. Alaina carried hers in both hands, as a shield. Meric ran up and knelt with another, as if he offered Kyrin a sweet, from bended knee. As if he were a slave. A slave . . . She was a slave no more. This

Sext saw it known by all. Though she need no longer look to him, this moment the wazir saw true skill.

Gathering a breath, Kyrin raised another board in her left hand. It's gold-white grain filled her vision. With one short, sharp yell, she snapped her hand back and forward with the knife edge of her palm. The dry pine splintered. Dropping the pieces, Kyrin spun to Tae. With every tired muscle, her foot shot up and snapped down in an axe kick. The wood parted with a *crack*. Alaina's shield split before a savage front kick, and she snatched up another board and spun into place. With a cry of challenge as if she faced Mornoth himself, Kyrin spun in a powerful back kick that sent Alaina reeling in a shower of slivers. Under hand and voice focused as one, a last hammer strike shattered Meric's platter. He looked at her, wide-eyed.

The entire sequence took the space of a long-drawn breath. A breath everyone was holding.

Jaws dropped. Men and women cheered in a rising wave of jubilation. Kyrin bowed, spent and shaking. She had broken every board with one strike. It was enough.

Tae nodded dismissal. Kyrin moved to one side of the square, glad for the rest. Alaina took her place with the boards, and also broke every one with the first blow. Kyrin yelled approval, grinning. Her sister's journey in the great Al Ramlah had hardened her in all the right ways. Too soon, Tae called them again.

In the middle of the square they knelt and bowed over their knees, offering the courteous trust of the bared neck in the way of the East. Alaina bounced to her feet, a dagger winking in her hand. She struck swifter than thought.

Kyrin deflected the blow and used Alaina to pull herself up. She tucked and pulled Alaina over her shoulder, following her to the gorund to drop a knee in her chest and an elbow to her throat. There was at least one a shocked cry, until the watchers realized the blows were pulled short of injury, under precise control. Then they leaned forward, eyes gleaming.

For each attack, Kyrin put Alaina in a different lock or hold, stripping her dagger and adding a deadly mock strike with it. After the last, panting, she bowed to Alaina and then Tae. Would he judge her worthy? Kyrin's blood hummed in her ears. She was dripping, every fiber pushed to the edge of endurance. But he was not looking at her.

Hooves thudded. Kyrin turned. Her first armsman rode Lord Keffer's white stallion toward the square. Meric and Cor ran to lower the rope. Berd wore Tae's chest armor of leather, the cane strips shining in the sun across his chest. He wore her bracers, and had her recurve bow in his hand, arrow nocked. His feet were out of the stirrups. *Twr.* Berd had been speaking when he ought not. Kyrin's jaw locked. She looked at Tae, who inclined his head. He wished to show them this.

Berd kicked the stallion straight for her at a trot and circled, lifting the bow. Kyrin sprinted five steps and jumped, her feet rising higher than the horse's belly. The hook kick swept Berd's bow arm across his body, her other leg driving a solid round-kick to his shoulder. With a meaty *thwack* he was propelled from the saddle, the blow not hard enough to break bone. She took a chance, seeking to land in his saddle, and made it.

There was staring silence—and then a thunder. Caps rose. Cierheld shouted. "Cieri! Lady of Cieri, first daughter!" While the boy at the rope screamed with the rest, the old man yelled in his grandson's ear, "That's our Kyrin!"

Smiling, Kyrin bowed over the saddle. She was not sure she could dismount and keep her feet. But she was absolutely sure it was worth the strained muscle in her protesting right leg, the faint ache in her head.

On the ground, Berd sat up with a grimace. Kyrin slid down and found she could give her first armsman a hand to his feet, though she also gave him a dark look. "You would do better to speak of Twr's deeds than mine."

"All the same," he said, unrepentant. "That was well done." She could not stop her smile.

"Kyrin Cieri!" It was Tae, commanding a warrior. Quiet fell.

She handed Berd the white horse's rein and went to Tae. They faced each other at formal attention, eyes meeting, and it was as if he knew her fear, the haunting step of the tiger, every cry of the falcon—and what her answer had been. "Well done, my daughter."

Kyrin flushed. Her test was completed, with honor. Alaina beamed at her side, still in her white sash. But she had earned the black already. Why did she not wear it now?

"Kneel."

They obeyed. Tae knelt opposite. Celine approached, reverent, and Tae took from her hands a black silk sash. He spread it wide and lifted it high. 'Kyrin Cieri' was stitched on the black in gold thread. At Tae's motion, Kyrin loosed her white sash and folded it carefully on the ground before her. Tae leaned forward and looped the master's black twice around her waist, cool and firm and right. He tied it in a neat knot in front, the same as his.

When Alaina also wore her sash of first mastery, Tae motioned them to rise. Kyrin picked up her white sash for safekeeping, and Alaina's for memory. Her eyes stung. She knew. Her sister had waited to receive her sash until Kyrin could also. Kyrin bowed with all respect to Tae and then Cierheld. The test for first mastery was ended.

A ssome applauded and others surged up to exclaim over bits of scatered wood and apple, not dring to touch the blade, Kyrin stopped Alaina with a hand on her arm. "Alaina, if you ever have need—you may call on me." She swallowed the lump in her throat. "I know you waited for me. No one can ever—ever take your place. That spot at my back will always be empty."

"As will mine be," Alaina whispered, blinking hard. "Burn it." With a little laugh, Kyrin hugged her a long moment and walked out of the square on rubbery legs. Men and women flooded around her, smiling, just wanting to touch her back, or give her their salute. Tae spoke with her father. Elinor was on her feet, hands before her mouth, staring at Kyrin, white a ransoms. From the benches, Lord Bergrin and Kem gave her rather awed salutes. Meric jumped up and down and asked "how did she *do* it." She smiled. With her Lord of a higher hall, and the falcon he gave. *My skill questioned what many lords thought they knew.* Meric had kept the falcon dagger for her. It slid beneath her sash as if it belonged there. Nell smiled, as if she'd always known Kyrin could kick a man off a horse.

Kyrin stopped in front of Elinor, who sat white-lipped and still. Kyrin touched her arm. "My mother?" Elinor was shaking.

"Well done, first daughter," she whispered through stiff lips. Her eyes dark with pain and wrath, she rose and stumbled for the hall, shoulders shaking. Stunned, Kyrin looked after her.

"I will be back in a moment, my lady." Cernalt bowed, and Kyrin inclined her head and he hastened to Elinor's side. Frowning with concern, Kyrin wiped sweat from her face.

Seated among his crimson-clad guard, Sirius Abdasir stared at her, his face remote. Kyrin gave him a little bow. Did he mean to give her the writ of her freedom this even'? If only she could be sure he was not thinking of Tae's death touch. One of Sirius's men approached, and the wazir turned. Beside him, Hala kept her veil close. Kyrin grinned at her. What a talk they would have.

But what ailed Elinor? It might have been the sight of Kyrin's leap to Lord Keffer's horse, since Penni had fallen to her death from one. But surely Cernalt would tell his first lady that last test surprised all but Tae—and she could not rightly refuse it.

Dain interrupted. He swept her up and whirled her around, hugging her fiercely. "That's my first daughter! Well done!" Kyrin hugged him back, and there was no need of more words.

"Will you show me?" Talik demanded, coming up behind them.

"Show you what?" Kyrin asked, lips twitching in suddenly wicked amusement as her father released her.

Talik mimed her jump with his hands, swiping at her nose and head with a grin. Kyrin slid aside, around his arm, and ended at his back, knife-hand lightly tapping his neck. He playfully caught her wrist and pulled till she faced him. The smell of oat straw, sweat, and bluebells mingled. Her father's eyes twinkled. He cleared his throat, waving away Talik's apology. Then his gaze snapped aside.

Beyond the square, Cernalt stood, the file leaders of five ten-squads ranged before him. Kyrin stiffened. Had they had word of Margye's brigands?

Two of the men mounted and led their squads toward Cierheld. Berd and three others swung into their saddles and rode for the trees, mud flying. Kyrin knew their squads guarded the pass and held sentry posts along the road. The rest of Cierheld's force had marched with Nith and the regent's men for Fenwrd, for large-scale maneuvers. They had been sorely disappointed to miss her test.

Weary to her bones, Kyrin sighed and slipped her hand from Talik's. Despite her regret over Twr, never once had his squad companions looked askance at her. Now Twr's file, which Nith had placed her in at Cernalt's request, rode without her. Mayhap it was nothing more than a boundary check.

31

Tested

It is I who put to death and give life. ~Deuteronomy 32:39

"Lord Wyman!" Cernalt strode up, his eyes on Talik. "Those blades need secured." He indicated the swords Tae had left on the field amid crushed apples.

"Yes, sir." Talik turned to Kyrin with a smile. "I must go secure the blade *you* left in the dirt. You will teach me how to do that—the kicks, not the sword thoughtlessly left to rust."

"It will be my pleasure, my *lord.*" Kyrin curtseyed deeply, laughing.

Nearby, Dain touched Tae's arm, asking about training, drawing him once more into conversation. Kyrin rubbed her eyes. Her second father had taken the whip for her when she was first captured. Soon he would be gone, gone to Huen and his son. All at once she felt alone. Some quiet moments with Alaina would be welcome.

At the bottom of the hall steps, a swift hand on her arm stopped her. She tensed on instinct then forced her mucles to loosen. "Yes?"

Umar and another in red and black flanked her. The second man eyed her sash, and the falcon blade. "Is that the one?"

In answer, Umar gripped her sword hand with fingers of iron. "Sir, your grip is hard," Kyrin said. She stepped in and twisted.

She was free and they were in front of her. She backed toward the kennels. A sharp pain in her back stopped her, where another of them held a blade.

"Yes, it is what we seek, see the eyes?" Umar stepped aside, pointing at the falcon dagger in Kyrin's sash. She clenched her jaw. The guards' hands closed on her arms like a vise. "What is it, sirs?" she asked in Arabic, and shifted her weight minutely.

"Kyrin?" Meric's call was tight. A distance behind her, he eyed Umar and his men in doubt.

"Get Father, I am sure we can find out what this is about." As she spoke, Kyrin stared at him in silent warning. *Lord, help us!* Meric strode away. By the tenseness of his back he wanted to run.

The wazir's guards tugged at her, and Kyrin planted her feet. Umar might be acting alone, but he also followed the wazir's word as his Hand. "Will you hear me? Let the wazir speak with his host, as those who have eaten and drunk at the same table." The dagger pricked again, moving Kyrin toward the wazir's tent, raised in front of the smithy. A woman screamed, quickly cut off, and a wave of silence spread out around Kyrin.

Another dagger nudged her side as Cierheld men gathered, grim and silent, hands on their weapons. Women and children hustled away as Sirius's men urged her past the kennels. Archers in red thawbs poured out of the tent to surround them, armed with short-bows and swords. A raven cawed.

Neither her father nor Cernalt were in sight. But word would reach them quickly, and Tae. The guards prodded, and Kyrin stepped under the canopy, the sides of the tent rolled up and bound to let the light in.

Sirius Abdasir sat on a divan surrounded by cushions of crimson and blue, a crimson carpet on the floor with black vines crawling across it. Slaves stood at the tent's corner poles.

The guards forced Kyrin to her knees three lengths from the wazir, and drew their swords. She bent and touched her forehead to the rug without prompting, then gave Sirius the full weight of her stare. "Excellent One, why—"

He chopped her words short with a flick of his hand, not looking at her. Kyrin's heart thundered. This was a strange way to free a slave who had given honorable service, though she *had* displeased him in the matter of freeing Tae in Ali's house. What had Umar meant about the falcon blade being the one they sought?

Beyond the tent, the yard and the wall were eerily silent except for the sound of hustling feet. Cierheld was moving into position. But her father's men could do nothing while two armed guards held her. Her mouth was dry, heavy with the scent of old frankincense.

Steps sounded behind, and more of the wazir's men herded Lord Dain, Meric, and Talik in at lance point, carrying Tae's limp form in after. Kyrin's breath froze. But they would not be carrying Tae if he were dead.

She hoped Cernalt had the wit to get Alaina and the others out of the hold, if he could. Outside, one raven called to another. *Hyl's ravens.*

Arms rigid against his bonds, Dain cried, "What is the charge against my daughter—?" An archer drew on him, cutting him off mid-sentence. Dain gave a subtle flick of his fingers. On her knees, Kyrin watched two women at the edge of the restive crowd still growing outside the tent slip away, one toward the hall, the other to the kitchens. Talik stood unbound and wary among red-robed guards, his strong hands on her bewildered brother's shoulders. Early evening had begun to take the warmth from the air.

Sirius crooked one ringed finger. A slender figure in white appeared at his shoulder, face hidden by a tight-drawn kaffiyeh.

"Since you say you have found some honor in this person, speak to her of the nature of her wrong." The wazir's voice was quiet and full of anger. Kyrin stared at him, wordless.

"You, one Kyrin Cieri, a barbarian, possess the dagger of a murdered prince of Baghdad."

What? Kyrin shook her head. The wazir had seen the falcon dagger himself and given it back to her. And murder . . . but she knew that soft voice.

The kaffiyeh slipped down, and Hala stared over Kyrin's head, her face set and colorless as chalk. "The Most Excellent wazir wishes to know how the prince died. His death is to be paid for."

"I did not kill him!"

"Speak truth, your guilt is known," Hala said stiffly, her back rigid, her eyes red as if from weeping. Her mouth trembled. "If you did not, how did he die? Who hid the Damascus steel in bronze? I beg you, tell the Most Excellent wazir. Then mercy may be given." She dropped her gaze.

The guards' cold steel moved to Kyrin's throat.

What mercy, the mercy of the blade? Tae was five men from her, bound hand and foot with weapons warding him, and her father the same. Talik and Meric were surrounded. None could help her in time, all of them held hostage by her life. If she could take herself out of the way, and free the men of Cierheld.

Set the challenge. She raised her eyes to the wazir. "Most Excellent, I had heard you were here to uphold your word of a writ of freedom." *Give them time.* "This blade was my mother's. It came to me three years agone, after her death at raiders' hands. Once, I gave it into your hands. I have carried it since. I do not know of its finding, but I assure you, neither her family nor mine murdered your prince."

Sirius leaned forward, staring at her as if he could pierce her soul. He nodded, and a guard plucked the falcon dagger from Kyrin's sash and handed it to him. His nostrils flared and his hand tightened about the sheath. He gripped the falcon's head and his black eyes narrowed, watching her as he twisted it. With a click, the falcon head parted from the haft.

Sirius peered inside the cavity and looked up, his eyes burning dark. "Where?" The word was deadly quiet. He knew of the jewels.

She whispered, "I—traded them."

"What!" Sirius's face hardened to stone.

Kyrin flinched. No freedom, except mayhap to death.

The guards tensed, hands hard on her shoulders.

Before the wazir ordered her execution she would try for him. But the first to be slaughtered would be those without weapons, those behind her who would rise with her. Her gaze darted to Tae. If only he would wake.

But she was first daughter. This was her place, between Cierheld and danger, as it had always been, despite her blood of the hills. Mayhap because of it. She was not ashamed she was her mother's daughter.

There was a faint shout from the wall.

The wazir raised his hand—and the men around the tent lifted their bows. Surely he would not kill them all for the fault of one? The arms of one of the archers shook with strain. *Don't shoot, don't shoot!* Slowly, so the guards were not alarmed, Kyrin bowed flat on the black and red rug. "May this worthless one ask a thing of the Excellent One?" The slave words came hard; her voice was hoarse. *Fly high, stoop swift, take the heart.*

"Speak!"

She gave him full humility, not lifting her gaze to his. "Do you judge me worthy of death for an unproven slaying, and my father, a high one in our land, unworthy to speak?"

"It is so." Sirius' voice was flat. "You lie. You have the falcon dagger; you had it long. Your house is worthy of death. There is another who confirms it."

So, he meant to kill them—*but another who confirms it?* Kyrin lifted her gaze from the rug, her breath coming faster. "Who is this other?"

A low laugh sounded behind her. At the tent door, Umar grinned as she straightened on her knees, careful of the guards' blades. Stepping around Umar and smoothing his black Benedictine robe, Uncle Ulf strode before the wazir. He bowed. "I am."

Kyrin gaped at him. "You lie! And it is not lawful for you to be here, by order of the regent!"

"I was there the morn the Baghdad princeling died, witch." Uncle Ulf's smile was smug. "Truth overcomes mortal law."

"I would have heard of such a death—"

Her uncle's brow rose. "Had you heard of Lord Edsel when your father joined his ranks as—"

Dain's voice was cold. "You will not slander Lord Edsel in my place." He drew a step closer, sure and straight. Despite his bound hands, his bow to the wazir was graceful. "My lord, I found this dagger on one of a small band of strangers my squad found slain on the road. I thought it the work of a brigand who roamed then. Of all that the travelers had carried, the blade escaped, gripped in the hands of a young man who received his deathblow as he defended another. It lay hidden under him where he fell. I kept it after a year passed without word or knowledge of kin or friend."

Uncle Ulf's voice bore the ice of hate. "Ahh, at last the heretic speaks." He waved his hand. "The first of his words are a lie, the last is truth." He shrugged. "The young man died in his arms."

"In my hands, not by them!"

"I ask again, how did Hamal die?" Sirius regarded Dain with a wolf's steady gaze.

"A wound in the belly."

"Then his death was hard?"

"Aye." Her father's voice was steady, the sad memory in his eyes.

The wazir pointed outside. "Take him out and give him the same."

"But my father did not kill your prince!" Kyrin's breath came hard.

"I have spoken."

"There is another life, one I saved," Kyrin said, her voice low. "What of that?" Her hand crept to her throat and closed about the fish.

Hala looked at her father, tears in her eyes.

Sirius's mouth flattened. "I have spoken."

He would extract vengeance from the house of Cieri, beginning with her father. Uncle Ulf raised a brow and stepped aside. Umar smiled.

Kyrin forced her breath out, let one in. There might be an opportune moment if the wazir thought he could deal with her alone, at leisure. She wet her lips and said carefully in the Araby tongue, "Deal his death into mine."

"You can die but once," Sirius said, and looked away.

"There—are ways—to make it long."

"You would have it so?" His gaze whipped to her in disbelief.

"Yes." It was little more than a whisper. She knew what ran through his mind. Among many indignities and tortures, the beating with hot metal rods, the skinning, the staking out for the crawlers of night and day to devour her flesh, and at last the welcome blade. Uncle Ulf might be thinking of burning. A shudder ran over her.

"What did you say?" The wazir leaned forward, a glint in his eyes.

"I said yes!" She clenched her hands at her sides. He had seen her skill in Subak. There would be no opportune moment. Kyrin felt sick.

"Kyrin, no!" Dain did not understand their words, but he saw the wazir's expression and her shaking hands. Kyrin looked back at him. *I love you.*

Her father took one stride forward, pulling his guards with him. "You will not leave here alive, none of you! That is my oath as lord of Cierheld. My men hold the wall."

"My men hold *you* and all of your blood."

Dain's jaw was iron, his gaze molten with fire barely contained by two men on each arm. They wrestled him down.

Umar grinned and tilted his hand toward Kyrin, opening his fingers to show her the white scar across his palm. So, that debt was also to be paid. Kyrin could not swallow.

But the wazir did not yet hold the Lady of Cierheld. Women had gone to warn her, Cernalt, and Cook. Celine—Kyrin hoped she would forgive her. And dear Alaina, Nell, and Myrna and Bergrin. Though it would not take Umar long to bring them down if he found them. Cernalt . . . all of them. No one could fight against so many. Yet they would take many with them.

The tiger was far nearer than her back. His teeth closed on her heart, claws tearing with fear, anger, and despair. But she could not lay down the blade of right. Talik taught her that.

A raven croaked. Truthfinder cried it challenge in the oak. *Evil yawls across stronghold, dale, and daughter; death creeps o'er all. Heart, blood, and bone, beyond death I hear you call.*

Talik was moving to her side, his hands empty. Tae was yet a still, huddled shape beyond. If they'd hit him harder than they meant . . . Talik moved around a guard, and two lancers closed in on him. A weapon at his back and side in a moment, they grabbed his arms and kicked his legs from under him.

"Hold!" Sirius glared down at Talik. "This one is not of Cieri. He has naught to do with this debt."

"Kyrin, what are you doing?" breathed Talik, on his knees beside her, his head pulled back sharply, his throat bobbing. She could not look at him, or she would be undone. Her silence answered him. He went absolutely still.

Then he said slowly, "My lord. I do not know what she has been saying, but if you require a life, I ask you, do not take hers but mine."

Tears welled in Kyrin's eyes. *Hard choice my soul does wield. Love sealed, more precious than dragongield, rises up to take the field.*

Sirius shook his head in sharp negation. The heavier guard forced Talik up, fighting with all his strength. There was a thump and a gasp as they threw him to the ground beside Tae and held him there.

Her experience with the pike had not prepared her so well as it ought. If she could just touch Talik's hand, lay her head against his shoulder one more moment, tell him she loved him. In her mind's eye, wind whistled over Truthfinder's folded wings. The falcon plummeted from the sky, casting all aside, sure of him with whom she had to do. *Let me not fail you.*

"You know the law of the Medes and Persians, for Persia is in your blood!" Kyrin cried in the Araby tongue, pulling her gaze from Talik, from the storm of desperation in his eyes. "Seal it so! A day for each life." If she lasted so long. She took a breath. *Though we die, life is nigh.*

"You would die for so many of your blood, and invoke that ancient law?" The wazir steepled his hands and stared at her. "You would die—would you live in their place?"

Umar frowned, and his hand twitched toward his sword.

Anything that displeased him might have merit.

The wazir said slowly in common, "You return to my land, sworn to me, due coin for these lives justice would take."

A slave again. Sworn to him. Kyrin's bloodbeat faltered. To fulfill the oath of first daughter, she must give up her key—for a living death. The wazir would own her, and seek the death touch. But Cierheld, and her people.

"I will have the death touch at my command, either by your hand or by your teacher's." His voice was soft.

Kyrin's gaze burned into his. The death touch. Everything came back to that. "Tae will not give it to one untried. Still less for force." It was not wise to say Tae would never gift it to the unworthy.

"And for your life? Or these?" Sirius held out his hand with a slight smile. "When he wakes, we will see."

Uncle Ulf's eyes glinted. "Just so you cleanse Cieri's blight of evil from this land. That was our bargain."

The wazir leveled a stare at him. "Justice will be done."

Webs on webs. Kyrin drew a breath. Samson's Ode said it all. *The enemy's hand, never stilled, strives his ambitious heart to gild, schemes until he has killed.* It went further than Esther. But there was one who cut across all schemes of men, who directed the stars in their courses.

"Injustice is seen, and judged. There is one who is Master of all things." Kyrin grimaced. She had mayhap doubled her pain.

But somehow the words were there, forcing their way out in the deadly beauty of truth.

The hall door slammed.

Everyone looked toward the hall but the guards and Sirius and Kyrin, locked in silent struggle. Anger warred in his face against a seed of doubt.

"Let me pass!" Elinor's voice was clear. She walked toward them in strong, quiet beauty in a flowing kirtle of blue. Unarmed, his lanky frame staunch beside her, garbed in his Benedictine robe, Brother Rolf strode at her elbow, taking in the crowd, the archers on both sides, the wazir and his captives at a glance. Brother Rolf halted at the tent door, his lip curling as if he might spit at Father Ulf's feet.

No. Kyrin crumpled over her knees. Her second mother, too, fell to their webs. How long had the wazir planned this, how long had Uncle Ulf plotted with him? Though it did not matter now; she *would* pay what coin was required. If Tae did not wake and provide a diversion. If one of her father's men did not take the wazir's life, and then the guards take theirs.

Elinor trod the path those of Cierheld and Sirius's guards made for her, stepped delicately around Kyrin, and curtseyed before the wazir. With one graceful movement she lowered a golden loaf of bread and a cruse of mead before him. The decorative slices in the bread's crust overflowed with salt.

"How dare you?" Quiet were her mother's words. Starkly they accused.

Sirius held out his hand for a carved wood bowl from Hala. He held it before Elinor, unsmiling.

The lady of Cieri looked upon the pile of broken cakes she had offered to the wazir's men on their arrival, drowned in honey mead. Pale with condemnation, Elinor raised her head. "You have broken the heart of your law, though the shell of it stands."

"It is needful, when murder has been done," Sirius said.

"But you do not know the doer of the wrongful death. Yet you punish those you think close to it, dealing wrongful death yourself."

Sirius rapped, "Daughter of Cieri, who is this person who knows our ways—who is she to you?"

If she did not speak, Elinor would, mayhap rashly. "She is Elinor Cieri, my second-mother, Lady of Cierheld." As he very well knew.

"Ah." Sirius paused, his ringed forefinger tapping the falcon dagger in his lap. "She is a wise and brave woman." He leaned abruptly back. His guard's blades left Kyrin's skin. One of them gestured for her mother to stand beside Hala, on the wazir's left.

Sirius cocked his head. "My ruling yet stands. What say you, first daughter?"

Kyrin looked at him. "My word also stands." Beside Father Ulf, Umar's mouth worked. His breath fled harsh through his nose.

Hala bowed her veiled head. There was one who knew; living might be harder than dying. Never to see those she loved again, but endless strange or gloating faces in the caliph's court and Sirius's house, the fear and anger and hate of those who feared the sigil of evil in her ear or hated the Master of the stars. Or feared the death touch.

But at least her family and Cierheld would live, no matter how long Umar let her breathe. If the Master of the stars sent her back for this, so be it.

Kyrin wanted to collapse in a heap and scream and sob. Instead she forced her chin up, against the shaking of her limbs. She would finish her flight as Samson finished his. *In the strength of his eye is triumph without a sigh. Fly, falcon heart, fly.*

Sirius stood. A smile lurked about the edges of his mouth. "It is done. You give your life for all these." He lifted his arms. "Your first daughter has bound you by her word! You will live!"

Uncle Ulf pointed at Dain, shaking with anger. "You said this heretic would die!" There was a confused roar from the crowd.

That moment Umar threw himself toward Kyrin with a wordless growl. His dark eyes glittered. His sword whispered from his sash. Brother Rolf reached for him, too late. Kyrin's guards flowed aside.

Umar's blade came for her neck hard and fast. In a blur of motion, Kyrin rose from her knees, turning with him, inside the blow. The edges of her hands struck his sword arm in lightning succession. Her second blow pulled him into a knife-edged strike to the neck with all his force and hers. His sword dropped. She pivoted, and a tiger-mouth strike to the throat took him down.

His spine struck her knee. There was a *crack.* Umar sagged and slid to the ground. Kyrin was a pace from the wazir.

Sirius waited, unblinking, almost curious. Kyrin knew before the stench reached her that Umar was dead. She blinked, motionless. And then the guards had her facedown.

A sword point dug into her back, another drew a line of fire alongside her neck. Kyrin coughed, the breath knocked from her.

"Hold!" Sirius roared. "Your first daughter lives!"

"Do as he says!" Dain shouted. Weapons eased away from Kyrin. Everywhere about the tent, men shifted. Kyrin turned her head slowly.

Elinor's hands were over her mouth, her horrified eyes flicking between Umar and Kyrin. Hala clutched Elinor's arm.

"Umar disobeyed my command. Thus he broke the caliph's law." Sirius's embroidered shoes paced across the rug before Kyrin's nose. "Get up."

She rose, and barely turned from the nearest guard before her stomach rejected the sickness inside her. She closed her eyes, shivering. She was his slave. The warm breath of the tiger touched her face.

His breath smelled of mint. Her eyes opened. *Not* the tiger, though as unwelcome. Sirius's face was a hand from hers, his eyes dark. "Why did you not take me?"

"My people's—lives held me, if my word did not." Kyrin could hardly meet his eyes.

"Ahhh." It was almost pain, almost anger. His smile was sardonic. "I think not many men would hold to their word so far as you. They would not withstand the fire so well." The wazir paused and straightened. His voice hardened. "I judge the touch of death is not for common men. Such a deadly thing as you have shown me may not come near my caliph." His cold gaze rested a moment on Umar's body as it was borne out of the tent.

Distantly, Kyrin hoped he ordered her death away from her father and Meric, Talik . . .

Frowning, Sirius waved his hand. "Release them."

The words echoed in Kyrin's ears. Then she was shaking so hard a guard reached to hold her on her feet. Tears dripped down her chin. Her father's arms enfolded her from behind.

After a moment he gently released her to Talik and approached the wazir. Vaguely, she was aware of people speaking and moving around them. With her head on Talik's shoulder, Kyrin cried as she never had before. His hand touched her hair and then he crushed her to him.

At last things grew less blurred. Kyrin blinked and raised her face to Talik's. With a sniff, she turned, looked around blearily. "Where's Tae?"

His place on the ground was empty. His bonds lay where they'd fallen. Speaking with Sirius on the divan, her father looked up. Elinor reached for Kyrin with a lost look, and Hala moved beside her. Uncle Ulf was also gone, and Brother Rolf.

Every eye went to Tae's place. About the tent Cierheld men and Sirius's mingled, hands near their weapons, glances wary. Sirius rose.

Cernalt's command rang from the barracks. "Bring the horses!"

There was the sound of running.

Brother Rolf slid inside and gripped the nearest pole to stop his headlong rush, panting. He turned anguished eyes on Kyrin. "Ulf, he—and Thorgil—took Celine and Lord Bergrin's daughter, in the field. With your Nell. Then Alaina tried to help them—and Thorgil took her too." He swallowed. "Lord Bergrin woke from their coward's blow to see the traitors fleeing, and your Tae after them. Cernalt is readying men and horses." He pointed toward the barracks.

"I see. You have a traitor also." The wazir strode toward Kyrin, and Talik's arms tightened around her. Sirius nodded gravely to him and raised his voice. "I call all to witness!" He turned to Kyrin. "Honor has gone before you, daughter of Cieri. My brother's son and his seal received esteem at your hands. I absolve you of the blood of Hamal Abdasir."

Kyrin gaped. Seal—the falcon blade had belonged to the wazir's heir?

Sirius offered Elinor the falcon dagger with a formal bow, and gestured toward the bread she held close. "I would redeem your goodwill, woman, though there is little time. Bind us with cords that may not be broken."

Elinor hastily cut the loaf, and Sirius took a great bite and passed it to Kyrin, while Elinor poured honeyed mead into a cup Hala offered. The cup and bread went to them all.

Dain drank from the cup last and dashed it to the ground. "The fruit of the earth and the salt our Lord spoke of be witness to the peace between us! May it not be broken again." His face was terrible.

There was a croak, a sudden squawk, the scream of a falcon, and an explosion of black feathers fell from the oak like snow.

When the ravens gather, power will be seen. Though he knew it not, Hyl had spoken the Master of the stars's truth. He worked all things to his glory.

Thinking of the oath she had offered moments ago, Kyrin wrapped her arms around herself and bit her lip. She was glad that offering had not been taken. Her sister, Nell, Myrna, and Celine, had been.

Meric's hand crept into hers. "Courage," he whispered.

She gripped his hand hard and whispered back, "*De Re Militari.*" *Take the heart.*

32

Blades

Piercing as far as the division of soul and spirit. ~Hebrews 4:12

Tae spurred his horse faster. He'd woken from the thump on the head the wazir's men had given him and crept out of the tent after Kyrin took Umar down. Tae's mouth twitched up. His daughter graced the black sash.

He'd watched from the front of the crowd, hidden within an obliging Cierhelden's hooded cloak. When the wazir freed her, the treacherous monk moved out of the tent into the crowd. Tae followed. Uncle Ulf had trailed Thorgil, who rode across the fields for the woods with Alaina and Kyrin's companions bound on horses behind him. They'd been taken by surprise.

Now the group was slowing. He dismounted, touched a print, and sniffed the sweet oak smell of the leaf litter on his fingers. He must follow, close but not too close. By the earlier tracks, more men had met Thorgil and Ulf in the trees. Those of Cierheld would care for things there. His other daughter and those with her needed him now.

Thorgil had attacked Nell before. And he himself had a snake to kill.

Ware the asp. It never was the wazir's Hand, who was simply one of his coils. Tae mounted again and leaned over his horse's neck. If his thought was true, he would find the asp in his den, where it all began. He needed Berd and those three squads, somewhere on the road ahead.

§

Nell, her hands tied behind her, jounced on a trotting horse. A burly, long-legged man with a crown of thin red hair around his bald pate led her beast. Ahead, an ugly man with an axe slung across his back led Myrna, more in awe of her than anything else. He did nothing to torment her. Thorgil's fat friend held Alaina's mount and kept his hand close to his dagger, but that was all. Celine was blessed otherwise.

Thorgil's thin companion, who bore a sword, seemed to delight in laughing at Celine, pinching her when her horse drew up beside his, and slapping the beast to make it swerve, to try and unseat her. Celine endured it with the strength of hate, if her glares were anything to judge by.

Just ahead of Thorgil, Father Ulf turned in his saddle. "I thought we were to ride in peace." His quiet reproof stilled the thin man's grating laughter. "It will end soon enough."

It was rare a man of the Book held common cause with brigands. Nell smiled at their discomfiture, and Thorgil shot her an ugly look of promise. His heritage was plain to see in his flaxen, braided hair and mustache. Nell averted her gaze. She must remember, she was a rangdo.

Rangdo to her who helped capture the traitor monk who rode at their head, to her who retrieved the jewels that saved the north. She was rangdo to a true first daughter, who once brought Thorgil down. Nell tried to catch Celine's eye, but Celine avoided her gaze. So Nell watched them, riders and captives, and thought of all Kyrin had taught her, until evening and Vespers drew near.

Father Ulf kept his prisoners close. He slept between them and Thorgil and the rest until Matins. Then they rode again, keeping to the unused paths, the darkest woods, descending the mountains toward the sea.

The following three days were a torture equal to the rack and blurred in Nell's mind. At last she blinked awake in the dark. Her shoulders and back ached worse than her legs, which at least had some practice riding, while her arms had none at being tied behind her.

A stone wall rose before them, reaching too far on either side to belong to a church. There was a small door in it. A torch burned above as if it had been left for them. The sound of the ocean rushed in her ears. Starlight was bright.

What was this place? Few strongholds had stone walls, only two she knew of, both of them Lord Dain's. Cierheld . . . and Fenwrd. Where Lady Willa died. A moment, Nell's breath stopped.

Cernalt would never guess Father Ulf would come here, straight into Lord Cieri's own stronghold, where Dain had sent many of his men and a number of the regent's to learn company maneuvers.

Thorgil bundled Nell off her horse then moved toward Myrna. The thin man cut Nell's bonds, but left the cloth tied in her mouth. Her numb arms fell forward. The relief was short.

Thorgil laid a string of prayer beads between her palms and tugged a monk's robe over her head, then retied her, elbows and hands together. He looped the rope through the bonds and tightened it, drawing her hands up before her as if she were praying. The others were treated in kind.

Myrna was crying, tears shining on her cheeks; the axeman patted her back. Garbed in the same monk's robes, his axe rested grotesquely on his shoulder. The thin man shoved Celine, who jerked her elbow away from his hand and stumbled against Nell. "Rangdo," Nell whispered, "remember who you are." She could not be sure if Celine nodded or merely swayed, as exhausted as she. Nell's legs were damp with horses' sweat and blood from broken blisters long rubbed raw. But she could walk.

"Come, my brothers, the moment has come to pray for the dead who fell here." Father Ulf led the way to the door, guiding Alaina before him, his hand firm against her back, extended to help his weary brother, disguising the tip of the blade he held. He tapped a rapid pattern. The door opened.

The sentry on the other side watched them step through and move toward the yard. He silently bolted the door behind them. Fenwrd lay sleeping within the wall, much as it had when Ali's raiders took it, some three years agone. Nell shivered.

The thin man and the burly red-head with the dagger took up torches to light in the sentry's flame. The sentry glanced at the blade in the fat monk's belt in doubt; then his gaze moved to the woodsman's axe and the thin one's sword.

Nell gathered herself. If she tossed back her hood and ran to him . . .

Uncle Ulf hurried to the thin man's side, urging Alaina before him. "I *told* you this was a true place of God; they will not disturb us here where I am to be walled in. Come, Alard needs to find a place of rest." He gestured at Alaina, drooping on her feet, lifted his hands in apology to the sentry, and the sentry jerked his head curtly for them to move on.

Nell found herself panting, stumbling over flat ground, staggering over a jumble of stones. To be walled in? What did he mean to do? And there had never been any chance, one man against five, and one with an axe. The best she could hope for was that the sentry remembered the odd brothers who entered his hold this night. If any searcher who sought such oddities questioned the sentry in time.

Then there were steps up. Tumbled walls rose about the floor of the main hall, dark against the starlight. A stair led down. The flickering light and shadows of night tricked her eyes, and the burly man's hand dug into her arm, saving her a fall.

A dank passage closed around them, shutting out the stars, casting back Father Ulf's mutter, "At last I know where she fell, my Willa. Her false witch of a first daughter has been good for something." They passed dark holes and archways to chambers full of shadows and moss. A rat fled, squeaking. Nell shuddered. They turned sharp left through a rotten wood door.

Another turn in the passage, its damp stones crumbled across the floor, and on. Did Celine even suspect she walked in Kyrin's footsteps? Then another small chamber. Father Ulf led them inside.

In the bright torchlight, he slammed Alaina into the wall. Her head struck the stone and she collapsed at his feet with a slight gasp. Shock and horror held Nell in its own kind of stone. He leaned over Alaina and picked up her hand, twisting it to the light to see the ink stains on her fingers. He grunted regretfully. "A pity. What a scribe. But she chose her path with that witch. She would taint the Vulgate she touched."

The axeman cleared his throat. "Might she—might they have been deceived, Father? 'Tis said a witch's spells can—"

"No!" Father Ulf's hands closed in the cowl at the man's throat and he shoved him back. He calmed suddenly. "Keep your men in hand, Thorgil, or leave."

Thorgil glared at the axeman. "Do it!" he growled.

The axeman pushed Myrna to the floor and cut her bonds. Thorgil gripped Nell's shoulders and shoved her against the wall, stripping away her ropes. Cold stone dug into her back. Bewildered, she stared. Why had he loosed her?

He smelled of onion, his bearded face too close. "Do you know what happens when a walled-in anchorite does not eat for three morns? Eh? He is counted worthy of the ear of God, and men leave him to his contemplation. They look at the water undrunk and"—Thorgil shrugged—"of a certain, such a man of God took but a sip. Or if it is empty, then the rats drank it." He grinned, looking her up and down. "You *do* bear the witchy eye. Perhaps on the fourth morn they might wonder. The fifth will be too late. For you and for them." He leaned forward and whispered in her ear, "Cere was never enough of a man to tame you. Pray I come back, witch."

Nell would have spit at him if she could. Father Ulf did not need them alive long to draw Lord Dain into his snare. In the thin man's grip, Celine whimpered. Ulf cried, "Thorgil!"

With a growl, Thorgil released Nell. She heard the thud of his fist, and the thin man cursed. "I know you like to hear them scream, but not this moment," Thorgil said. "Out! All of you! Bring the stones." His men went.

Thorgil turned. She must seize the moment. Nell kicked his knee. He bent in pain, and she struck at the back of his head. It was her only chance, to take him quickly. But Thorgil had a guarding hand up. He grunted at her blow then backhanded her in the face. "Odin's breath, you'll pay for that, witchling!"

Nell staggered and fell, her head ringing. He tied her hands roughly behind her, then her feet, despite her dizzied, desperate kicking and muffled noises through her gag. "Your witchy eye will trouble me na' more." He fastened her hands to her ankles, and dragged her to a corner, where he kicked her until she retched. She choked. He purred in her ear, "Ye're blessed, or not, that the good Father wants you alive." He cuffed her. "Hunger and rats and your tongue sticking for dryness, that's a fit death. An your sister witch, she'll find a like fit end. The good Father's got all in hand."

Father Ulf saw to it that Alaina, still limp, and Myrna and Celine each had their own corner. Thorgil held the torch high. Father Ulf stood over them and said the prayer for the dying. Then he crossed himself and went out.

Don't panic. God's here. Breathe slow. Nell panted against the wall, her nose swelling, adding another obstacle to her breathing. Stones scraped as the thin man and the one with the dagger wrestled a first layer of stone into place across the doorway. The thin man was a mason by the way he set the stones just so and whispered directions to the others. No kicking that wall down. It rose steadily.

The stifled screams of her companions fell silent, and Alaina did not stir. Then the last light went out as a stone blocked the shelf left for food and water with a thunk. The men's footsteps died away. Nell counted them as best she could.

She thought the thin man had also gone, had not stayed to hear them scream. Her face was wet with tears, blood, and worse, and she could not wipe it.

"Nell?" Celine's voice was small.

Nell jerked. "'ere!" The cloth stole meaning from her voice. The thin man must have loosened Celine's gag just enough. With a whispering of cloth and a grunt, Celine rolled across the floor. Her head banged into Nell's ear. Nell bit back a cry. Nothing must complicate what she was about to say. "Shew!"

"What? That is all you can say? I'll see if Alaina is well." There was puzzlement under her forced, light voice.

"Uhhh." Nell shook her head violently.

"What then?"

"Shew!" Nell ground her teeth on her gag. If Celine could hear it . . .

"Oh." Celine twisted about for an age then Nell felt her mouth and teeth against the cords about her wrists. Bless her for being so sharp, never mind her words were too. Celine had gone for her hands first.

§

Kyrin topped the wooded hill with her father, Berd's three tensquads ranked around them. None showed themselves beyond the tree line. Even the wazir's men had donned pale thawbs. Far below the cliffs the sea was as quiet as if storm never touched it, rushing up and down the beach, glinting in the dawn light. Just before the woods, bright with spring green and the fresh scent of growth, Fenwrd's wall stretched across the gradually rising, grassy ground.

A horse thudded up from the left, weaving through the trees. Berd bowed over his saddle. "My lady, the steward knows nothing."

"Yet you followed this Father monk here?" Sirius looked over the water toward the sun, high in the sky.

"Yes," Berd grated. Kyrin did not let her grin reach her lips. He had not yet forgiven the wazir. Lord Bergrin Jorn also blamed the wazir for Myrna's capture. Umar had plotted with Father Ulf—but Sirius knew naught of it.

She sighed. They had caught up with Tae and Berd on the road before Bolton. They never paused more than a bell over hill, stream, moor, and marsh. It was a rushing ride on Ulf's trail through the mountains north of the Humber, down the Pickering Vale. She was weary to her bones.

Beside her, Dain lifted his hand and clenched his fist. Cierheld's men faded back from the crest. "We will do little good, tired as we are." Dain turned to Berd, ready at his shoulder. "Until Compline we will gather strength and watch. First armsman, send word to Nith to watch well inside the hold, without alerting all of Fenwrd. Tae searches for one among Nith's sentries who saw Father Ulf and his brothers. We will move with the night unless need dictates otherwise." Dain nodded to Sirius, who inclined his head like a northern lord. "Daughter," he added, "take your blanket and find a tree to keep the damp from us."

Kyrin turned Cauldron into the thicker forest, catching back a laugh. Lord Jorn and the others would likely meet Berd on watch, with Sirius, one of the reasons for their watchfulness, at ease in the midst of them. Berd considered the incident with Umar his fault, though he had been ordered to leave after her test. They did not yet trust the wazir. Strangely, she did.

§

Brother Rolf rode through the ranks, drawing near the front, and the wall. The night was dark, a mist coming in off the sea, chilling his nose and the mail he wore beneath his black robe. His sword belt around all did not keep out the wind, though he'd drawn it tight. He wished he could hug the pot of coals he carried, and wished also for a sheltered corner of the wall, with warm rugs around shoulders and knees.

But more, he wanted a piece of the man who'd betrayed a lady of a high house. Who'd betrayed him, as should not be done in the church; and much more, who betrayed God. Rolf grimaced. Not that his Lord needed his defense.

He sighed. No matter he'd argued with himself of godly charity and pity over the long road to Fenwrd, he yet wanted a piece of Ulf, or more. *Give me Your eyes to see.*

The three tensquads Nith had sent outside the wall at Dain's word joined them. They lit no torches, surrounding the hold at intervals. Rolf supposed the six alert squads left within would be sufficient to deal with matters there, if need arose. It was time. Nith opened the side door for Lord Cieri.

Talik and the others followed him inside. Rolf brought up the rear. A summoned off duty sentry told them in whispers of two abandoned ways into the passage of the ruined hold, to the chamber where Lord Dain's lady had fallen. He said, "The brothers were armed, some of them, that was what caught my eye. So I watched, and they came out again—the ones who were armed, that is. Father Ulf with them. They caused no trouble." The sentry looked down. "A lady with yellow hair met them with a basket of food. They ate on the steps, and went back below. They met the lady yesternight, before Matins."

"You heard nothing?" Dain asked. "No cry of any kind?"

"Nay, but the wind whistles about loud enough." The sentry shrugged, an anxious frown growing in his voice. "My lord, did I do wrong letting them in? I had heard of a new anchorite. Is—"

Dain gripped the man's shoulder. "Father Ulf tried to have me killed. The smaller brothers with him were four women of Cierheld whom he kidnapped, companions of my first daughter." He indicated Kyrin. "And one of them is Bergrin's sister."

The sentry stiffened to attention. "I am sorry, my lord—"

Dain raised a quiet, calming hand. "We will find them. You will lead Lord Jorn and Sirius Abdasir through the back and the longer passage. I will lead these the shorter way, from the front. If we take him, his brigands will scatter. But they may lie up in any of the chambers below." Though Rolf thought he smiled in the dark, Dain's voice held no amusement. "Father Ulf is no tactician. So I send you to block his bolt-hole. Thorgil and his men will be the greatest threat."

"Aye, my lord. I will not fail you." The sentry dipped his head, grim.

Dain's voice was quiet. "Good man. Go in the might of right." He tilted his head toward the ruin. "We will follow. Father Ulf prefers other hands to kill for him, but do not underestimate him. And be sure who you strike. The women may be held among them or apart, robed as monks or undisguised."

"Yes, my lord. This way."

At the entrance, Dain left half a tensquad to guard the great doors from the outside. In the hall, burned and broken, he slipped through a small door, ducking under a ruined stair. Tae scouted ahead. Kyrin paused, then ducked through, Berd and Talik behind her. Brother Rolf padded after. It would be close work in the passage. Kyrin was armed with all but her bow.

When they stopped to listen, he gripped the unlit torches under one arm, the pot tight in his hands. Voices would carry here. All was silent but for the distant drip of water. Rolf leaned forward like a hound, wishing he had a hand for his sword hilt. All he smelled was old stone, and fire.

The passage sloped down, black as pitch. Their enemies were as cautious as they. From what Kyrin had said, the first chamber lay off a straight stretch ahead. Not that he could see it.

Ahead, there was a scuffle. A muffled yelp and a grunt. They stopped. A shout rang further down.Light bloomed around a corner.

Quickly, Rolf thrust one of his pitch-laden torches in his pot of coals, lifting his own flame in answer.

At the edge of the light streaming from both ends of the fassage, Father Ulf lay motionless on the floor. Close beside his feet, Tae appeared to be wrestling with a rock in the wall. No, a chamber door stood before them, cunningly blocked with stone.

Kyrin gave a wordless cry, as Tae struggled. Rolf's heart ignited with cold fire. He could guess what was done here. Dain rushed to help Tae. Hand shaking, Rolf stepped over Father Ulf. Swords drawn, Talik and Berd sprang past them to guard the way, facing those heralded by the approaching light.

Kyrin's hand rested on the dagger in her black sash, the falcon's eyes dark as she glanced back at Rolf. He dropped the pot, drew his blade, and held the torch high, grim. They had but moments.

The first stone was out, guided aside by Tae and Dain. It thudded to the floor. The force shivered through their feet. A trickle of earth sifted over Brother Rolf's head, with a pebble. He shook it out of his hair.

A weak call came from the dark slit, and a cough. "Who—?"

His heart warmed. At least one was alive.

"Celine!" Kyrin lunged for the opening. "We'll get you out! Are you all there?"

There was a muffled sob. "Yes."

"It's a trap!" Nell's voice. "Get out!"

There was movement behind Rolf.

"A trap." Eyes bright, Ulf leaned against the wall. "Indeed it is. Though you spring it early." One hand on a protruding stone, he gripped it as though it were the crozier of his authority. "Where my Willa left this earth, so will you. Thorgil's stoneworker was inspired." With a horrible smile, Father Ulf wrenched the stone. It came out in his hand.

The passage behind him groaned, creaked, and the roof stones fell, one and three and a rumbling wave. Ulf darted past.

With a shout, Rolf swept Kyrin behind him, toward the chamber's strong wall. Dain and Tae pulled Talik and Berd close also. When rumbling fall ceased, the passage they had entered by was a heap of damp, chalky rubble. Someone coughed. Through the buzzing in his ears Rolf knew it came from before them. As the dust cleared a red-haired, grinning man edged up beside Father Ulf. At their backs Thorgil, a man with a wicked dagger, and two more blocked the way.

Dain prowled forward, his sword warding. "There is one here who could take you all. We stand six against six. Come then, if you are so ready to meet your maker."

White hair tousled, Father Ulf held out his arms. "Peace, peace. The church must be pure. Only you must answer for house Cieri, my lord. Then these will be freed, and I will have the ear of the regent, as I ought to have had from the beginning. Heresy must be stamped out in all its guises."

Kyrin stepped closer. "If our way out is through you, find it we will. It is not our will that you fall, Uncle."

Rolf almost smiled. She did not believe him either.

Ulf glared at her. "Witch!" he hissed. "It was never the will of God that *Willa* fall. *You* brought her here; she fell for *you,* a heretic's whelp!" He indicated Dain with scorn then his eyes burned upon her again. "Who was it who would not handfast a lord's son? If you had kept at home, her fall would have been of worth, a pure woman dying for her faith—"

Kyrin's breath drew in sharply. "Do you disregard her sacrifice so much, Uncle? She did it for love, the same love that burns in a martyr's heart, that gives itself for another." Kyrin leaned forward, tense as drawn wire. "That love is of most *high* worth."

"Such a death is nothing! Think you a fool's cap graces my head? Such sacrifice is for those who wear the fools' bells, but she fell to worse, to witchery, mayhap to heresy."

"Not witchery, not heresy. Defender! She fought with a blade of heart and hand. And her love reaches beyond death, for I am here." Kyrin was pale. "I was not quick enough, not strong enough, or brave enough to stop her fall. You speak truth in that." Her voice broke. "I would not see you fall. Will you give me your forgiveness?"

Ulf took a step, his voice dropping to a whisper. "She would use no blade. And do you ask absolution of me?"

"I ask for your forgiveness, Uncle. The Lord of heaven has already given me his absolution."

"Hah! I give no forgiveness to heretics or witches—unless they recant—then they still must burn to purity. Though burial under stone must do, this time," he said thoughtfully.

Brother Rolf could be silent no longer. "Traitor! You break the word of your regent, then think to gain his ear? You would deny the Book that says our Lord does not desire the death of the wicked, but that they turn from unrighteousness and live? And Lord Cieri has been examined by your own church and found innocent. Do you disregard all authority?"

Father Ulf raised his brows in faint derision. "When the law is twisted by men, someone must rise to thwart them, lay Brother." Beside him the burly man with red hair nodded.

"If you do not follow the law of the Book, whose law *do* you follow?"

The red-haired man frowned faintly. Ulf sighed. "I weary of this. Thorgil, take them."

Thorgil turned to Ulf in surprise. "You said we would but seal them in and kill tha' one." He pointed his sword at Dain.

Dain dropped the tip of his blade slightly, and Tae shifted behind him. Rolf wished he could wield a blade in either hand, but someone must guard the light. And those with him wielded swords much better than he. Berd edged around him, toward the thin man on the far side of the passage. Talik shifted to Kyrin's back.

Dain said, "Your men do not seem eager for the blade. They have not the mettle for a martyr's death. Nor do you, by your own mouth. You have another way out—"

It happened between one blink and another, as Brother Rolf had known it would.

Father Ulf shoved the burly man into Dain's blade. He yanked a dagger from the man's belt as he sagged, and drove the weapon toward Dain's side. Kyrin could do nothing but pull her father out of the way, opening her own body to the blow.

Then Tae was there, in one explosive motion. The wind of his passing stirred Rolf's hair. He deflected the blade with a yell that shook the bones. His other hand thrust straight as a spear into Ulf's lower chest. There was a ripping, wet sound. With a faint gush of air, Father Ulf folded over his arm.

No one moved. Tae raised his gaze from Ulf to Thorgil. "Taking a man's life is taking his life," he said softly. "This way is harder than some—for the one who takes it. Mark it well." It was stark warning. Tae let Ulf down to the floor and waited. His hand was covered in blood past his wrist.

Thorgil stared from Tae's fingers to his face. Lowering his blade, he backed away. The thin man followed, and then their enemies were running.

Rolf looked down. The wound gaped darkly under Ulf's ribs. Tae stared at him, white and weary. "It was a way—to keep us from death."

Rolf swallowed. Tae turned and took a staggering step past Ulf's body. "I will follow them, and guard the way out. Come when you can."

Talik and Berd looked at each other. Dain watched Tae, and Kyrin whispered, "Yes."

Brother Rolf lit a second torch for Kyrin to wedge among the rocks, and let Tae get some lengths along the passage before he followed with a light. After all, Tae would need it. Or maybe not. Rolf shrugged. Still, no man should be alone at such a moment. And he thought they might find a tunnel through the chalk.

§

"That—was the death touch." Berd said, barely a whisper.

"Yes. One of them. The death touch is not a single kind of blow." Kyrin wiped her face wearily. She ached for Truthfinder. But her armsman ought to know, and her father and Talik knew how to keep silent. She drew a deep breath. "The death touch the wazir thought he saw with Umar was but points of pain that take the senses—and then Umar fell on my knee where I broke his spine. That is often what is seen—many strikes done so subtly or swiftly men see one blow that kills," she whispered. "The death touch may be also be a simple blow given extremely hard to the head or a vital area that forms a clot and kills days later." She wiped her face again, and dropped to her knees. She stared at her uncle's body dully, an edge of lung glistening pink. "Not many have the strength and speed to pierce the skin in such a way, to take the heart." *Traitors rise and are downcast . . .* Tae had torn his heart mercifully quick. "Uncle . . ." she could not go on.

Berd gripped her arm gently, his voice low. "It is good you weep for what he might have been." At the same moment Talik touched her other shoulder. She looked up at them, and the men's gazes met. With a small smile, Berd turned away.

Kyrin swallowed. "First armsman, you always hold my back."

He grinned over his shoulder and moved to grab the other side of the large stone Dain was tugging from the chamber door.

Talik helped Kyrin lay Father Ulf straight. They wrapped him in a cloak, covering his face. Then between the four of them they pulled the stones apart.

Berd climbed over the last stones. First he helped Nell out. A great bruise spread across her swollen nose and cheek. She moved with one hand on her side, as if it pained her.

Kyrin hugged her, and Nell cried into her shoulder. "I fought Thorgil, I fought so hard, and I lost."

Kyrin clung to her harder. "No. You did not know enough, as I did not when my mother fell. You did not lose where it mattered.

You held fast the wall of your spirit. Some moments, that is all that can be done. Believe me, no fault lies with you."

Nell sniffed and gingerly wiped her face.

Kyrin gripped her shoulders. "You will hear such praise from me it will redden your ears. You endured."

Then Alaina slid out of the chamber, with naught but a bump on the head, and after tearful hugs all around, she went in search of Tae. Myrna bravely said she felt none the worse, except for a terrible thirst and the results of their long ride. And then Berd lifted out Celine, still bound. She had such a lost look, her red curls tangled and dirty about her white face, that Kyrin sat on the floor and gathered her in her arms.

"Forgive me, Kyrin." Her voice was thick, and she could hardly hold her head up. "I should never—he was wrong. Love is of most high worth. Please—"

Berd had his dagger out, and in a moment he cut her ropes and dropped them beside Kyrin. "Their ropes were chewed through. She loosed them first. Without knowing if their enemies might return." He knelt and brushed a bit of hair out of Celine's face, his dark gaze steady. "To keep going when your jaws are burning and you feel helpless, that takes spirit."

Celine cried harder. Kyrin patted her back, while Berd slipped within their prison again. There was a sliding, a thump, and Berd called, "My lord, would you bring the light?" Dain held the torch closer to the chamber doorway. He and Talik muttered with Berd, heads together.

Celine gulped down a sob. "On your next hunt, would—would you let me come with you and Truthfinder and Gwenich?"

It was the last straw. Kyrin stiffened against the tears but could not stop the crashing loss that poured over her, loosed by one heart she had thought lost—which began to care again. She shook with the force of her sobs. Alarmed, Celine gripped her tentatively. "Kyrin? What is it?"

"Oh Celine, you turned back and I am so glad of it, but they didn't."

"Who?"

"Umar and her uncle." Berd laid a long bundle wrapped in cloth beside them and put his hand on Kyrin's heaving back. "And as we have found out, mayhap Esther."

Talik knelt and pulled away the bundle's wrappings. It was the sword Kyrin had found in Samson's stream.

§

After Tae and Brother Rolf led them out of the chalk tunnel the brigands had dug, a search was made throughout Fenwrd. They found Esther. She confessed that she'd stolen the sword and given it to Father Ulf in return for his getting her messages to Lord Mornoth's nephew. Esther soon retired near Bolton Abbey, under an Abbess, against the will of her mother.

Standing at Bolton Church's altar where Alaina's Vulgate rested, Brother Rolf shook his head. "We'll never know how much she helped them, I think."

Kyrin nodded. "Mayhap she and Mornoth's nephew had to do with the brigands' escape. Or we would have found them." Cierheld's best had hunted long and hard. Alaina squeezed her hand. Kyrin smiled at her, then sobered. "Brother Rolf, was Uncle Ulf, well, was he mad?"

"No more mad than you or I, with our minds set on sorrow, hate, or greed." Rolf sighed. "Sorrow turns easily to bitterness, and bitterness to hate. Bitterness sees itself wronged, leaving a wide chamber for evil."

"That is true." Kyrin wished it were not true. As she wished the tiger were not. She'd had a long talk with Brother Rolf about her dreams. He did not think they would return. For she knew the tiger now where he roamed—in every morn's fears, the little jealousies, every day's worry. *A fall to worse than beast; where evils on us feast; nor we, evil becoming, ever cease; where the tiger hides under fleece; unless our hands take the blood of the least; revel in our Lord's sacrifice, joy, and love-feast.* Whatever ill shape the beast took, she could not conquer it alone. It rose from her oft treacherous heart, and the evil one, who sought to divide her from the Master of the stars. But his defeat was certain.

§

Kyrin stood in her stronghold's wide-open gate, those of Cierheld's house and hall gathered around her. The tensquads were drawn up beside the mill. A breeze wound about them under the bright morn, tugging at cloaks and flipping Kyrin's hair.

Their guests were leaving. Alaina, Tae, and the wazir stood beside some of Cierheld's finest horses. They would ride to Hyl and the *Howler,* where they would sail the ocean, cross the sands, and find their several ways home. Hala had promised to tell Hyl of the raven in the oak and the justice that conquered injustice, though he might think compassion only a tale. Kyrin smiled. It was a tale of truth he would have to discern.

In a white thawb and maroon sash, Sirius paused beside his horse. He turned to Lord Dain and Talik. "If you will permit, there is one last task . . ."

Everyone was smiling, and the tensquads drawn up before the mill gave a great shout, "First daughter of Cieri!"

Kyrin turned. Berd strode past the mews toward her, the smith hurrying behind with a pair of tongs. The wazir took the tongs from the smith's hand. He motioned Kyrin forward. She touched her ear thoughtfully and obeyed. The jet earring was cool. She'd near forgotten it these past days.

The wazir's archers and lancers drawn up on either side watched sidelong, with curiosity and caution. It was a ring of slavery and the eye of evil, after all. Her father smiled with pride and love, her rangdo grinned complete approval, and Celine smiled. A small, impish smile, with her hand on Gwenich's head.

None of their faces held fear. Meric wore his usual boyish grin. Elinor wiped her cheeks. Berd's deep eyes held his steady oath, and Talik's warm gaze held more than Kyrin could name.

Never again need she fear her scars, heaven's witnesses, or nakedness of soul. *Evermore he makes me stand, a daughter at his right hand.*

Kyrin tilted her head when Sirius reached for her ear. Talik's hands closed on her shoulders. And Sirius Abdasir twisted the black ring. It snapped free. Berd took the earring from Sirius's hand and solemnly gave it to Dain. His hand closed around it, and his knuckles stood out.

Kyrin's head felt light. Sirius gave her a full bow, then rose to look her in the face. "Your task is done. Your writ of freedom is sealed. Let all witness!" She smiled at him.

"We are witnesses, daughter of Cieri!" It shook the air.

Kyrin bowed wordlessly. It had been a long road, a great circle of circumstance, wrought by a Master's hand. The Master of the stars called them all to this place. She became fit as he shaped her on the earth. And yet he had already made her fit for his heavenly hall. There all daughters were first daughters. As all sons were first sons.

First daughter *was* her place. She grinned up at Talik, and pushed a bit of straw-colored hair from his eyes. She was to handfast a lord's true son.

Samson's Ode grew within her. *You echoed my heart's desire, nor ever called it small. The board is wide, the trencher deep, the horn tall. Let our enemy rawl, the least as lord, sits in his hall. It is his ruling, truth at last to kiss peace.* She would follow the Master of the stars like the falcon, riding the wind of his Spirit. *Take up the blade and rest in victory.*

Every beautiful thing, and everything hard and troublesome, was made bearable by immortal promise. *Wonders ever increase, when he gives gifts apiece. Life to never cease.*

Sunlight sprang from the dagger in Sirius's sash. The bronze had been cleaned from the polished metal. But Sirius was drawing the falcon blade and turning to Tae. "It would honor our house and Hamal if you would take this gift."

Tae bowed and took the Damascus steel in both hands. His gaze on the wazir, he said solemnly, "I shall tell my Huen and my son, Ryung Suk. They will hear your story and learn how evil may be fought and wisdom gained."

Sirius inclined his head and swung into the saddle, his strong face split by a wolfish grin.

Kyrin held Alaina tight a last time. "My sister, bear well your scop's quill, and forget not the copy of my Chronicle that Brother Rolf asked of you."

"No." Alaina hugged her and stepped back, grasping her hands. "It makes my heart glad to see you healed. Never handfast a lord's son indeed!" She grinned. Kyrin smiled mistily. Alaina swung to her saddle beside Hala, who smiled at her, and it was well. Alaina had a friend.

Kyrin turned. Tae wrapped her in his arms. For her ear alone he whispered, "The asp will trouble you no more. Rule well, my daughter."

"Yes—Father."

Tae cleared his throat and turned to them all. "Though I may not stay to teach your Cierheld squads, I have left a book with Meric." He grinned. "Someday I may return to test that you have learned it well." He took leave of the armsmen in turn and shared a handclasp and a long look with Dain. Then he mounted.

In a storm of farewells, the company rode across the field, dwindling among the branches of green oak, ash, and birch.

Kyrin rocked onto her toes. She stared up at white clouds scattered across the blue sky, driven high by the wind that swept over her stronghold, tree and vale, and riffled Samson's stream among the bluebells. *True falcon heart, gone on, thou art. Rise undying, to dart, by wind and branch, free after the hart.*

She lifted her hand and stared at the teardrop of blood recorded there. Her heart had found its eyrie. She spread her arms, reaching for her family. Cierheldens edged in, and she embraced them. Joy cut like a sword. For a long moment they stood.

Then Kyrin loosed a hand from Meric's damp grasp, smiling at Cook. Truthfinder and the falcons needed fed. Cernalt always knew when she needed understanding quiet.

Talik joined her as she strode toward the mews. She looked at him—rescuer, wise one, lord's son, and soon-to-be handfasted friend. He put up his hands in mock defense, laughing. She put her arms around his warm frame and kissed him. Then blushed, and laughed, and laced her fingers with his.

Her falcon dagger went to witness a good man's return home. Samson's Ode was near finished. *Now your daughter wings by, swift as a glad sigh, to see my loves gathered nigh, in our Lord never to die.* Kyrin whistled. Truthfinder sped from the oak to her upheld arm with a thump, settling with a ruffle of her wings. There was a patter of paws on Cierheld's earth, and Gwenich put her nose in Kyrin's hand with an eager whine. Kyrin glanced at Berd and Celine, walking together behind, and at Talik striding beside her. *Love, loyalty, courage marks the steadfast. The moment is vast.*

Cauldron whinnied from the stable. Kyrin smiled. There could not be a better morn for the hunt. *Hearts rise and together we cry, full to the wide blue sky, in everlasting echo wild and high.*

Fly falcon heart, fly!

More Books

A reader of epic fantasy and new worlds, Azalea Dabill loves grand adventure and a satisfying, happy ending. Noblebright characters, the fate of the world, and tension between characters fascinates her. She will never stop learning about how words shape and hold meaning. Words wield power like a well-aimed bow.

Her debut novel was released in 2015. When she isn't writing you can find her growing things, raiding bookstores, or hiking the wild.

If you want to know more about her literary adventures you can join her here https://azaleadabill.com/ Her website is the hub for all her books, news, and reader resources. Kyrin's medieval adventures continue in Falcon Flight, and you can get your signed books from the author's website store and support her directly at https://azaleadabill.com/store/

It's usually cheaper than Amazon with shipping.

She is active on her Facebook page Mythic Fantasy https://www.facebook.com/azaleadabillmythicfantasy, or you can join her on Instagram https://www.instagram.com/azaleadabillauthor/?hl=en and GoodReads https://www.goodreads.com/author/show/13802917.Azalea_Dabill

Share Falcon Heart with a friend, Falcon Heart Wide Universal Book Link: https://books2read.com/u/bP1rpl. It's free!

Or tell me what could be improved or what you liked. Please leave a review on Amazon https://www.amazon.com/review/create-review/?ie=UTF8&channel=glance-detail&asin=B00VOEQXIO or at your favorite retailer. Thank you!

Lance and Quill Summary

In which Alaina flees the wazir's Hand, who pursues her and Tae even to the black tents of a Prince of the sands.

Foiled in her desire to rise as a renowned scribe in the court of the Caliph, Alaina finds herself tending an ailing sheik disguised as Tae's apprentice healer. But the prince pierces her deception, and soon has her scribing for him. Struggling to be worthy of his grandfather's seat as sheik, Prince Faisal has enemies Alaina would gladly shield him from. But she must keep her identity hidden from the tribe and the traitor among them, even as she faces Faisal's rival.

Alaina falls in love with the prince she is not worthy of, and fails him yet again before his rival's cunning schemes. When the wazir's Hand discovers them and their enemies converge in a last battle, Alaina must rise and break the webs of deceit. If she can discern her uncertain heart before it is too late.

Story Chat

*If you have read other Falcon Chronicle books, how did this look into the deeper mysteries of the falcon dagger change how you see Kyrin? How do you think you would face losing a loved one in your life?

*At first, Kyrin has a low opinion of lords' sons. How do you know this? What does Bergrin do that affects this? How does Kyrin's relationship with Talik change her opinion throughout the story? What does he do that makes her see him so differently?

*After she escapes Araby, Kyrin encounters many adversaries. What do each teach her? Have you ever had an adversary who taught you something? What was it?

*Does this book make you want to learn martial art yourself? Tae and Kyrin are good teachers. What do you think qualifies a good martial arts teacher? Do you want to teach something? If so, what?

*Have you ever been assigned one task that led to another, and turned out to be not what you thought? What is Kyrin's assigned task in the book, and what did it lead to?

*One theme in this story is finding your place in life. How does Kyrin find hers? Does her place change? What makes her place good? What about your place would you like to change? What is good about your present place?

*Another theme is leadership. How does Kyrin lead? How do you feel about leading? Have you ever had to lead when you didn't want to? What do you think are good ways you can lead?

*Different beliefs about who God is and who we are become apparent in this book. In the context of the story, what is the conclusion of who God is, and who people are?

*There is also a thread of poetry throughout Kyrin's tale. How does it reflect the story? Why does the poetry carry deep meaning? In the poetry, where does the falcon lead your mind?

Glossary

These terms and names span the world of the Chronicle. Not every entry or book will have every word. Mispronunciations and mistakes are my own. For easier pronunciation I have reduced some words to phonetic spelling. May contain slight spoilers. Enjoy the adventure!

Britannia:

Armsman—"Arms-mun" a lord's sworn man who protects the lord's person and stronghold

Bells—Lauds "Lawds" (just before dawn), Prime (just after daybreak), Terce "Terse" (third hour), Sext (sixth hour), Nones "Nons" (ninth hour), Vespers (eleventh hour), Matins (just after midnight)

Britannia—"Bri-tan-ee-uh" ancient name for Britain

Brooch—"Broach" a pin often worn in pairs, used for cloaks

Death touch—Possible with a strong man trained in Subak—a death thought to be brought by a single blow. Most often the culmination of several deadly nerve points or blows

Eagles—"E-gulls" an ancient name for Romans

Evil eye—Ali believes Kyrin can bring evil with her dark stare and brands her with a jet earring in her ear, besides his bronze ring of ownership in her other ear

Eyas—"Ee-ass" a young falcon in the nest

Eyrie—"Ear-ee" a falcon's nest high on a cliff

Falcon, Peregrine—"Pear-uh-grin" the bird Kyrin loves, which draws her to follow the Master of the stars

Falcon dagger—a mysterious dagger shaped like a falcon that Kyrin finds hidden in a cloak on her murdered mother's breast

Girdle—"Gir-dul" a kind of belt for women, often braided of leather or linen

Hose—like leggings but for men, usually fastened by cross garters attached to leather shoes

Mantle—"Man-tul" a woman's wrap, with a central hole for the head, like a poncho

Stronghold key—a large key that signifies authority over a stronghold. Women often wore them on their girdles

Tunic—"Tune-ick" a medieval shirt-like or robe-like garment worn by men and women, worn over an under-garment or shirt, often of linen, flowing to the knee for men and the feet for women

Names of important characters:

Aart—"A-art" Kyrin's horse, means like an eagle

Alaina Ilen—"A-lay-nuh I-len" Kyrin's peasant sister, closer than blood, means one who harmonizes, noble, stone

Aunt Medaen—"Ma-day-en" her father's tart-tongued sister, who Kyrin hears in her head more than she'd like

Father Annis—"Ann-iss" an important monk who opposes Kyrin

Brother Rolf—"Rawl-f" a sympathetic monk who plays a part in Cierheld's fate

Father Ulf—Kyrin's uncle, pivotal to events in Falcon Flight

Berd—a young armsman in training who becomes Kyrin's armsman

Celine Loring—"Suh-lean Lore-ing" a childhood friend who antagonizes Kyrin. I liked the name for a red-haired girl

Etain—"E-tain" Alaina's mare in Araby, means fairy

Esther—a stronghold daughter, and Kyrin's beautiful rival

Cernalt—"Sir-nalt" an old armsman and hawkmaster to Lord Dain Cieri

Dain Cieri—"Dane Si-eery" Kyrin's father. His name fit the time and place, to my mind

Willa—"Will-a" Kyrin's mother. The connotations of the name fit her gentle strength

Elinore—Kyrin's stepmother in honor of Sam's Elinore in LOTR. It sounded right

Gwenith—"Gwen-ith" the saluki pup that Alaina gives Kyrin, means blessed

Hal Loring—Celine's father and Kyrin's first student in Britannia

Kyrin Cieri—"Kai-rin Si-eery" I liked the sound, the name reminds me of dark hills, Celtic times, and Elizabeth Moon's Paksenarrion

Lord Bergrin Jorn—"Bur-grin Jorn" Myrna's brother, who holds Kyrin captive for a time, and is an ally in war

Lord Ludwin Mornoth—"Lud-win More-noth" who is Cierheld and the strongholds' nemesis

Lord Nidfael Keffer—"Nid-fi-el Keff-er" Mornoth's second in command, and Kyrin's nemesis

Meric—"Mare-ick" Kyrin's stepbrother. His name fits his scholarly bent and nature

Myrna Jorn—"Mur-nuh" Kyrin's friend, means tender

Nell Trinley—a girl with mismatched eyes that Kyrin rescues, who becomes a healer

Nith—an armsmaster, first in command of Cierheld in *Falcon Flight*

Ragad—"Ra-gad" shipmaster of the Howler, Sirius Abdasir's ship that brings Kyrin on her task to find Hamal

Seliam—"See-li-am" the wazir's slave, an askar who threatens everyone Kyrin loves in *Falcon Heart*

Sirius Abdasir—"Sear-ee-us Ab-duh-sir" wazir to the caliph, who holds the secret of the falcon dagger and threatens to destroy Kyrin and all of Cierheld

Talik—"Tal-ick" a messenger between the strongholds who rescues Kyrin, loves and quarrels with her

The Master of the stars—the meaning of this name is for you to discover

Wolf-ship warrior—another name for a Viking

White Christer—a Viking's name for one who follows Christ

§

Araby/Arabia:

Aba—"Ab-uh" an Arabian women's cloak

Aneza—"A-nez-uh" a tribe of Araby people in Kyrin's world

Askar—"Ass-car" means fighter, warrior

Bisht—"Bi-shit" an Arabian men's cloak

Bedu/Bedouin—"Bed-du" or "Bed-o-in" a name for those who live in the desert

Caliph—"Kal-iph" Araby ruler in Baghdad

Dalil—"Dal-lil" a caravan guide, often across the desert

Djinn—"Jin" jinn, genie, jinni

Empty Quarter—Al Ramlah, the ocean of sand south and inland of the coastal mountains

Hattah—"Hat-tah" the desert women's light head covering. Not a veil, though it can be used to cover the face

Kaffiyeh—"Ca-fi-yuh" Araby men's head covering

Mahr—"Marr" a desert maiden's dowry, often precious metal anklets, bracelets, and coins sewn into a bridal headpiece or veil

Nargeela—"Nar-gee-la" a water pipe

Nasrany—"Nas-rany" an infidel unbeliever

Nur-ed-Dam—"Nur-ed-dom" oath of the Light of Blood, or blood-feud oath

Reem—the black-horned gazelle and others of its kind

Shaheen—"Sha-heen" Arabic for a falcon, also the name given to Kyrin

Sheyk—"Shay-ick" a desert leader of a tribe, such as Gershem Ben Salin of the Twilkets

Souk—"Sook" an Araby market

Thawb—"Thaw-ub" an Araby tunic

Twilkets—"Twil-kets" an enemy tribe until events bring unforeseen secrets to light

Umar's Hand—"Oo-mar's Hand" Umar's pack of salukis he trained against their gentle nature to hunt men

Wadi—"Wad-ee" a watercourse, usually dry except during the rainy season

Wazir—"Wah-zeer" the advisor to the caliph

Names of important characters:

Ali Ben Aidon—"Ali-ben A-don" Araby slaver, a common Arabic name

Basimah—"Bass-i-mah" means one who smiles

Cicero—"Siss-er-o" Kyrin and Alaina's saluki, named after a wise man

Faisal—"Fie-sel" desert prince of the Twilkets, loves both Kyrin and Alaina. Means a wise, just judge

Farook—"Fa-ruke" the wazir's slave forced to betray Alaina, means one who discerns right and wrong

Gershem Ben Salin—"Ger-shem Ben Sa-lin" Twilket sheyk and Faisal's grandfather. I liked the name

Hafiz—"Ha-feez" first warrior, and Alaina's opponent in Lance and Quill. Means the guardian

Hala—"Hall-uh" Sirius Abdasir's daughter, means halo around the moon

Hamal—"Ha-mall" the wazir's lost traveler, means gentle as a lamb

Jachin—"Ja-chin" Ali's bodyguard and Tae's friend. I liked the sound for a friendly Nubian

Kentar—"Ken-tar" caravan guide and Tae's eyes and ears. I liked the name from *The Blue Sword*

Mey—"May" Shahin's wife and Rashid's mother. I liked the sound of the name

Nara—"Nar-uh" Umar's Egyptian mother, Ali's cook, and Kyrin's friend in Ali's house, meaning unknown

Nimah—"Nim-uh" first to welcome Kyrin and Alaina to Ali's housem, means blessing

Neddra—"Ned-druh" an Aneza girl who admired Kyrin's falcon dagger, the sound drew me

Qadira—"Ka-deer-uh" head concubine in Ali's house, means powerful one

Rashid—"Ra-shid" the young sheyk's son, means the well guided

Sahar—"Sa-har" Faisal's red saluki, means the dawn

Sarni—"Sar-nee" the name a desert prince gives Alaina, means the elevated one

Shahin—"Sha-hin" sheyk of the Aneza, shelters Kyrin during the desert war for saving his son, Rashid

Truthseeker—the falcon eyas the Aneza tribe gives Kyrin

Umar—"Oo-mar" Ali's treacherous and unacknowledged son, means flourishing, long-lived

Zahir—"Za-heer" Faisal's stallion, means shining, radiant

Zoltan—"Zol-tan" Nimah's brother, means a ruler

§

Land of the Morning Calm/Korea:

Ap bal Chagi—"Op-ball-chagi" front-kick—a snapping kick that best attacks the groin or stomach

Barow—"Ba-row" means return to starting position

Chin-gol—"Chin-goal" means true bone. It was one of the highest military ranks after head-rank five.

Choson—A name for the early Korean culture, specifically applied in my books to the Silla dynasty.

Death touch—death thought to be brought by a single blow. Possible with a strong man trained in Subak, but more often the culmination of several deadly nerve points or blows

Dwi Chagi—"Dwee-chagi" a back-kick. The strongest kick, this one stops an attacker like a stone wall

Hwarang—"Huh-waa-rang" flowering warrior or leader of 500 to 5,000 hwarangdo—one trained in martial arts, literature, the arts, sciences, and one hundred and eight different weapons

Jun be—"June-bee" stance ready for attack. There are several variations

Kum-sool—"Come-sool" means sword skill

Kuksun—"Kook-sun" a commander or general, a lord who led by example

Naryu Chagi—"Nari-yu-chagi" an axe-kick or spinning kick often used to attack enemies on horseback

Open hand—attack with the fingers, palm, or knife-edge of the hand to the eyes, temples, neck, etc.

Pil Sung—certain victory through courage, strength, and indomitable spirit.

Poomse—"Poom-say" a sequence of training techniques done in flowing order, often with multiple techniques hidden within

Hwarangdo—"Huh-waa-rang-doh" or "Rang-do" a martial art student who learned under a hwarang master and followed Sesokokye

Seajok—"Say-jock" a command to begin (the fight, etc.)

Seon—"Say-on" Tae-shin or Tae Chisun, after his name was changed—left Seon to follow the Master of the stars, means the way of Zen

Sesokokye—"See-sok-o-kye" be loyal to your country, honor your parents, be faithful to your friends, never retreat in battle, use good judgment before killing any living thing.

Silla—A dynasty spanning the first century B.C. to 935 A.D. Our story happens around 830 or 840 A.D.

Subak—"Soo-bok" a component of Tae-shin's way of the warrior, means hand technique

Tiger—a beast of terrible power that haunts Kyrin's dreams

Yeop Chagi—"Yee-op chagi" side-kick. This can cripple, used against the knee at an angle

Names of important characters:

Cho Seung—Tae-shin's treacherous hwarang master, means candle, beginning, or second, and rise or achieve

Jeong Jin-ho—"Jee-ong Jin-ho" the rebel kuksun who honors Tae-shin when he is cast outside his clan as a traitor. Means quiet or loyal, and great, brave, heroic, or chivalrous.

Ha-nuel—Tae-shin's brave student who carried an essential message for the life of his people, means sky

Kim Jin-dae—"Jin-day" the name of Tae-shin/Tae Chisun's wife, means truth, or jewel, and greatness. "Hu-en" (pet name) may be associated with judgement. "Kim" means gold. I liked the sounds of these names

Kim Paekche—"Kim Pack-chi" is Tae-shin's father-in-law who exiled him. "Kim" means gold, "Paekche" is thought to mean one hundred crossings

Ryu Tae-shin—"Rue Tie-shin" where "Ryu" means willow tree, "Tae-shin" means great, and belief, faith, or trust. He came to be named Tae Chisun "Tie Chee-sun" by his captor, in his exile. Tae (great) is the first name of a grandmaster, Tae Hong Choi. I also liked the sound for a hero's name. Choi, as in Master Choi in *Path of the Warrior,* means governor of the land and the mountain, or high, superior, lofty.

Young-sool—means dragon or valiant one, and martial art technique

Acknowledgements

There are too many wonderful people who assisted me on my writing journey to name them all. So, if your name is not here and you dropped a word of encouragement or helped me on my writing journey, know that I appreciate you very much.

My thanks to my dad, mom, and family for their support in so many ways, and to Sandy Cathcart, Lynn Leissler, Jeanette Windle, Susan May Warren, and Kathi Macias for their teaching and encouragement at pivotal points in my writing.

And I could never get far without my crit group, Fantasy for Christ. My deepest thanks to you.

More recently during the book updates, I thank Charlotte Lesemann and Emily Moore for their encouragement, beta reading, and help with the things that make a book worthwhile.

And I also thank you, my readers. You're the best! I deeply appreciate your invaluable advice and honest reviews!

If you have not reviewed this book yet, you can leave a review at Amazon https://www.amazon.com/review/create-review/?ie=UTF8&channel=glance-detail&asin=B00VOEQXIO, GoodReads, or at your favorite retailer if you want to let the world know how you liked it. As the author, I highly value your feedback and insights, as does the rest of the reading world. Thank you!

Azalea Dabill

www.ingramcontent.com/pod-product-compliance
Lightning Source LLC
Chambersburg PA
CBHW020323030826
48979CB00022B/961

* 9 7 8 1 9 4 3 0 3 4 1 8 5 *